Hayner Public Library District-Alton
W9-CAA-069

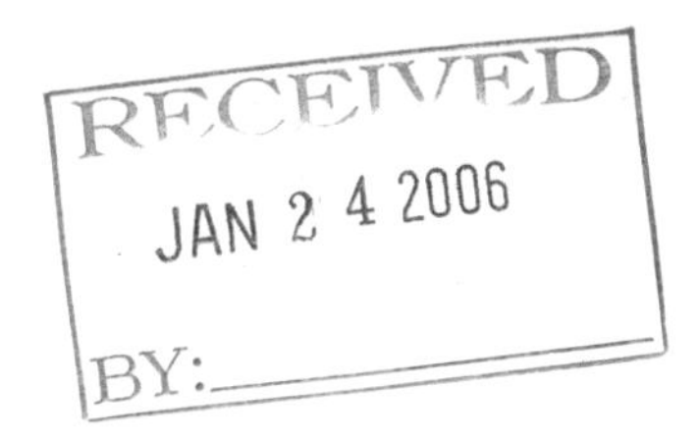
RECEIVED
JAN 2 4 2006
BY:

AFTERLANDS

Books by Steven Heighton

FICTION

Flight Paths of the Emperor
On Earth As It Is
The Shadow Boxer

POETRY

Stalin's Carnival
Foreign Ghosts
The Ecstasy of Skeptics
The Address Book

ESSAYS

The Admen Move on Lhasa

ANTHOLOGIES

A Discord of Flags: Canadian Poets Write About the Gulf War (with Peter Ormshaw and Michael Redhill)

Musings: An Anthology of Greek-Canadian Literature (with main editor Tess Fragoulis, and Helen Tsiriotakis)

STEVEN HEIGHTON

AFTER

HOUGHTON MIFFLIN COMPANY

LANDS

A Novel

BOSTON NEW YORK 2006

First published in Canada by Alfred A. Knopf Canada, 2005

For information about permission to reproduce selections
from this book, write to Permissions, Houghton Mifflin Company,
215 Park Avenue South, New York, New York 10003.

Visit our Web site: www.houghtonmifflinbooks.com.

Library of Congress Cataloging-in-Publication Data

Heighton, Steven, date.
Afterlands : a novel / Steven Heighton
p. cm.
ISBN-13: 978-0-618-13934-7
ISBN-10: 0-618-13934-6
1. Polaris (Ship) — Fiction. 2. Arctic regions — Fiction.
3. Wilderness survival — Fiction. 4. Survival after airplane
accidents, shipwrecks, etc. — Fiction. I. Title.

PR9199.3.H4443A68 2006
813'.54 — dc22 2005046223

Printed in the United States of America

QUM 10 9 8 7 6 5 4 3 2 1

AMUSEMENTS.

BARNUM'S AMERICAN MUSEUM.

THURSDAY, Nov. 20, 1862.
ONLY THREE DAYS MORE
ONLY THREE DAYS MORE
OF THOSE WONDERFUL

ESQUIMAUX INDIANS,
ESQUIMAUX INDIANS,
ESQUIMAUX INDIANS,

Which have just arrived in this country.
FROM THE ARCTIC REGIONS,
Whence they were brought by
C. F. HALL, Esq., ARCTIC EXPLORER,
Being the first and only
INHABITANTS OF THESE FROZEN REGIONS
ever brought to this country, they are objects of universal interest; but they can remain only this week.
SEE THEM NOW, OR YOU'RE TOO LATE.
They are on exhibition from 10 A. M. till 12 M., from 2 till 4, and from 7 till 10 P. M.
A few days more of
COMMODORE NUTT,
THE
$30,000 NUTT.
One of the most extraordinary wonders of the world. As he is preparing for a trip to Europe, and is nearly ready to sail, he cannot possibly
REMAIN HERE BUT A FEW DAYS.
REMAIN HERE BUT A FEW DAYS.
He will be seen
AT ALL HOURS, DAY AND EVENING,
and at intervals, and on the stage, during each dramatic entertainment, he will
GIVE A VARIETY OF PERFORMANCES,
including songs, dances, military drill, relate his history, &c., &c. Also to be seen,
THE MADAGASCAR ALBINO FAMILY,
New and beautiful life-like
WAX FIGURES
OF
GEN. HALLECK, GEN. BURNSIDE,
GEN. BANKS, GEN. McCLELLAN, GEN. POPE,
GEN. CORCORAN,
and the glorious old hero and patriot,
COMMODORE FOOTE.
Also, an exact likeness of that curious creature, the
WHAT IS IT?
in consultation with
JEFF. DAVIS and BEAUREGARD,
regarding the cause of this rebellion. *What Is It?*
Also, life likenesses of
QUEEN VICTORIA and the PRINCE OF WALES.
OLD ADAMS' CALIFORNIA
PERFORMING BEARS,
THE BEAUTIFUL COLORED TROPICAL FISH,
LIVING MONSTER SNAKES, LIVING HAPPY FAMILY, and a million other Wonders.
BOUCICAULT'S GREAT DRAMA,
PAUVRETTE; OR, UNDER THE SNOW.
THIS AFTERNOON, at 3 o'clock; EVENING, at 7½.
Mr. WM. B. HARRISON, Impromptu Comic Singer, appears at each performance.
Admission to all, 25 cents; children under ten, 15 cents.

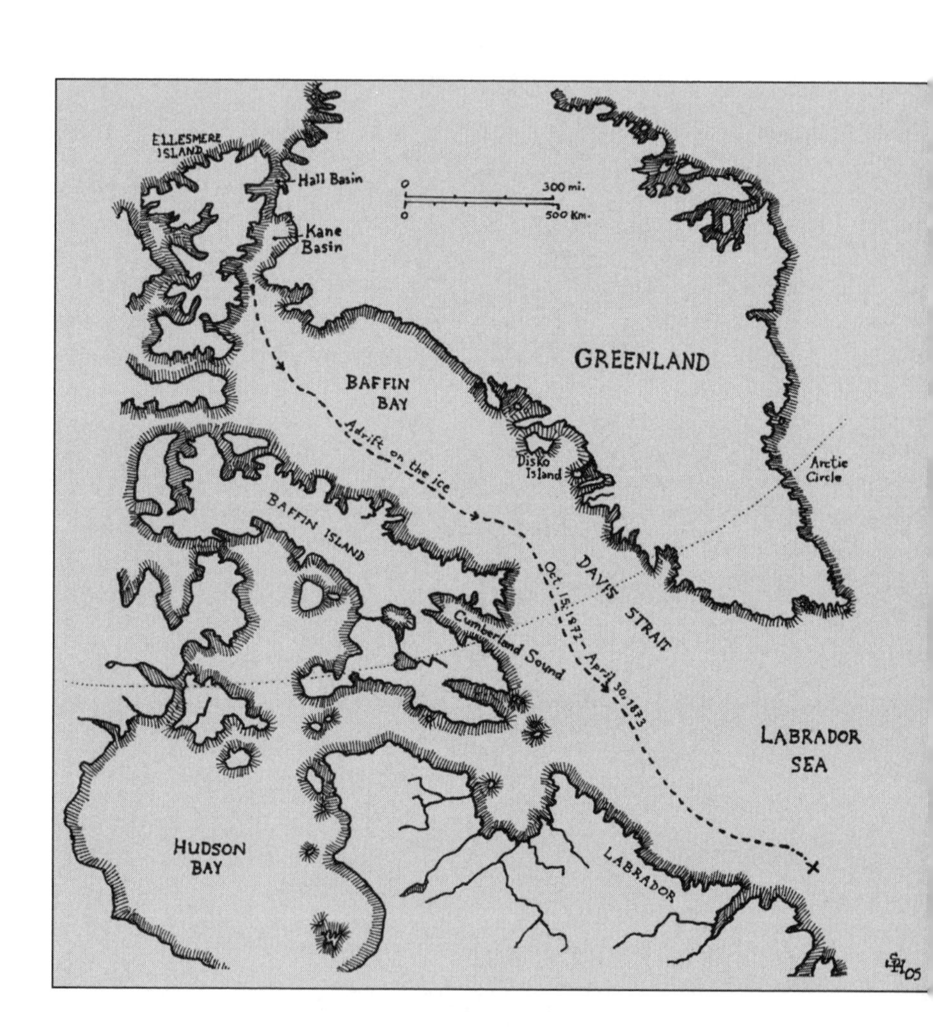
ELLESMERE ISLAND
Hall Basin
Kane Basin
0
300 mi.
0
500 Km.
GREENLAND
BAFFIN BAY
Adrift on the ice
Disko Island
Arctic Circle
BAFFIN ISLAND
DAVIS STRAIT
Oct. 15, 1872 – April 30, 1873
Cumberland Sound
LABRADOR SEA
HUDSON BAY
LABRADOR

CONTENTS

I have no patriotic illusions.
I have only the supreme illusion of a lover.

—JOSEPH CONRAD, *Nostromo*

ONE

BURY ME

AT SEA

But what thinks Lazarus? Can he warm his blue hands by holding them up to the grand northern lights? Would not Lazarus rather be in Sumatra than here? Would he not far rather lay him down lengthwise along the line of the equator . . . go down to the fiery pit itself, in order to keep out this frost?

—HERMAN MELVILLE, *Moby-Dick*

Wanted to shadow the three of you, all scattered
by the one storm. Tracked you (or some sediment,
cinder of you) to churchyards along the seaboard
near Mystic, or indio *graveyards above the gaunt*
gorges of Sinaloa—a search party of one, a mere
century-plus late. No, more—with every resource
I searched, clue traced, a shade more of your oblivious
withdrawal, waning to ash, as I scrawled my course
(it seemed) ever nearer, through tiered detritus
downward, by the spadeful, a volunteer
unwilling to leave the warlike scene—
recovering just fragments, fallout, DNA.

Dawson City, Yukon, September 2001

Hartford, Connecticut, September 1876

AN ESQUIMAU PLAYING MENDELSSOHN is a tremendous novelty. The local gentry fill the seats of the Main Street Memorial Hall, whiskery gentlemen in frock coats and wing collars, the ladies in gowns and layer-cake hats trimmed with ribbon and mock flora. Their elegant figures are shored up by trusses or corsets—synthetic exoskeletons fortified with whalebone. If any members of this audience make a connection between their own underclothes and the presence onstage of a child from the Arctic whaling grounds, they don't let on. They are effusive in their praise of the little Esquimau. She is clearly a prodigy. She is only ten years of age! She has been playing the piano for only three years! How charming she looks in her cream cotton dress with the puffed sleeves, the ends of her braids joined at the small of her back with a red ribbon bow. As they whisper and nod, a lush welling of self-appreciation and security warms their chests.

In fact, Punnie is not playing as well as she did when rehearsing for the recital with her teacher, Mr Chusley, who will be performing after her and before the chief attraction, a master recitalist from Leipzig who is said to have known Mendelssohn personally. This lean and tousled master, seated severely in the front row, will be aware that the girl has committed a few slips.

What he doesn't know is that her playing also lacks its usual earnest, beguiling zest. Punnie is dizzy and has to concentrate to suppress the dry scraping cough that has been gaining on her since April. Throughout the summer holiday she has been practising, as much as four hours a day. There is something unnerving, quietly violent, in her discipline. She's the sort of only child who lives for the endorsement of adults. More and more these days she coughs while she rehearses. She and her parents, Tukulito and Ebierbing—Hannah and Joe is how they are known to Americans—came down from the Arctic after the rescue over three years ago, but the poor child still carries the Far North in her lungs. So Mr Chusley puts it. He even urges her to practise less.

Actually Punnie's cough began not in the Arctic but after their journey south.

Stiff in the aisle seat of a middle row, Tukulito sees that her daughter is struggling, but the audience is so caught up in the spectacle of this oddly pallid Esquimau child playing one of Mendelssohn's *Songs without Words*—op. 30, no. 1 in E flat—that they don't notice. Tukulito's face has the waxen stillness of somebody watching the last stages of a shipwreck, trying to contain her alarm—a stillness that could be mistaken for calm. This is her usual expression. Only her eyes, sharp with practical understanding and quick sympathy, lend life to her face; enough life for a dozen faces.

In fact, the child *is* something of a prodigy. Mr Chusley, a soft little man with sombre brown eyes, rumpled clothes and clove-scented breath (and, unluckily for his dreams, stumpy hands and fingers), has said that he foresees fine fine things for the girl. Very fine indeed. And Tukulito grasps that this is not a man given to flattery. A stutterer, he keeps his utterances short. I've never yet tutored a child possessed of such a, such a faculty of silent concentration. Your Punnie seems to me utterly undistractable. Chusley does not then detour into ethnological conjecture, like some of the well-meaning Groton neighbours, on whether this is a specialized trait—a result of the savage's need for vigilance by the seal's breathing hole, or his wife's Oriental patience, acquired in the igloo waiting with the children for her mate's return. . . . For some years the life of the Esquimaux has gripped the romantic imagination. They've become a staple of polar adventure novels, which emphasize their fortitude, their loyalty, their stealth, their rare inscrutable lapses into cunning and violence. In the 1860s the fascination with Esquimaux even hatched a short-lived fad for duelling with bone harpoons. The *Polaris* debacle and Lieutenant Tyson's subsequent drift on the ice with eighteen other castaways have made them even more popular; Tukulito's husband Ebierbing was in some ways the hero of Tyson's published account of the drift (as Second Mate Kruger was its villain), and this Esquimau family have been celebrities since settling in the port town of Groton, Connecticut.

Tukulito still thinks about Mr Kruger but has not heard from him in some time.

The child is small for her age, no grand piano ever looked huger. She will start a piece straight-backed on the bench but as she plays she will tip gradually forward so that by the last bar her face is just above the keys. (Mr Chusley has tried to correct this.) Her playing is stronger now, op. 67, no. 5 in B minor, "The Shepherd's Complaint." Those firm-pacing, stately notes in the minor until, just as the ear is tiring of the solemnity, the tune resolves into major.

Two rows ahead of Tukulito are a pair of gentlemen who arrived late and claimed these last seats in the house. The man on the aisle has black hair of collar length, pomaded and combed straight back to cover a bald patch. The rims of his ears stand well out from the sides of his narrow skull. The other has a shaggy head of white hair and, fuzzing the slabs of his claret cheeks, side-whiskers that Tukulito sees whenever he turns to address his companion. His voice is genial and raspy. The black-haired man doesn't turn or even move his head when he speaks, but she hears him too: the ponderous baritone of a butler or mortician. Her hearing is the talent not just of a quiet observer used to being discussed, but also of the Arctic's first professional interpreter, sought after by expeditions for the last twenty years.

The black-haired one's accent is difficult to place, though she gathers he is a visitor, from Canada. She swallows her own impulse to cough so that she can keep listening to him as well as to Punnie. He might remark on Punnie's playing. It matters to her as much as ever that the white people regard her family as something more than a sideshow attraction.

He says softly, I would agree that the question of the Esquimaux' nationality is a highly vexed one. But I maintain that the girl must be deemed Canadian, because her home, in Cumberland Bay, is in Canadian territory.

But that would make her a subject of the British Empire, wouldn't it?

Indeed it would, sir.

The white-haired man chuckles. You can hardly expect us to accept that, Mr Wilt. As you know, the family resides down here in Groton now. And the *Polaris* expedition was an American enterprise. No, no, Mr Wilt, our claim is thoroughly staked!

Hush! This from a beard and monocle in the next row.

For a few moments, they hush.

Then: Some have declared, sir, that your *Polaris* expedition was in fact a German one.

The shaggy bear's-head shakes wryly. So now you're claiming the Esquimaux for Germany!

Wilt gives a formal snort and then, as if conscious of being overheard, he whispers, It must be remembered that her parents enjoyed their first contact with civilization in *England.* They took tea and dined with the Queen herself! The accent of the mother, I am told, is still English!

True enough, Wilt, but—

I understand furthermore that her husband has returned to the *Canadian* Arctic.

Returned, Mr Wilt, with another *American* expedition! And he is expected home within the year. Home, Wilt, to *Groton!*

This last phrase, inanely disembodied, hovers in the brief silence as Punnie completes her third of the *Songs without Words*—the "Cradle Song," op. 67, no. 6 in E. Its dying trill is deftly executed. She stands under the soaring proscenium arch, buffeted by applause. Her hands dangle at her sides. The tight hard line of her mouth, which always gives her an aspect of stern determination, so adult, now suggests barely contained discomfort. She looks out at the crowd. As if overcome by the response, she brings a hand to her mouth, a fetching gesture, it appears, of bashful pleasure, astonishment at these accolades—but Tukulito understands. Her daughter's coughing can't be heard over the ovation. The two patriots surge to their feet with the rest of the house, and while continuing to clap heartily they go on hauling the child back and forth across international borders.

Some, of course, might submit that they are a nation unto themselves.

Well, but the Danes have also laid claim to that region, haven't they?

It is news to me, sir, but I would be little surprised.

Tukulito remains seated, sheltered in the dark cavity formed by the people standing around her. The gentlemen's words are not unamusing; still, shame flares along her collar and prickles her scalp under the hairpinned Brussels cap. After twenty years she is still not hardened to being spoken of as if absent or incapable of understanding. At first, in London, she quietly relished all the curiosity and attention, accepting it as evidence that her people's faith in their own specialness was not misplaced. The Chosen People is what any nation thinks it is, until history disappoints it; or destroys it. In time her growing knowledge of English allowed her to grasp and forced her to brood on the commentary of onlookers, especially during her and Ebierbing's tenure as fur-clad "Living Exhibits" at P. T. Barnum's American Museum in New York, in 1862. By and by her outlook was changed, her pleasure in public life reduced. This shame is familiar. This shame is the trite undertow of her adult life. But now it forms part of a new and hybrid emotion as her corseted chest floods with the heat of her pride, and anxious love. *These Sons and Daughters of the Distant North, Ladies and Gentlemen, possess some ninety words for Snow!* Yet only a fraction of human feelings are clearly nameable. Most feelings are complex chords, like the ones Punnie plays, minor or major or suspended, each composed of many notes, a current joy, a lingering shame, a hunger, a loss, all sounding together in a pattern never to be revived. In New York during the war her first child, Butterfly, then later up north King William, slipped from the bone-crib of her arms, and Captain Hall, their beloved American sponsor, died up there as well. Punnie, her Punnie, is adopted after the custom of her people. Her Punnie, her pulse, the very spark in her eyes.

The North took her last baby, let the South preserve this one. She rises to join the ovation but is too short to see her daughter on the stage.

New York City, November 1876

SUICIDE IS ONE OF THE FEW WAYS for a ruined immigrant to go home.

The East River seems to be exhaling cold, and how Kruger hates that. Hatless and coatless, shivering, he leans on the taffrail of the South Ferry crossing toward Brooklyn, the Atlantic Street pier. Big rawhide hands gripping the top rail. One battered boot up on the lower rail, as if on the rung of a ladder he is hesitating to climb. This aft deck is lit by a single lantern. Alone, he watches the skyline of Manhattan recede. It's apt that a suicide be looking backward in the moment before action.

The skyline is low except for the west tower of the unfinished Brooklyn Bridge, which now in the dark resembles the Gothic facade of the Marienkirche, in Danzig, where Roland Kruger was raised. He's solid, middle height, a trimmed black beard, dark escarpment of standing hair, high forehead carved with horizontal lines. Heavy brows like lintels over blue eyes that in his weathered, fighter's face seem transplanted from a more schooled and studious one. His bluchers, though battered, are polished. A small book bulges in his vest pocket. Even now there's a jut to his chin, an inclination of profile that suggests someone who was once of another class. Or, who has made a habit of defiance.

Kruger was intending to climb the scaffolding around that granite tower, and from there—within sight of the Harper's building—throw himself away, as scores of others had done since the Panic of '73. The authorities, however, had begun posting night watchmen at the fenced perimeter of the worksite. Not wanting to loiter by the fence for several years until the bridge was finished and he could hurl himself off, Kruger decided to bury himself at sea.

He takes a final draw on his pipe and jams it into his waistcoat fob. He swings his left leg over the top rail, then his right, perches on a middle rung, hesitates, then leaps, trying to clear the eddy of curdled water above the steam-prop ten feet below him; still selective. He slaps through the river's dark membrane. After a spell of surrender—making no effort but to empty his lungs of air—he is thrashing, pulling at the icy water white with froth, clawing his way upward. Partly it's the cold, a bitter smack to the face, reviving the instinct of resistance that kept driving him through half a year on the ice. Partly it's how his memory of the ice summons Tukulito's face back to him: her expression near the end, while he and the others braced the lifeboat on what remained of their "island" and the night's giant swells lunged over them. Seemingly calm, even then, blessing him with her stamina, she'd ruddered and renewed him.

He thrusts through the surface and gulps air. The ferry's taffrail lamp is surprisingly far off, leaving him to his own resources much as the *Polaris* had, withdrawing into the night and stranding him and Tukulito, Tyson, and the others. The icy water clamps his throat and lungs so he can only suck in partial breaths. He dunks under the rolling wake and tries to undo his bluchers. His fingers, swarming the laces, appear worm-like in the gloom. They're too stiff with cold to make headway but he's a strong swimmer and the eroded boots weigh little. He aims for the gothic monolith of the tower. Starboard lamps of the Montague and Fulton ferries in mid-crossing cast wobbling spikes of light on the river. He can see his hands churning but not feel them—not feel whether his boots are still on or have worked themselves off.

Over the tower the moon is a paring short of full. A sky of fathomless depth, of dreadful neutrality. He can see her wide face there, lunar; and the face of her husband, to whom she'll always be loyal.

After the rescue and return, some three years ago, Kruger too was a minor celebrity. Lodged in a small but unembarrassing boardinghouse on Fulton Street in Brooklyn, he was a focus of some pride and comfort for immigrants—Germans, Italians, Irish, Poles—struggling more than ever since the Panic of '73. A *Polaris* survivor, the Second Mate, here among us! He was a sort of living exhibit, a popular one, although many found him difficult to class—as he preferred. He was rugged in appearance but reflective in manner. People found him friendly in a somewhat contained, distant way, which they mostly attributed to his ordeal on the ice, although others thought he seemed like a man unhappily in love (and yet surely too philosophical, too ironic for love!). He smiled often enough, though with lips closed on the stem of his pipe. He seldom laughed. He measured his words and he delivered them with a satiric glitter in his blue eyes—though more in self-mockery, it seemed, than in mockery of others. He seemed wholly uncomfortable only around cops, wholly unguarded only with children.

This is how he struck his fellow immigrants. And in fact he did prefer the company of children, mostly for how their minds hadn't yet congealed to the point of thinking within borders.

He knew what it was to be frozen and starved. Like his heroes Voltaire and Goethe he would share whatever food he had in his various pockets (stuffed like the cheeks of small, hoarding animals) with the skeletons haunched down on the stoops of nickel lodginghouses, urchins asleep in shitty areaways, families camped under the awnings of failed shops on Atlantic or Dock Street where he became known as the Chestnut Man, having discovered that filling his pockets with hot chestnuts, a penny the bag, would help fend off the Atlantic's winter chill. . . . It was a wonder, many felt, that his ordeal had not made him stingy, but then maybe he'd acquired the ways of those Esquimaux, who were well known to share everything, even their wives.

Urged enough, he would tell his story. In his version, Tukulito, or "Hannah," with whom he still exchanged occasional, formal letters, was the heroine. Once embarked he was glad enough to tell it, their story, for much the same reason a person secretly in love will bring up the name of the other in conversation on the thinnest pretext: to invoke a closeness. Actually he was long resigned to the impossibility of his feelings, and the stoic in him, the student of Marcus Aurelius, had come to accept it with a certain grace. Loss was the world's final law.

It never struck him that he could lose the very fame that made his love-loss easier to bear. Celebrity, like grief, feels permanent—a verdict, not a passing state—and day after day he did remain a hero, an inspiration to people who felt like starved castaways themselves. They too might someday reach a lardered shore. They too might emerge battered but whole, a kind of success, like this Kruger. . . .

All this he found quite gratifying in spite of himself.

There were no jobs to be had, yet people found him jobs. Unready to return to sea, he would take only the ones on land. He became a lector at the Seamen's Reading Room at the foot of Atlantic Street. While the literate read in the pine carrels, lips moving in their beards, Kruger read aloud whatever books the unlettered requested. The selection was meagre. There was a little Cooper, Longfellow, and Scott, but no Dickens. The Methodists who ran the Reading Room out of the Seamen's Bethel next door considered Dickens subversive. They stocked *The Pilgrim's Progress* (three copies) but not *Gulliver's Travels.* They supplied Carlyle but not Voltaire, and when Kruger was caught translating his own copy of Lessing's *Nathan the Wise* to a huddle of scruffy deckhands, he was warned, hero or not, to stop.

Tired of solo nights and brothels, starting to crave a simple life of hearthside meals and family, even a dog, he was uncertainly courting the daughter of a Dutch minister—a man who never would have stood for his only child's betrothal to a seaman, and a freethinker into the bargain, had Kruger not been a small-time hero as well.

The publication of a book changed everything. From Lieutenant Tyson's version of the story another Kruger emerged: a thief, a rebel, a foreign provocateur. Everywhere a sound of slamming doors. The most contagious sound in the world. He'd been embraced as a "German-American," even a "New American," but after Harper & Brothers unleashed *Arctic Experiences* he was soon recatalogued, first to "German immigrant," then to "German," then to "Prussian." Then simply "Squarehead." Mentally, Kruger—whose sense of the puerility of patriotism and the ways of the herd had been much deepened on the ice—observed this obliteration with grimly amused detachment, but in his guts the blackballing sat with a primitive, sickening weight. Neighbours who'd laurelled and fed him and found him dry work and placed their own daughters in his path now cut him dead in the street. Other Germans who'd deemed him a credit to the pack swiftly disowned him. At the Reading Room he was no longer required. Marijke had broken off the engagement by mail, likely at her father's insistence, although there was no way to establish the truth because Kruger was not permitted to see her, and she would not, or could not, reply to his letters. For three more Sundays, like a man suffering with piles, he wriggled through Pastor VanHuffel's rhinocerine services, vainly willing Marijke to turn toward him in the back pews, hoping to speak to her after. On the third Sunday, while the pastor with his glowing pate and bobbing red beard denounced "that Teuton" who with "other foreign crew" of the *Polaris* had brought down on the heads of all New Americans a fresh wave of contempt, Kruger watched Marijke's nape and the backs of her tiny ears burn while his armpits prickled and his cheeks blazed: two almost-lovers intimately linked for a last time, although by shame. At the end of the service a delegation of bearded elders had helped Kruger down the steep front steps of the church. Former admirers watched him topple and roll.

He fled Brooklyn for the Bowery.

Hoping to clear his name, gain Marijke back and support himself without returning to sea, he began approaching American publishers, starting with Harper & Brothers themselves. None of them expressed interest in the notes he'd hurriedly produced—notes toward a fresh account of the party's months on the ice. Of course, Tyson himself might be responsible for the Harper & Brothers rejection, but he couldn't be behind all of them . . . could he? Kruger pored over the letters he got in prompt response to his inquiries. He soon realized that beyond the local streets there could be no interest in the version of an immigrant seaman already discredited by a native of rank and prestige. And perhaps his written English was not so correct as he believed? In Danzig he had been a talented pupil—if sometimes lazy, stubborn—but after all, he had had to leave school at thirteen, for employment on the docks, where his older brother

Armin already worked to sustain the family. 1858: of this he recalled most a forest of mast tips stabbing at the early morning stars, also a lamplit cabin porthole, secure and inviting, seen from the quay where he hunched with Armin cranking the windlass, for hours. How he longed to be aboard and casting off! Papa himself could no longer work. Even if he had been allowed to teach again at the *Gymnasium*, he was too weak. A Prussian radical, he had written pamphlets and broadsides for the liberal reformers of 1848, and when the movement collapsed he had been exiled to France. In '52, trying to slip back early, he was caught and imprisoned. He was released after three years but returned to his family ailing and heart-spent. Some vital thing had vacated him and was not coming back. The struggle for democratic reform—that rational yet romantic impulse that had swept across Europe in '48—was likewise shattered. Papa could no longer bear to look at his shelves. He no longer believed that all men would be brothers one idyllic day as Lessing and Schiller and Goethe had proposed. *Roland, this country doesn't care to be just. This country wants only to be strong.*

Kruger had little sympathy, at the time, for this embittered, gin-doused, disintegrating failure. There were worse things than wanting to be strong. Worse things than not failing! At seventeen, his rage clotting into patriotism in just the way that recruiters have always found convenient, he did the thing best suited to punish Papa for his helplessness: he joined the Prussian navy. He soon grew to loathe its strictures but to love the borderless sea, so that later, having fled Prussia for Amerika, he continued to work as a seaman, then as a second and first mate, on packets and coal-steamers out of Brooklyn, up and down the Atlantic seaboard and as far south as Panama. Yet more and more, hearing tales, he conceived a strange longing to see the Arctic.

In the Bowery, in the Pell Street flophouse where he slept in a bunkroom on a cot, with a deal locker for his effects, Kruger pondered his fall. He could not even return to work at sea—not after what Tyson had said of him. He was still collecting a remittance from the Kaiser's navy on account of the serious wound he had received in '64, but the amount would buy little with the current inflation. He became a client of the stale-beer dives, swilling four-cent Choctaw punches of hot rum, benzine, camphor and cocaine dregs. Telling his story to any who would listen.

Kruger had his story, but Tyson had a Book.

At last he tried publishers in Germany. The country's ever more nationalistic public did hanker for an account of the fiasco, especially as some American newsmen had implied that the Germans on the *Polaris* might have been "secret agents" planted in hopes of usurping the expedition and raising the Black Eagle at the Pole. And in the minds of some Americans, the German doctor, Bessels, remained a suspect in Captain Hall's mysterious death. Hadn't Bessels, soon after the burial, attempted to reach the Pole himself? And on the ice-island hadn't the Germans actually tried to seize power? Germany, now unified and with a growing sense of itself, did want its own rendition of affairs. But evidently not from the ruined Kruger. Still lacking America's selectively democratic ways, Germany would *much* prefer to hear from a man of rank, and that would be the ship's meteorologist, Friedrich Meyer. The Count, as he came to be known on the ice. But the meteorology of the Count's mind, already so unsettled during their ordeal, had lapsed into chronic storm soon after the rescue. He now resided in a fairly new, well-appointed asylum in the Catskills. So it could never be known for certain if it was only delirium that had once made him whisper to Kruger, But we *are* agents of the Kaiser, you see. All this was arranged! We *are* spies!

Kruger's numb, kicking feet jam in the slimy rocks of the inshore. He wobbles in through the shallows, hauls himself shuddering onto the pier under the tower. The watchman with his raised storm-lamp squints noncommittally at this wild-eyed amphibian stinking of sewage, then tosses down the stub of a cigar, turns up his collar and saunters off. It seems a night of receding lamps. Kruger picks up the stub and warms his lungs. It's unexpectedly marvellous, this long and re-inflating puff. He finds his briarwood pipe still in the fob, although his book—Voltaire's *Littlebig*—is gone. There's nothing more to lose, it seems. The past few years he has been adrift, swept along on the current of history, part of the race to the Pole and the contest of rising nations, and this is where he has washed up. To hell with history. He will flee south, somewhere warm, Mexico, where his naval remittance will go farther—not face another winter of womanless cold and disgrace.

Next day at noon, sneezing, clothes still damp under his overcoat, he stumps up Fourth Avenue to the Grand Central Depot to buy a ticket for as far south as he can afford. En route he collects a waddling entourage of scavenger-pigs—the city's trash disposal system—who seem appetized by the smell of the river still on him. A further odour of disgrace. People glance or stare frankly as his following grows. Hugging his overcoat tighter around him he accelerates, trying not to inhale the food-smells as he passes a child wrapped in a shawl with a pot at her bare feet, calling hoarsely, Hot corn, here's your nice hot corn!, then a newsboy with a cherub face and town-crier voice blocking his path, walking backward, shaking a *Herald* up at him as he screams, Sitting Bull and Injuns in full retreat from the army, Mister, you can read it yourself here!

Thank you, he says, no. He has given the papers a wide berth for some time. Still trailing a wake of pigs he passes Madison

Square Garden, where a vast amputation is on outdoor display: the arm and torch of the Statue of Liberty. To get any closer you have to buy a ticket, apparently a way of raising money to finish the enormous plinth and assemble the statue. It looks as if the full statue has been buried in the earth by some disaster, only the arm and torch now showing, five storeys high. Dapper men and women strolling around it.

The cheapest train ticket is for a week later and can take him as far south as Mobile and leave him a couple of dollars besides. He writes a letter to his brother Armin, in Danzig, though he has not heard from him since after *Arctic Experiences* appeared—and, of course, he writes Tukulito in Groton, a simple, formal note, telling of his departure and wishing her and her family well. Nothing more, nothing to embarrass her. His first note to her in almost a year.

In disgrace you feel certain nobody wants to hear from you.

As ever, I remain your most loyal, and obedient,

R. K.

Two days later a letter arrives at the flophouse, the first letter Kruger has had in weeks. It's postmarked *Groton*, but the *Mr R. Kruger* on the envelope is not inked in her stiffly perfect cursive. With his penknife he edges it open, breathing little, as on the morning six years ago when a reply came from his mother's house in Danzig, but his name and address were not written in her hand.

Tukulito's neighbour and American sponsor, Mrs Budington, has written some lines on a piece of vellum cardstock, in a crabbed, shivery script:

My Dear Mr Kruger,

"How the Lord doth try our Strength" Punnie is dead, & Hannah inconsolable. O I fear for her as well, truly I do! The Child took ill with Cold but a week ago, & this Cold it went all to her Lungs. Sunday night she passed on Yes, on the Lord's Own Day He gathered to Him this gentle Lamb of the North. She will be interred this Friday next at Noon at the Starr Burying Ground on Starr Hill. I do hope, as does Hannah, who is indisposed, that you will attend! She & also the Child would speak so fondly of you, & often! Mr Tyson I hope will not attend, tho he may read of the Child's passing in the News-papers, & no help for that.

In shared Sorrow, & in sincere hope of Welcoming you soon,
For 'Hannah,' & for 'Joe,'

I am your truly faithful and trusting Servant,

Mrs Sydney Budington

Starr Burying Ground, Groton, Connecticut, 23 November 1876

THE SMALL CEDAR COFFIN has been eaten by the earth. But the gullet of lead-coloured clay remains open, as if hungry still. On the lip of the grave, see Tukulito in her black veil dropping in her handful of dirt. She does not direct it, just lets it slide through limp fingers. Her sobs turn to coughs while she stands swaying, as if to the slow bass of an inward dirge—unable to turn from the hole and walk away. Easier maybe just to topple forward, to follow the dirt now spattered over the bed-like lid of the coffin, homeward. Down there it's always the Arctic. Her face veiled, a doll in the crook of her arm and standing barely five feet tall, Tukulito could be a schoolgirl playing at grief.

The afternoon is unseasonably warm and so still that the straws of hair poking from the Reverend Cowan's bald scalp do not stir. The Ground is on the eastern face of Starr Hill so that the light of the sun foundering into the stripped hardwoods on the hill's crest skims downhill, level with the slope. Shadows of mourners and monuments are fantastically elongated. The beams ignite little bonfires of colour amid leaf-drifts that gales have piled against the west-facing stones.

Beside the Reverend Cowan, the piano teacher Mr Chusley stands dabbing at his nose with a handkerchief. Next, there's Kruger, in his tight-buttoned black seaman's overcoat despite the weather, his derby in his hands, mussed hair upright like breaking surf. A rumpled skeptic, but his eyes are red. Beside him Miss Crombie, the schoolma'am, glares upward with a look of perplexity and something like indignation: the look of someone whose beliefs are in tumult, maybe about to change. A handful of the child's white classmates are clumped around her. The largest set of mourners is the Budingtons: Sydney, who captained the *Polaris* and, although not present on the ice, was also accused in Tyson's book and disgraced, his wife Sarah, and the Budingtons' many grown children. For years the Budingtons have been "Hannah and Joe's" hosts in the South, and after the rescue assisted them in buying their own house, close by. But Joe—Ebierbing—is now absent. After two years' settled work as a carpenter, farmhand, and fisherman, he grew restless and returned to the Arctic with another expedition.

To think he knows nothing of this, muses Tyson, who's stationed apart, stiffly squared, as if policing the event, in the dress uniform he has just received as captain of a ship taking yet another expedition north next spring. His tight, guarded eyes like isinglass in his florid face. Greying mutton-chop whiskers. He's brawny, looks like a man of few sympathies, and yet. *Think of poor Joe peacefully digesting his dinner, picking his teeth with a fish-bone, smoking his pipe . . . my God!* Feeling himself watched, Tyson glances over, again receives from Kruger that fixed, incriminating stare. He looks away past the grave to where the goat-bearded sexton stands by a young elm, hands folded atop the long spade handle, chin propped on his knuckles. He's humming softly. One soiled boot rests on the blade-back as if on a tavern foot-rail. When he sees Tyson glaring, he straightens up fast.

Tyson is the sort of man who has to be testing his power all the time. He never can resist a test. If none arises, he will find ways of engineering one. Without constant proofs of strength and competence he feels himself fading, shrivelling into something less than himself—less than solid. He must keep ramming himself up against the world to make sure he is all there. He still longs to perform one grand, strenuous feat that will make his name, imprint it on the upper zones of all maps, win him a respect he will no longer have to prove himself worthy of, day in day out—his own misgivings like wind-driven snow filling in the tracks. In leading the floe-party to rescue, then publishing a book on the ordeal, it might seem he has succeeded perfectly. But *Arctic Experiences* has not done especially well. Worse, certain newsmen have doubted elements of his account. And at the naval inquiry after the rescue, Kruger, among others, while praising his courage and resourcefulness, had also embarrassed him. *Yes, on board I saw the Lieutenant when he was drunk like old mischief. I saw him when he could scarcely move along.* (There wasn't much of this talk, but it's what Tyson recalls best.) In the battle of narratives that followed, Tyson's own did prevail, and he is widely revered as a hero, but not in the unassailable way he desires.

Tyson is the sort of man who will always feel himself assailed.

Now Chusley is guiding Tukulito back from the rim of the grave, encouraging her in a mild, stammering voice: Come, Hannah, please, you must. You must have some tea. Some tea now. She moves as if newly blind. Anyone can see he is in love with her: a married woman, dark and rather plain, her head too large for her tiny sloped shoulders. Yet she gains loyal admirers—such as Tyson himself, on the ice. Such as Kruger, who may also have been her lover.

Tyson is pained and also surprised to see Kruger here, having heard rumours that the man had returned to Europe, like some of the other crewmen. Soon after the publication of *Arctic Experiences* Tyson received a letter from Kruger and, deeply offended, had not replied.

To disregard the wishes of the dying can be an act of love—so the Reverend Cowan told Tyson before the burial. The father, especially, will need a body to mourn on his return. And Cowan explained how the Esquimau child, delirious in fever, had made her mother promise to bury her at sea, like a certain crewman who had died of the pleurisy on that sealing ship that plucked them from the ice. The *Tigress*, Tyson said. Yes, he remembered that man. Pockets weighted with shot, body swaddled in his own blanket. While the sealers stood by, bowing rain-drenched heads, the man's three brothers had lugged him over the gunwale and let him drop into seas still scraping and rattling with ice—slabs and pashy floes and slurry. Tyson had watched, grim-eyed, yet with a survivor's numb detachment, his belly packed, mind dulled. . . . Cowan reported that at the time it had not seemed to Hannah that Punnie had noticed the event, yet three years later as she lay burning in bed—fingers scuttering over the counterpane as if at the keyboard—she remembered. Why, she even remembered the dead man's name: Obadiah Squires. I want to be buried in that cold water, Mama, she'd said in English. She would only use English now. Poor Hannah feared that she was forgetting her mother tongue. But my darling, you are getting better! she'd said, laughing and crying at the same time—you will not need to be buried on land or at sea!

Promise me, Mama.

Hannah, just do as she asks! Cowan had told her. Promise her! Perhaps it will calm her!

And she'd glanced at the physician, who nodded soberly, then at Chusley, who was watching the child's moving fingers with wide, blood-rimmed eyes, perhaps reading a familiar tune in their motions. The mother was known to all as quietly decisive, but at that moment she seemed utterly lost. At last she leaned close to her daughter's ear, stroking the freshly shaved head, and gave her word.

They file down the gravel path to Pleasant Valley Road. Mourners will walk more slowly from the grave of a child, but because it's downhill the numb-legged gathering moves with some clumsiness, faster than it means to, as if fleeing the site. Sarah Budington and Sydney in his stovepipe hat support Tukulito, dwarfing her, one on either side. They help her into the funeral brougham waiting by the churchyard gate and get in after her. Four black horses draw the brougham away. Cowan and Miss Crombie and Chusley and the other mourners climb into chaises and buggies and follow in a straggling procession back to the Budingtons' parlour.

There will be a wide selection of spirits, knowing Budington, thinks Tyson, who is now a teetotaller. He knows that Budington will be unhappy to have him in his house, but this is New England and the man won't want to make a scene—at least not until he has absorbed a few drams. There's also the German to consider. His letter all but challenged Tyson to a duel. Still, Tyson wants to be able to give Tukulito his heartfelt sympathies, and after what they went through together on the ice, he must.

Of course he's also drawn by the prospect of another test.

He declines an invitation to board a neighbour's buggy, meaning to walk, then realizes that Kruger, behind him, has already done the same. The final buggy rattles past Tyson and he walks steadily up the middle of the road, inhaling the wheel dust that hovers in the sun's last amber. The creaking of the buggy's axle fades. Kruger's footfalls sound some dozen paces behind. Tyson stifles a cough. It seems important not to accelerate, either. He slows down. In silence the last buggy rounds a curve in the road, vanishing behind a stand of black cypress-like pines.

Tyson stops, plants his feet, pivots from the waist up.

Well, shall we walk the rest of the way together, Mr Kruger?

For a moment it seems that Kruger will sweep past the larger Tyson without a word, but he halts abreast, gives Tyson a challenging look from under his hat-brim, then turns his eyes up the road.

Yes, and why should we not. And he strides on with his rolling, wide-stepping sailor's gait. The German accent is faint, although he still pronounces *w* like *v*, says *und* for *and.*

Especially on a day like this, says Tyson, catching up. His tone, while hardly fawning, is mild enough to broach the possibility of peace. Why revive finished battles? A sentimental part of him has always yearned to be liked as well as feared.

You're referring to the weather, Mr Tyson? *The veather.* Yes, a fine day to make amends.

I refer to the funeral of a child who shared our suffering and all but died with us. And I have no amends to make.

As they walk in silence on this road even the tiniest stone has its shadow. For a moment, their stride rhythms merging, they're in step.

Still, Tyson says softly, the weather is a true mercy. It's a harder thing to watch a body laid in frozen sod.

Ah, poor Punnie! Kruger exclaims.

That's it for a while. At last Tyson ventures, I do recall how you would often play with her and the other children on the ship. . . . German games, were they not?

Children's games are children's games. Leave your borders and uniforms out of it.

Tyson bolts a look at him and then down at his own moving, side-striped trousers. *You think a life without uniforms is possible, Kruger? How naïve that is of you. Who would protect our settlers under threat in the West? Who kept this country together, North and South, and emancipated the slaves?*

I didn't suppose you would come, says Kruger.

I shared their snowhut, Kruger.

Yes, and expressed disgust over Tukulito's housekeeping in your book. Also her habits. I didn't suppose you would dare coming. You disgraced her too. Disgraced everyone but yourself.

You retain a special concern for her, I see.

Ah, and you not? Kruger's smile is chilling. You can go to hell.

Tyson holds his composure. Slowly and earnestly self-educated, he feels awkward around the Educated, easily out-manoeuvred, an elephant trying to stamp on a panther. In fact Kruger has little more real schooling than Tyson—who as an orphan went to work in a Newark foundry, then escaped to sea—but Kruger is from a once-bourgeois family with bookish leanings, and his manner on the ice provoked Tyson sorely. But he had to harden himself to insolence out there, where at first the foreign crewmen were armed and he was not, and he desperately hoped to avoid mutiny and get the lot of them home.

The book was a journal, Kruger. We were all of us fighting to survive. Surely you felt moments of disgust with the men of your snowhut?

You said that your journal was lost—there in your prologue it said so, that you had to re-complete it from a few notes. You scarcely took any time at it, either. There were as many stories as there were castaways but you fed yours to the public first. They ate their fill, then they left the mess-hall. You received my letter?

You could hardly have expected a reply. You seemed to be hoping for pistols at dawn, in Central Park.

Kruger actually laughs. Damn lucky for you there was none of that. I seem to be increasingly unkillable. The polar seas couldn't manage it and last week also the East River failed.

I've no idea at all what you're saying.

But you ought to, you above all! On the ice I kept you alive. Count Meyer wanted a war. There was that time also, the one night when you were about—

Tyson stops, stamps his foot on the road and cries, God damn it, man, have you really come to the funeral of this poor child just to chastise me? I kept *you* alive. I was your ranking officer. Don't pretend you've forgotten our last weeks out there!

Kruger stares from under his hat-brim, arms stiff at his sides. For a moment it seems he is trying to nerve himself to draw a weapon from his packed pockets. Well, he says finally, I shall be leaving here—then looks down at his scuffed but polished boots, dusty now, and turns and walks up the road. It takes Tyson a moment to realize that he means he will be leaving the area, perhaps the country, not merely the spot where he was standing.

Tyson walks the rest of the way behind Kruger, who gradually pulls ahead. They pass a grey farmhouse set back in a stubble field. A clutch of crows peers up in silence from a furrow where something intriguing lies out of sight. In a woodlot there's a teetering rank of headstones, like a frozen demonstration of the force of gravity; Tyson's sharp eye distinguishes a date brought out by the sun's last rays, maybe victims of the Indian chieftain, King Philip. The English settlers in this area were exterminated. But they had sprung back. And in June of this year Custer and his bluecoat cavalry were wiped out, but many more soldiers had come after them to drive the Sioux and the Cheyenne and the other hostiles farther back into the wilderness—farther back, Tyson feels, into the human past that is their true habitat. He likes Hannah and Joe very much, he admires them truly, but he takes it for granted that they are unusually advanced members of a primitive, doomed race. The child's death is a heartbreak, yet in some parlour of the mind it gratifies the vision of racial destiny that Tyson shares with his era. The Esquimau has no resistance to the ailments of civilization, and that is telling. *The native is but an episode in the advance of the Caucasian.* Where did he read that? A recent editorial, perhaps in the *Tribune.* The tone was neither hostile nor contemptuous. It was simply the pragmatism of progress.

Tyson's wife and son were to have accompanied him to the funeral, but he and Emmaline had quarrelled again and he had left for the train alone. Of all the things that had kept him alive on the ice—fear of disgrace and the hope for fame (the two are really one), duty to the flag and to God, old habits of discipline, hopes of exposing Budington, hopes of punishing the crew, dreams of a bath and fresh oysters with horseradish and vinegar and her hot crusty bread, richly buttered, dripping with molasses—none seemed as important as Emmaline and little George. He had his duty to them too. Above all, he had his Love. In the breast pocket of his shirt he kept a torque of strawberry blonde hair with a circlet of the boy's auburn hair linked through it. Only let me return and I'll never again look complacently, or with bored aversion, on the comforts of home. On the ice he'd contemplated Home so avidly. And somehow in the fragrant, copious kitchen of his meditations he'd altered it—or his absence had. On his return as a hero he seemed to feel, naturally enough, that some kind of reward was in order, but the boy seemed a changeling, his wife a disappointing impostor. Stern-faced, stolid, thorough—not the imagined bride who'd helped keep his heart beating in that hell.

Clearly she found him changed as well. His faith had been fractured. Because God had not been out there. He couldn't tell her that in the Arctic an interstellar cold and darkness dipped down to touch the planet's bare scalp. As a whaler, then a mate, then a captain, Tyson had been up there often before, but never in such a naked way. He was struck through by that cold and darkness and carried them back to the human South like an infection. The house became a chambered vault of ice. In recreating his journal for the book, he'd often referred to God's watchful Providence on the ice, and the repeated act of writing the words had seemed to trick back some faith—though never for long. He has constructed himself around various loyalties, and his fame is built on just that, yet now it seems he's destined to fail—to leave on the ice—his wife and small son. It's an era when such an act can destroy you. There's a mistress now too. But the new expedition he will lead (to initiate a white colonization of the Arctic) will remove him from the scene for now and allow him to go on convincing others that he's still what he's thought to be.

What he's thought to be is a man of his time. The ice has made him a man of our time.

As the coloured maid admits him to the vestibule he can hear Kruger being introduced in the parlour. When Tyson finally enters, a hush falls. Kruger, in his overcoat, is kneeling in front of Tukulito, who is collapsed, dwarfed, in a deep wing chair by the hearth. Kruger holds her hand in his two hands—an almost courtly posture. Now, seeing Tyson, he rises, releasing her hand, and steps back, though not far. His fists disappear behind him and he averts his face as if to study the Civil War lithograph hung over the sideboard. Tyson's scalp burns. The house seems very warm. It hits him that perhaps the German has still not removed his overcoat because he means to pocket some of the lesser crystal by the decanters. That or it's the only black thing he owns. The Budingtons receive Tyson with frosty correctness. Their mouths are compressed as if the glasses between their fingers hold not sherry but vinegar. The mourners stare with bright indecisive eyes, as if torn between interest in Tyson, fresh from the lecture circuit, and fealty to the ruined Budingtons. Tukulito draws herself out of the chair and stands—Tyson begging her not to rise—and whispers his name. Face shrunken with sorrow she smiles a little behind her veil to pretend she is all right. On the ice he never once heard her complain. In the crook of her arm is a battered Esquimau doll—Punnie's doll, Tyson recalls it well, with its pouting sinew mouth; boy dolls smile, the child once informed him, the girl ones they all frown. Tukulito sets out across the carpet toward Tyson, who moves to intercept her before she can faint.

Chihuahua State, Mexico, New Year's Day 1877

He emerges from the wine-cellar dimness and chill of the cantina and lifts his face to the sun still afloat over the plaza, still parching its border of adobe shops and acre of rusty dirt with such severity that it seems this town, Maria Madre, has become the sun's exclusive target. Even now, late afternoon, the throbbing air hits him like a draft from a boiler-room hatch. And the roar of the fiesta—the hollering, the song and the talk, the blurting of trumpets and fast strumming of guitars—seems the peculiar and complex clamour of that heat.

He follows a troupe of drunkards merrily shouldering their way to the front. They are got up in tight short jackets, broadcloth trousers, boots whose blacking holds the cayenne dust. Around Kruger young women in hoopskirts, tortoiseshell combs in their blue-black hair, press together on tiptoe in their cliques or stand perched in side-on embraces, two to a wooden chair, a half dozen to a bench. Passing them he breathes more deeply, not so much to inflate his chest as to take in as much of them as he can. A man with a cigarillo and tusky moustaches as white as his hair shoulders a grandson who squints stoically through the flies. The man offers the boy—perhaps five years old—a puff of his cigarillo. The boy gravely accepts.

Toward the front, seeming to hover above the crowd, a stout

matron sits sidesaddle on a mare, her sun hat as broad as a parasol. The bridle is held by an old Indian in livery who stands at attention by the mare's head with his heels together, dirty feet fanned out, eyes closed. He's snoring. A wide, acorn-coloured face, like Ebierbing's poised above a seal-hole.

Kruger strokes the drowsing mare's forelocks and muzzle and tucks his hand into the nosebag. At the bottom he finds untouched corn and scoops and pockets a handful. The mare twitches, shies her head. Her gummed, blinkered eye, brown as syrup, pops open and considers him. A reflection in the eye makes him look behind: three other Indians, all in white blouses, have laddered themselves rump on shoulders in the manner of circus acrobats. The top man surveys the chaos from under the brim of a hawk-feathered bowler, the middle one gnaws at a tortilla, and the bottom one, squat and husky with cannonball calves, his bare feet planted, has no view of anything but still grins with buck teeth as sweat courses down his cheeks. Giving Kruger a second look—everybody does that here—he grins bigger and Kruger realizes he was not actually smiling before, the teeth project so sharply that he can't close his lips.

Kruger reaches the crowdfront where children in blossom-bright outfits festoon the crux and boughs of an ancient pecan. Massed along the eaves of shops across the plaza more onlookers, sharply defined by the back-sun, stand or hunker or sit with legs lolling. Far behind them, bordering the world to the southwest, a grey reef of barren peaks.

The plaza itself is vacant. Kruger is unsure of what's to come. In the cantina various revellers had competed to explain matters, gathering around this compact gringo with his heavy brow and hands, pipe with a curved stem, ratty bow tie. At last two drunken rancheros, despairing of his Spanish, began to mime a confrontation involving on one side a bull—a man planting the ends of two soup spoons on his lowered brow and lurching around the cantina, butting at a ring of giddy onlookers—and on the other side . . . what? A man with a broken nose raked sideways at a drastic angle stood swaying, head back, hands raised with the fingers curled, as if clinging to a precipice. Eyes in a blind squint. Clearly insensible to the pain it should be causing, he kept pursing up the nose and forcing out rough, bestial snufflings. Onlookers slapped at thighs and tables. A bear, Kruger assumed, but then the bull huffed and charged and the bear, roaring theatrically, snatched the bull's horns and lobbed them aside and cinched its opponent round the waist from above and the two men, near spastic with mirth, started grappling wildly, the circle of spectators yipping and cheering. So perhaps it was to be some kind of contest between men in animal costume? Some annual indigenous rite. Kruger drained his mug of gluey *pulque* and chuckled around his pipestem as the men, now locked in earnest, wheeled as one over the clay floor in the manner of a keg rolling over a ship's tilting deck.

Waiting with the crowds Kruger dips into his waistcoat fob and takes out a few of the almonds he shelled during the siesta, sitting on the side of the pallet in his ten-centavo room. In these almonds, pinched last night from a torch-lit stall in the thronged portico beyond the church, Kruger tastes most of all the fat. For the last four years he has not stopped craving fat and now expects he never will.

Through a growing gap in the crowd at the southwest corner, blurred through the heat's liquid shimmerings, a complex apparition is entering the plaza. Kruger, slowly chewing, squints against the sun. For a moment it seems that some immense animal is being torn apart for sport, files of men like centipedes heaving on opposing ropes, the animal already in two large pieces. Kruger stops chewing. There are two animals, he sees, a black bull and a brown bear. They are twisting, thrashing stiffly, a length of rope stretched between them—no, a chain, like the grapnel chain of a sloop, five or six feet of it linking one of the bull's forelegs to one of the bear's hind legs. Radiating round the animals like spokes are teams of barefoot men in the white pyjamas of peons. Three teams fan out from either animal, hauling on ropes attached to each of their free limbs, keeping them apart. The teams closest to Kruger on either side tug rhythmically, pulling the animals into the heart of the plaza.

Other men appear through the dust and miraging heat: a fat officer waving a sabre and yelling orders, behind him five men elongated by the heat into uniformed scarecrows, barefoot, with rifles and bayonets. Kruger looks down. A mestizo girl in a stained smock held up at the front with both hands as if to keep it out of the dust is skirting the crowd, yelling up at the faces. A ranchero next to Kruger responds, tosses a coin that the girl receives by unfolding her smock and catching it in the pouch. The pouch contains little cobs of scorched Indian corn. With a grubby hand she passes a cob and then a second cob to the ranchero and scutters on.

The man turns to Kruger with tiny drunkard eyes like bullet holes in a door.

You American? he shouts over the din, offering the bigger cob. He smiles with gold fangs under wax-pointed moustaches. Kruger, taking the corn with a half bow, says, I am from Prussia. Germany. *Muchas gracias. Habla usted* . . . You speak English? Perhaps you might explain to me. . . .

The man thrusts out his bristled chin, clucks his tongue. No have English. *Poco, poco.* You . . . no Espanish?

I am sorry, *no hablo mucho español.* I crossed the river only three days ago.

The man smiles, spreads his palms in a shrug, nods vehemently at the corn. Kruger never has to be exhorted, but now his mouth is too parched. With his tongue he tests the corn's luscious glaze of salty grease and charcoal, but can't bite in. It's the nearness of the first bear he has seen—and now smelled, a dense feculent waft of confinement and squalor—since the Arctic. And the presence of soldiers. Uniforms.

The peons have manoeuvred the animals into the heart of the plaza and are holding firm, leaning back on their ropes. Limbs spraddled out by the lines, the scrawny bear gnaws at the knots around one paw, then the other, back and forth as the moulting hide billows over its bones, the hump of the shoulders. The bull, small but fit, its front-heavy shape sleek and lean, is yanked back by the ropes onto its haunches. It brays like a train, tossing a maul-shaped head at the sun.

The officer holds up his sabre and performs a sort of slow pirouette, on tiny feet. He has spurs, a frogged and braided green jacket, gold epaulettes, a cocked hat with a plume. Medals, of course, winking on his breast. Apparently he means to slaughter the animals while they're helpless. He steps toward them, blade over his shoulder. The mob is coaxed to roaring of a fresh fever. He nears the bear. Its piggish snout is wrinkled back, lips peeled off the lathered fangs, jaws gaping. The peons haul back on their lines: with a choked moan the bear seems to offer its paws, like a schoolboy submitting to the cane. The officer hefts his sabre and slashes. As the blow falls, the line of peons staggers backward, some of them laughing as they stumble and the crowd is laughing too and Kruger can see that the bear is uncut, his left front paw now free. The officer has severed the rope, a foot from the knot. With a new spryness, maybe a sign of faltering nerve, the man nears the bull as it puffs and lurches, eyes rolling, left foreleg flared out and held taut by the line. The man hacks at the line, rushing the effort, needing several blows to finish. He yells something shrill as he backs away. His preposterous plumed hat on the ground like a dead rooster. The foremen on the remaining ropes skitter in with knives in their teeth and crouch just out of the animals' range, carve quickly, rise and flee. The peons and soldiers scatter wild-eyed, laughing.

The bear and bull in their separate ordeals have seemed mutually unaware but they turn on each other instantly. The starved bear writhes around, rears up and lunges at the bull with shaggy arms open like a hunchbacked wrestler. The little bull lowers its muzzle to the dirt as if ducking, then rockets its head up at an angle, hooking with the outer horn. The bear drapes over the bull's shoulders, gripping with its fangs and rending with its claws, and the bull bucks, lifting its attacker off the ground again and again, the bear's hind paws dangling, chain and rope-ends swinging, as the bull thrusts a horn into the bear's groin.

Kruger can hardly hear the animals' slaughterhouse roaring over the din of the mob. He's moved forward by the pressure of people frantic to get closer, while he himself wants to retreat. The chain confines the animals to their own small island of intimate struggle; like the castaways on the ice. Kruger turns and realizes he's trapped. He's pushed, loses his balance. The ranchero grabs his arm and hollers something close in his face and Kruger smells *pulque*, peppers, Indian corn.

The bear, bleeding from the groin, rears onto trembling hind legs, searching the air with its snout and eyes as if the bull were not right there, planted a few steps away, as distant as the chain allows, its head stooped and the flayed muscle-hump of its shoulders heaving. Around the animals' other limbs the knots have loosened. Lanyard knots, Kruger thinks. The rope-ends will soon drop off. Like dazed human fighters they're holding back, considering. The crowd is muted. The bull chuffs sharply and then, hoofing up blood-sodden dirt, it charges the bear, who moves or stumbles to the side where the bull sticks him with a horn, but the bear wrenches free and grapples onto the bull's exposed flank. The bull whirls, bellowing. The bear is thrown loose but hangs onto the bull's hindquarters, wrapping itself over them as if covering a she-bear in a violent mating. It buckles the bull's dainty hind legs, trying to topple it in stages. But now, as the bull hauls and kicks out with its forelegs to keep upright, the chain wrenches the bear's back leg and it totters and flails, slamming onto its back in the dust. Laughter teems through the plaza as if at the antics of sideshow buffoons. The bull doesn't turn on the fallen bear. For a moment it seems to want to flee, or gain room to manoeuvre, its red crescent horns and bloodied shoulders straining toward the gap in the crowds, but, hobbled, it lurches, hops in place, the drag of the bear's weight too much for its foreleg. Recovering its fury it swivels and catches the bear in the act of righting itself. With a short, concise thrust, it hilts a horn in the bear's neck. Blood pumps into the air. The bear sits back down with a despairing, human howl.

The ranchero next to Kruger and others around him are yelling and bouncing, particoloured bills fanned in somebody's waving hand. Others groan and hang their heads. But the bear is still active. With a paw it cuffs the muzzle of the advancing bull and as the bull recoils with a small, stiff jump, like a fired howitzer, there's a clank and both animals are still. The crowd's clamour changes—gasps, here and there. The bear turns from the bull and starts waddling away. The chain has snapped at the attachment to the bear's manacle. The bull stands at a loss, twitching bloodied nostrils, snorting gore.

Leaving in its wake the officer's trampled hat, rope-ends, a spoor of blood graphic in the sunlight, the bear veers toward the north side of the plaza. A vacuum spreads around Kruger as spectators retreat, falling over each other like a mob fleeing a collapsing building. In a matter of seconds only Kruger remains, feeling nailed to the spot. Across the plaza the crowds also dissolving. In the middle the bull, head erect, trailing the snapped and clanking chain, canters in lame, crazed, tightening circles.

The bear moves in Kruger's direction, dragging itself with pigeon-toed forelegs. What is it about fear that makes the feared thing so often come about? As if you secretly desire and invite what you think of as deepest aversions. *You . . . German!* He half turns and there is the ranchero's sweating face, mouth working, the words nonsense. His friends are trying to drag the man away. They soon do. Kruger is alone. The bear sags to a halt a dozen steps short, its hog-small eyes dully measuring him, the barrel of its snout probing the air, wounds in full flux. From somewhere a shrilled command, then a stippling of flame and the ragged crash of rifles. The bear is blown onto its side; Kruger the last thing it has seen.

SLEEP ON THE ICE was protracted but shallow, shredded by jittery dreams and wakings, but that night Kruger and the men in their snowhut must have slept better, the seas below the floe almost placid, because later nobody could say whether the domed roof had caved in and the white bear had found them there exposed, or the bear with black-razored paw had sliced away the peak of the dome, like the top of a boiled egg, meaning to scoop out the insides. Kruger came awake to a Babel of panic, everyone reverting to his own tongue. The bear's eyes in the lamp's glow were reptilian and its massive skull outlined with stars, but had it really been slavering and roaring down like a fairy-tale dragon through a castle's shattered roof? Others would later describe a medley of horrific sounds, but, as Kruger retold it, the bear had gone about its business with a sort of laconic reserve, a demeanour of unhurried and routine competence. If there had been any roaring it had come from the men. The bear's jaws never opened and its eyes never blinked; its face was thoughtful, roman-nosed. Something almost surgical in its manner as it worked a white-coated arm over the edge of the hole and started probing down at the men trapped on the bed-ledge, their backs flinched up hard against the walls. Count Meyer (he was still addressed as "Mister" then) was trying to pull on his spectacles with one hand while jabbering orders. Who had moved his revolver? He was rummaging in the furs. Kruger and Anthing and Lundquist and Lindermann were all driving their fists into the walls, trying to punch through into the outer cold and feel for the rifles staked butt-down in the snow. This was before the rift between the parties—or the Nations, as the Count was to call them—deepened to the point where the men began keeping their firearms inside with them at night, despite the moisture, and a week after they had roasted the last of the dogs that would have warned them of the bear.

Jackson, the Negro cook, had dug out his cleaver and was waving it experimentally at the paw. In that cavernlight the blade looked rusted, dull and small. It was a yellowed, plush paw about the size of a young seal. It foraged closer while the men who had guns—all but Madsen and Jamka, who seemed paralyzed—kept reaching outside, arms through to the shoulders like horse doctors feeling for foals, and Kruger as he groped was swearing *Scheiße, scheiße, verdammt nochmal, wo bist du . . . !* The casual treachery of inanimate things. Now Madsen was yelling for help to Ebierbing and Hans and Tyson in the other snowhuts and Jamka was whimpering, giggling. Somebody sneezing repeatedly. Lundquist leaning back with his Springfield angled up, loading, he must have just pulled it inside, a clump of snow still on the sights, and the bear got its claws on the jerking leg of the steward, Herron, who started poking at it with a penknife. Kruger's hand outside closed on the freezing stock of his rifle. Lundquist's rifle, aimed at the bear's head, clicked coldly, nothing, and Lundquist cocked the hammer again and again nothing. Get me another fucking round, he said hoarsely in Swedish and Kruger understood him but was too busy twisting his own rifle in through the wall butt-first and cracking the breech and fumbling a cartridge into the groove and swinging it round and up and cocking the hammer with the side of his palm because his thumb was too cold. He aimed at the bear's cool, attentive face, beneath which little Herron was squirming and making farm-yard sounds, dagger-like claws barbed in his breeches, dragging him down off the bed-ledge into the centre of the hut, upending the lamp so that it flared up and then died.

The rifle fired in the dark. The brace-plate thumped Kruger in the starved hollow of his gut. He curled on the ledge, both hands gripping his navel with its old scar and renewed pain, while the men around him, on their feet donning their furs, began the celebrations. There's a pitch of joy, fierce and pure, primordial, unique to the truly desperate. They would butcher the animal now in the middle of the night and they would feast, their beards and teeth and lips lacquered with blood, greedy faces underlit by the refuelled blubber-lamps. A paleolithic scene. Ebierbing and Hans could be heard outside conferring in their clicking tongue, and now Tukulito was there, her composed, melodious voice, the first thing about her Kruger had loved—Are all the men quite well, Mr Meyer?—and then Tyson—I warned you this snowhut would not hold, Mr Meyer!—and two of the Esquimau children, likely Punnie and Succi, crying *Nanuq! Tuavilauritti!* Kruger sat up to receive a mug of foaming blood from a jolly-looking Herron—Herron whose squinty eyes used to vanish into his plump, port-coloured cheeks with every grin. Now his hag-face with gory lips and beard leaned in to kiss Kruger on the nose. A ghoul! In English Kruger asked after his leg and as Herron replied at length—again his garrulous self, though his teeth jittered and his Scouse accent had thickened—Kruger nodded, winced a smile, and drank the blood.

TWO

VERSIONS

OF LOYALTY

To understand desire, one has to be, or remember having been, hungry.

—JUDITH THURMAN

The world loves to be fooled.

—NICCOLÒ MACHIAVELLI

The image is an aerial view—night—the round
eroding icefloe glimpsed from the level
of clouds sweeping low and huge like ice-
bergs in the atmosphere. (Clouds that diffuse

the moon's searchlight beam—we're in a search plane.)
Through rifts in the gale, a gunblue fragment
lies coldly lit, adrift in black waters,
and the notion comes of remoter views:

blue planet in the deeper night of inter-
planetary seas, with stars of white shards,
faint sheddings, an image caught by satellite.
Now lampglow through the domes of separate

snowhuts seems the flicker of burning cities
glimpsed from space, by stationed personnel
served sudden notice of a deeper exile
at the start of some vast squabble of tribes.

THE VOICE IS BOTH MUFFLED and urgent in tone, like the voices of rescuers digging down to you. Tukulito works her face out from under the snow-covered pelts. Still dark, the morning sky has cleared and air of a searing coldness funnels down out of the high, dazzling altitudes of the Milky Way. On all sides, dimly visible, a pale and stately escort of icebergs drifts with the floe.

At the sea's edge, not far off, Lieutenant Tyson stands in his cap and cotton jacket, mumbling phrases of a song through chattering teeth, pulling at a tin flask of something, humming some more. Now passionately he bursts out, *O drill, drill, ye tarriers!*—then stops himself, glances around. Tukulito has never understood that line of the song, which the lieutenant and some of the other men would sing often aboard the *Polaris*. Since Captain Hall's death the officers have spent much of the expedition drunk. Many of Dr Bessels' prize specimens—a skua hatchling, three lemming embryos, the fist-sized testicles of a muskox—were left to spoil in their jars as the officers, and sometimes the men, helped themselves to gallons of taxidermic alcohol. Drunk, Captain Budington was the sort to turn sentimental, a devotee of table and song, hearth and all humanity, while Tyson grew more tight-lipped and flint-eyed by the dram. After Hall's death Budington was for sailing home, Tyson for slogging on to the Pole.

Somebody is moving under the pelts beside Tukulito and she feels for Punnie's head and slips her hand into the child's hood, resting it on her warm brow: Punnie is asleep, her breath slow and moist on Tukulito's wrist. It's Ebierbing who is stirring, not the child. His firm hand on Tukulito's backside, moving. Now, just a few body lengths away, Mr Kruger's hood pokes up out of this human snowdrift—the castaways lying together for warmth. He tugs back the hood with a white chuff of breath. His rumpled hair stands stiffly. He doesn't look toward her, he is watching Tyson, who is still searching out across the open water, sipping and humming. Kruger's mouth opens as if he will speak, but then he waits, apparently giving the lieutenant time to slip the flask back into his jacket. Kruger's beard tightens around his mouth and Tukulito senses his irony, his temptation to deliver some irreverent remark. She has heard him do so often enough. He is kind to the children, he is respectful to her, but she very much dislikes this irony. It makes it impossible to know what he really thinks about things. Usually with white people it is easy to know (their overt expressions, their spilling words)—essential to know! Kruger clears his throat and with untypical earnestness calls out, Sir? Allow that I take the watch now. Come in and take shelter, sir.

Tyson twitches, wheels around. By the time he is fully turned—that fast—he has pulled himself together. He always seems to gain inches of height and pounds of solidity whenever he feels himself under observation. Ebierbing's other hand squeezes the good fat of her belly and tugs downward, commandingly. Being freshly adrift, jammed here in a midden of sleepers, is nothing new to him, no sexual deterrent. He has never been as discreet as she would like. She pushes the hand away; she needs to observe this exchange. Lieutenant Tyson is now in command and much depends on him. Twice crushed by the loss of a son, Tukulito means to ensure her daughter's safety one way or another.

Ah, Kruger! says Tyson, as if clearing his throat with the name. Come in and find shelter, sir. Room can be found.

I mean to scout a little yet. Go back to sleep, Kruger.

Giving up on sheer force, her husband is easing down her caribou pants, stroking between her thighs. She swats at his hand. He grips her hand and tugs.

Any sign of the *Polaris*? Kruger asks hoarsely. Again no trace of irony. In fact, fresh from sleep like a child, he looks dazed and anxious.

Nothing! By God, when I lay hands on Budington again, he'll . . .

You're shivering, sir.

Never mind that. You rest now, with the others. At dawn I'll call you—all of you. And he strides off along the floe's edge, as if on a morning's brisk constitutional in a city park. Lunar rounds of breath rise and dissolve above him. Ebierbing's caresses are diligent and Tukulito is beginning to sag down to him, into the stuffy warmth under the pelts; Kruger turns, noticing her face, and stares for a long second. She stares back while Ebierbing's hand smoothly continues. Kruger nods, says stiffly *Madam*, then ducks back down into the snowdrift, as if in some children's game.

She is back in her husband's silent, barely moving embrace.

Above, massed stars droop and arc down to the horizon where the calm sea-leads around the floe are slick and milky with mirrored light. The floe seems to slide not over the sea but through the heavens. One of the men moans and babbles in German, the sounds muted through this huddle of bodies buried in the night's snow. They will never again sleep, or think, as a single group like this; for now they all believe that the *Polaris* must return for them at any time. It's silent. Snow cloaks the sleepers like quicklime over a mass grave.

TYSON, FROM *ARCTIC EXPERIENCES*

Oct. 16, 1872. Blowing a strong gale from the north-west. We are adrift on the ice, and the *Polaris* is nowhere visible.

I think it must have been about 6 P.M., last night, when the vessel was nipped with the ice. The pressure was very great. She did not lift to it much; she was not broad enough—not built flaring, as the whalers call it; had she been built so she would have risen to the ice, and the pressure would not have affected her so much. But, considering all, she bore it nobly.

In the commencement of these events, I came out of my cabin, which was on the starboard side, and looked over the rail, and saw that the ice was pressing heavily. I then walked over to the port side. Most of the crew were at this time gathered in the waist, looking over at the huge floe to which we were fastened. I saw that the ship rose somewhat to the pressure, and then immediately came down again on the ice, breaking it, and riding it under her. The ice was very heavy, and the vessel groaned and creaked in every timber.

At this time the engineer, Schuman, came running from below, among the startled crew, saying that "the vessel has started a leak aft, and the water is gaining on the pumps." The vessel had been leaking before like this, and they were already pumping—Anthing and Esquimau Joe, I think, with the small pump in the starboard alley-way. I then walked over toward my cabin. Behind the galley

I saw Captain Budington—who appeared again to have been drinking—and told him what the engineer said. The trembling wretch stood there apparently oblivious to everything but his own coward thoughts. Then, he threw up his arms and yelled out to "throw every thing on the ice!" Instantly all was confusion, the men seizing every thing indiscriminately, and throwing it overboard. These things had previously been placed upon the deck in anticipation of such a catastrophe; but as the vessel, by its rising and falling motion, was constantly breaking the ice, and as no care was being taken how or where the things were thrown, I got overboard, calling some of the men to help me, and tried to move what I could away from the ship, so things should not all be crushed and lost; and also called out to the men on board to stop throwing things till we could get what was already endangered out of the way. But still much ran under the ship.

It was a terrible night. It was snowing and drifting; the wind was exceedingly heavy, blowing strong from the south-east, and it was fearfully dark, and so bad was the snow and sleet that one could not even look to windward. High seas were striking the ship and the floe, and the air was filled with freezing spray, like hail, so that I could scarcely see the unloaded stuff—whether it was on the ice or in the water. Now and then the full moon cut through the clouds, but for a moment only, enough to show the great bergs bearing down on us, with the current and against the wind.

We worked for three or four hours, I sometimes on the ice and sometimes on the ship. On the ice Hannah was working beside me; and we worked till we could scarcely stand. They were throwing things constantly over to us. Then at last I went aboard—where I found that the engineer's statement about the leak was a false alarm! I asked Budington "how much water is the vessel making?" and he told me "he feared now that we had been mistaken." The vessel, it seemed, was mostly sound, but when the ice had nipped her and she had heeled, the little water in the hold was thrown over, and it made a rush, and Schuman thought a new leak had been sprung. Budington and I went below decks to check one more time. Finding she was making no more water, I returned to the ice to try and save the provisions. While we were so engaged, the ice commenced cracking; I warned Budington of it, he meantime calling out to "get every thing back as far as possible from the ship." We did not know who was on the floe or who on the *Polaris*; but I knew some of the children were with us, for at that moment I spied a little heap of musk-ox skins, lying across a widening crack in the ice, and as I pulled them toward me to save them, I saw that there were *two or three of Hans's children rolled up in one of the skins!*

Moments later, the ice seemed to explode under our feet, fracturing in many places, and stern ice-anchors broke loose. I saw the steward, John Herron, trying to leap from a pan of ice and grab the ship's loose hawser, but it swung away from him too fast. "Good-bye, *Polaris!*" he called, as the ship broke away in the darkness, and we lost sight of her in a moment.

Much, perhaps most, of the goods were lost in the floe's breaking, and now some of the men were on separate pieces of ice, all crying out for help. They could scarcely be heard over the storm. I took the "little donkey"—a small scow—and went for them; but the scow was almost instantly swamped. Then I shoved off one of the whale-boats, and took off Herron, Jamka, and Mr Meyer, while Kruger, Lindermann, and the coloured cook took the other whale-boat and helped their companions back; so that we were all on firm ice at last.

We did not dare to move about much after that, for we could not see the size of the floe we were on, on account of the storm and darkness. Fortunately we had the two whale-boats with us. The men had also saved their firearms and ammunition—a fact at which I was initially pleased—as well as their clothes bags. I had only the light clothing I had been wearing aboard the ship: my old sealskin breeches, an undershirt, wool shirt, cotton jumper, and "Russian cap." And now all the rest, the men, women, and children, sought what shelter they could from the storm by wrapping themselves in musk-ox skins, and so lay down to rest, huddled together. The dogs slept curled in the snow nearby. I walked the floe all night, keeping watch.

Around three in the morning the gale and snow abated, and by the light of the full moon's setting I could see all. This was a nearly circular piece of ice, about four miles in circumference. It was not level, but was full of hillocks, and also ponds, or small lakes, which had been formed by ice-melt during the short summer. The ice was of various thicknesses. Some of the mounds, or hills, were probably thirty feet thick, and the flat parts not more than ten. It was very rough; the hillocks were covered with snow; indeed, the surface was all snow from the last night's storm. Those who lay down on the ice were all snowed under—but that helped to keep them warm. Perhaps I should have lain down too, if I had had any thing to lie on; but the others had taken all the skins, and I would not disturb them to ask for one.

I should think the ship would soon be coming to look for us.

Why does not the *Polaris* come to our rescue? This is the thought that now fills every heart, and has mine ever since the first dawn of light this morning. At that time, I scanned the horizon but could see nothing of the vessel; but from a large hummock, the floe's highest point, I saw a lead of water which led to the land. The sea had become almost calm. I looked around at the company with me upon the ice, and then at the provisions which we had with us. Besides myself there were eighteen persons, namely:

Frederick Meyer, meteorologist (German); John Herron, steward (English); William Jackson, cook (Negro)—*Seamen:* R.W. Kruger (German); Fred. Jamka (German); William Lindermann (German); Matthias Anthing (German-Russian); Gus. Lundquist (Swedish); Soren Madsen (Danish).—*Esquimaux:* Joe; Hannah; Punnie (child); Hans Christian; Merkut or Christiana (Hans's wife); Augustina, Tobias, Succi (children); Charlie Polaris, new baby of Hans's; and there were as well six Esquimau dogs.

Now, to feed all these, I saw that we had but fourteen large cans of pemmican, eleven and a half bags of ship's biscuit, one can of dried apples, and fourteen hams; and if the ship did not come for us, we might have to support ourselves all winter, or die of starvation. Fortunately, we had the boats. As soon as I could see to do so, I walked across the floe to find where was the best lead, so that we could get to shore; and in the mean time I ordered the men to get the boats ready, for I was determined to make a start and try and get to the land, from which I thought we might find the ship, or at least, if we did not find her, we might meet with Esquimaux to assist us.

I wondered if perhaps the *Polaris* had foundered in the night, as I could see nothing of her.

On my return, I told the crew—who were up but had not yet seen to the boats—that we must reach the shore. They thought so too, but seemed very inert, and in no hurry; they were "tired" and "hungry" and "wet" (though I think they could not have been more tired than

I, who had been walking the floe all night while they slept); they had had, it is true, nothing to eat since three o'clock the day before, and so they concluded they must get a meal first. Nothing could induce them to hurry; while I, all impatience to try and get the boats off, had to wait their leisure. I might have got off myself, but I knew in that case, if the *Polaris* did not come and pick them up, they would all perish in a few days. So I waited. Not satisfied to eat what was at hand, they must even set about cooking. They built a fire of some broken gaff-poles which they had found in the whale-boat. They had nothing to cook in but a few flat tin pans, in which they tried to fry some of the tinned meat, and also tried to make coffee and chocolate. Then some insisted on changing their clothes. At last I got started about 9 A.M.; but, as I feared, the leads were now closing, and further I feared a change of wind which would make it impossible to reach shore.

The piece of ice we were on was now caught fast between heavy ice-bergs which had grounded, and we were therefore stationary. The wind had hauled to the north-east. I had no means of taking the true bearings, but it was down quartering across the land, and it was bringing the loose ice down fast. But though it seemed to be too late, still I determined to try. At last we got the boats off, carrying every thing we could, and intending to come back for what was left; yet when we got half-way to the shore, the loose ice, which I had seen coming, crowded on our bows so that we could not get through, and we had to turn back and haul up on our floe.

Within minutes we saw the *Polaris*, and I was rejoiced indeed, for I thought assistance was at hand. She came around a point above us, eight or ten miles distant. Yet she did not make for us. Thinking, perhaps, that she did not know in which direction to look—though the set of the ice must have told which way it would drift (and the small ice, though it had stopped us, would not stop a ship)—I set up my flag, and laid a square of India-rubber cloth on the side of a hummock. Then, with the spy-glass, I watched her.

She was under both steam and sail, so I went to work securing every thing, thinking she would soon come. I could not see any body on deck; they, if there, were not in sight. She kept along down by the land, and then, instead of steering toward us, dropped away behind what I suppose was Littleton Island. Our signal was dark, and would surely be seen at that distance on a white ice-floe. I do not know what to make of this.

I sent some of the men to the other side to keep a look-out there, and in going across they saw the *Polaris* behind the island, and so came back and reported; they said she was "tied up." I did not know what to think of it; but I took my spy-glass, and running to a point where they said I could see her, sure enough there she was, *tied up*—at least, all her sails were furled, and there was no smoke from her stack, and she was lying head to the wind.

And now our piece of ice, which had become stationary, commenced drifting; and I did not feel right about the vessel not coming for us. I began to think she did not mean to. I could not think she was disabled, because we had so recently seen her steaming; so I told the men we *must* get the boats to the other side of the floe, and try and reach the land—perhaps lower down than the vessel was—so that we might eventually reach her. I told them to prepare the boats. We would leave all of our supplies behind, taking only a little provision—enough to last perhaps two or three days.

I told the men that, while they were preparing, I would run across the ice and see if there was an opportunity to take the water, or where was the best place, so that they would not have to haul the boats uselessly. I ran across as quick as I could. I was very tired, for I had eaten nothing but some biscuit and a drink of blood-soup; but I saw there was an opportunity to get through, and that seemed to renew my strength. The small ice did not now appear to be coming in fast enough to prevent our getting across. But it is astonishing how rapidly the ice can close together, and I knew we were liable to be frozen up at any moment; so I hurried back to the boats and told them "we must start immediately."

There was a great deal of murmuring—the men did not seem to realize the crisis at all. They seemed to think more of saving their clothes than their lives. They said they feared we would be crushed by the small ice. But I seemed to see the whole winter before me. Either, I thought, the *Polaris* is disabled and can not come for us, or else, God knows why, Captain Budington don't mean to help us; and then there flashed through my mind the remembrance of various scenes and experiences aboard in which his indifference had nearly cost me my life, and those of the crew. But I believed he thought too much of little Punnie, Hannah, and Joe to leave us to our fate. Then the thought came to me, what shall I do with all these people, if God means we are to shift for ourselves, without vessel, shelter, or sufficient food, through the dark winter? I knew that sometime the ice would break into small pieces—too small to live upon. From the disposition which some of the men had already shown, I knew it would be very difficult to make them do what was needful for their own safety. Then there were all those children, and the two women.

It seemed to me then that if we did not manage to get back to the ship, it was scarcely possible but that many, if not all of us, would perish before winter was over; and yet, while all these visions were going through my brain, these men, whose lives I was trying to save, stood muttering and grumbling because I did not want the boats overloaded to get through the pack-ice. They insisted on carrying every thing. They were under no discipline—they had been under none since Captain Hall's death. Anthing and Kruger were especially stubborn on this point. The men loaded one boat full with all sorts of things, much of it really trash, but which they would carry. We were going to drag the boat across the floe to where we could take the water. I went on, and told the Esquimaux to follow me across. I had not gone more than two hundred yards before a fresh gale burst upon me. I nevertheless persevered and got across the ice, and when I got to the lead of water saw that the natives had not followed! Whether they thought too much of their property, or whether they were afraid of the storm, I do not know; but the coloured cook, Jackson, *had* followed me, and when he saw that they had not come he ran back for them.

The men, finally arriving with the boat they had dragged over so overloaded, now quibbled about getting in. I would have shoved off as long as I had the strength to do it; but when I looked for the oars, there were but three, and there was *no rudder*! I had told them to prepare the boat while I was gone; I had told them to see that all was right, including sails; but in truth they did not wish to leave the floe, and that probably accounts for it. I am afraid we shall all have to suffer much from their obstinacy. Perhaps we would not have reached either land or ship, but it was certainly worth trying. Why they prefer to stay on this floe I can not imagine; but to start with only three oars and no rudder, the wind blowing furiously, and no good, earnest help, was useless. I tried it, but the men were unwilling; and in the crippled condition of the boat it was no wonder that we were blown back like a feather. I was compelled to haul the boat back on to the ice. The men by this time were, I think, truly exhausted, and I could not blame them so much for not working with more energy.

Night was coming on; our day was lost, and our opportunity with it. We must prepare for another night on the ice.

We had to leave the boat where she was; we were all too tired to attempt to drag her back. We also left in her the clothing and other things the men had been so anxious to save in the morning. I went back toward the middle of the floe, and put up a little canvas tent, and then, eating a little frozen meat and ship-biscuit, I was glad enough to creep in, pull a musk-ox skin over me and get a little rest, drifting in the darkness I knew not where; for I had had no rest since the night before we parted with the ship. Now the ice-floe proved a refreshing bed, where I slept soundly until morning, when I was suddenly awakened by hearing a loud cry from the natives, and the barking of the dogs.

It had snowed during the night; but that was nothing. *The ice had broken!*—separating us from the boat which we had left, being unable to haul it the night before. Our cache of six large bags of biscuit remained with it on the old floe, and we were left on a very small piece of ice—the thick part where we had made our extemporized lodgings. As soon as I saw the position of affairs, I called the men out, desiring them to go for the boat and bread. It could have been done with safety, for there was no rough sea running between the broken pieces, and they had not separated much at the time; but I could not move them—they were afraid. (I noted that Hannah also by this point seemed quite unhappy with the men; I believe she has been so for some time.)

And so we drift, having but one boat on our piece of ice, while the other boat, and a good part of what provisions we have, remains on the main part of the broken floe. We drift apparently to the southwest, for I have neither compass nor chronometer with me; my compass is in that other boat, and even my watch is on board of the *Polaris*. Our piece of ice is perhaps one hundred and fifty yards across each way. Quite a heavy sea is running; piece after piece is broken from our "raft." God grant we may have enough left to stand upon!

Tukulito is melting snow in one of the big Schuyler Pemmican tins over the fat lamp, constantly checking the wick, adding more snow, stirring and now scooping in hunks of half-frozen pemmican from the tin Jackson has just opened. The walls of the snow cookhut are yellow with lamplight, damp and soft with the heat. Toward mealtimes everyone crowds into the cookhut. It's the warmest spot, of course, but also everyone wants to keep an eye on the food.

The bread now, please, Mr Jackson.

I suppose you mean this here wormy tack.

In pieces the size of playing cards, please.

He pushes his forage cap back on his head, where it rides lightly on a froth of curls.

This one here went along on Sherman's march, I wager. And I bet they wouldn't of et it then either.

Grimacing with the strain Jackson starts hand-breaking slabs of ship's biscuit to stir into the stew. On the *Polaris* he was in charge of the galley, and Tukulito was an unofficial assistant, but since their stranding on the ice, with no discussion and no fuss, they have exchanged roles. Sea ice is a constantly shifting extension of the Esquimau homeland; this is Tukulito's ancestral kitchen, as Jackson himself seems to realize.

God damn it half to blind, he cries, flinging down a chunk of biscuit. It's like cracking a god damn ox bone by hand, and for spoiled marrow.

He reaches for his cleaver.

Mr Jackson, Tukulito says with her soft English accent, I ask you again please not to swear so. The children often hear.

Well, but it ain't even their language!

It is mine, sir, by adoption. Hers as well.

Punnie is on the snow-bench poking eiderdown into Elisapee, her scowling doll, and sewing up the tear in its belly, her face bent close to the tip of the needle. She doesn't look up. For a moment Jackson stares at Tukulito. In his ginger-coloured face his green eyes are fixed hard; his mouth, fringed with a wisp of beard, is sullenly slack. At last he starts chuckling. Well, I am sorry, Mrs Ebierbing. I know I keep telling you this same sorry, then I keep saying them words again.

You are better than most on the ship.

What *ship*? says Anthing in his thin, breathy tenor. He's playing euchre, teamed with Jamka against Herron and Kruger, all the men stripped to grimy drawers and heavy, high-necked sweaters. Tukulito's impression of Anthing is always of a large pair of bloodshot eyes bulging under pressure, as if meaning to pop out at you. They give him a constantly indignant look. He has a snub nose in a broad pink face, curly blond whiskers, a head of wiry curls. A lower front tooth is missing, adding to the impression of a cranky, bearded boy.

She thinks we are still on a Gott damned ship, Anthing goes on, as if Tukulito's slip of the tongue, with its reminder of where they are not, makes her somehow blamable for where they are. *She thinks* comes out as *She sinks.*

Spiel weiter, says Kruger. Just let her alone.

Never disturb a working cook, Herron adds lightly, yet with hunger edging his voice. What's trump again?

Pik! says Anthing. The spades. You know this.

Jackson pauses, cleaver upraised over the stubborn biscuit. On this here chunk of ice, he says, with all this other ice around, I reckon we're safer than on any ship. Like can't hurt like, not so easily.

The bread, please, Mr Jackson.

Not to say *we're* all like here, are we, lads? says Herron.

Jackson brings the cleaver slamming down. The biscuit shatters with a fearsome crack. Everyone looks over, startle-eyed, except for Punnie, who goes on stitching with grave concentration, and Anthing, who could well be deaf, all sense-energies funnelled through those great, globular eyes that go on searching his cards. A boy's impatience, but also a boy's intense competitive focus.

After a moment Kruger lays the jack of spades on the snow.

Hah, lads! cries Herron, snapping down two more cards with a grin. You're considerably euchred!

Herron, raised in Liverpool, a recent emigrant, is the only crew member who is liked by everyone, even by those who dislike each other, and so like an axletree he has helped to hold together the spokes of this varied wheel, so far. Though still in his twenties he's as florid and portly as a middle-aged squire. Though never drunk or profane—he's a Quaker and teetotaller—he always seems to be in a state of mild, comradely intoxication. He's one of those who give kind words and compliments not out of strategy, but simply for the pleasure of spreading contentment. One of life's natural harmonizers. His good cheer compels belief, seeming to defy fate to do its worst; as if fate, thinks Kruger, ever needs an invitation.

Kruger has read somewhere that "character is fate" but to him, now, fate is simply People in Power—Budington, who seems to have deserted them, and Tyson, who has tried to make them quit the floe's relative safety for what seemed, to Kruger and the other men, certain death in an open boat stripped of supplies. What chance would they have stood in a gale, or if the milling ice had crumpled the boat? Well, brave men love to roll the dice.

But at least when fate takes human form, it's resistible.

On their sixth morning adrift, a piece of good luck from bad. Kruger, Herron, Jackson, and Jamka, reasoning that several hunters will be more effective than one, discreetly follow Ebierbing to the banks of the small floe in a glacial twilight. Knowing stealth to be vital they conceal themselves in back of a small hummock thirty paces behind Ebierbing, who is prone on the floe-edge beside his kayak. Jamka's presence makes Kruger uneasy. His service in Bismarck's recent war with the French has left him damaged. Kruger is baffled as to how he got past the immigration agents in Battery Park, then hired on for this expedition. He is shaggy and gaunt, as if cast away for years already. Sometimes he looks cross-eyed and his gapped teeth are stumpy and brown. He fidgets, startles at the slightest noise.

Ebierbing lifts onto his elbows and aims his rifle at a vague form on an ice pan some way off in the dimness. The crewmen also take aim and slowly, in near silence, thumb back their hammers. Let Joe shoot first, Kruger whispers, nodding toward Ebierbing while trying to catch Herron's eye—because Kruger is wary of him, too, his exuberance. There is no endearing trait in anyone that's not also a liability sometimes. Ebierbing holds his aim, motionless for minutes, in wait, it seems, for the ice pan to drift nearer, as it appears to be doing, if slowly. Breezes riffle the wolf-fur fringing of his hood. Kruger's forefinger starts to prickle with the cold. There's a sharp report and the four deputy hunters open fire and continue shooting as quickly as their fingers can lever and jam the trapdoor-breeches with rounds. The ice pan disintegrates in a fountain of snow and its passenger lurches or falls off with a splash, merging into the black sea. *Hab'n wir's erwischt?* asks Jamka—but Ebierbing is not leaping into his kayak to retrieve any seal. In fact, he is staring over his shoulder at the men. His brown face, fringed with the hood's grey-white fur, shows surprise veering toward exasperation, even disgust—a frankness of anger completely untypical of him.

Have we a seal to our breakfast then? asks Herron as he rushes toward Ebierbing, who without a word gets up nimbly and seems stanced to dodge out of the way should Herron try to embrace him—Herron's custom with everyone—thus possibly propelling both men into the sea. Now Jamka with his strong accent bellows, WE HAVE WAITED UNTIL YOU HAVE FIRST FIRED!—

and though Ebierbing usually just shrugs and grins whenever Jamka tries to address him, he now says curtly, I never fire my Spencer. You hear the ice break. I wait for this seal be much more closer—seal gives a hunter just one shot!

In silence Kruger and the others study their sealskin boots. After some seconds Ebierbing seems to chuckle and Kruger looks up: the man is shaking his head, laughing broadly, stub teeth under his long Mongol moustaches. Kruger offers gruff apologies while Herron, as if wishing to make reparations, starts gesturing upwind. Look! I believe it's a walrus, something big! All turn: another dark shape on the edge of what seems a much larger piece of ice, looming. Herron and Jamka seem keen to start blasting away at it. Ebierbing raises his hand. After a few seconds of level study he says calmly, By golly, boys, it's the boat.

The rest of the party soon gathers with them while the larger floe, with the lost boat aboard, glides toward them, as if conjured and hauled in by their collective will. Herron and a few of the men cheer—a small, hollow sound in the face of the floe's vast and silent approach. Hurrah. They cheer on, Kruger now, too, as if this were the ship returning, the *Polaris* whose mainsail they still spy in every passing berg. But there is no one to cheer back.

Thank God, says Tyson, his face taut with emotion.

That evening in the big communal snowhut Tyson stands as straight as he can under the dome and says that tomorrow they will re-establish themselves on the large floe. With the five hundred pounds of biscuit recovered with the boat, he says, they now have about 2,400 pounds of provisions, but, considerable as that may sound, they will have to commence rationing tomorrow. Meyer, Kruger and the others grudgingly consent to the necessity, but Anthing, Jamka, and Lindermann grumble. (The Esquimaux remain silent—unconsulted, and, it seems, unconcerned.) Anthing: Surely the *Polaris* must soon come for us, or we will arrive at the shore? Tyson stares at him without a word and Anthing can find no more words of his own, at least in English, although he does mutter something in German to Jamka, his bulbous eyes scanning the other men's faces. Kruger can't make out the words. An uneasy silence follows.

Still, for the first time since the stranding there is some cheer in their camp. They eat a last, large meal of pemmican stewed with biscuit, then canned apples, then coffee and chocolate, all prepared in cleaned pemmican tins by Tukulito and Jackson. After dinner the men play euchre while Ebierbing tells the children a story in their language, deftly animating it with hand-shadows on the snowhut dome. At one point Kruger makes out a dancing fox, then a large bear rearing over the card players' bowed heads. Tyson and Meyer are scratching and correcting a rough map on the wall, discussing their position. Herron suggests that as Greenland is receding from view, they must be drifting toward the west-shore, and God willing tomorrow or the day after they might find themselves aground on the coast. It's muskox loin to our dinners then, lads, he says. *I* hear as they'll just stand in a circle and let you walk up and shoot 'em.

Jackson says, I don't reckon we'll hit one any other damned way.

When Kruger goes out to the floe-edge before sleep, a half moon is peering through long louvres of cloud over the snowy summits and blue glaciers of Greenland. There's Tyson, standing at the earthquake-seam between the small and large floes, apparently checking one of the ice anchors they've dug in to hold them fixed. A glint of moonlight on tin as he cants back his head to drink from his flask.

Kruger starts pissing as noisily as possible, aiming at a swath of hard ice. Tyson spins around, slipping the flask back into his jacket.

Mr Kruger! I did not hear you come out.

That preservative is not known to sharpen the senses, sir.

After a beat or two: I *beg* your pardon?

Your plan for rationing is a good one, sir, but you may not always make such good plans after consulting with your bottle.

Folding his arms across his chest, Tyson lowers his brow like a bull. The visor of the Russian cap hides his eyes. His hands are bare. Mr Kruger—you were second mate aboard the *Polaris.* Out here you're simply a castaway. Don't forget yourself.

It appears to me, sir, that you also are a castaway here.

Kruger shakes and tucks his frosted member back into the fur trousers.

If you will forgive my frankness, sir.

Go back into the snowhut, Tyson says, and Kruger nods once and turns away.

Oct. 22. We have now given up all hopes of the *Polaris* coming to look for us, and this piece of ice will never do to winter on. So today I got the boats loaded, harnessed on the dogs, and so sledged all of our supplies across onto the big floe. It is fortunate, indeed, that we have these boats. Humanly speaking, they are our salvation, for in an emergency we can use them either for the water or as sledges.

Have had another talk with Mr Meyer about the locality of our separation from the *Polaris.* He thinks we were close to Northumberland Island, but I believe it was Littleton Island; he says "he ought to know," for he took observations only a day before, and of course he *ought* to be right; but still my impression is that Northumberland Island is larger than the one the *Polaris* steamed behind. I wish I had a chart, or some means of knowing for certain. Meyer has now taken to reminding me that he is a "trained meteorologist," by which he means "educated man"—and educated "in Europe," too! Apparently books and diplomas count with him for more than experience. He has little of *that.* What with his blond, retreating hair grown somewhat long in the back, his full moustaches, and his hawk nose, he looks somewhat as the famed Colonel Custer might if that gentleman wore spectacles.

The weather has come on very bad; but, fortunately, we have got our new snow-houses built. We have quite an encampment—one "officers' hut," or rather a sort of half-hut, for Mr Meyer and myself; Esquimau Joe's hut for himself, Hannah, and Punnie; a hut for the crewmen; a store-hut for our provisions; and a cook-house, all united by arched alley-ways built of snow. There is one main entrance, and smaller ones branching off to the several apartments, or huts. Hans has built his family hut separately, but nearby.

Joe did most of the work building these huts, or *igloos*—he knew best how to do it—but we all assisted. We have to do things fast, because there is not much light to work by; only about six hours a day, and not very clear then. On cloudy or stormy days it is dark all the time. Tomorrow, according to Mr Meyer, we shall see the last of the full sun until well into the New Year.

We only allow ourselves two meals a day now, and Mr Meyer has made a pair of scales, with which to weigh out each one's portion, so that there should be no jealousy. We use shot for weights. Our allowance is very small—just enough to keep body and soul together; but we *must* economize, or our little stock will soon give out altogether. Our present daily allowance is eleven ounces for each adult, and half-rations for the children. Already the men visibly suffer, and I am so weak that I sometimes stumble from sheer want of strength.

Hans has just taken two of the dogs, killed and skinned them, and will eat them and feed them to his family, for they ate their full allowance at breakfast and have nothing tonight. I give each of the natives the same amount of biscuit, and whatever else we have, as

I deal out to myself; but the Esquimaux are, like all semi-civilized people, naturally improvident; while they have, they will eat, and let tomorrow take care of itself. I do not suppose an Esquimau ever left off eating voluntarily before his hunger was fully satisfied, though he knew that the next day, or for many days, he would have nothing. Sailors have some kind of idea that a ship's company must, under some circumstances, be put on "short allowance"; but that is an idea you can never beat into the head of a native, and yet of all people they are the most subject to fluctuations of luck—at times having abundance, and then reduced to famine. But there is no thrift in them. Still, they do seem free of the selfishness that commonly goes along with thrift, and they will share all they have with a stranger; and, also true, they will sometimes store away provisions, and build *caches* on their travelling routes, but this is always when they have more than they can possibly consume—as when they have been lucky enough to kill a whale or walrus, and by no means can eat it all. Only Hannah, I imagine, is more like a white person in this regard.

Then a short day of oasis. The sun rises, late, in the southeast and skims low and remote over the horizon like a hot-air balloon unable to lift free of the lower atmosphere's gravity. Yet today its depleted rays can be *felt.* A mild breeze blowing from the southwest since dawn has swept the giant skies clear and is melting a little fresh water in the ponds so that rills begin to purl again in their summer channels, down from the modest heights of the floe's interior and between hummocks and ridges to tumble over the wave-smoothed ledges of the "shore."

Frederick Meyer, hatless, hair flying back, bustles about the floe with his crane-fly strides, taking measurements, scratching data, with the air of an aristocrat-scholar. The walrus moustache that frames his weak chin also hides his mouth, but through bottle spectacles his eyes shine in a fever of excitement. Four degrees centigrade and rising! Extrapolating from the known tendency of the human organism to manifest a last surge of energy in the moments before death, he wonders to Kruger if perhaps he has discovered a new polar phenomenon: the sun in its annual death throes issuing a last, defiant blaze of warmth.

The Meyer Effect.

Men are collecting fresh water in whatever will hold it and drinking their fill, rinsing faces darkened by the fat-lamp they still haven't mastered, and which often flushes them out of their hut, swearing in their tongues, pursued by coils of greasy smoke, to the huge amusement of the Esquimaux. Soren Madsen, a slender and nervous Dane, hands on hips, scrupulously toes snow over the bloody patch by Hans's snowhut, which the remaining dogs now avoid. These dogs are frisking on a hillock closer to the floe-edge, their barking, along with the shouts of the children and the piping of dovekies (whirring little airborne propellers), crowding the air with sound. Around the edge of the camp goes a game of Dogs-and-Bear, the children (Dogs) pursuing Kruger (the Bear) and pelting him with snowballs. The oldest child, Augustina, broad and chubby, the size of an adult, hurls devastating sidearm shots. Her mother Merkut sits mending in a southward angle of the snow walls with Charlie Polaris drooling in her hood.

Weak from the rationing, Kruger retreats before a unified assault and slips away. Punnie waves her tight little wave goodbye. Her solemn, stern-lipped face. Kruger waves back with a grin. He relights his pipe, gulps the dizzying fumes like food. A white-masked husky trots after him and they walk "inland" through a miniature mountain chain of upthrust ice. On top of Mt Hall he turns full around, in part to absorb the panorama in this constant sunset, but mainly in hope of spying a sail. People may say they've given up hope of something—at times that seems rational enough—but the heart and guts keep their own stubborn vigil. To say I give up hope is really to plead with life and luck to prove you wrong.

His eyes devour this last wafer of sun. Eastward above billows of tidewater fog the glacial tongues of Greenland are lit up vermilion like flumes of molten ore; to the west, the tors of Ellesmere Land in the glassy air seem touchably close; southward Baffin Bay under pack ice fans out like a pink desert studded here and there with bergs, like crags and mesas of salt rock—a vast coherent landscape drifting south. Then there's northward. New weather on the way. The pack ice scraping around the floe gives a sort of constant whimpering, as of a pod of seals bobbing at the surface in pain or unease.

Meaning to deflect his hunger with a drink, he slogs over a hummock toward Lake Polaris. It's barely a pond. The castaways, inspired by Herron, have been taking lyric liberties in naming the floe's "landforms," which amuses them but also gives comfort, making it easier to fool themselves and pretend that Great Hall Island *is* an island, and stable, out here where nothing is. Spike bounds ahead and stoops to lap water at the pond's edge. Kruger stops short. In profile, kneeling straight-backed on the shore, working the ice with her knife, is Hannah—Tukulito. She gives no sign of knowing anyone is there. It's disorienting to see her out here, in a long-tailed white-trimmed parka, like an Esquimau woman. On the *Polaris* they had grown used to her in the layered hoopskirts, poke-bonnet and fringed caribou cape she preferred, or seemed to, speaking with her mild English accent, each word placed as carefully as a foot along a seacliff path.

Good afternoon, Mr Kruger. She has not looked up; he must

be reflected in the membrane of meltwater on the surface. A kind of spectre, with no belonging out here.

He removes his watch-cap and bows slightly.

Good day, madam. May I ask what you're doing?

I am cutting new windows for our houses, sir. The others have melted somewhat. Please feel at liberty to smoke.

He realizes his pipe has gone out again. The men often jibe him for having it in his mouth and not noticing it is cold.

Thank you, but I haven't much left. I fear soon I'll be rationing this also.

She works in silence, not looking up. Her small brown hands are bare. He has never yet seen her use this knife of hers—a half-moon copper blade with a toggle-shaped handle—on anything but skin or sinew.

Is your husband off on a hunt, then?

He is, sir, yes—and then, as if reading his mind, she adds, And gone with his snow knife, sir, so I must use my own at this.

Her downturned cheek seems flushed, but then her cheeks are always ruddy, red on brown. That vital blush and the strength of life in her eyes cancel out her plainness. She moves with a simple grace of purpose; she's one of those who perfectly fill whatever space they occupy. For some time after you speak with her, her features will return to your mind in clear flashes.

The sound of Spike's lapping tongue fills the silence. Kruger nods northward at an encroaching rim of overcast.

I hope your husband means to return soon. It's turning colder, I think.

I believe it is, sir.

Hannah, you and your husband . . . you have been lost before on the ice as we are?

Never like this, sir. This is no common occurrence, among Inuit.

Around his pipestem Kruger smiles. I see, yes. A matter of white stupidity.

She looks up and meets his eyes, a rare thing.

I say nothing, sir, of white stupidity.

No, I say this myself. Our leaders are all drunkards and at odds with each other, and we—

Father Hall was not like that, sir, no drunkard! And we must give the lieutenant some time.

Yes, says Kruger, time to run dry, then time to dry out.

I do not understand you.

One's leaders are always drunk on something. Mostly themselves. In the meantime, we underlings hope for the best.

Mr Kruger—are you proposing that we . . .

Oh, I propose nothing, he says, regretting his irony. She's not amused by his banter but instead seems perplexed, wary. So, he sees now, he did intend to charm her, does feel drawn to her. The Meyer Effect, perhaps. They might well be dead, after all, before the month is out.

Mr Kruger, I shall finish my work here, if I may. And breaking gaze she draws from the shallows a dripping, finger-thick oval of ice. Turning away she holds it up to her face like a mirror and peers through.

Oct. 27. Weather cold, and growing colder for some days. Should judge the latitude to be about 77°30'. We have now lost sight of the sun's full disk, though at noon he showed a quarter of his diameter above the horizon—

"Miserable we,
Who here entangled in the gathering ice,
Take our last look of the descending sun,

While full of death, and fierce with tenfold frost,
The long, long night, incumbent o'er our heads,
Falls horrible!"

We are all very weak from having to live on such scant allowance, and the loss of the sun makes all more or less despondent. But still we do not give up. To-day with the "little donkey," transformed into a sled, the crewmen have brought in a load of stuff—one of the *kyacks*, and some poles and canvas, thrown from the ship on that terrible night—but the ice is very rough, and the light so dim that they can fetch but little at a time. There seems now no chance of reaching the Greenland shore, we have drifted so far to the west. Yet we *must* try for land one more time.

The sled has been followed home by two additional dogs—"Bear" and "Chink"; these animals have been lost for three days, perhaps searching for fresh meat. May the great and good God have mercy on us, and send us seals, or I fear we must perish.

In early morning darkness the lieutenant leads the party west toward Ellesmere Land: a line of basalt crags and spurs rearing out of the coastal icefield like fangs embedded in bloodless gums. Grudgingly the men cooperate. They load one of the boats, and with the starved dogs helping to haul it, they cross a broad adjoining floe with surprising ease, so that suddenly, amazingly, the land seems within reach. It's at this point the ice fractures almost beneath them and a well-timed gale funnels shrieking out of the northwest, a perfect ambush, forcing them to retreat in disorder to their camp.

Tukulito feels some relief at this. She knows that the coast of that land can offer them little comfort, being uninhabited and all but empty of game. God can only provide where there is something to provide. On the floe at least there are seals—and, beneath the floe, the spirit that governs them. This drifting ice rests on the meeting line of the white God and the darker, hidden gods of her people. In America, and aboard the ship that was really a northbound fragment of America, God was dominant and the old powers in abeyance; out here, the Woman under the Sea has equal power, perhaps more power. And, as if to further reclaim Tukulito from Hannah by sending a token of that power, the Big Woman dispatches a small seal for her husband to capture at its air hole some hours after their return to the floe.

To trust now in that spirit, Nuliajuk, is only sensible. Still, the ice can only be depended on to a certain point, and the current is bearing them ever farther from shore. Worse, they now have only one whaleboat to resort to when the ice does break up, for soon after their retreat to the encampment the men took hatchets and began to chop up the second boat—at first gingerly, as if in spite of themselves, then with a mounting, almost giddy excitement.

Downwind in the stinging snow Tukulito and Punnie watched with Merkut and her children as the beat of the hatchet blows accelerated and splinters and wood chips flew. Ebierbing and Hans were off on their hunt. In his little cotton jacket and cap Tyson lurched among the men, ordering them to stop. The faces—Tyson's pale, the men's blackened by their lamp and with darting bloodshot eyes—were contorted in their various intensities as if performing some grotesque, melodramatic minstrel show. Those soot-black faces amused her no longer. Over the storm Tyson was roaring *Listen to me, all of you—you are leaving us with only half a hope!* Anthing, his pistol in a belt cinched tight around his parka, yelled back that Tyson was a damn drunken fool, he must let the men alone. Tyson turned paler, stiffening into a statue of helpless rage. The men now hacked with a will, in the grip of some collective madness, and apparent elation; she had noticed before how white men could derive a curious pleasure from harming their prospects. Yet these men had seemed dependable—mostly. Lindermann, a mild giant, his long bangs almost hiding his surprised blue eyes; Lundquist, mutely respectful, a boy, his lumberjack jaw almost hairless; Soren Madsen, frail but methodical. Even Mr Kruger, Herron, and Jackson were in the thick of it—although for a moment Kruger lowered his hatchet and with a dazed, half-absent look, raising his voice over the wind, told Tyson that since they had abandoned this boat anyway in their push for shore, clearly it had been thought unnecessary and was therefore as good as gone. Why should the men not enjoy a little warmth from it, their lamp being useless?

Now Meyer, who on the party's return had crawled weakly into the officers' hut, emerged in his hooded parka and spectacles and pitched into the argument, on the men's side. Three times in the slashing snow Meyer and Anthing turned away from Tyson to confer in German, the words too faint for Tukulito to hear, although she was trying; a gifted linguist exposed to a tongue daily for over a year will naturally acquire some.

Mostly the way of her people is to allow adults to disagree as equals, then act as they see fit—as the men were doing themselves—yet she was deeply troubled by this scene, not only because of the loss of the whaleboat but also because the crewmen were white (Jackson too she considers white) and the custom of white men is to obey their superiors. If these men were already acting in such an erratic manner, who could say what other laws and customs they might be willing to violate, given time? An answer was not long in coming—as if the men, having supplied themselves with fuel, now felt that it should be set to use for more than just heat. As if all prohibitions had collapsed at once. While Tyson, helpless and trembling, stamped off to the officers' hut, and Meyer looked on, a line of men began crawling in and out of the storehut like beetles, taking provisions back into their hut along with the freshly cut wood. Lindermann stood outside the storehut holding his rifle with both hands at an angle across his chest. A mutiny, then. Tukulito sent Punnie back with Merkut and her children but remained to watch as Kruger, now putting himself in the way, sealskin boots planted, argued with the men in harsh German. Herron and Jackson, who spoke no German, stood looking confused, noncommittal. Anthing thrust a long shard of ship's biscuit—half weapon, half temptation—right under Kruger's nose and said something. Tukulito edged closer. She seemed invisible to these men, or irrelevant. Finally Kruger shoved the biscuit away and trudged stiffly back to the crewhut, tearing off his cap as he went.

In disgust she bent and began salvaging wood chips from the deepening snow.

For hours afterward the men could be heard feasting. Eventually some of them became ill, vomiting and coughing outside in the storm. A keen ear can identify the tone of a cough; one of the sick feasters was Kruger. And why should she have expected any better, after all? Travelling far from home without women and children, as white men do, has always struck her people as odd; yet now, as Punnie by the lamp feeds a supper of imaginary sealmeat to Elisapee, one could certainly wish to God that one's only child were somewhere other than here.

Oct. 29. Night. This is very bad business, but I cannot stop them, situated as I am, without any other authority than such as they choose to concede to me. Armed as they are, it will not do to thwart them too much, even for their own benefit.

Mr Meyer to-night joined the men in their hut, for their banquet. This too is a bad business, for we appear to be drifting into a future where all and any barriers of rank will be broken down; and where there is no authority, there can be no order; where there is no order, no survival. On Mr Meyer's return, when I asked him why he did not help me to enforce order, he replied haughtily, "That he had signed on with Captain Hall as a meteorologist, and it was not his look-out to help me to control the men," adding that in his view I was "not fitted to command them anyway"—which, given his imperfect English, could be a reference to my inadequate clothing, which does indeed weaken my position, or, more likely, another reminder that he alone of the men on this floe—and in this officers' hut—has the benefit of "higher education." But it is an education which, I observe, has not provided him with the moral scruples to resist the pilferers' feast from which he has just returned. His belly full, he sits combing his blond hair and moustaches—in want of nothing so much as a mirror—and not deigning to answer further.

May the one Authority, that none can challenge, continue to watch over and help us all!

Oct. 31. Cold and blowing. Since the men's feast, there has been no more *open* pilfering—indeed, several of the men have looked rueful and sorry—but a worse symptom has appeared: some one, or some group, has secretly made free with the store-hut. We have only had chocolate prepared for the party four times, and it is *nearly all gone*! It is far too cold to set a watch; but it is plain enough to be seen that things have been meddled with. May God keep the watch for us, or we may soon have nothing left.

Crawl into the new and larger snowhut that the crewmen have just built, fifty paces north of the other huts. The men lie jammed on the bed-ledge in caribou bags and muskox hides. For the sake of warmth and space they lie head to foot, head to foot, Madsen and Lindermann closest, as always, like duelling pistols in a lined case. The air is rife with a humid, heady stench. In the pemmican-tin lamp a few embers still glow, projecting a dim aurora over the dome of the raggedly built hut. The storm scouring the walls outside sounds like a waterfall. The men see and hear none of this, all asleep, some maybe dreaming in their several languages of differently dressed women, different cuisines. Differently undressed women.

Sailors, the professionally homeless.

The sounds wake Kruger first. A low grunting along with a moan of wind, then a blast of icy air. In the flickery womb-light an immense grey wolf, bunched flat to the floor, is creeping in through the entry tunnel. Kruger's scalp and forearms freeze and then the vision reforms: Ebierbing in his parka has just crawled inside, pushing through the grey wolfskin that blocks the tunnel. He stands, props his rifle on the canvas floor and peels back his hood, the hair plastered flat on his forehead. Looking around the hut he grins, a master stoneworker tickled by a child's ambitious house of blocks.

Gott steh mir bei! Jamka hisses, sitting up. He wakes anxious with every warlike crack or boom in the ice, and they're constant; and he doesn't hide his fear that the natives may intend to slaughter them and feed on their raw flesh. (Raw, not cooked—somehow it is worse.) He has a long face, long black beard, tiny lobster eyes set too close together. Others are waking now. Anthing's eyes pop open in the gloom. He digs in his sea-bag for his revolver; the unloaded rifles are all staked outside, on Ebierbing's strong advice, to prevent damage from the moisture.

Good evening, boys! Ebierbing says thickly. Excuse me, but you boys will all please come and help.

Is it morning, Kru? asks Herron, next to Kruger.

Well, it's early.

Night still, says Ebierbing. Hans Christian is lost. It's many hours now since. I look and look everywhere, but nothing. You boys now please come and help.

The awake ones seem unable to meet each other's eyes. The others, far from being disturbed by Ebierbing's intrusion, seem soothed by it into deeper states of repose, nestled in their bags with a sort of mortuary stillness. Herron recedes deeper into his bag. Only a tousle of his hair shows. As Kruger watches, others do the same—oddly furred, larval creatures in the grip of some obscure tropism. From inside his bag, Madsen's cough asserts itself with tubercular urgency. Jackson decides to see to the lamp. Ebierbing is no longer grinning, yet neither is he frowning. His steady gaze and posture suggest that he's merely waiting, as if for a seal to surface, and will remain that way until somebody does.

All right then, Kruger says gruffly, sloughing himself out of his bag in his woollens. Small amends. He grips the mouth of Herron's bag and shakes it, saying Johnny, come on now! But Herron retracts further, disappearing.

Outside, Ebierbing takes Kruger's mitten firmly in his own and they push into the white-out, hand in hand like schoolchildren lost in a forest. Kruger blushes; as if anyone can see them out here. In fact, nothing can be seen, even a few paces ahead. Rifles across their backs they lean steeply into the storm as if climbing a gangplank. Snow burns into Kruger's eyes like whipped sand on a beach, then freezes on his lashes, sealing them shut. He staggers blindly, still pulled by Ebierbing. After a moment the healing pressure of a warm, bare palm over his eyes, patiently thawing them open. As the hand withdraws he passes from a dark sort of blindness to a white one. A face leans in close to his own: Ebierbing yelling, a mittened hand shielding his mouth. *Head more down, Mr Kruger, like this!* Kruger opens his mouth to reply and is gagged by the snow-sharpened wind.

They crouch behind a hummock and Ebierbing tries to explain what became of Hans. They were hunting in the twilight of midday when Hans, hoping to find seal-holes on a large floe that was bumping into theirs, crossed a narrow lead, promising to return soon. But Ebierbing may not have understood; Hans's Greenland dialect often gives him trouble. Hours later Ebierbing returned empty-handed to the camp, expecting to find Hans there, but was disappointed, and so had gone straight out again into the rising gale and spent some hours searching. At last he came to the crewmen to ask for help.

Kruger realizes that Ebierbing has been out walking the ice for over fifteen hours.

They push on for some time and reach open water, black and steaming in the dark, small whitecaps clipping across it. The edge of the map. They turn around and trek inland with the wind, driven at a run among the Central Alps, and now with the wind behind them they call out for Hans, puny syllables swiftly absorbed: *Hans Christian! Hans Christian!* Twice, at a slight lull in the storm, Ebierbing fires his rifle into the invisible sky and pauses to listen.

On the shores of Lake Polaris they hear something. Turning back to windward they peer into the swarming snow. A little less dense than before. Ebierbing signals Kruger and they bunch down behind a small hummock. The hunter, his moustaches glazed silver, levels his rifle and cocks the hammer and Kruger does the same with his Springfield, now seeing what Ebierbing must see—a white bear clambering down over a hummock on the far shore of the pond and crossing the ice toward them, reared up on its hind legs to attack. In the flying snow it's impossible to say if this is a small bear very close, or a huge one farther off. It comes on swiftly with the wind at its tail. Kruger squints against the snow and waits, his heart jolting up into his throat, for Ebierbing to fire. The bear is almost on them. Ebierbing lowers his Spencer and jams the tip of his mitten under the hammer of Kruger's rifle and then begins chuckling, *laughing*, a sound almost stifled by the wind. This laughter clears Kruger's eyes. They have come within a trigger's breadth of shooting Hans Christian. There he stands tottering, his fur clothing and hood impastoed with snow, completely white. Ebierbing rises and shouts something at him and then continues laughing hard, his eyes glistening and welling with tears which freeze on his cheeks, while Hans himself, who has been lost in the storm for a dozen hours and has just barely escaped being shot dead, merrily joins in.

Ebierbing leads them back to Hallburgh, apparently navigating by the wind and the contours of the ice. Hans crawls immediately into his own hut. The squat silhouette of Merkut seated before her fatlamp appears to them as if on the wall of a magic lantern. For a moment Ebierbing studies Kruger obliquely, then invites him into his own bright snowhut, for tea and food. They enter on all fours. How difficult it must be, Kruger thinks, for a native to put on airs, or to play the returning hero, when nobody can barge or strut into a room. Everybody crawls.

In parka and fur pants Tukulito sits cross-legged before her fatlamp, her long braids swinging around the flame but never touching it. The neat and smooth-domed hut is filled with the aromas of tea and burning blubber—a smell like rancid cod-oil, but Kruger would gladly guzzle every hot, stinking drop of it. Ebierbing mutters something to Tukulito in their tongue, seeming to nod toward Hans's snowhut, then toward Kruger. At her husband's safe return she is coolly formal, not openly relieved;

maybe on account of an outsider's presence. She will not meet Kruger's eye. Well, she must wish her family to herself, at this hour. Or is she simply exhausted? Broad, brown Esquimau faces don't betray fatigue the way white faces do.

Good evening, Mr Kruger. She is carefully pouring tea into tin mugs.

Must be near morning now, he says weakly.

So it is, sir. Good morning, sir. She passes him and Ebierbing mugs of pemmican tea and chunks of biscuit. The men fall on their meal, Ebierbing's strong jaws working noisily at his slab, Kruger impatiently dunking his in the tea to soften it. How wonderful the tea steam feels on his cheeks! How warm and bright and orderly the hut, compared to the jammed barracks of the crewhut! Little Punnie lies among ox furs on the bed-ledge, only her face and the yarn-haired scalp of her doll's head showing. She sleeps with her eyes half open, flickering with lamplight, the way Kruger's baby sister Elke used to sleep in her cradle beside the coalstove. The heat, the food and the cozy closeness and the sight of the child sleeping and the strain of this night overcome Kruger and he brings a hand to his face and fills it with a number of hard, fierce sobs.

Heim. Heimat.

When he has mastered himself, he looks out at Ebierbing, Tukulito.

Forgive me.

With averted eyes they nod.

And thank you for this.

I believe you will need more in a minute, sir. Perhaps some meat.

Thank you.

I know that you crewmen have excellent appetites.

He looks up at her. Her liquid eyes, calm and clear, are fixed on his.

After a moment he says quickly, I hoped my going with Joe tonight could make some small apology for my . . . weakness of the other night. Apparently it does not. Of course it's not enough. I'm ashamed, and I offer you both my truest apologies.

Another studious pause, then she says, To the contrary, sir. It is more than enough. Your help may have saved Hans Christian. And she smiles, fleetingly, an astonishing sight—a small but explosive release.

Ebierbing looks at her in puzzlement, as if awaiting a translation.

This is the one place on this island, Kruger says, moved, where I see no weakness.

In the eyes of God we are all equally weak, sir.

Weak, we eat more, says Ebierbing, taking two of the grey strips Tukulito has set to warm on the rim of the fatlamp. One of these he hands to Kruger with a cordial grunt. Kruger hesitates. Presumably this is a leftover fillet of either Sambo or Poodle, and so far the men have declined to eat such meat—another small "justification" for the other night's open theft. But before long they may have to accept whatever comes; Tyson has said that since the "secret pilfering" is occurring almost every night, he may soon be forced to tighten the ration.

The strip tastes a little like stringy, dried-out pork.

Hans Christian is a barrel-bodied little man with a benevolent gnome-like face—large snouty features inherited from the Danish grandfather he proudly cites. His chin and cheeks are as hairless as a girl's. Seen from behind, he has the stubbed, bandy legs of a terrier. In noon's blue twilight, a few stars twinkling, Kruger watches him kick and drag Spike by his salt-and-pepper scruff away from the camp. The dog gives a few shrunken barks and whimpers but is too starved to do more. For a moment Spike seems to hold Kruger's gaze—*Help me, you!*—and Kruger can only look away from those hazel, human eyes. The remaining dogs sit clumped together by Hans's snowhut, howling as they watch, and the Esquimau children cluster nearby. The crewmen by their own hut watch intently. Meyer stands with them. Ebierbing is off hunting seal, the lieutenant is indisposed. Meyer has told Kruger—whom he seems to see as a kind of subaltern—that his cabin-mate has been feeling poorly since finishing the "liquid provisions" to which he had grown accustomed on the ship. When Meyer adds that he, Meyer, has decided to move in with the men, perhaps tomorrow, Kruger guesses that while Meyer has been willing to share a bit of Tyson's drink, he's not prepared to share a small hut with a man in the throes of withdrawal.

The air is frigid and still. Human and animal exhalations rise in pale, fading verticals. This is the third day running that Hans has slaughtered a dog. The crewmen now eagerly partake of the meat. The men seem ready to eat almost anything. When Kruger told them how close he and Joe had come to gunning down Hans, a brief, ambiguous silence had followed, and Kruger had felt, had known, with a sort of tribal intuition, that some men were pondering what would have been done with the remains. What they'd have been willing to do with them.

Hans draws a gutting knife from his belt and with the hand that grips Spike's scruff he tries to upend the dog and expose his throat. With a whiplash twist of the body Spike breaks free and, lips peeled back, leaps snapping at Hans, who recoils, falls. In silence Spike turns and hobbles quickly away, favouring the left front paw. Without a word Hans gets up and starts after him at a plodding lope. Hurry! cries Herron. Jamka lifts his rifle and Anthing his long-barrelled revolver and they fire on the dog, but miss.

Kruger joins Hans in pursuing Spike, now well ahead but slowing as he limps over a steep hummock of rafted ice. Both men are winded—just standing up winds them all these days—and Kruger feels as if he is running on stilts, way above the ice, numb and tottery, as in a sickbed dream. They reach the hummock and scramble up and then slide and stutter-step down the backslope. Two starved men chasing a crippled dog on a doomed ice floe. Spike stops and glances back at them: the white mask of his face, the ears pricked. He has reached the eastern rim of the floe, the very shore of the world. A blood and emerald aurora billows faintly. In the dimpled gloom the men slowly approach. They make soothing sounds. Kruger trembles from head to toe. Spike checks them over his shoulder, his backside to them, scrawny haunches tensed, his anus seeming to watch them like an eye from under the erect tail. He leaps. The white corona of a splash in the black sea. *If only I had my rifle, and Hans his kayak!* Spike has been his favourite among the dogs, but now he thinks only of that gristly, life-giving flesh.

They run to the edge as Spike scratches up onto a teetering cake of ice barely large enough to hold him. He turns and faces them: a rug of matted fur draped over a rack of ribs. When he shakes himself, droplets fling around him and tick down, beads of ice by now, on the darkly smoking sea. The lead between Great Hall Island and the ice cake widens as the island drifts on to the south, and the ice cake, amid other pans and patches of grey frazil, recedes westward, pushed by the side-wake of the floe. Shivering on his flake of ice, staring with limpid eyes as a breeze riffles the tufts frozen between his ears, Spike watches the men in silence as he drifts out of sight.

Nov. 19. I am down sick with rheumatism, hardly able to hold a pencil. Our island is now entirely encircled by water, and I judge we are drifting to the southward very fast. Today at noon, only a faint streak of twilight in that direction. The natives tell me that they saw two bear-tracks and five seal-holes; but they brought home nothing. How I wish they had better fortune.

Here we are, and here, it seems, we are doomed to remain.

Nov. 21. The last few days the weather has been clear and cold; I have been confined to the hut with a heavy cold and rheumatism; but, thank God, I am around again. It has been very difficult for the natives to hunt this month, except the few times the moon has shone, on account of the darkness; but today, thank God, they have brought in two seals. Without them we should have no fire, with one boat already cut up. It will never do to touch the other, for the time must come—if we live to see it—when the boat will be our only means of safety. As for Captain Hall's writing-desk, which is all we have left of him, and which the men might also cut up, two weeks ago I asked Hannah and Joe to keep it safe with them in their hut.

We are living now on as little as the human frame can endure without succumbing, and suffer much from the cold; when the body is ill-fed the cold seems to penetrate to the very marrow. Some tremble with weakness when they try to walk. Mr Meyer suffers much from this cause; he was not well when he came on the ice, and the regimen here has not improved him. He lives with the men now; they are mostly Germans, and so is he, and the affinity of blood draws them together, I suppose. This is natural enough, yet such growing affinity is troubling. He joined them three days ago, and now I have joined Joe, Hannah, and Punnie. I prefer living with them, as they can and will speak English, which Mr Meyer and the men seem increasingly reluctant to do. *The biscuit has disappeared very fast lately: more of this hereafter.* We have only eight bags left. God guide us; He is our only hope.

Punnie, poor child, is often hungry, and indeed all the children often cry with hunger. We give them all that it is safe to use. And indeed, tonight, for the first time since separating from the ship, we have all eaten enough. I have fed heartily on seal—yes, and drank its blood, and eaten its blubber, and even the skin and hair; it will give me strength, I hope. The seal's blood was very savoury. For the last few days, being sick, I had eaten nothing—scarcely any thing for about a week. I really need and should have more, to make up for the days I ate nothing; but beyond this one meal, shall not ask for or take it. I must subsist as well as I may on the regular allowance. In our situation Joe is the "best man," for without him we should get little enough of this game. Hans is not so good, though he does well at times; and, as for the rest, they have had no experience. I am the worst off of all, for I have neither gun nor pistol, and can only make a shot by borrowing of Joe.

This is a disadvantage in other respects, and the men know it. After Captain Hall's death, for some reason unknown to me, arms were distributed among them, perhaps to organize hunting-parties; but, at any rate, while I was looking after the ship's property on the night we were cast away, the men secured their weapons. My situation is very unpleasant. I can do no more than advise them, and some now sneer openly at my advice. At times, this is close to unbearable; yet the insubordination is not altogether their fault, for after Captain Hall's death, Mr Budington allowed them to say, do, and take what they pleased. *And then, too, there appears to be some influence at work upon them now.* It is natural, no doubt, that they should put confidence in an officer of their own blood; but they will probably find that "all is not gold that glitters" before they get through this adventure.

We have discovered more bear-tracks on our floe, but have not seen the bears. Our two remaining dogs are very thin and poor, and unless we get more food, they will have to be killed. It is a great pity, for they would be very useful in bear-hunting.

Punnie is awake again, whining with hunger. The sound is different from other sorts of whining: at the same time more urgent and more feeble. Embracing the child, Tukulito lies between her snoring husband and Lieutenant Tyson. Customarily an Esquimau husband would sleep between his family and any man sharing their bed-ledge; this present arrangement is designed to keep the lieutenant, like Father Hall before him, from freezing to death.

Tukulito's gentle alto suffuses the iglu with a song of her people, a survivor's lullaby—*Aija aliannaittuqaqpuq inuunialiqtunga ijajajaja ijajajaja*—until, with no transitional pause, she flows on into the verse of a hymn that she has sung before in parlours in London, and New London, accompanied by local pianists, for salons of the curious, the amused and the moved:

I will sing you a song of that beautiful land,
The far away home of the soul,
Where no storms ever beat on that glittering strand
While the years of eternity roll.

The lieutenant seems to be awake and listening. He sniffs softly, as if needing to blow his nose. As Tukulito rocks, pressing lightly against both men in the process, Punnie's whining quiets and the child sobbingly promises Elisapee that there will be whale meat tomorrow. Oh, tomorrow, thinks Tukulito; *utarannaakuluk*, I would promise you the same if I could!

A few last, anxious hiccups and the child is asleep. Tukulito stops rocking. For some minutes the lieutenant continues to wriggle and shift his feet under the furs.

Are you cold, Lieutenant?

Forgive me if I've kept you awake, he says.

Perhaps we have kept *you* awake, sir, and she turns toward him under the furs. His body goes rigid, breath held, as she reaches for him, finding his shins and then his socked feet and pulling them toward her.

Your feet are like ice, sir!

In a choked, husky voice he says, I . . . try to get them comfortable, but can't seem to.

She is peeling off the wool socks, feeling the bare skin with her fingers. Soapstone.

These feet will have to be warmed Inuit fashion, sir.

She has instructed him on the importance of sleeping pressed up against others when on the ice, yet he resists. Father Hall was like that too, at the beginning, when first travelling with them on Baffin Island, eleven winters ago. She intertwines her feet with the lieutenant's as she once did with Father Hall. The lieutenant draws closer, as he should. And this is best. If the ship were to rescue them tomorrow, she would be glad again for her cabin and would allow no other man but her husband next to her—and the transition between these sets of customs would be seamless, graceful, and automatic.

Do you feel any better, Lieutenant?

Oh, yes . . . thank you!

His breath is on her face—the bitter-sharp breath of fasting. Burnt sourdough and greening copper. Her husband's breath is the same, and Punnie's too. Her own too, presumably. Hunger strips people of their own unique smells, good or bad, and makes them all one stinking clan. She is about to turn away when Tyson drapes a heavy arm over her shoulder, grips her braid and firmly draws her into him, ready in the way of men. She retracts her body and in the same motion removes his hand from her shoulder—all without disentwining their feet.

After a silence he says, Forgive me, Hannah. I thought . . .

He lets the sentence dangle. She has to cough, as is usual in the night. Turning her head away she politely covers her lips.

Please feel at liberty to leave your feet as they are, sir, she says finally. I trust it will help you warm them. Good night again, sir.

In the cold little storehut Kruger, Meyer, Tyson, and Hans kneel reverently around the ration-scales: two pemmican tins yoked together by a fulcrum of gaff wood. Rifle and shotgun cartridges are the counterweights. The daily rations now stand at six ounces of biscuit, eight ounces of pemmican, and two of ham. Children get half that much. Tyson divides and dispenses the rations in a silence that might appear surly if he were not so obviously weak. Saving his jaws for the food. Hans Christian nods and trudges off, along with Gumbo, their last shrivelled dog, who trails him closely with a slinking, crabwise gait.

Kruger, carrying his own burden, about the size and weight of a baby but feeling heftier, walks back to the crewhut with Meyer tottering alongside, precariously tall, his long bony nose and spectacles downturned in thought. Last night over supper he informed the men that he is in fact a member of the Prussian aristocracy, no less than a count, with a family seat in Torgelow, as well as a former captain in the Prussian army (Kruger understood that he was a second lieutenant, who emigrated because there were no prospects for advancement). Count Meyer has decided to reclaim his noble lineage—which he was obliged to set aside, he says, when he came to America and joined the Army Signal Corps, as a sergeant—so that the men will have greater faith in his fitness to command.

Mostly the men seem inclined, or determined, to take him at his word. At first aboard the ship the German sailors spoke proudly of being immigrants to Amerika and already part of a U.S. expedition. Now, in extremity, they're Germans betrayed and endangered by poor American leadership. In their own fear and hunger the Swede and Dane stand with them. Something is shifting. Even Herron and Jackson seem encouraged to have a man of natural authority here to guide and protect the group—and perhaps Jackson looks to Meyer for personal protection. He's anxious about the men's guns, which they now carry all the time. As a youth he survived the conscription riots in New York City, which produced the biggest and most lethal lynch mobs that the country would ever see, North or South. Jackson was raised in the South in a village of Free Blacks, near Asheville, his family fleeing north in 1860. As for Jackson's own weapon, Anthing has claimed it: *It is wrong if a cook have a rifle and a sailor but a pistol.*

Meyer assures Jackson that he is better off unarmed.

Herron's case is different. He has been allowed to keep his rifle. But he's the kind who, with friendly nods, will accept a story like Meyer's, not out of cowardice but out of kindness, a deep reluctance to deny or embarrass anyone. He's the kind who will swallow a great deal to avert discord. Who may love harmony too much for his own good. Besides—as he confides to Kruger, his bedmate—to cross Meyer or the others now would be foolish, reckless. For now he may be right. Meanwhile Kruger hopes to use his position to exert some moderating influence.

He and Meyer approach the crewhut in the still, bitter air. Kruger switches arms, cradling the food higher so as to catch faint, perhaps imaginary, whiffs of the biscuit. He's glad to perform this coveted task for Meyer. Everyone wants to see the rations allotted, to spend as much time as possible in the presence of Food.

Now Meyer pants in German: Last night I looked about me and reflected on what a rare opportunity our presence here affords!

The ice is lit dimly, gorgeously, by the aurora borealis, which Tukulito has told Kruger her people see as the spirits of those who have died by violence, with heavy loss of blood. Today the shivering involutions are coral, crimson, golden; is Meyer talking about the scenery?

Think of it! When ever have the descendants of so many different peoples been gathered in such a small space before? We have Esquimaux here, an African, an American, an Englishman, a Swede, a Dane, a Russian-German, and of course ourselves, Germans. What an opportunity for comparative observations, tests, measurements!

Meyer stops in his tracks, out of breath. The northern lights crawl slowly over his framed, upturned lenses. Odd to hear him speak of tests and measurements when he seems to have lost interest in his meteorological observations, rarely going outside with his sextant, or now and then just sending Herron and Kruger out with the thermometer and barometer. He does, however, spend more and more time jotting, rearranging, pondering the data.

. . . observations of the sort that Monsieur Gobineau was forced to travel far and wide to conduct! And of course he never did reach the Esquimaux . . . to say nothing of the Africans. . . .

I suspect you may find that folk starve in pretty much the same way, sir.

Ach, vielleicht nicht! We may well discover that the natives are naturally *adapted* to starvations of this sort . . . and should therefore actually receive a lesser ration than we.

Kruger glances back at Tukulito's snowhut: gently flushed from within by the lamp.

Their work is keeping us alive, sir.

I bear them no ill will, Herr Kruger. I am simply after the truths of Nature. In any case it can do no harm to view Great Hall Island as a kind of . . . floating laboratory. Important scientific work, even a book, might emerge from such research . . . one to supplement, or perhaps *improve* upon, Count Gobineau's work.

To speak frankly, sir, the Count's work would best be improved by obliteration.

Ah, but you would think so! I've seen you reading your Voltaire! I suspect our privations out here are likely to alter your views, however. You served well in the Danish war, as did I. I know you remain a loyal German. . . . Ah, here.

Kruger helps Count Meyer down onto his knees so he can crawl into the hut. *A loyal German.* He emigrated to find a country as free as his father once hoped their own country might become, and has said as much to the others on several occasions, but Meyer doesn't take him seriously. As if such a high concept is all very well, but Blood will sooner or later reclaim him.

Thanksgiving-day, Nov. 28. Having to live all the time on such scant rations keeps the subject of food constantly before one. It is one of the worst effects of our excessively "short allowance." While the stomach is gnawing, and its empty sides grinding together, it is almost impossible to fix the mind clearly, for any length of time, upon anything else. The scenes that have passed before my eyes during the last weeks were, many of them, worthy of the best efforts of the most accomplished artist, and of description by a poet's pen, but I have not the heart to enjoy or record them; for disgust at the way in which I have to live, and "command," overpowers every other sentiment.

We saved the can of dried apples for Thanksgiving. My breakfast consisted of a small meat-can full of hot chocolate (it was not a very delicate "coffee-cup," but I had used it before); two biscuits, of a size which takes ten to make a pound, with a few dried apples, eaten as they came out of the can. This was the "thanksgiving" part of the breakfast. To satisfy my hunger—fierce hunger—I was compelled to finish with eating strips of frozen seals' entrails, and lastly seal-skin—hair and all—just warmed over the lamp by Hannah, and frozen blubber; which tastes sweet to a man as hungry as I was. But I am thankful for what I do get—thankful that it is no worse. If only we can get enough of such food as this we can live, with the aid of our small stores, with economy, until April.

No doubt many who read this will exclaim, "I would rather die than eat such stuff!" You think so, no doubt; but people can't die when they want to; and when one is still in full life and vigor, albeit as hungry as we are, he don't want to die. Neither would you.

Evening. Tonight Joe and Hannah are sitting in front of the lamp, playing checkers on an old piece of canvas, the squares being marked out with my pencil. They use buttons for men, as they have nothing better. The natives easily learn any sort of game; some of them can even play a respectable game of chess; and cards they understand as well as the "heathen Chinee." If only we had two small chairs or stools to go with the writing-desk! Then we could sit properly, and also I could write there. As it is, the desk merely takes up space that we can ill spare, at the end of the sleeping-ledge; but still I am determined to protect it—as is Hannah. Punnie, at least, derives some amusement from it, constantly putting things in and out of the smaller slots, and even making a truckle-bed for her doll in the larger ink-drawer, where it slumbers alongside Joe's ammunition!

I have been thinking of home and family all day. I have been away many Thanksgivings before, but always with a sound keel under my feet, some clean, dry, decent clothes to put on, and without a thought of what I should have for dinner; for there was sure to be plenty, and good too. Never did I expect to spend a Thanksgiving without even a plank between me and the waters of Baffin Bay, and making my home with Esquimaux; but I have this to cheer me—that all my loved ones are in comfort and safety, if God has spared their lives; and as they do not know of my perilous situation, they will not have that to mar their enjoyment of the day. I hope they are well and happy. I wonder what they have had for dinner. It is not so hard to guess: a fifteen or sixteen pound turkey, boiled ham, and chicken-pie, with all sorts of fresh and canned vegetables; and celery, with nice white bread; and tea, coffee, and chocolate; then there will be plum-pudding, and three or four kinds of pies, and cheese; and perhaps some good sweet cider—perhaps some currant or raspberry wine; and then there will be plenty of apples, and oranges, and nuts, and raisins; and if my little son and his cousins have been to Sunday-school, they will have their little treasures, besides all their home presents spread out too. How I wish I could look in on them!

Well, I set down what I had for my Thanksgiving breakfast; I will give my bill of fare for my dinner also. For the four of us in this hut we had six biscuits, of the size above described; one pound of canned meat, one small can of corn, one small can of mock-turtle soup, making altogether a little over three pounds and a half, including the biscuit, for four persons; and this is an *extra* allowance, because it is Thanksgiving. Mixing all the above in one pan together, it was just warmed over the lamp, and our dinner was announced. Poor Punnie—the child is so famished that, while eating, she entirely forgot to "feed" her doll too, as she usually does.

Let us hope this feast may "satisfy" our thief, or thieves, for now; for the pilfering has certainly continued.

Talk and a laden table are ancient and natural partners. As the rations diminish, conversation in the crewhut grows sparser, more functional, less friendly. It's as if all motions of the jaw, even those of speech, are just an extension of the act of chewing food.

Thanksgiving morning the crew might be expected to feel less sullen, more festive, because along with their usual chunk of hairy sealskin they've had parings of dried apple, two biscuits, a drink of lukewarm chocolate, and a jerky-like morsel of Gumbo the husky. But they've looked forward to this morning for too long. These bonuses only taunt them. Now Herron, with a rare frown, contemplates the small helping of seal's intestine plunked in the middle of his bowl.

My father urged me to go to sea for the food.

A thoughtful silence is relieved by the sound of Lindermann, kneeling on the floor before the pemmican-tin piss-pot, rattling a stream into the tin. On his knees he is about the same height that Herron would be standing. His tiny head, perched on his bull-neck like a newel and capped with a tight lid of orange hair, grazes the dome. Over his shoulder he asks in a heavy bass: Also, Herry, do you English hold this Thanksgiving in your homeland?

When there was eatables enough on the table for the nine of us, we gave thanks.

Anthing brings a spoon down on his bare plate and snaps at Lindermann, *Warum sprichst du Englisch? Haben wir nicht beschlossen, dass in unserem Schneehaus nur Deutsch gesprochen wird? Wir sind hier in der Mehrheit!*

What's that he says, Kru?

Taking the pipe from his mouth, Kruger leans close:

He says German is the language in this snowhut now. Ignore him.

I've no choice, Kru, I don't sprechen-Sie.

Krüger! Was hast du gesagt?

Jackson quits stacking plates and peers around carefully at the white faces: Anthing bulging his reddened eyes at Kruger, Meyer perched on his new, private bed-ledge—about the size of a fireside settle—with withered legs crossed under him, his head stooped forward to accommodate the wall's inward slope. His spectacles keep slipping down to the top of the yellowed moustache that hides his mouth. In English he says, It is, however, what the majority has agreed, Herr Krüger. Herr Herron alone among us speaks English as his first tongue.

What about the cook? says Kruger.

That's right! says Jackson boldly, though ducking his head slightly at the same time.

The cook is the cook. He has his tasks. He need not speak at all.

Count Meyer, says Kruger.

You mean 'cause I'm so busy preparing all these here vittles, sir?

Meyer peeks over the top of his spectacles like a schoolmaster.

Are you being insubordinary, Mr Jackson?

He means because you are a nigger, says Anthing.

"African," I think, would be a more correct term, Herr Anthing.

Jackson's ginger-yellow skin reddens—darkens—as if to confirm his ancestry. This is the first time since the expedition started that anyone has said *nigger,* at least openly. Jackson has often said that he prefers working on ships—the men on whalers and so on, it's like they forget the customs of shore just as soon as they pass the seabreak. A ship's like a special island.

Herron speaks in a polite yet frankly puzzled tone: You're saying then, Mr Meyer sir, I'm no longer to speak my own mother tongue?

Not Mister, says Anthing. He is Captain now. Or Count—*Graf.* I say this to you in English for a last time. And what of that book you have borrowed of Krüger? This must be in English also?

English is all I speak.

Voltaire's *Littlebig*, says Kruger, teeth clamped on his pipe. This also will be forbidden—is it not so, Count Meyer?

Meyer weighs this, frowning. And Kruger can no longer squelch his natural impulse to expose any truth being conspicuously ignored.

But . . . I understood Count Meyer was most recently a sergeant, not a captain.

Yes, sir, and in the United States Army! says Jackson. This is a U.S.A. expedition!

Shut up, Anthing tells Jackson.

Shut up! adds Jamka, as if translating.

Ah, but we are not aboard an American ship now, says Meyer, still calm, pushing his spectacles back up his nose with a claw-like finger. And I am in command here.

A moment's silence. Then Kruger asks, Here in this hut? Or for the entire floe?

Meyer turns sharply to Kruger and again his glasses slide down. Apparently this very question already weighs on his mind. The pale and blond-lashed eyes seem exposed, undecided. He rubs his cracked, flaking hands together as if trying to thaw something between them. Kruger glances at the rolled fox-skin pillow where the man stows his pistol.

Lieutenant Tyson has showed himself . . . (Meyer short of breath now) . . . Lieutenant Tyson now shows himself to be . . . unfitted for command. By training, by character, and by class. In any case, not without help. Certainly he is unfit for command of the *majority* here, which is German. For now, then, we must . . . we will consider the command as . . . as *divided* upon this island. Which henceforth is to be known as—New Heligoland!

Wir grüßen den Herrn Grafen! cries Jamka with wide and mesmerized eyes. Anthing repeats this slogan with better strength and a moment later Big Lindermann, frostbitten hands still fiddling with his flies, throws in his lot. Lundquist and Madsen then add their voices, though with the forced, tinny fervour of conscripts. Kruger hangs his head. His pipe has gone out again. Meyer studies him, then looks seriously at Anthing, and Kruger realizes that without a word he has been demoted. Meyer has already given up on him. Anthing is his new lieutenant.

Some nights later Tukulito is awakened by the sound of Punnie, who always sleeps nested between her and Ebierbing, whispering in her father's ear: *ataataa, ataataa!* But he is exhausted from a long day's luckless hunting, on quarter rations. Nothing will wake him up.

Utarannaakuluk, Tukulito says softly. *Kaapiasukpiit?*

Yes, Punnie admits, she is a little afraid; footsteps in the snow outside. It might be that tall pale Qallunaat with the glass eyes!

Tukulito knows Mr Meyer is now too weak for night roamings, but somebody else might be outside to use the sheltered hole that they all squat over less and less often. It is not the lieutenant—she can feel his body warmth close behind her and hear his whistling snores and teeth-grinding muffled under the bed-skins.

But everyone is asleep, Tukulito says, drawing Punnie into her; Punnie in turn draws her ragged little *qitunngaujak*, Elisapee, into her. You sleep now too, says Tukulito.

There it is again, Anaana!

I hear nothing.

Maybe it's Nuliajuk, bumping the ice from below!

Nuliajuk does not trouble Christian people. Sleep now, little love.

Or maybe Satan-ee! Punnie adds in English.

The crewmen begin yelling in their various tongues. Tukulito sits up, shoving off the layered robes. She shakes Ebierbing's shoulder. The child seems no more or less frightened than she was before the commotion began. She whispers, Nuliajuk has come up through the ice, Anaana! She's eating them!

Lieutenant Tyson? Tukulito calls, switching tongues. Kindly wake up, sir.

He shudders and sits up, his eyes big in the darkness, teeth chattering. What is that? Are the men fighting?

She slips off the bed-ledge in her woollen nightdress—fawn, with its lace-trimmed collar and sleeves, the one, cherished article of southern clothing that she is still using—and drapes the bed-robes back over Punnie. I should think a bear means to eat them, sir, she says. She yanks Ebierbing's feet out from under the robes and into the cold air, calling firmly: Husband! She slips into her kamiks. The lieutenant is on the rim of the ledge trying to pull on his own high kamiks. The crew continue to scream and now there is another curious sound . . . sneezing? Then a frail voice addressing itself to Ebierbing, Hans, Lieutenant Tyson. *Help us!*

She had told her husband she considered it a mistake to kill and eat the last dog.

Ebierbing! she calls.

He sits up. *Suna?*

Even in the dark she can tell he is not truly and capably awake. Those who are most fully, perfectly awake in the daytime are the most perfectly asleep at night. A needle cry from the crewmen's iglu—the steward, she thinks—and this time it is a cry of pain as well as terror. She pulls out the ink drawer of Father Hall's writing-desk and takes a bullet from her husband's loonskin pouch and without donning her fur pants or amautik she crawls out through the entryway where he keeps his rifle and grabs it and stands up outside. The dense, pulsing stars and a bruise-green ribbing of aurora borealis thinly light the floe: fifty paces away the emaciated he-bear hunches over the shattered iglu, digging down with his forepaw as if for a wounded seal through the ice. Disembodied arms stick out through the walls, frantically groping for the rifles picketed around it. It looks odd, funny, as if the men are trying to escape through the iglu walls—to pull themselves through into the open. Loading the rifle, Tukulito kneels. One of those reaching arms has just found and dragged a gun into the iglu. The steward is screaming louder. She takes aim. A second rifle is pulled inside. The bear dips his long head, probing deeper still. The head comes back up. Again she aims, then pulls the trigger. The snapping report has an instantaneous echo, as if resounding off a cliff face near by, and for a moment she believes that a high berg, or even the coast of Ellesmere Land, is upon them; then realizes that somebody in the iglu has fired as well. Hit twice from different angles the bear straightens abruptly, as if hearing with astonishment somebody calling his true and secret name, then flops heavily backward onto the ice, head to the side, tongue lolling.

Tukulito stands up in her lace-trim nightdress. Punnie has followed the lieutenant out of the iglu; the two on either side of her now. The child takes her trembling hand. From his own iglu Hans has just emerged, armed, his whole family swarming out after him, always hungry for distraction. Seeing her friend Succi, Punnie scutters off to join her.

The lieutenant seems to want to reach a bare hand to Tukulito's shoulder, but holds back. I hadn't realized you could handle a rifle, Hannah, he says in a soft, awed tone.

I have not for some years, sir. But I have seen my husband use one often enough.

❧

Dec. 7. It is over a month since we lost sight of all land. The sun we lost even earlier, yet our eyes have become partially adapted to this dim light; as it has come on gradually, it does not appear so dark to us as it would to one suddenly dropped down on our floe from the latitude of New York. They would find it perhaps as dark as some of the shut-up parlors into which visitors are turned, to stumble about until they can find a seat, while the servant goes to announce them.

I have been over the floe, to the "shore" where our *Polaris* last anchored, after some canvas we had stored there. I called on the men for help and four responded—the steward, the cook, Madsen, and Lundquist. (Kruger, I noted, was not in the hut; the steward believed he had "gone out for air" or perhaps was "off trying to hunt.") This canvas I wanted to line the hut of the native, Hans. He has worked late and early to make the men comfortable, and they have their hut well lined, and the natives' ought to be too, especially as the children are there; and Hans's wife, like Hannah, is continually working for the men, by mending and making for them. Moreover Hans is sick, and can not hunt. Only Joe goes out sealing these days, although with no luck. Our day's allowance is now divided out by *ounces*: five of biscuit, six of canned meat, one and one-half of ham. These ingredients are mixed with brackish water to season them, and warmed over the lamp or fire.

I do not write every day—*it would take too much paper.* I had some blank note-books and ink in one of the ship's bags, but on looking for them a few days ago, found they were all gone. Some among these men will seize hold of any thing they can lay hands on; then, too, there are those who might prefer that I not keep daily note of what is happening out here, where I can scarcely get an order obeyed if I give one. The storehut—a smaller *igloo*—continues to receive secret visits. With the return of light and game, I hope things will be better; but I must say I never was so tired in my life.

Dec. 9. Last night, being clear, Mr Meyer was enabled to take an observation. He seems slightly stronger now, as if the men's fealty is food to him; which of course is not the only explanation possible. Several of his instruments, he says, including a compass and altazimuth, which he left outside "briefly unattended," have been mislaid or taken—and here he gave *me* a suspicious look—but he has still his sextant and ice-horizon, and also a star-chart; and so he took the declination and right ascension of γ, Cassiopeia. But he has no nautical almanac to correct his work by, so that he can only approximate our latitude. He makes it 74°4' N. lat., 67°53' W. long.; but I do not think it is any thing like that. If we are as far south as that, we have drifted faster than I consider possible.

We lie still in our snow burrows much of the time, partly because there is nothing to do—it is too dark to do any thing—and also because stirring round and exercising makes us hungry, and with the meat of our starved bear so soon finished, we can not afford to eat more. The stiller we keep and the warmer, the less we can live on; and, moreover, as I have said, my clothing is very thin and quite unfit for exposure in this cold.

Dec. 11. Increasingly Mr Meyer and I are in dispute as to the direction of our drift. He believes we are going to the east, toward Greenland; but we are surely going to the west. He judges, I suppose, by the winds being mostly from the north-west; but the ice does not obey the winds—heavy ice, I mean, like this. Heavy ice obeys the *currents*, and if they have not changed their natural course, we *must* be going to S.S.W. It would not matter in the least what opinion was entertained as to the course of the floe, only that it makes the men too hopeful, thinking they are approaching Greenland, and nearing the latitude of Disko, where they know there is a large store of provisions left for us. I am afraid they will start off and try to reach the land on that side; if they do, it will mean *death* to all of them. After living on

CAPTAIN TYSON IN HIS ARCTIC COSTUME.

such short allowance for so long, none could hope to bear up under the fatigue of walking and dragging their supplies over this rough hummocky ice. Moreover they would surely take the boat, perhaps loaded with all our provisions, thereby leaving us and Hans's family completely without resource, and likely ensuring our deaths as well.

I see the necessity of being very careful, but I shall protect the natives at all cost, for they are our best, and I may say only, hunters—though the *crewmen* seem to think them a burden, particularly

Hans and his family, and would gladly rid themselves of them. Then, they think, there would be fewer to consume the supplies, and if they moved toward the shore, there would not be the children to lug . . . I believe Mr Meyer has told them of the drift of the *Hansa* crew, and the gratuity of one thousand thalers donated by their Government to each man of that party, so they think if they should drift likewise they would get double pay from Congress. Little do they see the difference in circumstances! The *Hansa* crew had ample time to get all they wanted from the vessel—provisions, clothing, fuel, and a house-frame. And their drift was through less severe climes. However, these crewmen are organized now—swaggering about with their weapons, speaking loudly in German—and appear determined to control. *The fear of death has long ago been starved and frozen out of me*; but if I perish, I hope that some of this company will be saved to tell the truth of the doings on board the *Polaris*, and especially here on the ice. Those who have baffled and harmed this expedition ought not to escape. They can not escape their God!

Boredom and rage sound like opposite states of mind. In Tyson they're now states of body and they share the same cramped interior space. Restless and active by nature, he's now confined in the hut to a space a few feet square; a whaling captain and then on the *Polaris* lieutenant-captain, he can no longer exercise the deeply physical thrill of command; virile and accustomed to conjugal privilege, he's forced to lie in celibacy pressed against a near-naked, astoundingly warm-skinned woman.

He wakes from dreams where his voice can't project, legs can't move, hands won't grip. Now that he's awake certain thoughts creak into cyclic action and gather momentum, like a prisoner on a treadwheel. A drink might stop or slow them—God, if only!

There has never been a successful mutiny among the crew of an American ship. He signed on for glory and now faces ruin (and death, though that's a minor concern). If the crewmen flee and die on the ice, his disgrace. If they *succeed* despite his warnings and he and the natives should die . . . disgrace! There has never been a full mutiny among a USS crew, and now his name will go down in the schoolbooks as the first ranking officer to suffer one. His little son having to read, memorize, *recite* those words in the schoolroom, standing hot-faced at his desk while the children leer and the schoolma'am turns a blind eye to this cruelty—the boy's rightful legacy, after all. George Jr. thus loathing his father's memory. Emmaline, widowed, passing through a daily gauntlet of eyes, grateful for her black veil . . . or a black poke-bonnet laced tight around her shame. Widowed, yes, because he cannot imagine surviving such disgrace. For there has never been a full and successful mutiny among the crew of a U.S. . . .

A bitter draft breaks into this spiral, Tukulito shifting under the skins with a cough. Tyson's face is left uncovered. He opens his eyes: moonlight diffused through the pane of ice. She is on her hands and knees an arm's length away, Ebierbing kneeling behind her, rolling the lace hem of her nightdress up over her haunches. The exposed skin gleams like smoothed marble, strangely white in the lunar glow. Ebierbing's dark Mongol face is clenched. Her white buttocks block his shadowed groin from view. Like a Chinaman with a white woman, thinks Tyson. The couple is silent. Their breaths visible but silent. Tyson has wondered if they ever did this, yes, though he never wondered if they did it *in this way*, because it has never occurred to him that one might. Like dogs, or cattle; and in front of the child, who might wake at any time! Yet his physical response suggests less than complete disapproval. But then, shame and disgrace—both of which he feels as a witness to this moment—are for Tyson not sexual deterrents, but an inevitable part of sex, perhaps even stimuli. Poor Adam's birthright. Ebierbing grips her flanks, bucking his goat-hips faster, his lean torso, steaming in the cold, lapsing slowly toward her back. Tyson is relieved that both faces are in shadow. Especially hers. But as Ebierbing bends closer she pushes up on her arms, arching back to meet him, turning her face toward his so that the moonlight catches it. Her eyes are shut hard. She's biting her lower lip. Tyson means to shut his own eyes completely, but can't. Can't help holding himself hard, his shame, as he, Ebierbing, reaches under to grip her hanging breasts through the nightdress. He gnaws on her nape. Her braids dangle and swing. She puffs a short breath through her nose. She smiles, by God, Hannah smiles, she with her fine manners and proper accent, who had seemingly acquired all the feminine virtues, who had seemed so *white*. But the blanching moon is transforming her into a very different creature; or, perhaps, exposing a truer self. Ebierbing shudders and tightens and Tukulito cranes her head farther back to clamp her small teeth onto his throat and he lets out a creaturely moan, quickly stifled. And then her eyes part slightly. The wet, glinting pupils seem to fix on Tyson's squinted eyes. And he is certain that she knows, somehow, that he's present.

The eyes close and the face turns away, back into shadow. In moments the couple are back under the layered robes, again transfusing Tyson with their warmth. Her body exuding heat like a woodstove. A strong, exciting smell. Ebierbing starts snoring almost instantly. Tukulito's breathing slowly deepens. And Tyson lies awake for some time. At length, a weak, weary shudder of his own, mostly silent, but then the spasms turn into sobs and a few muffled ones escape him.

Lieutenant Tyson. . . . Are you quite all right, sir?

Hannah, you're not asleep?

I awoke just this moment, sir. When you shivered so.

I am only a little cold.

Then you must press closer, sir. That is the only way.

Tyson hears himself emit a tight, brittle laugh.

When he next wakens he is alone on the bed-ledge, feeling soiled in form and soul, a self-abusing peeping Tom, and there are sounds outside. Morning, presumably, though since the moon is no longer peering directly inside, it's darker in the hut. A moon that has not set for days. The children are at play close around the hut. It must be milder now. Their sounds make Tyson feel like a dead man in a country churchyard hearing the living above him—children playing tipcat, young men and women courting, spells of larksong. The din of a distant spring.

Rest now, sir! he hears Tukulito calling. She is standing outside the east wall of the hut. Her voice, being raised, has a different character, slightly girlish.

You mustn't tire yourself so, sir.

Ja . . . for the moment I rest.

It's Kruger.

Come play again, Mr Kruger! calls Punnie from a ways off, *soon!*

Soon! he calls back, panting as he approaches the hut, and Tukulito.

They do love when you play, Mr Kruger—their fathers must hunt all the time now.

Wonderful children, madam. A true refreshment. After some of my colleagues.

"Relief," sir, that would be the word.

Yes. Thank you. You must correct my English whenever it fails.

His voice is low and raw in a morning way. His English a touch askew.

And you, sir, might teach me some German.

He laughs—a rare sound, husky and pained. Well, as German seems now to be the official language on this ice floe, perhaps I must.

With almost teasing lightness she says, I do find it somewhat harsh of tone, however, sir.

Ah, it depends on the speaker—the words! He clears his throat. *Hast du die Lippen mir wund geküsst, so küsse sie wieder heil.*

This is poetry, is it not?

Ja, Heinrich Heine.

I think it quite lovely, sir.

You must call me—not sir. My name is Roland.

Will you translate, then, Mr Kruger?

You who bruised my lips with kissing, kiss them well again.

Just silence. Punnie and Succi a ways off, giggling weakly.

He says, I should like to learn similar words in your language.

Perhaps in time, Mr Kruger.

Tyson lies like a large fist under the skins. Is she not playing the coquette with him? Has she already been with him . . . or with some of the others? Of Merkut he could have believed this all—what he saw last night, what he is hearing now—but not of Hannah . . . *Tukulito*. She must be reverting. All of them reverting.

None of which makes him want her any less.

She says, I must take Punnie inside, sir. Children always play beyond their strength.

Of course.

Tyson sits up and grabs for his boots. He drapes a muskox skin like a shawl over his shoulders and crawls into the tunnel. He emerges on the other side of the hut from Kruger and Tukulito—who is calling Punnie in. The world is windless. Dim sapphire light. A waxing moon rides low over the pig-shaped hummock that marks the latrine. He stumps toward it. Catlike footfalls pad up behind. He stops and turns, trying to inflate his chest.

Ebierbing stands gazing up at him, a long moment, then edges closer. Is this about last night—some question of native honour? The man grins slyly in a way that strikes Tyson as deeply insolent. In shadow, a Colt revolver appears in his bare, black hand.

Joe, what the devil does—

You take this now, Mr Tyson.

Ebierbing glances over his shoulder, then thrusts the weapon toward Tyson. Tyson takes it at once.

But, you refused to give it me before, Joe.

Sure, two gun better for the hunt. Now, better you have one too. Again he glances toward the crewhut, then back at Tyson's beard. I plenty don't like how they looking. Too hungry.

The men?

The look out of their eyes, he whispers pointedly, as if to suggest Tyson be quieter too. He adds, If Joe get lost, or vanish, both guns gone. Better you have one too.

Yes, of course.

If Joe get lost, or killed . . . you watch out for Hannah and Punnie.

Tyson jams the heavy pistol into his belt. Already he feels a good foot taller, pounds heavier.

Don't worry, Joe. Now I have this—he pats the icy walnut of the grip—you need not worry.

On Tyson's striding return from the latrine, he digs out his notebook and scratches a few lines, as much as he ever writes now, knowing if their story is ever to be made public he'll have to rewrite and expand the notes, someday. *Whats becoming of us——God that any be tempted to that!——to become mere Brutes, biting & tearing each other to shreds!——But I have the Peacemaker now——will stop them & regain command.*

❧

Dec. 18. It is awful to contemplate what we may be becoming. God forbid that any of this company should be tempted to such a crime! If it is God's will that we should die by starvation, why, let us die like men, not like animals! However, I have the pistol now, and it will go hard with any one who harms even the smallest child on this God-made raft.

Dec. 22. We have turned the darkest point of our tedious night, and it is somewhat cheering to think that the sun, instead of going away from us, is coming toward us, regaining his power—though he is not yet visible. The shortest and darkest day has gone, and I am thankful; perhaps the worst may yet be averted. Friends at home are now preparing for Christmas, and so are we too. Out of our destitution we have still reserved something with which to keep in remembrance the blessed Christmas-time.

In Voltaire's *Micromégas—Littlebig*—an extraterrestrial being from Sirius meets another from Saturn and they embark on an expedition through space aboard the tail of a comet. The Sirian is 500,000 feet tall, the Saturnian a mere 15,000. Eventually, of course, they reach a "small and drifting speck" called Earth. In the course of their explorations there, they wade through the Mediterranean, and in the midst of this tepid rain puddle they find a ship returning from the north, after a polar expedition. Aboard the ship, a group of philosophers and scientists. When the Sirian plucks up the ship, places it on his fingernail and examines it with a magnifying device, he is dumbstruck to find "living atoms" aboard. In tiny chirping voices these inform him that they are "Human Beings with Immortal Souls," that they are "fashioned in the image of the Only God," and that they and their world are the "very Centre of the Universe." The bemused Sirian learns that these atoms have chopped up the planet into Countries and Kingdoms and spend their lives squabbling and killing each other over territory not owned by the killers themselves, but by Great Leaders, two of whom are called the Emperor and the Sultan. It seems these leaders "make the wars they do not fight, and the subjects fight the wars they do not make." The extraterrestrial guests are incredulous. The squeaking mites are insistent: "Why, even as we speak there are 100,000 of our creatures, all wearing helmets, trying to kill an equal number of their creatures, all wearing turbans!" This is war, and it is "Man's Supreme Glory."

The Sirian and the Saturnian board their comet and flee back to saner worlds.

Christmas afternoon, the crewmen awaiting dinner. Along with two biscuits each, there will be a small piece of frozen ham (the last of it), a few morsels of dried apple (the last of it), and a half-mug of seal's blood (the last, the last). Since breakfast the men have been telling stories and singing carols and songs, in a mood of truce even allowing Jackson to sing in English, and then Herron:

Herod the King, in his raging, ordered he hath this day,
His men of might, in his plain sight, all children young to slay.

The air is dense with pipe smoke, lamp smoke—a warm and lovely fug. And when Meyer and Anthing crawl outside to discuss their "New Year plans," the other men urge Kruger to read to them from *Littlebig*, the only book on the island. Sentence by sentence Kruger translates it into German while Herron and Jackson cook around the lamp and the men, supine in their bags, listen with the glassy eyes and slightly open lips of spellbound children.

Dinner is served and bolted in minutes. But the men are determined to prolong the feast. One by one they offer their ideal Christmas menus, and these become the main course after the brief appetizer of the meal. Herron's bill of fare, translated by Kruger, is heavy in roast fowl and beef, baked cod and herring, pheasant pies, black pudding, bread pudding, fig pudding, marzipan cream custard, mulled ale and Madeira and heavy port and hot gin punches. (The colours all dark and rich, like blood.) Eyes and cheeks shining he describes his table as a kind of busy harbour crowded with ship-like serving dishes, gravy boats, tall cruets of sauces, little varied bowls of walnuts, hazelnuts, prunes and raisins, all these like ferries or dories constantly on the move between plates. Jackson misses plainer stuff, like the beans and fatback he used to serve up as cook in the Federal Army during the war, but then he pictures the welcome-back from his own folks, now in Brooklyn: a pork roast, sweet potatoes glazed with molasses and then pickled okra and peas in vinegar and turnip greens and sweetened grits and hoecake and corn pudding and watermelon pickle and applejack. Lundquist and Madsen festoon their different tables with so many candles that it's no easy task to find room for the feast, but room is soon cleared for the roast goose or suckling pig and stuffed eels, the alebread or the *pytt i panna*, the platters of old cheeses, rye breads, balls of butter, bottles of apple brandy, urns of black coffee, cherry or lingonberry preserves and candied fruit heaped like soft gems in great glass bowls. Anthing, who before emigration lived near the Russian border, his long-dead mother a Russian, stocks his *Festtafel* with a steamed pork *pirog*, roast sturgeon, a great beet and cabbage soup made with beef stock and sweetened with thick cream, black bread, dishes of cherry and gooseberry jam . . . these along with the roasts, the *wursts* pan-fried and awash in hot fat, the platters of mashed potatoes with *senf* and butter, the stewed sauerkraut, the hefty fennel bread and pear and plum and apple cakes and *Glühwein* and *Kümmel* that the rest of the outcast Germans also include. . . . Yes, and as Kruger, mouth watering, renders this riveting list into English for a rapt Herron and Jackson, he yearns for his boyhood home with an intense monopolizing ache, like hunger, but throughout his body, a hunger in the cells and blood, and again he feels something like love for his countrymen, even Anthing, who sings the ancient carols so richly. The man is singing again now, in his effortless tenor, leading the others. He was an orphan choirboy, of all things, in Memel. Easy to see the boy in him anyway. *Es ist ein Ros'entsprungen.* Kruger is no singer, but he joins in. Not for the first time he reflects, How sweet, just to yield to sentiment and slip back among the mob, the Clan!

Out here where there's so little to tempt one, temptations are that much stronger. Yesterday the lieutenant informed Meyer that raids on the storehouse are continuing, and he believes "parties" in the crewhut to be responsible. Meyer himself blames the natives. Kruger knows this to be unlikely. Aboard the *Polaris* Tukulito once explained to him and Herron some of her people's taboos; to steal the food of others, or to refuse to share one's food, would bring about failure in the hunt, for the mistress of animals under the sea would no longer send the hunters any game.

But if the Esquimaux are not the thieves, and not Tyson, who looks increasingly thin, then who? Meyer has ready access to the storehouse, but if he has been taking extra food it hasn't stuck to his bones. Likewise Herron. Madsen always was girlishly slender and now is morbidly so—a skull with red lips and large, woeful blue eyes. He hardly ever goes out. Jamka is close to nervous collapse, alarmed by the slightest noise from the noisy ice, terrified of bears, so he too seldom emerges, except to rush to the latrine with the hunger-flux, gripping a few sheets of Tyson's spare notebook (that much, at least, the men have openly filched). Which leaves the less decrepit men: Anthing, Lindermann, Lundquist, Jackson, and Kruger himself.

Next morning breaks cuttingly cold, a gale from north-northwest blowing the snow into drifts. With Christmas done and its spirit of tolerance safely re-contained, Count Meyer is consumed by a new mood. Perched on his bed-ledge with Anthing standing beside him—Anthing's curly head stooped, eyes sweeping, pistol on his hip—he says, Henceforth all rifles are to be kept *inside* the snowhut, with us.

Kruger translates quietly for Herron and Jackson.

Herron says, But Count Meyer, sir, what of Joe's warning? About them rusting out . . . ?

Meyer, in German: We will not worry about such things. The native may know his country, but he knows little about the principles of metallurgy. Steel will never degrade at the rate he suggests. And I suspect he has other reasons for wanting us to leave our weapons out there.

Anthing: *Jawohl, Herr Kapitän Meyer.*

Kruger translates.

Jackson: Captain? Now he's promoted up to Captain?

Kruger: A holiday gift to himself, I think.

Herron: But sir . . . the ammunition's all indoors here, and Joe and Hans use different stuff.

Meyer: Let them rust a little anyway. We will soon reach Disko, and plenty.

Jamka: Disko! Disko!

Meyer: Meanwhile you are to drill outside with Sergeant Anthing. And from now on, we post a watch.

Kruger: To drill . . . to post a watch with the men starving and the weather like this . . . Surely this is somewhat—reckless.

Herron: What's that you said, Kru?

Meyer: But my dear Kruger, not only are such things *necessary*, they also afford science a rare opportunity to examine the resources of different kinds of human bodies under extreme conditions.

Meyer's hunger and confinement are affecting him even worse than the others. Underlit by the lamp's flame, his gums are lurid, cheekbones gouging through the white and loose-slung skin of a Walpurgisnacht hex-mask. But then, others have spoken before, on full stomachs, in just the way he speaks now. *Above all we must be prepared to defend ourselves and the honour of the young German Empire against the aspersions and encroachments of her enemies. We must be ready in body and spirit to depart for Greenland, and to fight, if necessary, for the boat and our share of supplies . . . which will, of course, be greater than our apparent share, as we will have to forgo the comforts of Hallburgh, and will no longer have the natives to hunt for us.*

Anthing: *Jawohl, Kapitän Graf Meyer!*

Anthing tries to click his heels together but the fur boots make no sound.

Jackson: Why ain't you translating no more?

Kruger: So then, you're preparing to come out in open mutiny.

Meyer: Ah, but how could there be any question of a "mutiny" where there is no fixed authority to rebel against . . . ? Well? For we are now our own authority.

The windstorm outside roaring, ravening like a crowd.

When Kruger translates, Jackson takes off his cap and digs his fingers into his hair. Well, that's secession, he says. I've seen with my own eyes what that means.

New-year's Morning, Jan. 1, 1873. "Happy New-year!" How the sound, or, rather, the thought—for the sound I do not hear—reminds one of friends, and genial faces, and happy groups of young and old!

We shall not make any "New-year's calls" to-day; nor will the ladies of our party have any trouble in ciphering up their "callers!" Some of the men, it is true, may be troubled to keep their footing, but it will not be with overmuch wine and revelry. A happy New-year for all the world but us poor, cold, half-starved wretches; though today, it seems, we shall at least eat well.

Yesterday Joe and Hans were out sealing, and Hans shot one seal, but lost him. It seemed very stupid, but I suppose he could not help it; if we were getting plenty we should not notice such an accident. Luckily, just now, Joe also shot a seal; as it floated away from him, he shouted as loud as he could call for his kyack, and a few of the men, who were attempting to place some kind of object, which I could not then identify, on top of the crewmen's hut, stopped their work and hurried it over to him—happy enough to assist if it might mean *food*. He got in and was fortunate enough to bag his game, which we shall dine on presently.

In dividing meat, suspicions among us are such that we now pick a "distributor" from one side of the camp, and a "caller" from the other; the distributor picks a portion at random, and the caller, standing with his back turned, calls out names in random order, so that each in turn receives his portion without any favoritism. But the men, who are usually somewhat appeased and more co-operative in the presence of fresh food, only grudgingly went along with this method today.

Now it has sometimes happened that when the Esquimaux have been tramping about for hours on the hunt for seals, and at last get one, they are by that time famished; and as, when they bring it in to the camp, they know they will get no more than those who have been "home" all day, they sometimes open the seal, and eat the entrails, kidneys, and heart, and perhaps a piece of the liver; and who could blame them? They must do it to keep life in them. They could not endure to hunt every day without something more, occasionally, than our rations. Yet the men complain of this, and say they do not get their share: so unreasonable and unreasoning are they. And now Mr Meyer, or "Major Count" as the men are calling him, advises me that "they will not stand aside for this practice again"! Well, we shall see.

But enough now; I must stop, and have my share.

Tukulito, Ebierbing, Punnie and Tyson have joined Hans's family in their larger snowhut to feast on a portion of the seal and to share Tyson's tobacco. Tukulito has not heard such laughter, if any, for many days. The fresh blood with its raw, iron smell, its sensational colour spattering the canvas floor and the filthy walls, is a token, to the being she was born as, of celebration and plenty, while the literate Christian she later became has to hold her revulsion in check. But this is no great feat, now, with her mouth full of the purple, lamp-warmed flesh, as sweet as she has ever tasted. As they eat or smoke—the adults and Augustina sitting on the canvas floor, the children on the bed-ledge—all eyes are fastened on the pemmican-tin qulliq whose white flame gives sign of a fresh abundance of blubber. The first strong light they have seen in weeks, it streams through the eyes into the dark brain to revive hope and joy: a June sun drawing life out of the tundra.

Increasing heat in the iglu brings to life other, worse smells. Tukulito doesn't care now, not even about Merkut, pipe chomped in her mouth, cleaning Charlie Polaris's bottom with her long tangled hair. Or Hans's ebullient belching. Or how Augustina—who was so fat on the ship that she still retains some fetching flesh on her bones, a blush in her cheeks, and who at twelve is the age that Tukulito was when she met her husband—is making eyes at the lieutenant, who shows no sign of noticing. He is devoting himself to his food, hunched over the dish, brow crumpled, eyes shut, jaw grinding. He holds his fork with a tight overhand grip, like a trowel. Now Tukulito feels Hans's slightly wall-eyed gaze on herself; as if one appetite satisfied must revive other hungers.

And what of Mr Kruger, off in the men's iglu—the way his eyes follow her? Eyes that can seem both mocking and rueful. And then that rare, flashing smile. *Is* he mocking her, and everything else? She understands her own people, and she understands most Christians—their curious mix of ambition and piety, pride and shame—but Kruger is neither one. Lately, on the rare occasions when he is near, her belly almost forgets its hunger. But as an Inuit wife and also as a Christian she is loyal to her husband, despite his own past infidelities, plenty of them. She loves him in her marrow.

To what is Mr Kruger loyal? she wonders.

Tyson peers up from his food with softened eyes, as if under a reprieving spell. He says, The little friends, they eat those seal's eyes with such relish! Paternally he smiles at Punnie and Succi—cross-legged on the ledge, chewing cheerfully, their little mouths and teeth slathered with blood—as if they're in pigtails and ribbons eating humbugs on a summer veranda.

But I thought the youngest would receive the eyes . . . ?

He takes only mother's milk as yet, sir, Tukulito says.

As if Merkut understands, she lifts her furs and slaps Charlie Polaris back onto her lax, pancaked breast. Tyson looks away, as if in pain, and his gaze collides with Tukulito's. Again he looks away fast. Ebierbing and Hans are setting buttons in place on the canvas checkerboard. Hans looks up with a startled face and says, Ahhh! We need drum! For dance now!

Or the accordion, says Ebierbing.

This drum we make now!

Ebierbing replies in Inuktitut and Tukulito automatically interprets for Tyson, who, like the other men, seems to find it quite natural that the natives should address each other in pidgin

English; showing surprise, and maybe suspicion, only when they revert to their own tongue.

Sir, my husband says that by the time we scrape the skin and make this drum, we shall all be too weary to dance. For lack of food.

Hans tilts back his head and slurs something emphatically. He appears drunk on the seal's blood—the regained bliss of it. He gives an extensive baritone belch that sounds like throat-singing, then a tight, quacking fart. Tukulito averts her face and covers her lips as she coughs.

Tyson: Is he saying they'll . . . they'll catch more seal tomorrow?

He says, sir, that by the time we finish the drum, we shall have to eat it. She smiles. Pom, pom, pom, goes Hans, puffing his keg-like torso in time. The sound of a man with a large drum beating in his stomach. The children giggle, even Tobias, the nine-year-old, who has been looking ill and absent, his posture concave, features pinched. Augustina with her jiggly laughter now seems a child once more—but then, taking a puff on her father's pipe and widening her eyes at Tyson, she is fully a woman. The transformation is borderless and Tukulito recalls how she herself played wolf tag and sledded on dogskins with her friends the morning after first sleeping with her husband. This was long before her Conversion; such an early union now strikes her as some years too young. But Merkut doesn't mind her daughter's flirting. Now the baby writhes free of her arms and begins crawling naked toward the qulliq. Always such an air of disorder in here.

There's a hard, air-tearing crack from outside.

Not the ice? Tyson plants his hands on the floor as if to rise.

Rifles, Ebierbing says calmly. Fire all of the same time. He yanks Punnie down off the ledge onto the floor beside him. Hans snaps some Greenlandic phrase that Tukulito has never heard and then starts dragging his own children down.

Might be for the New Year, Tyson says, though clearly with little hope as he feels for the butt of his revolver and dons his cap and then, looking weary but decisive, lumbers off on hands and knees, butting through the wolfskin blocking the tunnel. Charlie Polaris, gurgling happily, tries to crawl after him. Tukulito scoops him up and passes him over the qulliq to Merkut. Ebierbing and Hans are pulling on their parkas as they duck toward the tunnel. With his eyes Ebierbing signals Tukulito: Stay here. With her own eyes she relays the message to Punnie, and then, having passed it on and out of her, ignores it, slipping into her amautik and following Hans into the tunnel where he takes his rifle and emerges ahead of her into the dimness of midday.

Almost windless, not so cold, under a waning white moon. A few steps ahead, her husband and Hans and the lieutenant are silhouetted as if turned to stone, watching. Across the way stands Mr Meyer, a glare of moonlight on his spectacles, gaunt and tall beside the men's iglu, above which a flag hangs limply. Six crewmen are ranked at attention, anonymous in parkas, rifles over their shoulders. Hunched on the other side of the iglu, like a small chilly audience at the Changing of the Guard, are Kruger and Jackson. She knows them by their postures and the moonlight's shining on Kruger's curved pipestem.

Meyer barks something in German and the men awkwardly unshoulder and aim their rifles. Hans chuckles. They think they get the moon, he says. A breeze fans out the flag: the silhouette of something like a raven, though Tukulito guesses it is probably meant to be an eagle, the German totem, as she knows. She stands up. Another command and the rifles fire, more or less in unison. The orange muzzle flares are liquid, molten. Another command, the men turn, and with Meyer calling orders in a surprisingly firm voice, gangling beside them on his splayed-out feet, they troop single-file toward the floe-edge a few hundred paces north. Emaciation exaggerates the uniqueness of each man's walk. That will be Anthing first, with his tense, hunched, prowling tread, Lindermann with his loping forester's strides, Jamka shuffling like a convalescent in slippers. Lundquist still has the strength to lift his knees and truly march. Frail Madsen makes wary little steps, like an old man on bare ice. Herron lags, trudging and reluctant.

The children stream from the iglu and mill around Tukulito. Kruger waves, perhaps to her, and then, no doubt noticing the children, he passes his pipe to Jackson and bends forward, plants his mittened hands in the snow, kicks up his legs and starts walking on his hands, in time with Meyer's orders—in time with the marching men, as if pursuing them! Mocking them. Meyer doesn't notice but turns his head briefly at the children's throttled laughter. Tukulito, Ebierbing and Hans laughing too. Kruger's arms buckle and he lies in the snow with rapid breaths clouding around him. The children scoot away toward him. Tyson, Ebierbing, Hans and Tukulito stride close behind. Halfway over to the men's iglu they cross a deep, straight line carefully scored in the ice, up from the sea-edge and on toward the floe's centre.

Come to watch the parade? Kruger is asking the children, his mouth open in a panting smile. He totters upright and glances at Tukulito, seeming perplexed, or alarmed, at how badly his prank has taxed him. She gives him a wary smile, then grips Punnie's shoulders from behind and pulls her close. Jackson is puffing on Kruger's pipe, looking from Tyson's face to Kruger's and slowly retreating.

And why are you not taking part in the parade, Mr Kruger? Tyson demands.

I seem to be a . . . a pacifist objector, Lieutenant.

But we are not at *war* here, Mr Kruger.

But I object to parades.

Tyson's beard compresses around his mouth. Extreme cold thins and hardens all faces, but especially white faces, and these ones are all caving into their eyes, disappearing into their beards.

Well, if you have no further need of your weapon—Tyson nods toward the lone rifle propped against the iglu wall, a few paces behind Kruger—I would ask that you donate it to me and the two hunters who are keeping us alive.

I would like to keep it for now, Lieutenant. I sometimes try to hunt myself.

Sensing Merkut behind her, Tukulito turns her head and hisses in Inuktitut, *You should have kept the children inside!* Merkut blinks, hiding behind an impassive mask and her dialect. The baby bobbles in her hood. Tukulito has not snapped this way since long before the expedition began; her cheeks and nape blaze in mixed fury and shame. Punnie cranes her head back, her inverted little face peering up in astonishment.

There, says Ebierbing, I guess they shoot the guns again. Plenty waste.

Everyone looks toward the floe-edge. Meyer's men have formed up along the shore, ready to fire a third salute, this time in the direction of the northern lights which undulate like a phantom, windblown drapery. More bullets into the void. The crump of the volley is followed by a second rippling crack—a different, bigger sound. Meyer's troops begin to yammer. There is a splash. Tyson draws his revolver and leads the group at an arduous trot down to the floe-edge. A lead is steaming, widening between the floe and the crescent-shaped slab that has broken off, the men aboard it. In the sea somebody thrashing with wooden arms, head stiffly upright, eyes round and fixed. Lundquist. Meyer, across the channel, casts quick birdlike glances all around, as if trying to identify a cause and a culprit. His pistol hangs in his hand. Anthing glowers at Tyson. The other crewmen holler in their languages. Ebierbing offers the butt of his rifle to Lundquist, who grabs it and clings. Not a wisp of breath from his gaping mouth. Ebierbing, Hans and Kruger grapple him like a seal onto the ice, where his wheaten hair and few whiskers, then his fur clothing, instantly freeze. In seconds he becomes his own stretcher. Hans and Jackson bear him like a long box of supplies toward the crewmen's hut.

Save us, sir, cries Herron. Joe, save us!

Ebierbing is scrambling back toward his iglu. I bring the kayak now.

Get the boat for us, Lieutenant! croaks Meyer. Please, if you would . . .

Anthing turns a narrow look on Meyer.

The boat's too heavy for us to drag alone, Tyson calls, pushing the pistol into his belt. You must hang on.

Wir sind verloren, says Jamka, mildly, kneeling and laying his rifle across his knees and making the sign of the cross. Then he hefts the rifle and aims it straight at Tyson. Bring now the boat for us! Or, by Gott, as we drift to our end, we can kill you each by each! Tyson's mitten moves back toward his pistol, but stops short. He glances back—meets Tukulito's gaze—takes in the children now arriving on the scene with Merkut. Ah, Christ, he says.

Meyer mutters some order. Jamka lowers his gun. Tukulito widens her eyes in fury at Merkut, who this time does not pretend not to understand. The woman takes Punnie's and Succi's hands and briskly leads them back toward her iglu, ordering Tobias and Augustina to follow. The channel, still growing, is perhaps forty paces wide. Ebierbing returns, dragging the jouncing kayak by its painter, a coil of rope and a grapnel over his shoulder where his rifle should be. He launches and drives toward the men with high-armed, deep-digging thrusts of his paddle.

He throws the grapnel end of the rope to Herron, turns and paddles back to the floe.

In moments the two parties seem locked in a desperately serious match of tug-of-war. Meyer's men secure the grapnel well back on the ice, but also kneel along the rope's length and hang on to it, to be certain, while across the open water Tyson, Kruger, Ebierbing, Tukulito, and Hans lean back and dig in, bracing to pull the new castaways home. At first they make no progress. Then the rope starts coming, an inch or two at a time. And Tukulito hears Kruger, up the rope from her, speaking into Tyson's ear in a winded murmur.

Now's the time to act, Lieutenant. With Meyer so tired. And the men shamed. They've lost some faith in him.

For a moment, nothing. Then Tyson whispers back between grunts and gasps: Shamed men are unknowable, Kruger. Sick men more so. Scorbutic, I mean. Meyer has the scurvy, I think. Pull, boys—pull now!

He cannot stand up to you. Not now. Sir. Look at him. Assert your authority, or—

Can't risk starting a fight, Kruger. If Joe is killed, we're all of us dead men.

They know it, sir! And if Meyer is let to go on . . . we are dead anyway.

Heave through now, boys, they're coming to us!

This may be a last chance. You have no idea what he plans.

A shudder is visible through Tyson's thin jacket. He says, Only Hans and I have weapons here. And you—are you willing to go fetch your rifle, Kruger? Are you prepared to shoot down your own countrymen if need be?

Kruger is silent, grunting low in his throat as he works.

Just as I thought. You ask me to face them alone. You're . . . Tyson fades out and Tukulito instantly interprets the tone of his silence: it has struck him that perhaps Kruger, in the role of Meyer's unarmed spy, is trying to lure Tyson into a fight—one in which he alone will be killed. For a moment Tukulito wonders if it could be true. But then Kruger adds, in a pained, panting whisper, All right. You're right. I will get my gun. Meyer must be stopped.

No! says Tyson—perhaps still suspicious—more suspicious? That would be mad. With the children still in range. I am not saving these men so we can shoot them, and they us. I mean to bring them back under my command. All of them. To save them. And I *will* do so, Mr Kruger—here he glares over his shoulder and then yells full in Kruger's face, *Heave through now, boys, pull them home!* The rope is coming hand over hand. Tukulito feels dizzy and has to keep swallowing coughs. Through the fog of the men's breathing she sees the crescent with Meyer's armed skeletons aboard pulled back into place, like a piece of splinted bone.

Bad sign, sir, says Ebierbing. Now the ice it all start shrinking.

The lost men rise from their crouch and stumble back onto the floe. Tyson has his mitten off, hand resting on the butt of his pistol. Meyer, vacant-eyed, nods to him and wanders slowly back toward the crewmen's iglu. Anthing slings his rifle and marches behind, leaning forward stiffly, glancing neither right nor left. And Herron trails, sheepish and shambling.

I'm sorry, sir. I'm conscripted.

Tukulito lets the rope relax in her mittens. In her heart she had agreed neither with Mr Kruger's plan nor with the lieutenant's; for these crewmen are more than ever a threat to Punnie. She will not permit that anything should harm Punnie. Even as she strove to help pull the men to safety, something in her had hoped the line would part and the lot of them drift away into the night.

Stealing would be entirely permissible, says Meyer sociably—in English, so that all can understand—if only the booty would be shared! In fact, that could not even be deemed stealing. We must suspect the natives to be guilty, or the lieutenant himself—but if the thief, or thieves, is among us here, I ask him kindly, Make yourself known!

Anthing's wet eyes slew from face to face. Kruger coldly meets his stare. Jackson looks up warily, then down again at his work: boring a new hole in his chewed belt with the tip of a strake-nail. Lundquist rests under the heaped furs where he has spent the last week recovering. Since the pilfering has continued—has actually increased—he is no longer a suspect.

The Major Graf Meyer waits an answer, says Anthing.

I shall impose no punishment, Herr Thief, or Thieves, if you come forward now! And Meyer flexes his rotting mouth into the outline of a smile. Steady wind against the walls makes a gnawing sound, like rats in wainscoting.

Jackson looks up and cries, I know you all reckon it's me!

Everyone turns. With a dangerous softness Anthing says, And is it?

No! Well. A few times, I suppose, I been cooking and I et a extra crumb or two.

Meyer shakes his head tolerantly. That is not what I mean.

Well, but sir, says Herron, as you're talking in English, you must think it's myself or Jack?

Possibly . . . your loyalties are of course suspect.

Never stole a thing in me life, sir.

But, now you need only to confess!

Our stealer I think is here, says Anthing. This one who holds himself always apart.

Their eyes find Kruger. He looks around. Herron and Jackson are too frightened now to meet his stare, to acknowledge any link with him—not with Anthing there like an unburied mine. Kruger is growing frightened too. He does have a secret. But he says coolly, Gentlemen, as there seems to be no one else left to accuse, except perhaps our leaders, I believe I'll go out hunting again. I understand we're running short of food.

He reaches for his unloaded rifle. Anthing's hand rests lightly on the butt of his Colt. He blinks his heavy lids, then looks toward the Count.

Be careful, whispers Meyer.

Next morning when Kruger wakes—having seen and shot nothing again; having failed, again, to meet Tukulito by chance—his rifle is gone. The snowhut seems warm. He sits up in his bag. Meyer is still asleep on the private ledge, Jackson and Herron pounding biscuit. By the lamp, a thinly smiling Anthing presides, arms crossed over his chest, the others around him in sweaters and drawers toasting their hands over the remnants of Voltaire's *Littlebig*.

Jan. 9. The west land still in sight, just visible in the noon twilight, about eighty miles off. It keeps very cold, ranging from 20 to 36 below zero. For several days the ice has been firmly closed, and no water anywhere; so we drift with the pack. No water means no seals, nor the bears that hunt them, nor the foxes that follow the bears and scavenge their leavings; but at least the light is slowly returning.

The provisions are disappearing very fast. I would set a watch if it was possible for us to stand outside in the nights, but in our badly reduced condition of flesh it would be fatal; and my own clothing is too wretchedly thin to think of it. Meyer tried posting a "sentry," apparently, with a result of serious frost-bite to Jamka. Meanwhile Kruger—who I believe is a kind of "emissary" for Meyer—"warns" me that the men are still determined to cross the ice to land, and mean to go next month. (Kruger seems to feel that his issuing "warnings," or, to use the proper word, "threats," is a favour to us in this hut; but he is a German, after all, and I know his true loyalty must be to the "Count.") If they do set out, the poor wretches will go to the east, misled by false advice, thinking they can reach Disko, when we are all the time drifting to the western shore. If they were only risking their own lives it would be bad enough; but by divided counsels and divided action, the safety of the whole is imperilled, especially as they seem determined to take our last boat. I am more and more alone here; no one to assist me. Hannah seems changed by our struggles, in a number of ways. I fear even loyal Joe may be thinking of striking out for land, for in a few more weeks, by my reckoning, we will be at the latitude of Cumberland Sound—near his and Hannah's home settlement—perhaps about fifty miles off-shore.

Much as it goes against my temper, I must try and conciliate the men, and turn them from their purpose. There is some little time yet to operate; for they dare not start in January.

Jan. 15. A strong gale has sprung up from the westward, and is now blowing very heavy, with a thick snow-drift. We are compelled to keep in our snow-burrows. I am greatly in hope that this gale will open the ice, so that we can get a few seals. We have only enough blubber left to warm our little food for two or three days more. Now Hannah is pounding the biscuit, preparing our pemmican tea. We pound it fine, then take salt-water ice and melt it in a pemmican tin over the lamp (the time occupied in heating five quarts of water is from two to three hours); then we put in the pounded biscuit and pemmican, and, when all is warm, call it "tea." As Joe says, "Any thing is good that don't poison you."

Jan. 16, morning. The gale has abated; the wind has carried off most of the snow, leaving only enough to lend our little settlement a more cleanly appearance. The Esquimaux went off early looking for seals, which I hope in God they may find. The ice now is pushing and grinding, which will surely open cracks, as well as fracture more pieces off the edge of our "island." It seems strange to think of watching and waiting with impatience for your foundations to break beneath you; but such is the case. In our circumstances food is what we most want. Hans's little boy, Tobias, is sick, and from Succi one hears a constant hunger whine. Punnie will often say, when she speaks in English, "Oh, I am *so* hungry!" She looks every bit as thin and ragged as her sad little doll; no one who has been a parent could look upon her without feeling the most heart-rending pity, and foreboding. Joe and Hans say that they have often suffered before for the want of food, but they have never been obliged to endure any thing like their present experience. Considering that they are out of the huts so much more than the rest, walking and hunting, they really ought to have a larger allowance of food. I would gladly give it to them, but I fear it would cause outright mutiny among the men! This at least I must prevent. Notwithstanding my dark and dirty shelter, my bed of wet and musty skins, fireless and cheerless and hungry, without one companion who appreciates the situation, I shall be well content if I can keep this party—worthy and worthless—together without loss of life until April, when I hope for deliverance.

At ten in the morning a breathless Tyson calls the men out to help take the kayak to Joe, who has seen seals. The healthier men—Lindermann, Kruger, Herron, and Jackson—grope for their parkas. Meyer sits up and orders them not to move until he or Lieutenant Anthing gives the order. After a moment Meyer gives it, but tells Jackson to stay in and finish preparing breakfast. Anthing snaps open the cylinder of his Colt to check the load, then spins and clicks it back with a flourish. *Kommen Sie heraus!* He kneels and starts toward the tunnel. Kruger notes that the man now *crawls* with a kind of rolling strut in his wide hips and his shoulders.

Beside Ebierbing's hut, the crewmen form up around the kayak. Tukulito emerges with Punnie and sends her to Hans's hut. She flicks a loose strand of hair from her eyes. When it falls back again, she ignores it. She acknowledges Kruger with a tight-lipped smile. All this in the near-dark. She takes the bow, Tyson the stern, and two crewmen take either side of the hull. There's no question of dragging it, there's far too much rough ice in the direction they must go, across the Central Alps and to the far side of New Heligoland. With its skin covering and wood-and-bone frame the kayak is not heavy, yet after a few hundred steps it becomes a test to carry it. For six adults.

Anthing gasps at Herron, Come, Herry, hold up your side!

You and Lindy are the big men, says Herron, in too much pain to be careful. Feels like you ain't even there.

Krüger! Kannst du nicht mehr tragen?

Tyson: Enough, all of you! And he slips a hand off the stern to feel for his pistol. His eyes widen. In his excitement and hurry he must have left it behind.

Tukulito is next to Kruger, a little ahead. By her breaths, he knows she is working hard.

Are you all right, madam?

Thank you, sir.

The others begin to argue about who is or isn't slacking. Tyson is involved too. The cloudy green ice is awkwardly grooved and stippled. Under cover of the noise Kruger leans forward and murmurs, I may have to flee my hut. Would Joe help me build one of my own?

You cannot live alone, sir. One would freeze in a night.

But surely there's not room in your hut, or Hans's?

Not in his. And I fear the lieutenant would not have you in ours.

Kruger eyes the balding grey peak of her hood. Her aura of blue-white breaths.

He does not trust you, sir.

No.

Could you live with the steward, and the cook? Three would be enough.

They'll never let the cook or steward leave.

What's that you're saying, Kru?

Then you must stay where you are, sir.

Nothing! Kruger tells Herron.

Be careful, please, Mr Kruger.

They stumble to the shore and collapse there gasping and Ebierbing launches the kayak and easily retrieves the one beautiful grey seal he has killed. They retrace their steps like different beings, peaceably silent, bearing the triumphal kayak with fresh strength, as if they've already eaten some of the animal now shunting over the ice ahead of them, towed by Ebierbing, drawing them on. Its oily savour of beef and seaweed. And how different the camp looks as they approach in the twilight! The three glowing huts and the storehut seem to make a comfortable town or city after the featureless desolation they've been struggling through. But as they near and the two flags resolve into clarity—the makeshift Eagle over the crewhut and the Stars and Stripes now fluttering over Tyson's—the sense is more of two customs posts straddling a border in some mountain pass. It now strikes Kruger that there will be trouble, and it isn't slow to come.

Everyone but Hans, who is off hunting, spills out of the huts. They gather closely around the dark body lying in the snow, on the border. Jamka in his joy fires his Springfield into the air. Succi crawls in and touches the seal's stiffening flank. Tyson tells Ebierbing to take it into their hut, to be butchered and divided.

I'm afraid we cannot permit this, Lieutenant, says Meyer, drawing his pistol. Lindermann nods with a glazed look. Jamka reloads his rifle. Anthing steps toward the seal and puts his boot on the glossy head. A trickle of bloody snow is pressed from its mouth, or nostrils. Ebierbing's eyes widen, narrow, as if shocked and then gravely offended on the creature's behalf.

We will take and butcher this seal in *our* hut, says Anthing.

But Joe killed this seal! says Tyson.

Kruger can't take his eyes off the animal. The idea of its being butchered out of sight, in Tyson's hut, is hard to bear, although it has happened before—yet now Kruger is suspicious even of Tyson. How will he and Ebierbing—and even Tukulito—resist taking more than their share? His own thoughts amaze him. He's salivating so badly he has to spit before he can speak:

Let the seal be butchered here, then. In the open. So all can see.

The words bring sharp looks from the whole party. Tyson and Meyer both glowering. Tukulito eyeing him with a new mistrust—or simply returning his own mistrust?—or resenting his mistrust? Meyer holds up a partially unscrolled piece of paper and prods it with the long barrel of his Colt.

As this map does show, Lieutenant, the seal was captured off the German part of this island, and is therefore our property to dispense of as we wish.

Never! says Tyson and stamps his foot and looks around at all of them.

Nevertheless, says Meyer. Still, we intend to be fully fair in our allotment of the flesh—perhaps fairer than you yourself intended!

Jamka, Anthing, and Lundquist are not quite pointing their weapons at Tyson, but they're loaded and held ready, aimed at the middle ground. Tyson's drained face churns with emotion. He's trembling, though perhaps from the cold as much as from anger, or fear. Throughout this standoff, Kruger's mouth will not stop watering.

We can butcher this animal fairly right here, he says. Now.

A thick oyster of spittle lands an inch from Kruger's toes. Anthing. In German: Any more interfering, Kruger, and you'll be laid out beside the seal.

Let me have a look at that chart of yours, Mr Meyer, Tyson says at last. Meyer approaches stiffly and hands it over. Tyson makes a pretence of examining the map, then begins to grin. Finally he laughs. He can't seem to help himself. He looks up, his eyes red, laughing harder, a bitter grin in his matted beard. The *German* part of this island! he says with a sort of desperate mirth. You're losing territory to the sea every night, Count Meyer! How do you mean to fight the sea? And he tears the map to pieces and flings the shreds down over the corpse of the seal.

Take the Goddamned seal, then, and bring us our share.

He turns and marches away. Anthing grabs the animal by a back flipper and hauls it in the other direction. Ebierbing doesn't move. His gaze is fixed on the pink-stained shadow where the seal's body was. His eyes wider and stiller than Kruger has ever seen. Kruger tries to catch Tukulito's eyes again, to be sure she doesn't blame him for this crime, but she's already turning away without a word, shepherding the crying children back to their huts. I'm sorry, Joe, says Kruger. Ebierbing doesn't seem to hear. And already Kruger is turning from him, helpless—helplessly lured by the aroma of seal's blood and the thrilled mutterings of the crewmen pulling and shoving the meat down into their tunnel.

He wakes from a dream of stooped strangers thin as kindling, cowled and shod in dark rags, hurriedly roaming the streets of a city whose vacant, high houses and shops and Gothic cathedrals are all constructed of ice. Wartime. These figures—the demised, as the dream calls them—are solitary, their paths uncannily straight and intercrossing. Yet somehow no two of them collide. None stops to comfort or confer. They are foraging for supplies. But on the snowy, level ground, under the low and sombre clouds, nothing remains to salvage or to steal.

In childhood when you wake in the night it's often to fear; in adolescence it's to the engorging ache of lust. In adulthood, in the small hours, even a happy man or woman wakes troubled, and at first, before the full return of identity and causation, the feeling is sourceless and absorbing, as if part of a cosmic sadness every adult sleeper taps into. *Wo bin ich?* Where am I. . . . Waking on the ice, Kruger can never quite believe the answer. And then: How can he be who he is, this one swarming mind and this random name trapped inside *this* body, *here*? And trapped *now*, on the forward-moving edge of the raft of time—now, out of all the ages?

Jan. 19, A.M. Fair with light, variable winds. Joe and Hans hunting again, despite the outrage of our recent theft. Yesterday, five miles from the huts, they found water, and saw a number of seals; but it was blowing heavy, and very cold. Joe says he tried to shoot, but that he shook so with the cold that he could not hold his gun steady, and that his fingers could not feel the trigger of his gun, and so the seal escaped. The wind moderated in the night, but it was so cold that all the holes froze up. I think the sun must soon show himself above the line of icebergs to the south, and I hope it will cheer us, and give us all strength; for Joe, like Tobias, is not very well. I hope he will not get down truly ill, for we depend greatly on him. Were it not for "little Joe," Esquimau though he be, many, if not all, of this party must have perished by now. We survive through God's mercy and Joe's ability as a hunter.

❧

Night. Clear and cold, the glass showing from minus 35 to 38°. I stopped outside as long as I could, trying to keep an eye on the store-house, and also admiring the beauty of the stars. The northern constellations seem more brilliant here than I ever noticed them at home. Ursus Major and Minor—if I remember right, these regions are named for the Northern Bear, αρκτος—Orion, Andromeda, Cassiopeia, the Pleiades, and Jupiter, so bright—part of Draco too. What a splendid night it would be for telescopic observations! The air so clear and pure, there is neither cloud nor fog, nor any visible exhalations from this icy land, or, rather, frozen sea, to mar the crystal clearness of the atmosphere. I wish I could also take observations, so as to ascertain our position, but "Count" Meyer continues to refuse me the loan of any instruments. At any rate, the cold pinches, and I had to leave the stellar beauties, and my watch on the store-house, and crawl into my dirty burrow to keep from freezing.

Patriotism is the last refuge of a scoundrel. Yes, but maybe also the last haven of the hungry, the demoralized and the desperate.

These days Kruger rarely speaks. He and Meyer's troops find little to say to each other, and Jackson and Herron, who would have to speak to him in English, are afraid to use the *Verbotene Sprache.* Clearly Jackson sees this state of affairs as shameful. He avoids Kruger's eyes. Herron, meanwhile, tries to catch his eye whenever possible, to send him looks—rueful but helpless expressions of regret, furtive twinklings of amusement, even mockery. And a moment later he will be snapping to Meyer's command. Yet Kruger finds it impossible to dislike him. He is simply too well-meaning and sweet-natured, a natural talker now forced to imprison all his talk inside him. Besides, unlike Kruger, he and

Jackson have no choice but to collaborate. Being German is the only thing that has protected Kruger, so far, in his frank contempt of the Count.

It's late morning and Jackson, in long underwear, has risen to relight the lamp. His broad, wasted shoulders are bunched up around his face. He's sucking air in through his teeth. There's "breakfast" to be fixed. He shakes Herron's feet. The others are still asleep in their bags with their rifles. Anthing also sleeps with Kruger's and Jackson's confiscated rifles, as well as the cooking implements—an arrangement that forces him to lie stiff as a plank, inflaming his mood more by the night.

The sooted and bloody hut looks like an abattoir after a fire, yet now Kruger discerns a faintly glowing pink patch on the wall above Meyer's body. For a moment he assumes it must be a reflection of the match that Jackson has just lighted.

William . . . have a look at that wall.

Just noticed it myself, says Jackson, letting the match go out as he stares.

Herron sits up, starts to wiggle out of his bag. The glow is spreading across the wall like an aurora or ectoplasm over Meyer's foetal form.

Herron is up and pulling on his fox-fur breeches, yanking his parka out from under the rancid bedding. Come on then, lads! Euchre the lamp, we've the real thing now!

Kruger and Jackson crawl after him down the dark passage and emerge like half-blind whelps into the salmon dawn: sunrise and sunset at the same time. Fifty yards to the south stands Tyson, his back to them, silhouetted between the other huts. Herron gasps, stands and launches into a drunkard's wobbling jig. Jackson stays kneeling with eyes squinted, a broad grin distending his yellow face. For the first time in years Kruger whispers *Mein Gott!* He can't take his blinking, light-needled eyes off the sun's hallowed face, just as he could not look away from that dead seal. Now any source of heat is transfixing. Herron's jig is joyous yet also frantic—the capers of a condemned jester trying to placate a remote, inscrutable king. For the first time since Christmas Jackson sings in his wistful baritone, *From Greenland's icy mountains, from India's coral strand . . . Where Afric's sunny fountains roll down their golden sand. . . .* As the sun edges higher—as high as it will reach today—its colours subtly alter, persimmons and peaches shading into clover-honey, yolk-yellow, buttermilk-yellow, so the seamed and buckled pack ice spanning southward to infinity is steeped in rich new hues. *Can we whose souls are lighted . . . with wisdom from on high . . . Can we to those benighted, the lamp of life deny?* The light saturating the ice-plains glitters on the turrets and beryl palisades of icebergs massed to the south-east, and to the east and west as well—nothing but ice—although last night Meyer repeated that his navigational readings prove Greenland to be at hand. And the sun's return will surely make him eager to set off.

Herron quits dancing and tries to light his meerschaum pipe, his fingers shaking.

My God, Kruger whispers. As beautiful as the face of a woman you love.

What? My word, Kru, you're white as frumenty.

The sun, I mean.

I heard you right enough, Kru, I just wouldn't have reckoned you for the romantic sort.

It's the one sort of patriotism I can believe in.

You've been in love, then, a scoffer like yourself? Herron grins. You're in love now?

In a light tone Kruger says, A scoffer conserves his love, that's all. He awaits his occasion. A sentimentalist scatters his soft love over everything—a little here, a little there.

Well, tell us her name then.

You know what Goethe's last words were, Johnny? Goethe, the most rational of men.

Jackson stops singing and listens.

I do, says Herron. I've heard them reported. More light, more light!

That's just what the scholars pretend. The real words were Gretchen . . . Kitty . . . Charlotte . . . Christiane . . . Marianne . . . Charitas . . . Frederike . . . Eva . . . Heidi . . .

Jackson and Herron start laughing.

When I get home, says Herron, first thing I do is find a girl to marry me.

Jackson says, That's the last other expedition I'll ever sign on for.

I too, says Kruger. Though we'll not be looking our best.

Speak for yourself, Kru! Lads, where's your pipes, we've a celebration to make.

Finished, says Kruger, New Year's Day.

Well, I'll spot you both a puff.

You will indeed.

The other men emerge behind them one by one with gasps and choked hurrahs. The other snowhuts are also emptying. Merkut and her children—except for Tobias—appear, and Merkut begins a trilling and jubilant chant, *Aliannai, aliannai!* Tukulito and Punnie walk over to join Merkut, then Tyson leads the whole group across the no-man's land of snow between the separate camps, past the storehut. Without a word from Count Meyer, the men stroll south to meet them. Like a Christmas truce between entrenched armies of the future.

Good morning! calls Tyson with a brisk wave, a white smile—something of his old robustness. Only he and Meyer and Anthing are armed, pistols in their belts. The two groups stand civilly on opposite sides of the border, which the night winds have as usual erased, though by now everyone knows its position. Punnie and Succi smile playfully up at Kruger, who smiles at Tukulito. She looks down at the ice—not like herself. Her cheeks are the colour of the sun just now.

A good morning to yourself, Lieutenant! says Meyer.

For a moment it seems goodwill is going to prevail between the Nations.

Your readings, Mr Meyer, suggested we should not see the sun for four more days. So this surprise is a most welcome—

That is so! I have erred slightly. But given the conditions, Lieutenant . . .

You walk upside down again? Punnie asks Kruger, who laughs like a boy, his joy at the sunlight uncontainable. Tyson squints pointedly at him, then says, This error is benign enough, Mr Meyer. However, it means we are not where you have told the men we are—close to Disko. I bring this up only to ensure that—

But even with this error considered, we *are* close, Lieutenant. And if we should pass Disko, we lose our last hope. There is food there, tobacco, rum, all of it the properties of this expedition. We must . . . what in devil's name are you doing, Krüger?

I'm sorry, Punnie, I haven't the strength anymore.

Saluktualugavit! she tells him, nodding.

You're too scrawny, Tukulito translates, something like a smile tickling the corners of her mouth.

Aufstehen, Krüger! barks Anthing, *sofort!*

But only *look* in that direction, Tyson tells Meyer with the lightning impatience of a man unused to having to plead. All of you, look! To eastward there is not so much as a mirage. How can you possibly believe that—

We simply must have those provisions, Lieutenant. We set out tomorrow.

Mit der Sonne!

Punnie and Succi seem unperturbed by the rising voices. They amuse themselves trying to pull Kruger across the deleted frontier, one grabbing each of his hands. Augustina brazenly crosses the line, slyly circling round behind him, giggling.

Now listen to me, men! I have sailed these seas too often to be deceived in our course. The straits here are three hundred miles across, and Disko is a high, rocky island—think back to our stop on the way north. If we were anywhere near it, we *must* see it. I have been whaling many times there and I know all the coast south of it well. You would never manage, never—

Nevertheless! says Meyer.

Kruger chuckles—a younger and younger sound—as he is dragged and pushed south by the children. Meyer tears off his mitt and draws his pistol which makes Tyson do the same. Then Anthing. Merkut gasps. Tukulito moves with startling speed and grabs Punnie. Meyer is aiming not at Tyson but at Kruger. Kruger shoves Succi and Augustina well clear of him. Meyer thumbs back the hammer, the cylinder turns with a sharp click, the huge pistol shakes in his hand. The sisters lie stunned in the snow. Succi wailing. Kruger stands limp, staring up at Meyer from under the ledge of his brow. Even now it's all he can do to keep his mouth shut. Meyer speaks in German with an old man's weak and peevish quaver: This is the end of your insubordinations, Roland Wolfgang Krüger. Also of your stealing. You have shown yourself to be a traitor to your compatriots and to the Fatherland. We shall see to you shortly. Herr Jamka, Oberleutnant Anthing—take him into the hut!

Kruger casts a searching glance at Tyson. Tyson looks away. The man holds his own Colt revolver upturned by his cheek, but is not about to intervene. And Kruger sees it plainly. Tyson will not risk violence in order to keep any of these troublesome Germans from killing each other—or, he still fears they're trying to trick him into a fight, and is refusing to be drawn in. Only Tukulito, glancing back as she rushes off with Punnie, meets his gaze. Her eyes seem to swell briefly, to send a signal like two widening ripples in a pond. It feels like farewell.

The wind is gathering itself outside. Ebierbing, tired from hunting, has been asleep since after the evening meal. The qulliq is burning low, its flame a pallid amber. Little blubber remains. Faint sounds of discord drift over from the crewmen's iglu, but as soon as they're audible the wind erases them, a chamois wiping words from a slate. Tukulito keeps waking and dozing off. She wakes again. Ebierbing is easing her over, onto her belly, lifting her hips. She sighs, reaches a warm hand slowly back for him. This has not happened for some time. Cold dry drafts, then the shocking heat of contact. Beside them, the lieutenant lies very still now, snoring softly, no longer grinding his teeth. Ebierbing must be thinking the same thing as she—that Tyson is awake, a fact that she can tolerate, here, so long as Tyson at least pretends to see nothing. As her husband strains his way into her parched body he whispers to her in Inuktitut, This man suffers so without his wife . . . and his situation here is so difficult. You should comfort him some night. Maybe tonight, when I'm asleep again.

Don't nod toward him that way, she says, he may be watching.

He can't understand a word.

If we're speaking of what's on his mind, he might understand. The men all talked of it, after Hans lent out Merkut on the ship.

You say it with disgust. It's a custom—a kindness. He clamps her buttocks with both hands. There. Hold still.

It's not my custom. We are married, church married.

You always take what suits you of their ways and ours!

(This stings, especially now.) She says, Well, I won't do this thing.

And he's a good man, in his way. What use is a God that makes you so stingy?

But I *have* a husband, she says, reaching back to clasp his testicles. This stops his words, though not his sounds, his rocking. It's good to be fed in this one way, at least. Somehow she is certain the lieutenant is watching, has even caught the import of their words. At her furtive, worried glance he turns away, onto his side, still breathing too evenly, she thinks, to be asleep.

Later, Ebierbing snoring and Tukulito's mind at last starting to settle, Punnie whimpers, moans, clutching her stomach again. *Anaana!* Without a word Tukulito sits up and takes the child's hand and gets her upright. She wraps a foxskin over the bony, bare little shoulders and leads her to the pemmican-tin chamber pot by the tunnel. Punnie looks up quizzically, her brow furrowed, unbraided hair wildly mussed.

Go ahead, little love, just here. It's night-time.

While Punnie squats and strains, Tukulito listens: the voices louder now, the men outside their iglu. Punnie groans, then says how much it hurts, how she just can't. Then: Oh . . . I hear Mr Kruger's voice! I'm afraid they're going to hurt him.

Stay here, my love. Tukulito crawls up the entryway and looks out. The side of her face is slapped numb by the wind cutting out of the west. By the light of a waxing half moon among floe-like, driven clouds, armed crewmen are milling outside their iglu, the eagle flag above it flapping and cracking like a horsewhip. Meyer's voice calls out an order. The sound is faint, either because the wind carries off the words or because he is trying to be quiet. Anthing, rifle slung over his back, his mitten gripping Kruger's nape, leads him away from the group. At a short distance he stops and spins Kruger back toward the men, four of them, who have made a line with Meyer behind them, their fur-clad backs solidified into a single creature. Four—so

Herron and Jackson must be inside. Anthing swaggers back to join the crewmen, briskly unslinging his rifle as he comes. Kruger has on his head only a white blindfold and on his torso his high-necked grey sweater. The moonlight shows him trembling, all of him. Tukulito backs quickly up the tunnel, just into the iglu. Ebierbing now keeps his rifle here, with reluctance. Punnie stares at her, still haunched over the pemmican-tin: Anaana, I'm afraid they will hurt Mr Kruger! Tukulito takes the rifle and says calmly, Wake Ataata and the lieutenant. From outside, the sound of Meyer's next order. A thin clatter as the men load. *Meyer*, she thinks—perhaps one shot will be enough—will be best.

Don't wake them, she says. Bring a bullet from the loonskin pouch.

Ataata says I must never—

Now—two bullets! She crawls up the tunnel with the rifle. Another order, this time totally inaudible, and the men level their weapons. They seem to be aiming high, as if at Mr Kruger's face. How would she have felt, the question skims through her mind, had Ebierbing asked her to comfort *him* instead? Hurry. Punnie is scrabbling up the tunnel, she hears the child's clogged breathing—but it's too late. Meyer yells a word like *fire*. Already Tukulito is backing down the tunnel, to block Punnie's view and to protect her, from any number of things. Through the iglu's walls a flash like lightning, a wind-muted crunch of gunfire followed instantly by the wind's full return, like something arrived to cleanse things away.

Ebierbing and the lieutenant make no sound.

That is best now.

Anaana . . . will they hurt Mr Kruger?

Stay there. For a third time Tukulito edges toward the tunnel mouth and peers out. Anthing and Madsen are helping Kruger to his feet, Anthing brusquely, Madsen with a certain delicacy. On Kruger's white-masked face there seems to be no blood, and none on his sweater. His legs, though apparently unshot, will not function just now. At Meyer's hushed command the men turn and march in file back to their iglu and then, one by one, they kneel and crawl inside. Madsen leads Kruger in, half pulling him, while Anthing shoves from the rear; the way they brought in the stolen seal. Anthing glances over, straight at Tukulito, but apparently sees nothing in the dark tunnel mouth. She is about to go inside to tell Punnie that Kruger is all right when she feels the child at her shoulder. With what tiny voice she has left Tukulito says, There, little love, you see? He's all right. It was all just a little game.

Jan. 20. 1 P.M. Blowing a fresh gale today, which may open up the ice for the natives; and has also apparently delayed the plans of the Count.

I am now compelled to record an event that occurred this morning, after Joe had gone hunting, and Hannah and Punnie had gone to Hans's hut, to help care for Tobias; so that I was mercifully alone for a short time. Disgraceful though it be, it is part of this story, and must go in. It will also show the animus of some of the men, and is a specimen of what I have had to endure from them. Kruger, entirely unprovoked, entered my hut, and commenced to abuse me in the most disgusting language, even threatening personal violence; but perceiving, though I said but a few words, that I was entirely willing to afford him every facility for trying his skill in that line of business, he did not attempt to put his threat into execution; and finding he could not provoke me to assault or shoot him, he shortly subsided and left. I suppose the foolish fellow had been boasting of what he could do (aside from involving himself in public misdeeds, I mean, as well as covert ones, for here if ever is the proof)—and the others had set him on by "daring him" to do it. It is evident enough that he had his backers. However, he walked off feeling a good deal smaller, I think, than when he came in.

4 P.M. The Esquimaux have returned from their day's hunt, bringing a fine seal, one considerably larger than last time; he will furnish us all a fine meal; and, with full stomachs, I hope the men will find themselves in a better frame of mind. At the moment they are complaining harshly, and issuing threats once again, for the natives brought the seal in with some stealth, so that this time the men should not seize it; and we have made a fair division of the meat. They are more wary in their threats now, for with several of their number unwell, and Herron no doubt tepid in their cause—as his glances my way often suggest—they know they have not the numbers to bully us with their old ease.

The filth in this hut is truly incredible; I cannot allow myself to dwell on it for long. Hannah appears sadly to lack the inclination, or perhaps simply the strength, to keep it as she once did. It is difficult to believe that she has ever lived among civilized folk. But then, these days, I feel little more than the rawest of savages myself.

Kruger finally encounters her outside the latrine. She is leading the peaked, sallow child back to their snowhut. He almost collides with them. Reaching down he steadies Tukulito's small shoulder with his hand. She shrinks back at his touch.

Go now, love, she tells Punnie. The child peers up at Kruger, then scuttles off.

Sir, she says firmly, you must be more careful.

Yes, in this darkness I'm always—

No—I mean with the other crewmen. I know what happened the other night, sir. And the next morning, with the lieutenant.

One does get weary of being almost shot.

She blinks, impatient, or uncertain of his tone, then says, I tried, sir, but I could not help you. Forgive me.

He is moved to the core by these words, by their animating thought, but can find no way to respond, verbally. He swallows and says thickly, But does *Tyson* know what happened? He claimed to know nothing when I confronted him! (The man drawing his pistol at Kruger's advance, eyes orbed with fury, or fear, then seeming to squeeze the trigger—but either the proofcatch is on or the gun is jammed, rusted. Still, this second mock execution is enough to liquefy Kruger's limbs, force him to retreat. He tells her nothing of this.)

He was asleep, sir. I had not time to wake him.

Through that volley? I never heard a thing louder in my life!

Nor I, sir, I assure you.

If he means to command on this ice, he can't allow "his" men to be shot, whatever the . . .

She is edging back from him, his abrupt vehemence. He has been inching toward her without realizing.

Now you will have to forgive me, Hannah. I seem . . .

Not at all, sir.

He must think I'm being used to draw him into a fight.

So I believe, sir, though he no longer confides in us. You are trembling, sir.

Please, not "sir."

I was afraid to tell him what happened. As they did not shoot you really—I thought he would consider it a further ruse.

Do *you* at least trust me? He looks back over his shoulder.

I hardly know whether to trust myself any more, Mr Kruger.

Her eyes are elusive, blending into the dark.

But yes, she says, I do.

He finds himself extending his arms, trying to embrace her.

Please, they both say, in unison. She retreats, raising a mittened hand to stop him. The open hand is trembling.

Forgive me, sir. I must return to my daughter. And do be careful, sir.

Jan. 24. To-day is our one hundred and second day on the ice—one of the most wretched I have ever known. The monotony is fearfully wearisome; if I could get out and exercise, or hunt, it would help to relieve the tedium; but while this wind and severe cold lasts, it is not to be thought of. Fortunately it is also confining the men to *their* hut. I hope they have given up their plans to try and reach Disko. The glass tells 45° below zero. Both yesterday and today, the natives report, large pieces have broken off the sides of our floe; soon we may have to rebuild all the snowhuts further "inland"—and, if this shrinking should continue, build them closer together, whether we want it or not.

3 P.M. Joe has returned, in the same stealthy way as before, bringing a fine large seal. We already have our pemmican tea, made over the lamp; so we thankfully divide and distribute the animal, which is such a welcome addition to our meal, and eat a little raw meat, and a few mouthfuls of blubber, and then have a smoke. But that luxury will not last long; I am on my last plug of tobacco to-day. *The mercury is now frozen*, so we know not how cold it is. But the Count informs me, through his "over-lieutenant" Mr Anthing—for it seems that they have given up sending Kruger to me—that he and the other men will be setting out as soon as this cold spell passes.

Jan. 28. The moon changes to-day, or did last night, and there are now full tides; this may expedite the damage to the raft, but also opens up the ice for seals. The Esquimaux are off, as usual, on the hunt. We are all well but one, Tobias. I can doctor a sailor, but I don't understand what is the matter with this poor little fellow. His stomach is disordered and very much swollen. He can not eat the pemmican at all; so he has to live on dry biscuit, and we have nothing else to give him. At night we can hear him cry, and hear his mother singing to console him.

The wonder is not that one is sick, but that any are well.

The mercury is still frozen. The men are seldom seen out of their hut. From the nature of the food we live on, and the small quantities, there is seldom any imperative necessity which calls them outside—perhaps not more than once in fourteen days. Oh, it is depressing in the extreme to sit crouched up all day, with nothing to do but try and keep from freezing! For those accustomed to action and averse to sloth, I think Hell will be a place not of everlasting toil but of eternal inactivity. Sitting long in a chair is irksome enough, but it is far more wearisome when there is no proper place to sit. No books either, no Bible, no Prayer-book, no magazines or newspapers—not even a *Harper's Weekly*—though there are always more or less of these to be found in a ship's company where there are any reading men. Newspapers I have learned to do without, having been at sea so much of my life, where it is impossible to get them; but some sort of reading I always had before. I believe Kruger had a book here, but that he lost it somehow; more likely he and the men have "cannibalized" it for the paper, or burned it for the heat. *It is now one hundred and six days since I have seen printed words!* This engenders a kind of hunger, too, and one which the reader of these lines will be sore pressed to imagine.

As it is, the thought of something good to eat is apt to occupy the mind to an extent one would be ashamed of on shipboard or ashore. If this life should last much longer, we shall forget that we have brains and souls, and remember only that we have stomachs! Some of the ancients, I believe, located the soul in the stomach; I think they must have had some such experience as ours to give them the idea. We even dream of food in our sleep; and no matter what I begin to think about, before long I find, quite involuntarily, my mind has reverted to the old subject.

I miss my coffee and soft bread-and-butter most.

Still, I believe God is watching over us, unworthy though we be, and that He will guide us into safety. For although I am overcome sometimes with certain thoughts, as I think of loved ones at home, I am not without hope. God, in creating man, gave him hope. What a blessing! Without that we should long since have ceased to make any effort to sustain life.

Morning in a place where morning doesn't mean light: the lamp has gone out, so the various smells aren't overpowering, though neither are they comforting, as they can also be. And the hut is so quiet. Kruger lies alert, as always now, though there is nowhere to run to except the open ice. A raw, scraping hunger and the sear of thirst help to keep him awake. Also thoughts of gooseberries in custard-yellow cream, the steaming white fat beneath the parchment skin of a roast goose. Just to run your tongue over a palate slick and coated with fat! Meyer and Anthing have put him on half-rations. Half of next to nothing, that's what that is. It brings a deeper hunger that all but keeps his thoughts from turning, for reprieve, to Hannah.

The other men all seem adrift in their polar coma. He trusts none of them now, nobody. He is his own small country. At Valmy, Goethe had rejoiced as he watched the volunteers of the French Revolution repel the reactionary invaders, though the invaders were more or less his own people, Germans. How fine, to be a "patriot only to truth"! But Kruger is feeling beaten. Perhaps it's better to belong after all.

Ich hab' dein Fleisch gegessen, whimpers Jamka.

What's that, then? Herron speaks with something of his old lightness, clearly relieved to find somebody else awake. Eaten *my* flesh?

Jamka rises off his back, props himself on his elbows. *Es war ein Traum*, he says. A dream. So! he says, alert now, you understand German? *Oberst Graf Meyer—bitte! John Herron kann—*

Shhh! says Herron. Not to worry, Yam—I get nowt but the easy stuff. If I'm not allowed to speak my speech, it'd be a wonder if I hadn't gleaned a bit of yours, wouldn't it?

After a moment Jamka nods his scabbed, blotchy face. Meyer goes on wheezing. In a confidential undertone Jamka says, *Und so*, have you dreamed any such dreams, John Herron?

What—of eating human flesh?

Ja.

There's a prolonged, ruminating silence.

Well . . . perhaps the odd one.

In *my* dreams, Lindermann's voice jumps in, it tastes rather like pork.

But the children, Jamka says lovingly—they are more like lamb!

Well, I've et nothing but adults so far, says Herron. Big ones.

The tops of heads are poking one by one out of sleeping bags.

Bear meat, murmurs Anthing in a rapt voice. Very much like bear, I think.

Bear *is* rather like pork, however, says Lindermann.

Ja, ja, das ist wahr . . . und du, Kamerad?

Ja, says Lundquist. I too have such dreams. There is no taste but the taste of fat.

Und du, Kamerad?

Nein, says Soren Madsen, *nimmer!*

Jackson now says, Guess I've had a dream or two like that myself.

The lamp! Anthing orders him, it's out again!

You mean, says Lindermann, you have dreamed of eating the flesh of *white* men?

All eyes, wide and peering over the lips of sleeping bags, are fixed on Jackson.

Well, it was only meat. I don't recall it had any particular colour.

Meyer sleeps on like a giant foetus on his bed-ledge, withered knees sticking sharply over the edge, one eye squashed into the foxskin rolled around his pistol. Nobody consults Kruger about his dreams. From his exile a few feet away in the northwest corner he continues to watch things through tightly slitted eyes. Anthing wriggles out of his armoury of a sleeping bag and works into a sitting posture. He looks across at Kruger, who continues to feign sleep. Anthing says in hushed, rapid German, Of course it would be a very good thing to take some fresh provisions with us. When we set out for Disko.

Jackson and Herron lie still, rigid as hares in the snow. They can't possibly understand the words, though they look as if they get the drift of them.

But *Oberleutnant*, Lindermann says carefully, some of us are beginning to wonder now if . . . perhaps Disko really is farther off from New Heligoland than would be . . .

Nonsense, says Anthing.

It cannot be! says Jamka.

Sir, says Madsen . . . I am afraid I no longer have any real mittens to wear.

Have you lost them?

Well—not as such, sir.

Anthing's reddening face looks like it's being inflated with a pump.

You have eaten them, haven't you?

Little by little, sir. In the night.

Anthing juts his bloody beard toward Kruger. You'll just have to take his.

But now Lindermann, Lundquist, Madsen all speak together, pointing out that it's difficult to stay outside for more than a few minutes, let alone days, or weeks.

A good supply of fresh meat, says Anthing. That's the answer.

But surely we're not going to, to slaughter the children?

We go as soon as the weather improves, he says and Kruger can see how he's feeding off Meyer's decline, how it plumps and colours his bully-boy cheeks, sharpens the glint in his eye.

And no, we need not harm the Esquimaux. Not at first. Not the filthy parents, at any rate. I have another idea.

He slides Kruger's confiscated rifle out of the clanking sleeping bag and swings it round, Lindermann ducking, then slips the proofcatch and cocks the hammer. Krüger! While he holds his aim, the air of the hut almost clears of its fog as all the men except Meyer and the faking Kruger hold their breath. Kruger squints up into the muzzle, an arm's length away. Anthing's left eye bulges over the sights. *Roland?* Kruger shuts his lids totally and for a moment he prays. About God, too, perhaps it's better to be fooled. At twenty, he lay wounded by the taffrail of the *Königsberg* with snowflakes falling gravely onto his tongue and his eyelids and there was no pain at all, not yet. And he heard his messmates saying, Rolli's dead! He heard the stretchermen saying, Well, this one's dead! He heard the surgeons saying, Another one dead. Even the ship's chaplain believed he was dead. He began to believe it himself. He had died for his country and it had made him a part of nothing at all. He was perfectly alone. He'd become meat—nothing more than meat.

One's country was a cannibal with a vast, ceaseless appetite.

Peering out secretly he meets the rifle's Cyclops stare. Anthing, satisfied, is thumbing down the hammer, propping the rifle against the wall, and Kruger, with the insight of a man facing death alone, sees through him now, this truer threat—the hollow but cunning mediocrity in any group who waits his chance, then springs his putsch and grabs power.

Jackson. Light the lamp and roust Colonel Meyer. Herr Krüger for now we will let sleep.

Feb. 1. The wind still continuing to blow with violence, our "Lotos-Eaters" scarcely show their heads out of their hut. Still, Mr Meyer deems the presence of all the icebergs around us to be further proof that we are close to Greenland; *and* he promulgates the fantastic opinion that the straits in lat. 66 N. are only eighty miles wide! He would find it a long eighty miles indeed. Still, there seems something rather more tentative about the "Count" today, and his followers also. Perhaps they have at last become convinced that they cannot carry out their project. Their assurance of soon getting to a land of plenty has been the cause, I fear, of many raids upon the provisions, and of more being consumed than even they would have risked had they not been deceived as to the course of our drift; but now they begin to grasp that they did not know as much about these seas as they thought they did.

The Esquimaux inform me that the cracks in the ice where they have been sealing are not limited to the "young ice," but cut clear through the old—which is an intimation that our floe may split up completely at any time if the wind holds. Also, the huge ice-bergs are moving rapidly before the wind; and they are heavy enough, if propelled upon our encampment, to crush us to atoms.

On going into Hans's hut this morning, to visit the ill boy, I was sick at heart, seeing the miserable group of crying children. The mother was trying to pick out a few scraps of "tried-out" blubber from their lamp to feed them. Augustina is naturally a fat, heavy-built girl, but she looks peaked enough now. Tobias was in her lap, or partly so, his head resting on her as she sat on the ground, with a skin drawn over her. She seemed to have a little scrap of something she was chewing on, though I did not see that she swallowed any thing. The little girl, Succi, was crying—that chronic hunger whine—and I could just see the baby's head in the mother's capote. All I could do was encourage them a little. I have nothing at all to give them. I was glad, at least, to see that they had some oil left.

Our own hut is scarcely less filthy than Hans's. It is dark enough in here, but nevertheless I am compelled to shut my eyes on many occasions. We are all permeated with dirt—I have not had these clothes off *for over a hundred days*, and it sickens me to think of them, saturated as they are with all the vile odors of this hut, of seal's entrails and greasy blubber. I am trying to recall the pleasant sensation of putting on clean clothing, and how, while whaling, when I got my feet wet and cold, what a comfort it was to get on a clean pair of stockings or socks; yet, perhaps I had only worn the discarded ones a few hours, not months! Alas, we can spare no warmed water for washing. I know it is impossible to be clean, living as we do; but among the Americans Hannah has learned one thing that has been no benefit to her, and which has added many annoyances to our inevitable misery this winter. She observed among white folks that it was the custom for men to support their wives, instead of using them as slaves, as her own people do in their natural condition; and, in order to be as much like a white woman as possible, she has positively declined to do—has at least omitted to do—many things which would have made this hut more tolerable.

I comb my hair and beard with the only comb in the encampment—Hannah's coarse wooden one—and call it my morning wash. Well, but perhaps the waters of Davis Strait will yet wash me clean, so I won't grumble.

Feb 1st I cannot describe how nasty & dirty it is here. I know it is impossible to be clean living as we do but I must tell the thruth. This Esquimaux Squaw Hannah is the dirtiest most filthy thing I have ever seen. She is filthy for an Esquimaux. I have never seen her equal as a dirty & Lazy Squaw. And this Squaw has been back living with civilized people! How to continue I dont know. soiled to the bone. On my watch they will all die children & parents alike & seamen too & turn cannibal perhaps too & I can do little, beyond kill some.

My skin brown w. grime. God is gone & to die seems good.

In the middle of the night Kruger slips out of his bag. The lamp is out. For a moment he's tempted again to try stealing a weapon, but the only one he could possibly get would be Meyer's Colt, and lately the Count's skull is hardly ever off the foxskin in which it's wrapped. Kruger has died three times here: before the firing squad, before Tyson, and before his own confiscated rifle. A fourth time will surely finish the job. He fends for himself alone now, like the Gypsies.

He dresses in quick silent movements and crawls into the tunnel through the wolfskin, his parched mouth actually watering at its doggish smell. In the tunnel he grabs the snow trowel and slips it blade-first into his pocket. Outside, under a sky massed with tremulous stars, he steps over one of the tripwires strung around the hut. The four lines lead inside through small holes pierced high in the wall, where they converge on and suspend a tinny bell—an empty mock-turtle soup can with a bullet inside it on a string—that hangs under the peak of the dome. The Count's latest invention, rigged by Anthing.

He trudges inland, northward, hugging himself against the cold. Every muscle is gripped and held hard against the cold. His hood is drawn tight but through the fur-fringed gap in front of his eyes and nose the gusting wind lances at his face, layering new frostbite over old. His jaw and teeth ache and soon his legs are numb—wooden pegs from the knees down. His breath freezes to ice-crystal clouds that shimmer and fall tinkling at his feet. This is the worst cold yet. He beats his mitts together. Through all of this his mouth will not stop watering.

Scattered along the north horizon, icebergs frozen into the solid pack, molar-shaped, glitter in the starlight. Near Bismarcksee—formerly Lake Polaris—he stops beside a familiar hummock, walks a few paces west, a step east, kneels down out of the wind and digs urgently with the trowel. Soon there's a layer of ice to crack through. He does it with a savage jab of the blade. The cache, sunk deep in the side of the hummock, is exposed. There's a canvas sack jammed with biscuit, a half-dozen big tins of pemmican, two tins of powdered chocolate, frozen slabs of sealmeat, blubber, and skin. With the trowel Kruger cracks a biscuit in the snow and stuffs a piece in his mouth, the other shards in his pocket. He slips a fillet of sealmeat into his pocket and then plugs his cheek—the numb jaw still intently chewing—with a glop of blubber. Frozen, there's no taste, but as his gums begin to thaw the fat, the flavour comes, like a chunk of ice transformed, by pure force of desire, into a rich and oily food. Think of lard blended with dulse. Soft tallow with kelp.

A long sepulchral booming and the ice shifts like the deck of a frigate being shelled. He pockets another dollop of blubber to suck on the way back, then carefully reorganizes the cache and seals it, packing the snow down hard with his mittens, his boots. As he hurries south, markedly stronger and less frozen, he glances back to ensure the wind is erasing his tracks.

Punnie has a loose front tooth which of course she will not let alone, always testing it with her finger, just as the lieutenant, looking frail, stern and secretive, sits huddled among his muskox skins, chewing on his lengthening whiskers. At times he sneaks his field-book out from under him, scribbles a few furtive lines, then replaces it among the skins—first carefully squaring it with the wall, then sitting on it. Other times he removes and feels and even sniffs at the interwoven circles of hair, brown and blonde, that he keeps in his breast pocket. His red eyes well up; the right side of his beard twitches. *Pirliliqtuq*, thinks Tukulito. The madness of hunger and the dark months.

The child is happy to have a loose tooth, since Tobias has so many, but Tukulito, whose two born-babies died long before the tooth-losing age, worries that this could also be a first symptom of the scurvy. Again she tells Punnie to leave the tooth alone. This is the time of day when she will speak only English to the child, correcting her responses in a soft voice that now costs her a great effort to maintain. *Pirliliqtuq.* How the mind can churn with violence: a murderous irritation, but also this shame now, and guilt. There are so many customs to transgress. So move slowly, fixedly, from chore to chore. Against terror, only loyalty. On the ship she was teaching Punnie to read using her Bible, but that was left behind, so now for spiritual instruction she must draw on her large mental archive of hymns. Punnie has a good ear, a fine voice, and some of the strain seems to ease from the lieutenant's face as he sits listening to the two of them sing: *When I can read my title clear . . . to mansions in the skies . . . I'll bid farewell to every fear, and wipe my weeping eyes.*

Punnie sings in the way of small children, misconstruing difficult phrases into curious little poetries: *My Tight All Clear. To*

Man Shun Sin. Fear End White. Tonight as they sing together, Tyson joining in, hoarsely, there is a sort of echo, as if off the close walls of their iglu, and after a moment they realize that some of the crewmen are singing too. They seem familiar with the tune but have words in their own language. Their far voices are difficult to pry apart, and Roland Kruger's she cannot discern—which sharpens another fear—while Anthing, with his warm throaty tenor, seems to lead them. *O take me from the wilderness, and find my soul a home . . . O let me all my wrongs redress, and to your mansions come.*

High above them a raven or owl, blown off course and scavenging the ice in vain, might hear that small, still hopeful chorus, and looking down see a shrinking flake of ice barely lit by three lamped iglus, a raft of consciousness adrift in the impassive polar night.

Feb. 5. This evening the wind has hauled to the south; weather now thick and snowing. I can see but a few yards before me. Here in the hut, Joe is oiling his rusting rifle, Hannah mending his seal-skin boots; she will only repair those articles of clothing made from the skins of sea-animals. Yesterday, after we sang together, I asked if she would mend my deer-skin socks, and, when she said it was impossible, I made to do it myself; but in some consternation, she prevented me, explaining that to work on the skins of land-creatures while at sea might bring disaster. When I pressed her for a reason, she explained, with what seemed a sort of embarrassment, that such work might anger the goddess of the sea-animals, a jealous creature, who presides out here; so that Joe would find no game, and our raft might break up. To hear such irrational *tabus* from the mouth of an apparent Christian no longer much surprises me, however disappointing and disturbing it might be. Nevertheless, I had to mend my socks, and did so. Then, this morning, Merkut gave Tobias to Hannah and Joe to care for—apparently another custom, and last recourse for ill children; but for the life of me, I cannot see how we are to fit him in.

Feb. 7. Esquimaux returned, and we are all rejoicing over another feast of seal-meat! For Hans shot one about noon; but we had some little trouble over it this evening. Hans, if he gets a seal—which is very seldom—wishes to appropriate it all to his family's use, without considering that *he and his family get their daily allowance of biscuit and pemmican with all the rest.* Of course he must not be allowed to have more than an equal share; and, *had* I allowed it, Mr Meyer, Anthing, Kruger, and the other miscreants would surely have turned violent. Hans is a very selfish Esquimau; he is not a successful hunter, like Joe, nor has he his sense, and is proving a most miserable creature. He has threatened this evening "not to hunt any more." Well, let him try it! He was hired (and will be paid, if we ever get home) for the very purpose of hunting for the expedition; he will go very hungry if he continues to refuse, for I shall not allow him any thing more out of our stores. Oddly, he showed no fear at this threat, vowing that he will "somehow or the other" get enough to supply himself and his family.

Like the ice itself, it seems, our poor party is splitting into more and more separate parts.

Kruger can't tell if his plan is sound. He feels confused now, often. He looks back on events of just a day ago, or an hour, as if through a rum-drunk haze. Have the men really trussed Jackson's wrists and ankles with rope? Jamka and Meyer are terrified that the Darky means to kill and eat them in the night. Or *poison* them! (With what? Jackson objects. If they was any thing poison here,

I'd gladly eat it myself.) Was Kruger really stooping over Anthing in the lamplit gloom of a night or two ago (or three, or four?) with cold hands tingling at his sides like an assassin's? Until he perceived threads of crate-twine emerging from the mouths of the caribou bags, linking the Germans and Madsen and Lundquist by their wrists; Jamka's tremulous wrist half-exposed. If any are attacked, the rest will waken, armed to the eyelids.

Yet the measure that allows them to sleep harder also frees Kruger to leave the hut more often. His plan is to deplete the men's cache—because the secret cache is not his own—so that Anthing won't be able to draw the men with him, well supplied, on a trek to the east, taking the last boat, leaving the rest of the party to die.

Kruger discovered the cache just after the new year. Out trying to hunt—mainly to escape the hand-me-down air and sentiments of the hut, and in hopes of encountering Tukulito—he noticed a splotch of blood on the moonlit snow by a hummock, where the ice was disturbed. Brushing it, he exposed a hatchwork of crescent cuts, as from a trowel blade or the heel of a very large boot. And he dug there. But within a few days of his discovery Anthing confiscated his rifle, and he has been able to return only a few times, always careful to slip things inconspicuously from the back of the growing hoard, then reseal it with care. It must be Meyer's and Anthing's, he thinks—but if it is, why would Meyer have made his speech asking if the thief were any of them? Think. Simply to retain their faith in his probity until such time as they grow too desperate to care? Hard to follow any line of thought for more than a few seconds. But clearly Meyer, too ill even to groom himself, is not supplementing his own rations. Could the cache be Anthing's alone? He has kept stronger. Is now slowly assuming command. Think. Anthing, who knows he may never get another stab at power.

Of course by raiding his supplies Kruger makes it more likely that Anthing will have to resort to other sources of food. Yet for now he can see no other plan.

Cold not only slurs the tongue, it also muffles the mind.

He must get some food to the others. Tukulito, the children. Slipping any to Herron or Jackson seems impossible, for now. So give some to her directly. But when? He has only managed to encounter her once in the last few weeks, and he can hardly invite her, a married woman, outside. Leave some just inside the tunnel of her hut. No. They would think Poison. Especially if Tyson found it. *Ein Gift.* And he would confront the men and ask where it came from, and then Anthing would know Kruger was raiding his cache—*if* the cache is Anthing's—and if, if, if. Maybe Anthing thinks Kruger is raiding the storehouse on his own and has made a *separate* cache. *Which is why I am not trussed up like Jackson. So they can follow me there!* As his torpid brain works to triage the possibilities he hears Punnie and Augustina outside and it comes to him, another plan. The men seem to be napping. Jackson can do little else now. In a trance of apathy Herron is warming water. After some minutes, saying nothing, Kruger slips outside. In early dusk under a sky as low as a coffin lid the girls, one large and broad, the other tiny and frail, are tracing wide, slow figure-eights around their parents' huts, hand in hand. Hunger has stolen all the jump from their voices; they converse in a flat drawl, like weary adults.

He staggers away toward the cache. Easy to see why men in this state will fear they're being poisoned. He feels poisoned. There's a scuffling behind him—big Lindermann following, eyes to the ice, stepping with lumbering care over the tripwire, hunger's drunkard. Kruger climbs over a hummock and behind it he lowers his fox-fur breeches and squats, left hand cupping his genitals for warmth. After what seems a long time Lindermann peers over the top, puffing. The muzzle of his rifle beside his blistered face. His oddly small head has shrunken further and weathered darkly, like the trophy of a cannibal tribe.

Guten Tag, says Kruger.

Lindermann nods sheepishly, then lowers the rifle.

I wish I could join you in that, he says. I'm also in some pain.

So, is that why you've followed me?

I can see why you wouldn't want to use the old latrine shelter.

Actually, for a short time I considered living in it. Did Anthing send you?

Lindermann looks down, as if hurt. I am sorry you've been made to suffer so by the others.

Kruger stares at him pointedly.

Damn it, Roland, my heart is not with them! But they give the orders, Meyer, and Matthias—

So now you've tied up Jackson like a slave on a ship.

You should have organized us to resist them at the beginning! The men respected you . . .

But they revered the Count of Disko.

. . . but you always want to stand *alone*, Roland, that's why!

This stops Kruger. He wonders, in sudden pain, if his old messmate could be right. Still squatting over his dropped breeches, Sage of the Latrine, he murmurs: I thought it was obvious, no one can think freely in the middle of a shouting crowd. I've thought so for years. There's no glamour in sanity, Willi, but I believed in it. And now . . . now I can't get my head to think at all.

Lindermann says, The men—they don't really want to try for Disko—they now believe the lieutenant may be right. But they're terrified to disobey. And Roland, you must be careful!

His lower lip quivers. Big Lindermann, the mild giant, their strongman. And then it hits Kruger—this must be a trap. It might be a trap. His meatless knees are trembling and his hindparts are on fire with the frost. In a cool, neutral tone, he says, Thank you, Willi. I'll keep your words in mind. I may still be some time here.

Lindermann nods in a discouraged, heavy way, then sinks behind the hummock. After a few moments Kruger scrabbles to the top and peers over. With a weight on his heart he watches Lindermann slump back toward the crewhut. No way to know anything for certain now. Kruger turns and lurches on through the "Alps" to the cache.

On his return, Punnie, Augustina, and now Succi, all hand in hand, are heading around the back of Hans's hut. Kruger kneels in the aqua gloom and inters biscuits and sealmeat in the snow twenty paces behind Tukulito's hut, off the figure-eight trail the children are deepening. He marks the mound with a P. Then he staggers on, intercepting the children as they round Hans's hut. Punnie looks sad and pale, but at the sight of Kruger she grins: a lower front tooth missing.

Mister Kruger! Mother says they make you stay in your iglu now. She's worried!

Speak softly, Punnie.

Augustina, who has no English, stares at him vaguely, in her eyes the same torpor that Kruger feels behind his own.

Kruger holds Punnie lightly by the arm and tells her that she will have a treasure hunt. But the treasures must be shared with the other children, in secret. After her walking game is over she must look for her initial, beside her iglu, and promise to tell nobody of their talk. This prospect seems to delight her. Her mother is with Toby, she says glumly, and will hardly play with her at all.

❧

The warning bell does rattle, once, but only Kruger stirs. He has been awake, picturing and trying to taste his mother's dense buttery marzipan cakes, always served with scalding black coffee, to cut the fat. He dozed off once. Tukulito was bringing him a white porcelain side plate with the cake slice on it, swimming in a syrup of blood. It looked wonderful, and somehow in devouring the cake, he realized, he would be making love to her. He sits up. *You boys!* Somebody is yelling outside in the wind. *Roust now! Boys . . . ?* It's Ebierbing, not daring to crawl in as he did long ago—the night Hans went missing. *My Punnie lost now! Please help, come out, any boys of you!*

Kruger scrutinizes Anthing in the dimness, hoping to catch his unguarded first expression as Ebierbing's words hit home. Anthing has been asleep on his front. As he lifts his curly head and peers around turtle-wise, his creased face looks dull and slack. Kruger thinks, If you had something to do with this, you're a dead man, whatever it takes.

Wait for me! he calls in a cracked voice. He leans over the snowy no-man's land that borders him, to shake Herron, but everyone except Meyer is already awake. Hans is unpopular, Punnie is not. The starved men begin to rouse themselves, even the trussed Jackson, but Anthing, sitting up, says, I make the orders. This could be a trick. Why would the child be outside at night, in a storm? It could be Tyson and the natives waiting to shoot us as we come out.

Well, I'm going, Kruger says, pulling on his boots. Why not let Herron come, and Jackson as well? He can hardly boil and eat you while he's out there with me.

Jackson's bewildered eyes dart about, German words whistling above him like bullets.

You will all remain in here.

The devil I will. Kruger kneels and crawls toward the wolfskin.

As he pushes into the tunnel he half expects the grim *click* as Anthing aims his six-shooter at his ass, *fourth time will finish the job.* Instead he hears: Let him go. Let Herron go too. You others, you stay where you are. Prepare your rifles.

Outside Ebierbing and Kruger lean together. They have to be almost nose to nose to see and hear each other. Ebierbing's face betrays no emotion but his voice is a half-octave too high. Herron joins them. His face is tight and scared. It seems Punnie crawled out of the iglu a little while ago and the lieutenant woke up and saw her going out, then went after her, calling Ebierbing and Tukulito to wake, too. When he got outside he couldn't see her. Ebierbing, Hans and the lieutenant have been searching since then; Tukulito has to stay with Tobias.

Whatever would she have gone outside for, Kruger asks, the floor of his stomach caving.

We dunno. Tukulito think, maybe Punnie is, is, how is the word . . . of Toby.

Worried? asks Herron. Jealous?

That! Angry, too, so she run off.

Ebierbing ropes the three of them together, himself in the middle, and they spread out, groping through the whiteout with five paces between them, some slack in the rope, calling into the wind, or with it. Ebierbing says the lieutenant has attached a long leash to himself and is searching around their iglu, Hans around his own. On his end of the line Kruger feels almost warm, his cheeks and ears and nape blazing. It isn't Anthing who killed the child. She must have waited till after dark to be sure nobody would see her looking, and now the gale has buried the P.

Something grips his arm. He turns, blood thudding in his chin. Tyson leans at the end of his leash, his pistol in his belt. His cap, eyebrows, beard, and the muskox hide over his shoulders are plastered with snow.

I begin to fear the worst, he shouts, pushing his face up to Kruger's.

That the child is dead, Kruger murmurs.

No! That your compatriots have seized and eaten her.

Small icicles off his nose and beard tremble. Kruger takes a step back. Tyson strains against his leash, hanging onto Kruger's arm.

Lieutenant—how long since she went out?

The natives and I were coming in there to look for her, had none of you emerged to help. But then again—yes—perhaps you two are but decoys! In his quick-blinking eyes the same fever as in Meyer's and Jamka's, a hunger that trusts nobody. Yes—perhaps she *is* still inside your—

Lieutenant! How long ago?

What? Not so long. A half-hour.

But I was awake this past hour. The others were asleep. Your suspicions are un—

You admit you were awake! Pilfering again for Meyer, no doubt—

The rope tightens round Kruger's waist, then yanks him backward. Tyson hangs on.

Kruger! comes Ebierbing's voice, what you find?

I am not the thief, Lieutenant.

Don't lie to me! You've been courting the child's mother for months! Now I understand. This was the actual scheme. To gain her trust and use her like a whore, then seize her child!

Kruger tries to spit at Tyson's feet. His mouth is too dry. Tyson clenches the fur of Kruger's hood on both sides and jerks his face nearer. Kruger grabs Tyson's mantle and they totter together, pathetic wrestlers. The rope tugs Kruger hard. He reels back into the snow, Tyson toppling beside him. Kruger grabs Tyson's forearms to ensure he can't get at his pistol. Shouts are whirling in the frenzied air and white figures loom over them: Ebierbing, carrying Punnie who clings to him like an albino monkey, Herron hobbling behind, bent almost double against the gale. The child's face is pressed to her father's shoulder, her body pulsing with sobs under the caked little parka. Says she out looking for food! Ebierbing shouts, and his voice throbs and surges. Food in the snow, for Tobias! More food maybe make him better, he go back to his mother, hah!

Kruger lets go of Tyson and rolls onto his back with a sobbing laugh, then tears. Herron kneels, setting a mitten on his shoulder.

Food lying about in the snow, Kru! Now wouldn't that be grand!

The slight wavering of the qulliq's glow on the iglu's dome makes a miniature of the northern lights. Tukulito and Ebierbing are awake, Punnie and Tobias nested between them. The boy's breathing is quick and shallow. On Tukulito's other side, pressed close, the lieutenant lies straight and stiff as a cadaver, grinding his teeth. Before sleep he informed them that they are now at the approximate latitude of Cumberland Sound, their old home, perhaps a hundred miles to the west.

This they already knew.

Ebierbing reaches over the children and gently knuckles Tukulito's cheek, an uncharacteristic gesture. His fingers are oddly cold and dry.

Isumakaqaqpiit? Tukulito asks.

Saluktualugavit, he says. You've grown so thin.

Ahaluna!

After some moments Ebierbing continues in Inuktitut: He always sleeps the hardest before dawn. When he stops his teeth-grinding. We can set out then.

She says, I thought I'd trimmed it better.

What?

The wick.

I say that we can get home, maybe, across the ice now. This floe is wearing away and will soon be gone.

Oh, mother! Tyson moans in a stifled voice, the soilings! Yet you'd purged him . . .

Tukulito ignores Tyson and says, When the ice goes, there's always the boat.

You know that the men mean to take it.

I don't think they'll really try.

How can you know that? It's impossible to know anything about the Qallunaat!

Qallunaat wear their feelings on their face, she says, and draw them in the air with their hands.

But moments later they wear new feelings. If they take that boat, we're all lost.

No, not again! says Tyson. His entrails are a serpent!

She says, Father Hall would never want us to leave the others like that.

But he *loved* Punnie, says Ebierbing with some force, although he lies still. If Father Hall could see the way the men look at her and the other children, maybe he would want us to leave. We almost lost her last night. And where did she get that biscuit she was hiding? She didn't "find it in the snow." I'm afraid they're trying to lure the children to them. Maybe fattening them up.

After a few moments she says, Maybe it's Mr Kruger. I think he's a good man, maybe he saves some of his food for the children.

Maybe to use as bait. I don't trust any of them.

She falls silent. He is forced to go on: And now Hans says he won't hunt. The men may kill him soon. They'll never let an Inuk lie around in his iglu, same as they do, and eat up the stores—whatever they haven't stolen yet—without working. They'll kill him and his family and you know the rest of it. Our turn will come after, if we don't go. Wife, we've done our best.

If we leave, they all die, she says. You're the hunter here. And Punnie—

One hunter isn't enough.

Punnie is too small and weak to make the journey, Tukulito says with decision. Our best chance for her is to stay put—here, where we know there's food. Anyway, we can't return the boy to his parents unhealed.

We can return him dead.

What are you saying to me?

That he might not survive the night. Or tomorrow night. You can see as much. And then we'll *have* to set out, before the men do. When they leave, the boat will be full of the supplies, and our share as well.

She says quietly, Food could still be found somehow. You're such a hunter . . . and Hans would work again if the men were gone.

Oh *stop*! Tyson hisses, he will drown in those tidings!

Enough now, Ebierbing says. Consider Punnie and sleep with my words in your ear.

And my words in yours.

What a stubborn thing you are.

Ajurnaqmat, she says. *It can't be helped.*

Tonight as Kruger returns to the hut Anthing intercepts him, strolling out from behind the hummock where Kruger squatted with dropped breeches a few days ago. Anthing has his hood off. He looks focused and very awake. He rams the frozen snout of the revolver up under Kruger's chin.

Where were you?

The latrine.

It's not in that direction. Breathe on me.

Kruger shrugs fatalistically. He exhales on Anthing's face while the man trawls through his pockets.

I smell blood. Fresh meat. And what's this for?

Anthing holds up the snow trowel. Kruger ponders it for a moment.

I thought I'd make some minor improvements to the latrine.

Anthing flips the trowel to the ice. And this?

For the children. Sometimes I save a little of my food. One of the biscuits is for Jackson. As you seem to be starving him now.

His race can stand a little of that, they're bred for it. Anyway, we shall find out if that's so.

So now you're the Count's laboratory assistant?

Anthing twists the snout of the Colt and Kruger makes a gargling noise as if his throat has been sliced.

You're caught, Roland.

But the cache—Kruger stupid with cold and loathing—it's yours! I just took and allotted supplies that you stole already!

A carnivorous grin slides across Anthing's face, his cracked lips parting. So. This is not from the main store. Just as I thought. You've made a cache. Take me to this cache.

You know very well where it is.

Not at all! Please take me!

Those lewd, leering eyes—yet the heavy lids are blinking a touch fast, in agitation. He really doesn't know where the cache is, or whose.

You'll be confined on quarter rations until you do . . .

That seems a poor way to fatten me up, Matthias.

Anthing looks surprised, but then he says coolly: We've let you do that by yourself.

You'd be better to kill me now.

I will be killing you, you have my word. But not yet.

❧

Evening, a few days later, Anthing crawling into the hut with a disgusted face—out searching for the cache again, no doubt. Kruger asks in a dry whisper, How is the ill child?

As ill as he was and no better. He eats nothing. Are you ready to help us?

Poor starveling, says Madsen.

In the vapid mechanical way of a boy repeating something he has heard, Anthing says, It means that the strong get slightly more.

And—and if this child should die, Major Anthing?

Think of Napoleon and the deer! suggests Meyer in a crackling voice. He lies on his side and his eyes gape, blind without his spectacles, which seem to have vanished. The revolver is gone from his pillow as well, no doubt swallowed up in Anthing's arsenal of a bag.

The Count is awake! gibbers Jamka, the guard, cross-legged with his rifle across his lap.

Anthing studies Meyer.

Keep him well covered.

Yes, sir.

Wasser! croaks Meyer.

Herron—water for the Count.

With a tender look, as if his nature can keep no grudge, as if loyal to anything that suffers, Herron lifts Meyer's head and tilts the tin cup to his moustache. Meyer's wild tresses are now more white than blond. They look brittle as a storybook hag's. Kruger can't watch him sipping the water. Anthing has allowed Kruger and Jackson, trussed side by side against the north wall, no water for three days. The chips of filthy snow that Kruger claws from the wall and melts in his mouth are absorbed at once by the fiery lining of his throat. Jackson makes shallow rasps, staring upward—

still eyes hypnotized by hunger. His skin is sulphur-yellow. Only Herron will look at the two of them, and if sympathy were food and water they would be quenched and stuffed with his.

Seize the next seal and butcher her in here, Meyer whispers, and you'll see that it's true!

What! What is true, Graf Meyer? asks Jamka. He trembles constantly, all of him.

The words of Napoleon, of course. We seem to hear them again now . . .

He pants softly. He grips Herron's hand and holds it concealed inside both his own—huge hands, scaly yellow, orange-clawed.

"We were in the forest . . . on horseback in the forest, hunting, and we killed a deer, and I had the men cut it open, and I saw . . . inside it's the same as a man. Just the same. If I have a soul, so does it. If it has no soul, as we are told, then neither do I. I have no immortal soul. All is simply matter, more or less organized . . ."

Anthing, picking his teeth with a filleting knife, says, Time to rest, Count.

We need you well, sir! says Lindermann with a dab of panic, glancing at Anthing as the others nod slightly. Anthing looks quickly round at them.

What are you staring for, Kruger? If you want something wet, take me to your cache.

I tell you again, the cache is not mine.

The men seem unsure what to believe. Kruger fears that if he guides Anthing there, he and the men will finally set out with the supplies and the boat, leaving Tukulito and the children, among others, to die.

For the first time in days Count Meyer sits up. Leaning forward he squints toward Kruger.

But . . . I thought we had executed this man, Major Anthing?

You ordered me to have the men fire high, sir.

Ah, yes—so I did!

Still squinting, Meyer topples forward like a plank. Anthing and Jamka spring to his aid, propping him back up on his ledge. And now his eyes soften, as if discerning in Kruger—if in fact they can see him at all—a long-estranged comrade.

But, only tell me this much, my dear Krüger . . . Why have you stood against me? Please speak freely. You have my permission. I find that I . . . I rather long to know!

The Count's droopy lower lids are awash in tears.

Please!

Kruger whispers, Because you all think with your blood.

Anthing folds his arms over his chest. To him ideas, new things, are a visceral affront; but Count Meyer seems serenely thoughtful. With our blood! he murmurs. *Mit unserem Blut!* We think with our *blood.* . . . How *fascinating!*

Anthing and now Lindermann help the Count to stretch out on his snow throne. He's already asleep, a child's cozy smile on his hunger-eaten face. They drape furs over him. And next time Joe brings in a seal, Anthing tells them, you claim it and drag it in here. It's the Count's order.

Feb. 21. This morning, land became visible to the west, perhaps sixty miles distant. This should be more heartening; but, considering our weakness and the condition of the ice, it might as well have been a thousand miles. I have been cleaning house to-day, shaking the filthy "carpet," and bringing in ice to cook with; Hannah, I suppose, is too busy with little Tobias. She is doing all she can to maintain life in him, while Joe seems to feel the child is beyond help, and acts as though he believes Hannah's efforts are simply a kind of torture. As for me, I can not resist sometimes giving poor little Punnie a part of my scanty rations, and would do the same for Tobias, if only he would eat. Between our daily rations and the pilfering, which for now seems to have stopped, there is little left in the store-house.

Feb. 22, Evening. To-day, all over the United States, I suppose there have been military parades and rejoicing, and balls and other festivities in the evening, being "Washington's birthday" anniversary. We might have fired a salute to the flag, had I been in spirits to do so. But I forget; there is no one here who knows or cares any thing about Washington, or our flag, though they signed on to this expedition willingly enough, and took their false oaths of loyalty, doubtless tempted by the lure of a good wage.

I must be on the watch. There is a double game working around me; it is plain that the Esquimaux are anxious to get on shore to reserve their own lives from other dangers than scarcity of game. I think Joe feels that if he were on shore, without this company of men to feed, he could catch game enough; but to catch a living for eighteen discourages him, and indeed it seems impossible.

So this party seems set to disperse in three, perhaps even four, separate ways. God help me, I have never felt so tired! If men ever suffered on earth the torments of wretched souls condemned to the "ice-hell" of the poet, Dante, I think I have felt it here; living in filth, like an animal. Sometimes I feel almost tempted to end my misery at once—but thoughts of the divine restriction hold me back. Had our Maker left us free to choose, had not

"The Everlasting. . . . .fixed his canon
Gainst self-slaughter,"

I think there would be one wretched being less in this world.

To-Day is in remembrence of a great Hero for whom I am named What a mockery. Yet have tried as I have always! Is my God &

America then a lie for I have trusted to honest striving to raise my Fate from Foundling to Captain & it has come to this. Emmaline & George Jr forgive me. Let Hannah & Joe forgive too for any cruel words I spoke or in these pgs, they did there best in there ways. Devil take the rest for Thieves & Mutineers & Krueger for a Damned Spy. I can not stop them so weary my Colt has been useless for some time for the hammer & cylinder springs rusted what is more the Men must know, Krueger wd have told them after he burst in. & him unarmed, tho a Thief I almost killed an unarmed man & sparked a Slaughter. Not my self it seems I cant stop them. Food almost gone. At least they'll not get my Body. Hang them all for Canibals & Cowards.

After Tukulito has sung the children to sleep, the lieutenant emphatically scratches some lines in his field-book, then replaces it among the hides with his customary small adjustments and pats and flattenings—perhaps, she thinks, so he can detect if it has been meddled with. It will not be. Without a word or glance he crawls out of the iglu. He has not spoken for several days. As his crunching footfalls slowly recede, she and Ebierbing lean together above the qulliq.

Tomorrow we set out.

You know Punnie is too weak, she says.

We can keep her alive, he says. But here . . .

The thing is impossible.

Are you my wife anymore? I don't know. You're taking their ways too far.

In thought she taps her loosening teeth with her forefinger, swallows a cough.

We leave early, he says. The sky will be clear and the moon up.

But now I'm the boy's mother, too, and as long as he's alive, I can't leave him.

I don't know anymore what you're faithful to. Their ways, ours. Tobias, Father Hall, him, or me and Punnie. You seem so . . .

You'll wake them, she says. Who do you mean, him?

Him—the lieutenant. You seem so strange to me these days.

That may be, but I am still your wife.

Tomorrow then, he says softly, with finality.

She nods but says, Tomorrow is not here.

Under a humpback moon Kruger and Anthing slog inland through the puny "foothills" of the Central Alps. There's a groundswell groaning from under the ice—the ocean at high tide—with fitful snapping sounds from the shore of the floe where pieces are constantly breaking off. Anthing is forcing Kruger to walk slightly ahead, but because he, Anthing, is stronger, he keeps overtaking Kruger, then jabbing him forward with the snout of the pistol. It feels to Kruger as if no meat is left on his frame; the scavenging wind blasts through his skeleton. After days and nights of smoky dimness in the hut, this moon and its crystalline reflections are as dazzling as a July sun at sea.

Anthing has broken him. He agreed at supper—watching the men feast on their scant gruel of hardtack crumbled into seal-bone broth—that he would guide Anthing to the cache in exchange for a tin cup of water (which he drank instantly) and a return to full rations, for both him and Jackson, tomorrow. *It's all right*, a voice in his ear cajoled him. *With food you'll be able to think, and to act—to find some better way of stopping him! And Jackson is dying! He must eat!*

He has seen man defined as "the rational animal." Maybe "the animal that rationalizes" comes closer to it. But he is too hungry for shame.

How much farther? Anthing's voice, too, is breath-starved.

Not far now.

And were you never afraid of bears—sneaking out here unarmed?

Kruger is still sly enough to be silent. The courage of thugs is precarious, not built on long-weighed principles but on a fickle thing, animal vitality. And Anthing is running short. Once again he shoves Kruger forward, but it's little more than a sloppy ineffectual tap. This unremarkable weakling is the most powerful man on their shrinking little planet. They round a hummock shaped like an inverted whaleboat. Tyson appears a hundred paces off. He approaches from the direction of the cache in the slumped, plodding way of a man who has just had to shoot a favourite dog. The pistol Kruger knows to be useless is tucked in his belt. His head droops, the visor of his cap hides his face. He must be frozen dead through. Anthing, behind Kruger, doesn't see him, and clearly Tyson, upwind, hasn't heard the two men coming—or is he too deeply distracted? The weight of guilt, maybe. Yes: guilt and false accusation. To think it was him all along! Tyson's path takes him behind a long spiny hummock. He will emerge in a matter of seconds and Kruger is strongly tempted to let it happen.

Why have you stopped? asks Anthing.

Kruger stands frozen.

You see something? What?

Something looks wrong here, he whispers. I'm not sure.

Be sure and be quick about it.

Another moment's hesitation, and then: I believe it's over this way, sir. Along that line of hummocks. And he leads Anthing away from Tyson and the cache.

He has betrayed us again, says Anthing.

I couldn't find it, Kruger tells the men, a bead of sweat trickling down out of his armpit, under his sweater. It's been too long, the ice has changed. Tomorrow in daylight I believe I can find it.

The men don't look as disappointed or angry as he had feared. They seem, in fact, relieved, except for Jackson, whose swollen Adam's apple bobs as his eyes swing slowly away from Kruger.

Anthing says, It's bright as day out there. You're stalling. We leave for Greenland tomorrow anyway. You'll take us to the cache on our way east. If you won't, I'll shoot you myself.

So, you will come with us one way or another, Jamka says in a hollow monotone.

Shut up, Sergeant.

But sir, says Lindermann, we can't leave, not now. What if he really can't find it?

Then we take all of whatever's left in the storehut, not just half. And maybe some fresh meat also. The others can live off game, and Krüger's cache, when they find it.

A cautious grumbling starts and Anthing says sharply, You must understand that we no longer have a choice! If we ever got to the west shore with the others, and back to America, we'd be tried and hanged. East to Greenland and Europe, there's our only hope.

He pauses to let this sink in.

I suppose we could even leave Krüger here, alive. To help the others find the cache.

I was having a dream, says Meyer.

The Kaiser is awake!

We can't leave, says Lindermann, stubbornly frowning down at his hands. It's not only about food. It's the lieutenant. He must be right. If we can see the west shore, Greenland must be hundreds of miles away. We've all seen maps.

It's true enough, says Lundquist. Madsen nods and meets Anthing's glare.

Are you refusing my order? Sergeant Jamka—arrest this man.

Yes, sir! says Jamka. He sits staring.

Really sir, no need to wave that thing about, Herron says in English. He, and now Jackson, seem to be following the German argument. We can talk just fine without it, can't we?

Wasser!

Herron—water for the Count!

Jackson wriggles in his bag, props himself on an elbow and rasps out, You can't just go shooting the bunch of us. If you aim to, why, just start with me.

Or with me, says Lindermann.

You all address me as sir!

Kruger eyes the pistol. If Tyson's has rusted out, there's a chance that Anthing's has too, though Anthing has oiled his with lamp-blubber a few times. Kruger is on his knees beside Anthing who stands stooped under the dome.

Set the gun down, Matthias, Kruger says softly. Anthing aims it at him, frog-eyed.

Wasser . . . unter dem Eis! Everyone turns to Meyer, who is tossing off his robes, sitting up in his festering Jaeger-wear and speaking in a slow, clear voice: I was in the arctic lake, under the ice with the Teutonic knights, sinking with our horses. But the water . . . it cooled my fever. I will soon be well again. Very soon we shall continue our push to the east . . . toward Novgorod.

The Kaiser's dream is a prophecy, says Jamka. It means . . .

He's at a loss, pouting his lips, pleating his brow.

Well, I'm not crossing that ice, says Lindermann, and there's my last word.

I believe I feel somewhat better, Meyer says.

Set it down, Matthias.

And if you shoot us all, says Madsen, who will you have to command?

Kruger grabs for the gun with one hand and Anthing's forearm with the other, but he's too slow and weak. Easily Anthing slips back, although he holds his fire, glancing round at the men.

None of you move. Sergeant—your rifle!

Like I said, Jackson whispers, you start shooting, I'm first in line. Slowly but gamely he is sloughing himself out of his bag, an impossibly frail thing emerging from a pupa. His neck, his naked chest, his cankered arms as they emerge seem part of a Dürer allegory of Hunger, an engraving of Death. Jawslack the men stare at this perfected emblem, their collaborative work. On Anthing's face not horror but the frank and innocent sadism of a child.

Let me get you water and biscuit, Will, says Herron, quickly rising.

You will not touch this prisoner!

Fire away, sir, says Herron quietly.

Jamka? calls Anthing, angling round for any scrap of support. (Meyer, still sitting up, is snoring again.)

It means, says Jamka in an inspired tone, that we must not use *horses* to cross the ice!

With a grave and preoccupied expression, Anthing lays down his revolver.

Anthing has been accustomed to sharing his sleeping bag with a number of cold, hard, rusting firearms; tonight he sleeps alone, and Kruger, Herron, and Jackson have their weapons back. Kruger has grown accustomed to being on edge, alert in the darkness, so before long he wakes with a jolt. There's nothing to keep him from going out to raid Tyson's cache, and this time he can bring back extra for Jackson and the others. Tomorrow they will go together and retrieve all of it and distribute it among the huts. What he can't do, yet, is expose the thief. The men's unstable allegiance, now inclined toward Tyson, could still shift back to Meyer and Anthing.

The moon is in haze over the bone-glowing tors and spurs of that remote land to the west. Diffused milk-light makes colossal shards of tourmaline and turquoise of the bergs. He sets out toward the cache, then stops. Amid the faint snapping, gurgling, crepitating sounds, there is something else, gruff sobs, or growls, as of an animal in distress. He hunches, cocking his rifle. He squints toward the floe edge a few hundred paces off. A minute's careful walk and there can be no doubt. Tyson's silhouette stands on the edge: the cut of his cap, the muskox hide he drapes over his jumper. Kruger eases down the hammer and coughs softly. The silhouette jerks and shifts oddly and then, having turned toward him, resumes its shape. The face is blacked out, the moon behind. In a brief silence of the ice Kruger hears teeth chattering.

Stop. There where you are.

The voice is hoarse and small. Kruger lets his rifle drop on the ice but steps closer, to the edge of Tyson's long shadow. He eyes the moonlit water rippling coldly at Tyson's back.

Lieutenant?

I was out hunting. After a laden pause, he taps the butt of his pistol. Now that I have had this seen to.

It's the middle of the night, Kruger says.

I expect the dovekies to return at any time. I listen for them nightly.

You will have to rethink things, Lieutenant, the crewmen are now—

But I can readily guess what *you're* up to.

—the crewmen have had a change at heart.

Tyson's laugh is brief and brittle, teeth showing in the blackness of his beard.

You make a better thief than spy, Kruger.

After a beat: There, there *are* no spies on this fucking floe! And as for thieves, although you hardly—

Go back to your den, Kruger.

Although I'm none too sure you deserve your victory, you do have it, and must live to take the men back from Meyer. You're the only one who knows these seas well enough. When we take to the boat, we need yourself at the tiller.

The whites of Tyson's eyes are visible. He's staring intently, as if trying to believe.

Live? he says, as if there was ever any question.

As for your cache, I'm prepared to believe that it was only to protect the others. In case Meyer and Anthing took everything when they left. I only resented your accusations.

Tyson goes rigid. Squaring his skeleton shoulders he says, *Cache*? Mr Kruger, do you now have the face to accuse *me* of stealing the supplies?

Not steal. Put by.

I know of no Goddamned cache!

But this very evening I saw you, back there among the hummocks, returning from it!

After a few moments Tyson bows his head, then raises it, inhaling sharply. He says, I had only crossed to the far side of the floe—meaning to hunt there. So as not to disturb the others.

Kruger wonders if Tyson really does know nothing.

But the banks are all frozen there, Tyson says, no open water. So no seals. I came back here.

I thought you were looking for dovekies.

Tyson bristles. Paupers can't pick their meat, Mr Kruger.

Kruger nods, *touché*. Tyson's shadow now extends just under

Kruger's boots; he's fully upright, roused back into himself by his embarrassed lies—at least about the hunting—and by a renewed, bracing suspicion. Life-giving lies, as so many are.

But what of this "cache," Kruger? Suppose you tell me what *you've* been doing out here?

In my hunger, he says, I too was hunting. I too found nothing.

It's never too late to become the man you might have been. Where has Tyson read that? He sees an oval of lantern-light in his first mate's cabin aboard the *Seminole*, tacking north for the whaling grounds of Davis Strait in '58, '59. He forgets the book. He read so many in those years, an education scravelled together on the outskirts of long days, doing the world's necessary work, with stiff discipline, an orphan's resigned stamina fed by an instinct of cosmic grievance—a grudge with God, only sometimes conscious, which has kept him from acquiring the full Yankee optimism to go with his Yankee ambition and vigour. Now the collapse of Meyer's and Kruger's mutiny—no, near-mutiny—confirms his deep-laid belief that men of formal education (for this is how he sees Kruger, too) lack the gravel, the moral stamina, to back up their book-learning.

Very early he rises, claws his fingers through his ratty hair and beard by way of grooming and as if to rake away the shame that has accrued on him like caked filth. *It's never too late.* He shudders. If Kruger had waited just one day more to offer the men's surrender. . . . Tyson almost yielded to his own weakness. *Almost* yielded. *Almost* a mutiny. The natives are still asleep and for a moment his being first awake seems, in a small way, to further rectify his virtue, ratify his honour—until he reflects that of late they've generally risen before him. Still. It's never too late to become oneself. Maybe he's an optimist after all. The part of him that has striven since boyhood, like a pugilist's corner, to keep him fighting with confidence—to talk or whip or holler him through the hard parts—is already back in control, in command. George E. Tyson is back in command.

Ah, Joe, he says softly, seeing the man open his eyes and frown to focus.

What, Lieutenant. Why you up so? Something happen?

Tyson's split lips and cheeks sting wonderfully with the long-unaccustomed stretch of his grin.

He has them all congregate on the border. The morning is unclouded, the waxing moon low but bright, southeasterly skies softening to coral. Everyone is present except the ill child and the Count, though Jackson and Anthing, by the looks of them, should have stayed inside too. Crutched on a scarcely more hale-looking Herron, Jackson is lost inside his parka and trembling like a lapdog. Anthing is grey and shrunken, as if suddenly ill. Kruger stands a little apart. He seems to be trying to catch Hannah's eye. Her downturned face looks puffy, sleepless. Only Hans, Ebierbing, and Lindermann are armed—Lindermann with Anthing's pistol. Looming over Tyson with a sheepish air, he now offers it—resting on his upturned hands like a crown—and says, We are sorry that we let ourselves to be led to this mutiny, sir. We hope that this company may now be, ah, recounselled under your command . . . that is the word? He looks to Kruger (of course! thinks Tyson, Kruger has always been Meyer's true lieutenant—even if he too appears to have been ill).

Reconciled, Kruger says softly.

Tyson says, Thank you Mr Lindermann. But bear this in mind: there has never yet been a full mutiny aboard a ship of the United States Navy, nor will I consent to this being seen as the first. (How odd, disembodied, the words sound on the air after being scratched in the field-book and mentally rehearsed so many times!) If you men are truly prepared to work for me in the weeks to come, so as to preserve all our lives, for my part I am ready to overlook and forget all that has happened so far aboard this floe. However, your flag must come down.

Ja, sir, says Lindermann. The other crewmen nod.

Tyson turns toward Hans. Before Tyson can open his mouth Hans clumsily salutes, looking down at the ice and muttering, Yah, sure! I hunt again now.

Lieutenant? Perhaps both flags could better come down. (It's Kruger.) We have no real need for the flags out here, and now we must try to be a—

But this is an American expedition, Mr Kruger. The flag is an inspiration to those who are truly loyal to it.

Tyson looks at him fixedly and continues.

Last night I happened to learn of the food cache that you crewmen, I assume, have made with the pilfered supplies. I can but assume that many or all of you know where it is. I no longer care if one, or some, or all of you are responsible—I only wish to see the supplies returned to the store-house, and by tomorrow morning.

Tyson, fully inspired now, aware of himself, his body swept with shivers, bends stiffly to place the revolver on the ice at his feet.

I will not be needing nor using this weapon. And my own Colt, as you must know, no longer works. You have asked me to resume command and I will expect your cooperation without any resort to force.

For a moment the men gape in silence. Then they begin to salute—Herron and Jackson, Madsen, Lundquist. Lindermann snaps to attention and cries, Yes, *mein Kapitän*!

Lieutenant, says Tyson evenly, not Captain.

Jamka salutes. Anthing droops his head, as if for the hangman. On Herron's face a pallid travesty of his old elfish grin, but a grin all the same. Jackson's eyes glow like anthracite. Tyson's heart is engorged—exultant. He blinks to dam back his tears. He feels solid as a granite hero and yet light as helium. Second Mate Kruger can't seem to bring himself to salute, but he bows very slightly, on his thoughtful face a look that Tyson is at a loss to interpret. Impressed surprise, it could be, a sort of grudging regard—although this very appearance keeps Tyson's suspicions intact. Still, he'll take his chances and leave the weapon on the ice. Any of them can kill him if they wish, but now, it seems, they recognize him as their main hope of survival. And he will find a way to save them all. A new sort of hero for this modern, lawful era that people are talking of—the frontier all but conquered, new gadgets improving lives, democracy in advance—a hero who doesn't cut down his enemies like a savage, but gets them home alive. Having now reconfirmed himself in this high pledge, nothing will make him take up that frontiersman's Colt again. Which would seem an act of ignorant cowardice. And God, Tyson knows, hates a coward.

As the meeting breaks up, Tukulito quietly picks up the revolver.

23 Feb.——K. the Thief & I think Meyer's main Help has offered there surrender & at the last moment Thank God!! May be God does not yet forget us, or forget Himself, as I feared. This is one of the sweetest hours I have known ever. God willing I shall yet see your beloved Faces again.

So Kruger leads the stronger men—Lindermann, Lundquist, and Herron—out to the cache. They go that night, while the moon is low, because while Tyson and the crew may still believe him to be the thief, despite his firm denials, he doesn't wish to parade his apparent guilt in front of the Esquimaux too. Especially in front of her. To her people, he knows, stealing food is a heinous wrong. Of course Tyson may already have told her and Ebierbing about their exchange last night; Kruger tried to catch her eye this morning, to see if she knew, but their one mutual glance conveyed little more than that she was relieved to see him afoot. Or was that his imagination? The interpreter is herself unreadable. Again and again her controlled, noncommittal face seems to invite him to read there whatever he will, or must.

It's here, he says. He kneels out of the wind. With the trowel he makes a tentative prod at the mouth of the cache and it collapses inward, a thin pane of brittle snow. The men kneel around him. Herron lights a match. The walls and floor of the empty cave show a few pink stains, nothing more. *Scheiße*, Lindermann whispers, and Kruger nods. If the true thief has hidden a new cache somewhere, he himself will be blamed. The pink stains are making him salivate. Around the mouth of the cache the matchlight brings out in chiaroscuro a few more of those faint crescent slashes.

Like the lid of a pemmican tin, Herron says.

I was thinking so too, Kruger says; yet something he once saw out here flits at the margins of his memory.

It really was not you, was it? says Lindermann.

We were together all day, Kruger says. I told you, I just found it.

But Matthias did go out today, *ja*?

Not for long enough, I doubt.

I ask, Lundquist says—could it be really the Lieutenant Tyson? Or the Indians.

I doubt it could be the lieutenant. (Kruger feels he must say so, no matter how uncertain he may feel—so he has become a sort of spy after all, a secret intermediary.)

Let's return, he says, and hope the goods are in the storehut.

The men's responsive silence has the dense, charged quality of collective prayer.

When they squeeze back into the crewhut and announce that all has been returned, by somebody, Anthing, seeming delighted as well, edges forward in a posture of contrition. His thinned face looks shy and excited. As the other men happily confer, he puts his cheek next to Kruger's and wraps his warm dry hands, rusty with auburn hair, over Kruger's fist. I give you my apologies, Roland. You were quite right, in the end. Kruger seeks validation of the words in Anthing's eyes. To his surprise Anthing meets his gaze, unblinking, the deep pupils large and warm, blue irises soft as felted wool.

Feb. 25. Have had another long talk with the men, who now seem more inclined to listen. I have explained to them that I hope soon to get to the ground of the bladder-nose seal, which in March comes onto the ice, not far from where we are now, to breed. I have told them—what they already know as well as I—how little biscuit and pemmican we have left, even with the return of the supplies to our store-house, some time yesterday or night (an amount but a little short of what I knew to have been taken, so that it seems likely that whatever remained has indeed been returned). This restitution, I believe by Kruger and the men, is a great relief and a boon; but still I suggested, in case we are later than I expect in reaching the sealing-ground, that we ought to subsist on still less than we have been doing. It seemed hard to ask them to live on one *short* meal *per diem*, but if we do not, we will most certainly exhaust our small store too soon.

The mountainous west-land is still visible about forty miles off, due west, and now, with the supplies returned, I am tempted to try to reach it. But I fear it would be too much for Meyer, Jackson, and little Tobias; and to-day a deep fall of snow has rendered it impossible for even the most fool-hardy to think of starting, although Joe still speaks as if he is willing. We went off hunting instead. About noon found one little hole, and Joe, again our "best man," shot the only seal that has been seen to-day. The edges of our floe still continue to crumble off in bits; the sea moves in on us from all sides, like a besieging army. Our little continent is now *considerably* smaller than when we first took up residence upon it. Still, we do not despair.

Feb. 26. The sun is shining through our little ice-window! It is the first day that the sun has gotten high enough to penetrate our burrow directly; but there is no blessing without its drawback; though the sun is welcome, it reveals too plainly our filthy condition. I thought I knew the worst before, but the sun has made new revelations. The crewmen are actually infected with spring-fever, and except for the weakest—Mr Meyer, and Jackson, whom I visited to-day—they are *cleaning house.* I should think a good cart-load of black, smoky ice was taken from their hut, and clean snow taken in. This morning, too, Punnie seemed to be enlightened by the sun. She sat looking at me for some time, and then gravely remarked, *"You are nothing but skin and bone!"* And, indeed, besides will, I am not much else.

Feb. 27. Clear and cold. The mercury has gone down again to 38 below zero F. Such a set of skeletons as we would have had a poor chance camping out on such a night without the shelter of our huts. We are now on our allowance of one meal a day; but I have insisted on a little supplement for both Meyer and Jackson, to speed their recovery. The men's co-operation is heartening, of course, but our trials are far from over; we are still all starving; and now this group of formerly stubborn crew-men is my full responsibility once again. Command is best maintained by one of strong body and clear mind;

in these conditions, as "Count" Meyer appears to have discovered, it is a test both day and night.

March 1. 5 P.M. Our Joe has shot a monster oogjook!—a large kind of seal—the largest I have ever seen. Luckily most of the men were present, on the hunt, to help drag him to the huts. Herron and Jamka fairly danced and sang for joy. The warm blood of the seal was scooped up in tin cans and was relished like new milk. No one who has not been in a similar position to ours can tell the feeling of relief which his capture produced. How we rejoiced over the death of the oogjook it would be impossible to describe. Hannah had but two small pieces of blubber left, enough for the lamp for two days; the men had but little, and Hans had only enough for one day. And now, just on the verge of absolute destitution, along comes this monster oogjook, the only one of the seal species seen to-day; and the fellow must weigh six or seven hundred pounds, and will furnish, I should think, thirty gallons of oil! Truly we are rich indeed. Praise the Lord for all his mercies!

March 3. We eat no biscuit or pemmican to-day—oogjook is the only dish; and it does me good to see the men able once more to satisfy their appetites. And they are bound to do so—they are cooking and eating night and day. We have had oogjook sausages for breakfast, the intestines being stuffed with blubber and tied into links, and with these some of the meat stewed. After such long fasting the men cannot restrain their appetites, and some of them, like poor Herron and Jackson, have eaten until they are sick. And yet we make few inroads on this great hill of flesh. Our glorious oogjook has proved, on measurement, including the hind flipper, fully nine feet and seven inches long! What a Godsend!

They are coming, sir. Tukulito squints into the southern light near sunset. Kruger visors his brow with his hand. He can see nothing, but on faith he levers open the rifle's rusting trapdoor and jams in a cartridge. Herron and Jackson do the same. The four of them crouching on the level summit of Mt Hall. Ebierbing and Hans, distantly visible, are on a for-now adjoining floe hunting seals; every other adult, even Merkut, is outside on the home floe, waiting for dovekies. Small neckless globular clumps of down, they've begun to appear, helpfully peeping as they dart and dip northward on their short, pointed wings. The main flocks, Tukulito has told them, are somewhat overdue.

This here gun don't feel halfway so heavy as it did just Sunday, Jackson says.

That's thanks to our lovely oogjook, Will. Herron works the word into his conversation as frequently as possible, lips puckering with delight around the juicy, oozing syllables. *Ooog—joook.* He says, Even if we shot a dozen brace of these fowl, still it's oogjook I'd be eating.

It's the richest meat I ever had, Jackson says.

I feel fit as a butcher's dog! Herron exclaims, and his full-lunged laughter triggers their own. It sounds uncanny out here in the open—an openness spilling past headstone bergs to the west-land (farther off today, it seems) and to whistling distances of ice lit by lateral citron rays.

Kruger and Tukulito are side by side, about a body's width apart. She has left Punnie in charge of Tobias, who is rather improved, she says, by the fresh provisions. Kruger has so many things he wants to say that the words jam in his throat like river ice in a thaw. Now that his belly is crammed with good meat, other appetites are fully resurging. He tries to edge closer, just to feel her solidity—a galvanic contact, nothing more—but she maintains the slim boundary. It's windless, not too cold. She has her hood down and the smell of her hair comes to him, rich and slightly bitter, like walnut oil. Her naked wind-cracked hands, with the pistol Tyson rejected, are tucked in the apron-front of her parka. Tiny hands! Her presence is such that it's easy to forget how tiny she is.

Still no sign of the birds that she has sighted, then it's as if the flock has swooped out of a cloud or a rift in the sky. The four brace themselves, each on a knee, raising their weapons as the black-and-white birds, clumped tight as starlings, bear down on them with shrill tittering cries. Tukulito with both hands lifts the butt of the huge-looking pistol. Kruger shuns the absurd impulse to ask if she needs help. In fact he and the others wait for her to fire first, as if sensing that she controls these dovekies somehow, even conjures them out of the south. The pistol snaps and bucks in her hand. Jackson fires into the dense flock and a bird starts spinning like a small propeller, plunges. As Kruger fires, the brace-plate kicks into his fleshless shoulder; another bird slips from the flock, resumes flying for a moment, dives. The dovekies streaking overhead. Tukulito calmly squeezing off her shots. Kruger reloads in a fluster. He's wildly impatient, starting to sense how for the rest of his life no store of fresh-killed food will ever be enough.

No need to hurry, sir, she says, methodically refilling the pistol's cylinder. Kruger looks up. The flock, as if attracted by the gunfire, which must sound to them like ice cracking, opening leads where they can alight and rest, are assuming a tight circle pattern, like chimney swifts close above. Kruger fires and brings one down. They're packed so tight it's hard to miss. He levers the breech—the ejected casing flying at his cheek, hot as a bee sting—and lets out a throttled cry, not of pain but of joy. A sound he hardly recognizes. They're killing together, that's what it is—he and the men, but most of all he and she, and now, as the dovekies go on offering themselves to the hunters, it starts to feel like a kind of sacrament. Every bird he sacrifices is for her—his gift of warm flesh, of fat, of heat. And if he never gets any closer to her than now, perhaps this fierce and primal joy, seemingly shared, can be remembered as enough.

They shoot faster into the cyclone swirling above. A dismantled bird, black, white and blooded, thumps down on the trampled snow among them. It lies still amid the brilliant brass casings. Heat smoking off the barrels of the guns. Food, life, raining down on the ice. Of this there can never be too much. Yet already, like sexual pleasure, the moment has crested, is in decline. It's more and more unsettling the way the birds, frantic yet unshakeably patient, will not stop revolving above their killers, transforming the air into an orderly abattoir, awaiting their turn to be culled. Some suicidal instinct has them on a tether. It's their own nature. The ice is cobbled with little round bodies. The ammunition running low. At last, it's almost too much, something in this mass mania, the birds' mania, he almost wants to scream at them Stop now, stop it! Go on, fly on! *Because you all think with your blood.* But the birds are helpless and, as long as they stay up there and a single bullet remains, the hunters are helpless too.

March 10, morning. Our three days of calm have been shattered by a gale. These storms seem endless, and continue to eat away at our raft, which is now only perhaps a quarter of its original dimensions. There will be no hunting to-day. Fortunately we have still much of the oogjook remaining, as well as a good number of dovekies, small though they be. Little Tobias, whom I have tried to help Hannah and Punnie to nurse, continues to improve. This morning he has been returned to his parents; so there is now a little more room inside our hut. As for Hans, he again is working hard for us, in part, I think, to counter-weigh the men's apparent belief that it was *he* who was our store-house thief. I assume Kruger convinced the men of this; and I suppose it is not entirely impossible.

March 11. Last night was one of great anxiety. The gale raged fiercely throughout the day, and at 5 P.M. the ice began a great uproar. Our heavy floe commenced working, cracking, breaking with a succession of dismal noises, like distant cannon-fire, mingled with sharp reports and resounding concussions; and these noises seemed to have their centre immediately under our huts. Commingling with the raging storm, the crushing and grinding from the heavy pressure of the bergs, and heavy ice around us, these sounds gave us good reason for alarm. They startled me from my sleep; several times I thought the floe was going to pieces. In the swirling snow we had got every thing ready to catch and run—but where to? That was the question. There is precious little room left.

About nine o'clock, hearing a heavy explosive, then grinding, sound, Joe and I felt our way outside in the darkness and some twenty yards to the rear of our hut, while Hannah stayed with Punnie, who was clinging to her pathetically. There we found the floe had broken. The sides of the severed pieces swaying back and forth, then rushing upon each other and grinding their sides with all the force which sea and gale could give them, caused the alarming noises I had heard. We crept back inside, then had to stay alert all through the night—and with such feelings as I leave the reader to imagine—but nothing more serious occurred. At some point, I went out to check on the other huts.

The gale still blows this morning, and there is some rough seas under the ice. We have never before felt it move up and down like this; but then, our raft is only a fraction of its original size. Should the ice break up still farther, and we be obliged to abandon our little snow-burrows or be turned out of them by farther disruption, it would be very hard upon the party, with such weather prevailing. *But a kind and merciful God has thus far guided and protected us, and will, I trust, yet deliver us.*

Mar. 10?11?—Calm shattered by Gale. Raft groans as tho' to go to pieces yet I feel myself near whole. Am now but little distracted by her, whether charms or defects, being wholely concerned with survival of Party. & God being unwilling it appears, to let us off without farther Trial. But surely Hardships some times are sent to rescue us from baser things? So be it. She thinks now but little of K I believe for when I told of my discovery he was prob. main Thief she appeared v. disturbed. Well he is Trouble & this may help her to avoid him.

The prospect of execution doesn't so much concentrate the mind as make it scan inward for any escape, any distraction. The uproar outside is like the sound of immense jaws crunching something inedible. Kruger keeps returning to a certain windless evening, a sharp V of red-breasted geese appearing, with joyful cries, above Danzig Harbour.

Was ist Trumpf? Lundquist speaks in a falsetto bass, a boy with something to prove to men, as the floe tilts and pitches like a large raft in an ocean storm—exactly what it is. *Kreuz, ja?* He, Kruger, Herron, and Anthing, shawled in pelts, sit on the bed-ledge playing euchre in a silence better fit for solitaire. Two a.m. Jamka, Bavarian by birth, has been kneeling on the canvas floor for hours chanting monotone Ave Marias. He's refusing to wear his boots. His feet are blackening like a mummy's. For the first hour or so Kruger was moved by the chanting, returned to boyhood and his wonderfully fat mother who prayed mainly for her husband to glimpse the Light and the Lamb beyond his free-thinking. Count Meyer is murmuring in his sleep. In Lindermann's bag, Lindermann and Madsen lie cramped together, unmoving, all pretence abandoned. Beside them Jackson in his fingerless gloves holds the lamp and gazes down at it, face skulled by the underlight; what if the ice should open under them and their lamp slip through, into the sea?

We dasn't lose this lamp, he repeats.

Well *that* was a loud one, lads! Herron's stumpy fingers tremble as they hold his cards; the worse things get, the more he chatters. Like a broadside at Trafalgar, he says. Lord help us.

After this hand, I go to check on the others, Kruger says.

I think I know what concerns you, Anthing says, his features bland, illegible as a valet's.

That it will split between us and her! Herron babbles—then he adds quickly, I'm sorry, Kru.

It's natural enough, Anthing says with a neutral shrug.

Kruger eyes him narrowly over the cards.

Swam in the Hiwassee when I was a boy, Jackson says. I always could swim.

Nunc, et in hora mortis nostrae . . .

Water there, it's like demerara cooked in butter—just that colour. And just as warm.

Well, Matty, the good hands are all to you tonight, aren't they?

I can swim too, Kruger says absently, tossing his cards onto the pile.

Bitte . . . komm her! It's Meyer, ogling Kruger with one open eye. How hard that makes it to ignore his plea, though Kruger would prefer to remain where he is—gaping up at a chevron of red-breasted geese, their stained-glass panes of rich colour, beating low over the harbour, north toward the Arctic, as he emerges for the first time from a dockside brothel, now apparently a man.

Ja, Graf Meyer? He crouches beside Meyer's private ledge. Under his knee the floe sways and shudders and his quivering muscles accent the effect.

I have been meaning to let you in on a little secret, Herr Krüger.

The eye, all pupil, stares unfocused. Kruger nods reluctantly.

All this talk of spies, Herr Krüger . . .

Ja, I understand it to be nonsense, Graf Meyer.

Ah, but to the contrary!

A pause while Meyer fights for breath. That one staring eye—it's like being addressed by a determined octopus. Kruger has to incline an ear to catch Meyer's phlegmy whisper: Because we *are* all secret agents of the Kaiser, you see. All this was arranged, by Bismarck! We *are* spies!

Anthing is peering over sidelong, but Kruger doubts he can hear over the chaos of the ice. Lundquist is quietly retching into the pemmican tin he keeps handy tonight. In a patient, almost parental tone Kruger says, *Herr Graf*, we are *Ausgewanderte*—emigrants, hired because Americans didn't want the job. They're all going west, American men. Wise of them, I now feel.

But Doktor Bessels and I—we *arranged* for Germans to be hired! We believed we could count on such men, to help plant our flag at the Pole! We even armed them, after Hall's death.

Sleep now, Kruger urges. *You drooling lunatic.*

We and America will be the Great Powers of the century to come! We must begin now . . .

He trails off. His other eye opens wide and also regards Kruger, but, unlike the first eye, it doesn't seem to recognize him. In fact, it looks frankly hostile. The first eye remains almost affectionate. Profiting by this confusion, Kruger retreats to his sleeping bag and slips his parka on. If there's any truth to the Count's fevered ramblings, it would mean that Captain Hall, in his own delirium, may have been right to loudly accuse Bessels and Meyer of poisoning him, just before he died. But who can say? It would be very like the Count now to imagine himself as Bismarck's right-hand man. Out here in such extremity you would expect everything and everyone to be stripped down to a hard, pure essence—all lies laid bare—yet with every hour the Truth grows more uncertain and unstable.

He crawls into the dark tunnel. Something is padding, panting its way in from the mouth of the tunnel and he and this other come face to face, as if deep underground. It's Tyson, his laboured breaths smelling like copper pennies.

I've come to see how you men are doing.

Sir. I also was coming out to see how the rest are.

Well—Tyson's voice bristles slightly, as if upstaged somehow, or challenged—we are all fine. The natives, of course, can take care of themselves.

Of course, Kruger says. And neither man moves. Clearly enough Tyson doesn't want him to visit Tukulito. It has become clear to Kruger that every white man on the floe believes them to be lovers, and that they all hate him a little for that. Even

Herron, perhaps. Hated for a love that he seems to have no chance, or right, to consummate! Like burrowing, brute creatures, minds stalled with terror and fatigue, the two men remain unmoving for some time.

March 12. Another twenty-four hours of care, watching, anxiety, and great peril. The gale has been terrible. For sixty hours, amidst this fearful turmoil of the elements, with our foundations breaking up beneath us, we could not see ten yards around; but this morning at last the wind has abated, the snow has ceased to fall, and the terrible drift stopped. We can now look around and see the position we are in. In a vessel, after such a storm as this, the first work, with returning light, would be to clear the decks and set about repairing damages. But how shall we repair our shattered ice-craft? We can look around and take account of loss and damage, but we can do nothing toward making it more sea-worthy.

We see a great change in the condition of the ice; the "floes" have become a "pack," and great blocks of ice, of all shapes and sizes, are piled and jammed together in every imaginable position. On my last extended walk before this storm, the large floes had appeared to extend for many miles; they are now all broken up like ours, and the pieces heaped over each other in most astonishing disorder. Moreover, we are still surrounded by the icebergs which have drifted with us all winter—though of course they are now much closer on all sides, and hence seem higher, our floe being so reduced. Though they are a peril to us, and may well end by destroying us, yet their familiar presence is also a strange comfort.

With the winds more moderate, we recommenced shooting. Seals are scarce, but, there being open water around us and between the cracks, we can now shoot all we see. Indeed, we can stand in our own hut door and shoot them, for our floe is *so* diminished that it is only forty paces to the water. Today Joe shot two, Hans one, and the former thief Kruger, one as well. Then, espying another oogjook, not as large as our first kill, but still very considerable, I asked to borrow Hans's rifle, after which I crept as close to the animal as I dared. My first shot went true, thank God; and as we dragged the oogjook onto our floe, the sun appeared for the first time in days, as if further to encourage us.

And so it seems that one danger—that of starvation—may be receding even while another, more urgent one, closes in; but now that we are no longer "a house divided," the odds do not seem so unbeatable. The sun will enter the first point of Aries in just a few days, and be on his upward course. Spring is here, according to the astronomers; but oh how I wish that another month were passed!

It is mild enough in the sunshine in the lee of the hut that she can butcher the huge carcass outdoors. Though the noon sun is not high the atmosphere is alive with light, as if charged with dazzling particles—the sun's rays reflecting off the ice and the hut and the slow, dignified armada of icebergs convoying them south. This light is inebriating. So is the sight and the smell of fresh meat. With her woman's knife she flenses the body, its grey-furred "blanket" heavy with fat peeling off smoothly as a ripe peach skin. Beside her Kruger is haunched down, holding the cool blanket clear of her gory hands while she cuts deeper, in toward the spine, pivoting her wrist back and forth, her braids swinging. It's only the two of them. The recent abundance has made everyone more trusting about food. Heat radiates from the cleft flesh as if from a bank of raked coals; the blanket has retained the inner heat for hours. There's a raw smell. The scalloping incisions of her red-daubed blade—a half-moon of steel with a toggle-shaped handle.

What is the word in your language, Hannah, for this knife you use?

It is called *ulu*, Mr Kruger.

He nods slowly. I'm surprised that without a whetstone you have kept it so sharp. But I suppose that cutting ice with it might help. Once I saw you doing that, at the pond.

She doesn't look up from her work. She ducks her bare head nearer to the carcass, into the shadow of the blanket, which Kruger lifts higher as she cuts inward. He shifts closer to her, wanting to keep his voice down.

But I don't suppose you often use it that way?

As you know, sir, my husband has tools better suited for such work.

There's a squelchy, sucking noise as she swivels the crescent blade side to side. Her shiny hair is parted above the nape, tight-spread, tapering to the drooping braids. The furrow of scalp is oddly red.

I believe he had taken his snow knife with him that day, the day you saw me.

Yes.

Please pull the blanket farther back, if you would. I am cutting over the spine now.

His wasted shoulder muscles burn as the blanket grows heavier. He has to stand to hold it up. His hip bone presses into her working shoulder, through the parka. Somehow, with no appreciable movement other than those of her cutting, she recoils from him slightly.

He eyes the moving blade.

It took me until now, watching you work, to know what made those marks. In the ice.

Be careful, sir, I have to cut over this way.

A glottal sound and a rich stink as more of the blanket works free. The animal is still on its side. She leans, reaches under the blanket that Kruger holds high, his arms now trembling, and frees the skin over the abdomen. Then she digs lower.

I owe you my apologies, he says, looking down at her back, the loose, jiggling hood. For taking from your cache. I believed it was Meyer's—or maybe the lieutenant's. (He doesn't add what now occurs to him: that in his hunger and aloneness, he might have raided the cache even if he had known it was hers.)

In that case, she says calmly, you don't know the lieutenant very well.

I begin to think I don't know anyone very well—yourself included. Still, I'm sure that your reasons for hoarding were good. You must have realized the men intended to leave you nothing.

Please move to the other side of him now.

Yes. And Hannah, I know—Tukulito—I know how much you love your daughter. I did try to give back something to the child, you know. Some of what little I stole.

He now stands across from her, the blanket held high, like a man allowing a wife some modesty on a bathing-beach as she changes. Her lowered, crimped brow is reddening, upward to the hairline. It could be from the work; from anger; from shame. She's freeing the skin and blubber from over the retracted genitals. Kruger looks away. The animal's right eye, dark and soulful as a spaniel's, meets his.

Yes, she says, I thought it was you. Otherwise I would have moved it. Her flat sun-shaped face is squinting up, the direct light hardening her look so it's impossible to know whether her sternness is real or just an effect of the brightness. Still, she allowed him to eat from her cache—which she made and kept against her own people's taboos—and although in the end she could have let him shoulder the blame for it, she must have taken the risk of returning the supplies herself, thus helping him clear his name, at least in the crewhut. If love is just deep respect fused with desire, then that's what absorbs him now. Bellyfuls of meat for days have revived his other hungers. Even the other men have begun to look almost fetching. At the same time they look truly awful. Everybody looks awful. Only Tukulito, he thinks, has retained something of her inward and outward grace.

I am in love with you, he nearly says.

Help me roll him onto his spine, sir, so we can slit open his belly.

After a moment or two he mutters, Yes, of course. And he returns to her side. They return to work as though nothing important has been uncovered—but there is one more suspicion that he wants to confirm. He says softly, Why then did you not use your husband's snow knife at the cache . . . ? Her silence gives the answer he was expecting. Her husband knows nothing about the cache.

After various small, hidden surgeries, her hands deep inside the body, she tenders the crescent knife like a salver. On it is a slice of steaming, plum-coloured meat.

From the front of the heart, she says, meeting his eyes.

He wonders if the heart means the same things to her people—more than meat. He wonders if she could be trying to bribe him, buy his silence. He's in a position to blackmail her, he supposes, to gain her favours. Of course he would not, but still this longing, this toppling forward into her eyes; and are Esquimau husbands not said to follow old traditions of erotic hospitality? So the other men used to point out, often enough.

Please, Mr Kruger, help yourself. Or have you no appetite now?

He leans into her, almost bringing his throat against the red blade-edge, and kisses her on the lips. She pulls back and slaps his face with her free, bloody hand, her ring leaving a lightning-thread of pain along his jaw.

Mr Kruger. I am a married woman.

He stares at her frankly, helpless. Her widened eyes seem to show a contained desperation.

If you're not inclined to respect my husband, sir, or Inuit marriages, consider also that we were married in London, before God, by a vicar of the Church of England.

His hand comes away from his face bloody, though with his blood or the animal's, he can't tell. He grins with the pain.

Of course, you care no more for God than you do for Inuit ways.

But it was *you*, says Kruger, stung and no more able to ignore an apparent hypocrisy than to quit thinking—it was you who went against your people's laws in taking the food. Was it not?

A facial flicker of shame as she looks down and he is sorry for his words.

As for Joe, he whispers—Ebierbing—I respect him very much. Only, love trumps respect, I now find. But forgive me, all the same. I shall trouble you no further.

I did not eat any of that food, Mr Kruger! She looks up at him with something close to passion. Not a morsel! I reserved it as a final store for us, should the crewmen leave us bereft. And still, it felt like an evil thing. Still it feels so, like a savagery!

No, he says quickly, no, you may well have saved us. I think you've saved all of us. He wants to reach out and console her. There are further things he should say here, but he can't seem to complete a thought, let alone express one. He can't help eyeing her smoking bloody hands and wanting to kiss and lick them clean. Nor can he help grabbing like a child and pinching the slice of heart's meat on the blade and shoving it into his mouth.

One day at dusk Tukulito takes Punnie out to the new latrine, the old one having vanished the night the ice disintegrated. In a year or two, bemused whalers might discover it mysteriously bobbing along on its own tiny floe. The new facility is a too-shallow pit dug behind a hummock, which forms a kind of sloping back wall, with two side walls of rough snow blocks extending out from it to stop the wind. The sea-edge is just a dozen paces off, though in the latest cold snap the leads have all frozen over and the floe and the towering bergs are again part of a solid pack inching southward like a glacier.

As mother and child approach the latrine hand in hand, a low muttering is audible from back of the hummock. German. This although the crewmen have their own latrine.

Tukulito stops and calls, Yes? Who is it?

You know very well whom!

She can't place the voice: shrill, scolding. Mr Jamka staggers from behind the hummock, crab-eyed, hoisting up his fur trousers with grubby hands. His feet, purple, swollen and hairy, are bare in the snow. He wears no parka, just a sailor's jumper. Above his matted beard the sharp nose is burgundy against his white, white face. She has not seen him outside in weeks.

You have been looking straight at me! he says with a crafty expression.

But you were in the latrine, Mr Jamka.

Ah! he says triumphantly, and how can you have *known* such a thing without looking?

And perhaps you are mistaken in the dusk, sir. This is not your latrine.

But it is not at all dark, Madame, look about you!

A sighing crack runs through the new ice and Jamka peers around with rolling, primitive eyes, the whites clear and luminous in the twilight. From beneath the floe comes an enormous gulping, belching sound. When it subsides Jamka looks wily again. The knee-length trousers give him thick furry thighs under a shrunken torso, like a satyr. He still seems not to notice Punnie.

Perhaps all along you knew I was here, he says with a look of pride, delight in his own shrewdness. We know so much about the squaws, *mein Gott, ja!*

He comes at her, sets hands on her shoulders and draws her to him. Punnie, holding her mother's hand, is tugged closer too.

Stop this at once, Mr Jamka, we are here because the child needs—

Oh do not *speak* to me of childrens! Jamka is pressing bearded kisses on her cheeks while trying to topple her back onto the ice. She mashes the heel of her palm into his gluey nose. Scrawny though he is, he dwarfs her in every way. He wrenches her down hard and Punnie, still a ghost to him, tumbles with them. Anaana! the child cries, wriggling out from under his furry thigh and leaping up. He is on top of Tukulito, trying to pin her by the wrists, his long nails gouging her skin, his lower body thrusting at hers through the layers of clothing. A braiding of veins, purple on white, stands out along his temples. His breath is hot and hideously sweet.

Stop this—my husband will kill you—

He may try, pants Jamka, continuing to thrust. So also your lover.

You are wrong—please—stop!

For I am protected by the Count.

She tries to butt him, bite at him, but he cranes his head back, limpid eyes staring down at her, straight through her, on through the ice and the green sea and the sluggish weeds to the bottom, as though possessed. Nuliajuk, she thinks: this might, must be the Old Woman's judgment on Tukulito, for her stealing of the food. Then comes the thought that the Lord God would never permit the Old Woman to enter and control the soul of a Christian, like Jamka, even out here.

Get help, she tells Punnie in Inuktitut, though she knows Ebierbing is off hunting. In her spine she feels the receding thumps of the child's running steps. Tukulito slips her right wrist free and while Jamka gropes to pin it again, she digs in her amautik pocket for her ulu, but it's not there, slipped out. Jamka now pins the wrist beside her squirming hip, then tilts his face toward hers with an expression that is suddenly wistful, tender. He is trying to kiss her eyes. She bites into his cheek along the beardline and tastes blood, raw flesh. His face opens with horror, then fury. *Du Kannibalin!* he hisses—I knew this! Through her flattened spine she feels steps coming fast and tries to twist her head to look, but Jamka's moist forehead is clamped against hers. He seems to stretch and warp, like a monstrous limpet, to cover every inch of her. There is a sharp grunt, a thud, and Jamka arches and flies back off her as if yanked by a shaman's puppetlines. Kruger stands over Tukulito, his face red and distended, gripping his rifle like a cudgel.

Has he harmed you in any way?

No, Mr Kruger.

He lets the rifle fall. She sits up quickly, flushing. Punnie emerges from behind Kruger and embraces her at a run. A few feet away Jamka lies on his back whimpering, rolling stiffly, his face bloody, eyes shut, hands under his arched spine clutching it. Tukulito almost whispers *I am grateful,* but then it strikes her: that Mr Kruger might possibly have arranged this attack, yes, and heroic rescue, in order to win her good regard, her body. Who knows? It is vile, and childish, this infectious lack of trust, which she would prefer to think of as a White malady, or at least as a winter sickness, yet it's worsening still, in her. Henceforth she will keep the revolver with her. People can be heard stirring in the camp. Briskly she lifts Punnie off herself and gets to her feet, retrieving her ulu, straightening and brushing her amautik.

Lieutenant Tyson appears, then some of the crew. Kruger crouches beside the weeping Jamka. And watching everything, the child: who trusted Kruger enough to bring him here, even if her mother does not.

Mar 26. I know not what to make of this. Was Jamka forcing self on her or she "entertaining" him? Will not shame her farther by enquiry. The men protect their own by silence. However, Krueger saw & in jealous, or righteous outrage interfer'd. I have now Jamkas health to worry me too for he is struck in the face & spine. I have insisted K be responsible for him & tend to him carefuly wch he seems willing enough to do.

If I told Joe about K & now Jamka I suppose he wd soon rid us of these Damned troublesome Germans, only they too I mean to bring Home alive.

March 28. The bladder-noses are here! I thought they could not be far off; and their appearance, after my prediction, appears to solidify the men's faith in my command; they are beginning to act as helpful as raw ratings. Shot nine large seals today, and saved four—five of them sank. Three were Joe's, and one Hans's. Thank God, we have now meat enough for eighteen or twenty days. Our whole company feel cheered and encouraged, knowing we have now got to the promised seal-grounds, where great plenty can be obtained; and our ammunition holds out well. Mr Meyer has actually been out of his hut, and took an observation; he makes the latitude 62°47' N, showing a drift of thirty-two miles in three days. We are now in the strong tides off the mouth of Hudson Strait; and because of our drift we again can see no land. Huge bergs—and I do not in the least exaggerate when I say hundreds in number—are plowing their way among the floes, almost as if they were sentinels, or guides; but our little ice-craft is making its way through the sea without other guide than the Great Being above.

One of the men, Jamka, received in a mishap a bad, but not mortal, couple of injuries; he was in considerable distress, but now appears to be mending.

April 1. We have been the "fools of fortune" now for five months and a half. Last night there was a heavy sea, water all around us, and scarcely any ice to be seen; today's sun, pale and sick, shows our shrunken home to be entirely detached from the main pack, which is far to the west of us, and which would be "safer" than this little bit we are on. And so, last night's winds having abated, I determined that we should take the boat and try to regain it.

I did not make any conversation with either Meyer or the men about abandoning the floe, for the time had come when it was absolutely necessary to do so, and the men seemed to know it. We got launched, towing the *kyack* behind us. The boat was laden very heavy, and was, of course, low in the water, with nineteen souls aboard, instead of the six to eight it was intended for, and also ammunition, guns, skins, and several hundred pounds of seal-meat; so that the sea began to break over us, and the men became frightened, some of them exclaiming that "the boat is sinking!" Meanwhile our home of some five months receded behind us, the huts where we had lived so long soon resembling, at a distance, mere hummocks or slabs of raftered ice. The seas were such that for a while our "island" came in and out of our sight, and then vanished altogether, as if having passed over the lip of a cataract.

The men rowing did what they could, but we made little headway, having but four oars, and their every movement impeded by the heads or bodies of others. We were in fact so crowded that it was difficult for Hans and Joe to bail, which they did constantly, and I could scarcely move my arms sufficiently to handle the tiller yoke-ropes without knocking into some child—and these children frightened and crying almost all the time. I could not leave the tiller to eat—there was not room to leave anyway—so that Hannah had to feed me pieces of raw seal-meat as I steered.

Of course I wished to reach the pack without losing any thing more than was completely necessary, for we really had nothing to spare; but the boat took water so badly that I saw we must sacrifice every thing, and so the seal-meat was thrown over, with most of our rusted firearms, and other things; but the boat had to be lightened. After all was done, however, the boat was still overloaded fearfully. It was with much difficulty through these changes that I preserved Captain Hall's small writing-desk from destruction, as some of the men were bound to have Joe throw it overboard; but I positively forbade it, as it was all we had belonging to our late commander. Hannah, who reciprocated my feelings in this regard, argued in untypically open fashion with Kruger, who declared that she and I were being sentimental. One might expect a native to put survival before human sentiment at such a time, but Hannah in many ways is civilized, and she and Joe loved Captain Hall like a father. She rightly made the point that it is only our "sentiments," at a time like this, that keep us from barbarism.

Soon afterward, however, a wave broke over us to larboard, and, as the boat rolled, Kruger contrived to push the little desk in the direction of the roll, and over it went in a moment and was lost to us in the waves. Hannah's feelings can be imagined, although she said nothing; Joe actually looked as though he might approve of this crime; and, in reply to my angry rebuke, Kruger declared that "The desk would soon be swimming at any event, it being only a question of whether we wished to swim with it, or remain in an upright boat." Well, he can phrase things as deftly as a lawyer, but he knows less of boat-craft than I; Captain Hall's desk was, if a risk, a minor one, and well worth taking for reasons of morale. Calling him a thief and a scoundrel, I warned him that he could expect to keep double watches for the next few nights.

Having, by hard work and some luck, got about twenty miles through open seas and reached the pack, we were compelled to hold up on the first piece of good ice we could find. There we spread what few skins we had, set up our tent, and ate our ration of dry bread and pemmican. We were all exhausted—too weary even for argument or complaints. On the morning of the 2d we started again, still pushing to the west; but the wind, with snow-squalls, was against us, and we made but little progress. Hauled up on another piece of ice, and encamped.

April 4. After a day spent in repairing the boat, and fitting her up with wash-boards of canvas to keep the seas from dashing over the sides, we rigged up and headed west again; and after a desperate struggle, we at last regained the "pack." We are now encamped on a heavy piece of ice, and I hope out of immediate danger. But there is no ice to be trusted at this time of year. The sun showed himself at noon, but we are again "blessed" with a heavy wind from the north, and snow-squalls. Our tent of course is not as good a protection from the wind as the snow-huts. Joe, with a little help, can build a hut in an hour, if the right kind of snow-blocks can be procured, but on this floe there is little but bare, scraped ice. Still, he intends to try. In the mean time, nineteen souls crowd into our tent, and the noise of the luffing canvas is terrible. If one attempts to rest the body, there is no rest for the mind. One or other of the men will often spring up from their sleep, and make a wild dash forward, as if avoiding some sudden danger.

Blowing a gale from the north-east tonight, and a fearful sea running.

❧

Kruger paces the tiny floe on the last of the night's one-hour watches, his straddling gait helpful as the ice teeters and wallows over the stricken sea. He feels his marrow congealing in this cold, his nose-hairs frozen, lips swollen as sausage. Now and then the moon slides into view between rags of animated cloud to show the glistering ice-pack for hours westward rippling and seething like . . . not something alive, but something dead and aswarm with corruption.

Is facing death harder for the lucky or the unlucky? Somebody who has tasted few of life's blessings, realized few hopes, has little to lose and yet much to regret—a future where those dreams might still be gained. Somebody who has lived fully, who has what he wants, will have little to regret but knows how much he's losing. (A wife, children, simple work ashore, a small house full of food and books in a peaceful, sunny country; and tobacco, anything now for a plug of it.)

Halt die Leiter, Jamka blurts in panic from the tent, *damit er das Bild aufhängen kann!*

Hold the ladder, so that he can hang the picture!

Kruger passes between the tent—the whaleboat is right beside it—and Ebierbing's crude little snowhut. From inside, a muffled chorus of breathing in which he tries to distinguish Tukulito's breathing, her high, clipped cough. The sky is brightening, warm tinges of orchid edging the black tatters of cloud on their disintegrating southward dash. He walks on. In silence a crack zips toward him across the floe—like watching a centipede skitter across a deck. It passes just to the right of his boot and squiggles on under the snowhut. With a dry, tearing sound the crack widens, exposing a stratified cross-section of ice like a bed of shale. In time with the groundswell, black seawater pumps up in the gap, sloshes over onto the ice. *Kommt raus!* he yells, everybody up! He runs to the hut which Ebierbing is already crawling out of, fully dressed, Punnie under his arm like a bundle of furs, and under Punnie's own arm, her doll. The entrance faces the tent. Kruger scoops the trembling child up in his embrace, *Shh, shh! keine Angst!* and when Ebierbing stands—a wide grin on his strained grey face—he passes her back. Guess I lose another hut eh, Kruger? he says, and one can only think: This is a man. Kruger offers Tukulito his glove as if she is climbing up into a carriage after a ball, absurd gesture in this extremity, and he helps her to her feet, her fatlamp cradled, red eyes assaying him, while Ebierbing hunches and crawls back inside. The rift widens. Tyson is now out of the tent, shouting orders to move everything farther back, toward the new centre of the floe. Ebierbing is backing out of the hut with his rifle and the dripping bedskins as the rift, now too wide to step over, undermines the hut. It buckles like a sand castle in a tide, ruined walls left on either side of the lead as it spreads, white blocks dissolving in the steaming water like sugar cubes in tea. The men, even Anthing and Jamka—barefoot, still limping from his injury—are out and following Tyson's orders without quibble. He has them loading everything into the boat where Hans and his family have been sleeping.

Stand by for a jump, men.

Aye aye, sir!

Women and children in the boat. Men for now in the tent. And Mr Jamka, for the last time, on with your boots or I'll reef them onto your feet.

Jackson and Herron are trying to warm water in the tent while men sprawl or hunker on the canvas and try to rest, to steal their way back into interrupted dreams of elsewhere. Kruger stretches out by the lamp, wishing she, her family, were in here, not in the boat. He's jolted from a doze by a familiar tearing sound, then men's grunts, rough hands dragging him. The hissing as a tinful of broth meets the seawater fuming in a sudden crack. Herron and Jackson heave him out the door through which men are fleeing with whatever they can hold, Anthing and Lindermann helping the half-blind Count, who looks perplexed and testy. And Jackson: I warned you all, this was sure to happen! His pemmican-tin lamp floats wobbling on the dark water, still alight, but nobody wants to approach the widening gap to retrieve it. Then Jackson and Tyson crawl forward. The gap slams like the steel sides of a steam laundry press, oil sparks shoot up and when the jaws open, the crushed lamp, blubber flaring within, welters on its side, settling in the water, spitting and disappearing.

Oh boys, says Lundquist, we are all goners!

Shut up now Gus, Herron snaps, his voice squeezed thin and tight.

What?

Shut your . . . g-g-g-Goddamned gob, please!

That's enough, men, Tyson says. We've work enough here.

They watch the pegged tent deflate as the centre pole, unseen, thrusts down into the crack, and now the canvas stretches over the widening lead until it looks taut enough to bridge the weight of a crossing man. For a few seconds the canvas halts the process of splitting, keeps the halves of the floe close. Then on the far side it starts ripping around the eyelets through which the peg-lines run. It snaps free with a whipping sound. The far half of the floe, unmoored and trailing peg-lines, drifts loose and the men scramble to the new edge of their toehold and pull in the canvas hand-over-hand, fishermen hauling home an empty net.

Tyson and Jackson cut ragged new eyelets and, using an oar for a peak pole, with Kruger helping, they pitch the tent again. Tyson grunts as he lashes the Stars and Stripes to the protruding oar handle. His chest is barrelled, fire behind his eyes. And Kruger sees it now—how Tyson takes this all personally, how he feels himself engaged, more or less alone, against forces that badly outrank him, and perhaps has felt this way his entire life. The kind of man who spends his life waiting, or searching, for a moment of supreme testing. He has something to prove to the universe. This makes him invaluable now.

Day passes in a kind of shared delirium . . . Ebierbing, Tukulito and Punnie join the men in the sodden tent . . . from its walls a chill, brackish drizzle drips. A mild wind has come up. Then heavy rain. Hans's family, also finding the boat too wet, squeeze in as well. There is not room for everyone to lie down and Tukulito, with Punnie furled in her lap, sits cross-legged on the edge of that borderless human mass, against the tent wall. Her eyes are closed. Her husband lies on his back alongside her, wheezing. Kruger would offer her a place to stretch out if he had one, if she would accept it, which she would not do, now, he supposes numbly.

It's salty, Mama . . . the walls are weeping!

Sleep again, *utarannaakuluk*.

In the night the crew sit propped back to back. It's opium blue with moonlight and many are feverish. The thin walls of the tent frozen hard as sheeted zinc. He wakes, no idea who is at his back. It's Anthing, shuddering with cold, grinding his back into Kruger's for warmth. Tyson and Meyer are likewise twinned—Tyson's brow knotted in sleep, while from Meyer's lips a stalactite of frozen drool runs down to his clasped mittens.

Tukulito's nodding profile is moonlit, terse coughs at times puffing open her lips.

Like a cell ceaselessly dividing, the floe splits again at dawn. The crack quickly separates the tent and the boat, which were close together—so close, growls Tyson, as if to himself, that a man could scarcely walk between them! He's hunkered in the tent door, Kruger beside him. The way he shakes his head, knuckles his pouched eyes as the boat recedes, says: If *this* is the precise work of God's jigsaw, then he is toying with us, cruelly.

Tyson perhaps is starting to see his own god as an antagonist—not a tester but a teaser—a trickster. Perhaps disillusionment need not induce apathy, as with Kruger's father, but could be an active thing, galvanizing.

Tyson's baffled expression hardens, narrows.

Wake up, all of you! Now where the devil is Meyer?

The tent is so crammed it takes the occupants several seconds to ensure that Meyer is not mislaid somewhere among them. Blank faces turn back to Tyson. A drunk-sounding voice rises over the wind—a tuneless voice, mock-operatic. The words are German but garbled. The men crowd into the door. The smaller floe, with the boat and kayak aboard, is pulling away fast, and Meyer is arranging himself in the boat, sitting with great ceremony on the bow bench, facing the stern, then slowly reclining so the back of his head rests on the prow. His white-blond locks dangle down over the gunwale and the hull. He folds his huge mittens over his bosom.

It's a Viking burial.

Mein Graf, Graf Meyer! calls Jamka as if his heart will burst. Meyer is singing softly, eyes closed. His falcon profile beneath the dramatically red skies. The men shout at him but he makes no answer. Without a word Ebierbing and then Hans push out through the tent flap, grab two of the staked oars, trot to the end of the floe and simply leap out into the craze of small ice-pans bobbing in the growing gap between the floe and Meyer. They start to copy across, leaping from one tilting pan to the next, each with an oar held athwart his chest like a high-wire artist with his pole. Tyson says, Two men will never get that boat back alone—to launch it. Who'll come with me? I, sir, says Kruger. I also, says Anthing. Now the others volunteer as well but Tyson orders them to stay back: Two men is enough. He takes an oar and Anthing and Kruger reach for the last oar at the same time and for a moment they both grip it. They say nothing. Exchange no glances. At last Kruger, seeing Tyson staggering ahead, leaves the oar to Anthing and hurries on.

The slippery wave-washed cakes of ice dip underfoot and teeter and you have to step or hop quickly onto the next, moving steadily to keep from falling, like a goat on a cliffside. Fear revives some of the spring in Kruger's joints. Ebierbing and Hans are well ahead, but Tyson is right in front of him, so now he has to keep from bounding onto Tyson's pan before the man jumps onto the next. Arms extended for balance Kruger holds up on a low, broad pan and it settles under him, seawater closing around his ankles, freezing through the sealskin, and then his footing is gone: Anthing has plunged down onto the same piece, jostling him, crying out Hurry, we must catch them! as he leaps onto the next, his oar held high overhead with both hands. Kruger is left flailing on the wobbling pan. He hurls himself in the direction of his fall, onto a smaller chunk a few feet off the men's path. He lands on his chest and hands as his legs dunk up to the thighs and his boots fill with water. The cold of it almost stops his heart—a slow heavy thud in his ears. Anthing glances back. Are you all right? Hurry! Again he has yelled the words in English. Kruger looks back toward the main floe. Their fragmentary path is diffusing, open water now behind. He crawls upright and tries to follow Anthing, muscles tight with cold, tries to get back the rhythm of it. A seal buoys up between pans and for a moment he meets its intrigued, beagle-like eyes and looks away but feels it watching, revolving its whiskered head in the dark slush as he passes—this awkward, forked being, Roland Kruger—something it could never have imagined and will never see again.

Ebierbing and Hans are on the floe ahead, apparently trying to haul the boat over the edge with the dormant Meyer still aboard. Kruger breaks sweat in his armpits and over his back while his sopping legs freeze. Anthing keeps him going, in pursuit—though when Kruger reaches the floe-edge, Anthing turns and offers his hand and yanks him aboard the ice. I'm sorry, he says softly and quickly in German, but you paused there! I was in step behind you, I couldn't stop.

Help us try to launch here! Tyson calls hoarsely. Kruger—over there. Anthing—speak to Mr Meyer. Implore him to get out of the boat until we launch.

Aye aye, sir! Anthing hollers.

On the way back, Meyer insists on standing in the bow, waving solemnly like a returning monarch as they approach the castaways lining the shore of their home.

That evening the sea sweeps over the floe and washes them out of the tent. Tyson orders everything and everyone into the whaleboat, where they slump together in a democracy of terror and cold. Through a haze the setting sun appears grey and hollow and cold, and the wind seems to be howling straight out of it, as if from the mouth of a pale tunnel. She sits on the middle bench with Punnie on her lap, in a ready boat on a hard surface, waiting for the flood to lift them. The Flood, this is the story she tells the child now, sometimes quoting verses word for word. How those good people with their mated animals—yes, lions and camelopards as well—drifted for a long time over the floodwaters, but then they sent forth land-birds, and at length the dove returned not again unto Noah, and he and his family came safely unto shore. Punnie, whispering, relays the story to her glumly staring doll, interpreting into Inuktitut; for Elisapee, she affirms, speaks no English.

Soon the Gosling Moon will begin, little one. The land-birds will lead us home, too.

They were lucky to have so many pairs of animals to eat, the child says.

They try to sleep as the night engulfs them, and Tukulito hears Mr Kruger clacking his jaws, shuddering over his frozen feet. In her heart she feels the wrong of the lieutenant's believing him to have been the thief. Two days ago, or perhaps three—nothing is quite clear anymore—she confided to him, the lieutenant, that Mr Kruger was innocent of this charge, for she herself was the thief; and then she quickly related her full story. At first he was silent, but his beard had a bitterly smiling look. Then he said, I can't credit that you would break so with native custom, Hannah. You mean to protect him, I see. When she replied, And why should I wish to do that, sir? he only smiled in the same chilling, cheerless manner, the pupils of his eyes sinking into the deep-fathomed blue around them. So he too appears to hold this false belief about herself and Mr Kruger. Of course she said nothing on the matter; but she cannot help wondering if Mr Kruger has made some lying claim.

From time to time high seas swamp the floe—not enough to lift the boat, though they rock it a good deal—so that all are confined aboard. All are throttled with thirst; the freshwater ice is now polluted with brine and there is no blubber to melt it anyway. The men are again famished. It has been days since Ebierbing has taken a seal. Tukulito can read their hunger in the way several of them consider her and Punnie, and especially in how they look skittishly away: Jamka, with his green-scabbed cheek, who now takes pains to avoid her, trying to keep a crewman between himself and her at all times, which is easily done, for Kruger always quietly inserts himself, though whether to protect her, or to be closer to her, or both, she is unable to interpret.

At dawn she wakes in the boat with Punnie right inside her amautik. Somehow the child has burrowed up inside it in the night so that Tukulito looks, and feels, massively pregnant. Feels even the warmth of pregnancy. She takes the revolver from her outer pocket and pushes it into her boot. It is consoling to know that with this, her third child, death will not be able to separate them, and they will sink as one flesh: what they never really were. How wrong some people are to suppose that one does not love a *paninguaq*, adopted girl, "pretend daughter," the same way. As if the warmth of flesh and blood could ever surpass the fire of the soul's love. Behind her at the tiller, Tyson, demoted to boyhood in his joy, cries in a breaking voice, Oh, Hannah, look! A raven is gliding toward them not far above the ice, inspecting them. In the wake of the straggling dovekies that have passed lately, this bird looks enormous, a thing considerably too large to be airborne. Updrafts dance in the finger-like feathers off the backs of her wings. So, here is the land-bird that her story has promised Punnie. Punnie!—wake up, little one, come out and see!

Her voice is in the same condition as Tyson's, but the child will not emerge.

Fevered with hunger and familiar since childhood with the spirit of such creatures, Tukulito is now peering down from high above, through the raven's shrewd, currant-black eyes, on a floe where everything is still alive and, for now, there is nothing to scavenge. With a coarse, scraping call—having astutely noted the company's position—the bird circles back toward land.

Easter Sunday. Conditions increasingly desperate. We seem forgotten here. Men obeying still but some wear dangerous Looks. This Hunger is disturbing every Brain. Last night the Stars looked heartless to me & the Aurora a gawdy & vacant show! Can right no more now. Must sleep.

❧

April 14, Morning. I think this must be Easter-Sunday in civilized lands. Surely we have had more than a forty days' fast. May we have a glorious resurrection to peace and safety ere long!

Last night, as I sat solitary on my watch, thinking over our desperate situation, the northern lights appeared in great splendor. I watched while they lasted, and there seemed to be something like the promise accompanying the first rainbow in their brilliant flashes. The Auroras seem to me always like a sudden flashing out of the Divinity: a sort of reminder that God has not left off the active operations of his will. So we must continue to trust. This, with my impression that it must be Easter-Sunday, has thrown a ray of hope over our otherwise desolate outlook.

April 18. Blowing strong from the north-east. There is a very heavy swell under the ice.

At 9 P.M., while resting in our tent, we were alarmed by hearing an outcry from Lundquist on the watch; and almost at the same moment a heavy sea swept across our piece, carrying away every thing on it that was loose. This was but a foretaste of what was to follow; we began shipping sea after sea, one after another, with only a few minutes' interval between each. Finally came a tremendous wave, carrying away our tent, skins, and most all of our bed-clothing. Only a few things were saved, which we had kept in the boat; the women and children were already there, as they were every night, or the little ones would certainly have been swept to watery graves. All we could do now was to try and save the boat. So all hands were called to man it in a new fashion—namely, to hold on to it with might and main, to prevent its being washed away. Fortunately, we had preserved our boat warp, and had also another strong line, made of strips of oogjook-skin, and with these we secured the boat to projecting vertical points of ice; but having no grapnels or ice-anchors, these fastenings were frequently unloosed and broken, and the boat could not be trusted to their hold. All our additional strength was needed, and we had to brace ourselves with all the strength we had.

As soon as possible I got the boat, with the help of the men, over to that edge of the floe where the seas first struck; for I knew if she remained toward the farther edge, the gathered momentum of the waves as they rushed over the ice would more than master us, and the boat would go. It was well this precaution was taken, for, as it was, we were very nearly carried off, boat and all, many times during this dreadful night. The heaviest seas came at intervals of fifteen or twenty minutes, and between these came others that would have been thought very powerful if worse had not followed.

There we stood all night long, from 9 P.M. to 7 A.M., enduring what I should say few, if any, have ever gone through and lived. Every little while one of these tremendous seas would come and lift the boat up bodily, and us with it, and carry it, and us, across the ice almost to the opposite edge of our piece; and several times the boat got partly over the edge, and was only hauled back by the strength of mortal desperation. Then we must push and pull and drag the boat right back across the floe to its former position, and stand ready, bracing for the next sea. Had the water been warm and clear of *débris,* it would have been hard enough. But it was freezing and full of loose ice, rolling about in blocks of all shapes and sizes, and with every sea would come an avalanche of these, striking us on our legs and bodies, and bowling us off our feet like so many pins in a bowling-alley. Some of these blocks were only a foot or two square; others were as large as an ordinary bureau, or larger.

And so we stood, hour after hour, the sea as strong as ever, but we weakening from the fatigue, so that before morning we had to make Hannah and Hans's wife leave their children and get out to help us. I do not think Mr Meyer had any strength from the first to assist in holding the boat, only that by clinging to it he kept himself from being washed away; but this was a time in which all did their best,

A FEARFUL STRUGGLE FOR LIFE.

for on the preservation of the boat we knew that our lives depended. If we had but "four anchors," as St Paul describes in the account of his shipwreck, we could have "awaited the day" with better hope; but "when neither sun nor stars appeared, and no small tempest lay on us, all hope that we should be saved was then taken away"—nearly all. That was the greatest fight for life we had yet had. For twelve hours there was scarcely a sound uttered, save for the crying of the children and my orders to "hold on," "bear down," "put on all your weight," and the responsive "ay, ay, sir!"—which now, thank God, comes readily enough. I am afraid that a sealing ship is our only hope now; and though the season is right, we have still a ways to drift to the sealing grounds.

Kruger grips the gunwale amidships, bracing his numb feet on the ice in stance for the next assault. Through the moonless dark the sea is distinguished from the sky only by its pale-glowing, incessant cargo of ice pans and chunks and pash and frazil which, like phosphorescence, chart out the violent flexing of the waves.

When the larger swells approach, the floe dips lower and lower and Tyson at the bow yells, Hold on, men, here it comes! while beside him the soft-spoken Ebierbing hollers over the uproar, Big wave, boys, big! The hardest thing is to keep both hands on the gunwale while the sea thrashes over with its rattling barrage of ice—not raising a hand in self-protection. To do so would mean getting swept away. So the men tortoise their heads down and scrunch their bodies into the gunwale, as if under fire. Such cold and fear, Kruger's testicles press upward hard as if trying to cringe back up inside him. His throat burns raw with salt. Every time a wave lifts the boat, flushing it clear back across the floe, he wonders if his boots will light again on ice or in the sea on the aft side.

But he has Tukulito to see him through. She is seated in the boat, on the middle bench beside him, Punnie a large bulge inside her parka. She has to grip the gunwale too, her mittened hands next to Kruger's. Her face calms him like a full moon seen through a window on awakening from a nightmare: expressionless and benign. Sometimes her eyes are closed and she is silent and then they are open and staring ahead as she sings steadily to the hidden child—to Kruger—English hymns, and then, later, in the keening depths of the night, lullabies in her own language. By then he is hallucinating freely. Assigning German words to the lullabies, hearing a clear translation in his mind, much as lovers will instantly adapt each other's words, even when they speak the same tongue. One time in the short spell between big waves he dozes off and wakes to her mittened hands clasped over his, holding them tight to the frozen gunwale. Then a shove from behind: *Wach auf, Roland!* It's Anthing. *Ja,* says Kruger, *danke.* And Tyson's voice again: Bear down, bear down . . . ! Minutes later Kruger in turn has to kick Herron awake. Tukulito's head, in its pointy hood, is now resting on her mittens, on the gunwale.

Kruger feels such an ache of tenderness that he can't be sure if the salt taste on his cold lips is only brine or tears as well. How ever did the others get through this night without a woman beside them? At one point her tired eyes mesh with his and in that breath of time it seems to him that she weighs him critically, comes to some difficult decision, then thanks him for his efforts with her gaze, a slow tender blink of acknowledgment, as if to say, You are a man, or, I trust in you. His eyes are choked with tears, for some time. Some time later the highest swell yet and on its surface a thin sheet of ice like a pane of glass comes slicing downward. Kruger ducks and when he opens his eyes the boat is surging backward as if airborne, and ahead of him John Herron, cleanly decapitated, still clings to the side; then Herron's drenched head, still attached, sticks back up from inside his parka.

Near dawn, the churning seas visible, icebergs riding the storm like agate galleons, Tukulito forces Punnie down out of her parka, under the thwarts with the other children. She and Merkut clamber over the side to help the exhausted men. And for the rest of the battle she is there in front of him, between him and Herron, the jaunty point of her hood, still stained with Jamka's blood, giving an impression of strength and surety. In the crush of the bigger waves they're often shoved together, front to back, the way her people are said to prefer fucking, and he believes, will believe for the rest of his life, that the warmth and solidity she exudes through her layers, and her animal smells, blood and smoke, fishy seal oil and sweat, are what keep him going and alive.

Tyson looks gaunt and grey but unyielding, pure will. *Bear down, men. We can beat this one too.* In any life a moment must come when one gets nearest to satisfying an ideal image of oneself—reaching that state we might always maintain if we were more, or less, than human. A lucky few might even excel their ideals. This must be Tyson's moment now. To Kruger, whose distaste for the colonels of the world is in necessary abeyance, he now merits total loyalty.

In the grey-green morning light he orders them to launch for a much larger floe, adrift downwind. He rearranges them round the boat, himself at the stern by the tiller, Kruger and Ebierbing at the bow. With a game cry they shove off the floe-edge and haul themselves and each other in over the side as the bow bucks over a lesser wave, spray like birdshot stinging Kruger's eyes. Oars! shouts Tyson, now! Behind Kruger an urgent grunting. Anthing and Jackson are trying to grapple in over the same part of the gunwale. Anthing has one leg inside the boat, Jackson now clinging like a giant barnacle, his knees curled under the gunwale, trying to keep his feet clear of the sea. Don't! he cries. Half-blind with the salt Kruger can't see what is happening. The boat heels to starboard, dunking Jackson, and as it rolls back up he loses hold. Anthing swings his other leg into the boat before the falling man can grab it. Jackson disappears, then finally bobs up thrashing and reaching amid the ice-wrack, already a rope's throw away and drifting south. He will surely go down before they can row to him. But then he drags himself onto what looks like a small slab of blackened ice studded with weirdly upright shafts. Table legs. Captain Hall's writing desk will not let itself be discarded, it seems. Jackson waves and yells something inaudible. A sheen of triumph on Tyson's face as he orders them to row toward the overboard man, and the desk.

On their latest floe they're resorting to a snack of dried sealskin that has been saved for patching clothes, when Ebierbing, atop a hummock a snowball's throw away, ducks and slides down the scarp on his rump and dashes toward them. Everyone but Meyer gets up. A steamer! cries Herron. Joe, t-t-tell us, it's a steamer?

Ebierbing says that a bear is on the way. You boys, he says—you all look like seals now. Lindermann and Madsen glance at each other in quick inspection. Meyer gurgles with amusement. With a rare note of impatience Tukulito says, He means you must all lay yourselves down, scattered about, and remain still, as seals do.

The crewmen hesitate, exchanging looks.

Do it, says Tyson.

So, so one of us is to be the bait then?

Hans lovingly thumbs a cartridge into his rusted rifle. *Tuavilauritti!* he says.

Please do hurry, Mr Herron, the men will slay the bear. And she lies down where she is and pulls Punnie down beside her. As the child again tunnels up into her parka, Tukulito bares her right hand and rests it on the gun butt protruding from her boot. Merkut and the children make a group with them. Kruger lies so as to come between the bear and the women and children. Meyer sets a fine example by simply maintaining the seal-like posture he assumed on arrival at this floe.

The crewmen arrange themselves around Meyer like a basking herd; there's some difficulty as they compete for inner positions.

Stop that, all of you, lie still where you are! Tyson says. Not another sound!

A tarnished sun glows dully through the haze. Hans and Ebierbing are flat on the hummock, their hoods off and back so that the points don't break the skyline. The bear is visible, ambling over a neighbouring floe with its pigeon-toed gait, nose low and engaged. The yellowed fur stands against the white of the old ice and the cloudy absinthe of a looming berg. Jamka whimpers, holds his breath. Merkut's soiled hand is clapped over Succi's mouth. The bear, snout angled up, silently swims a lead, eases onto the floe without stirring it, and then bounds directly toward them. The rifles fire together and the bear plunks its nose straight into the ice and its body follows, caving. The floe flinches with the weight of its fall. Everyone leaps up, shouting. A little mob of skeletons races toward the bear, Jackson and Jamka and Anthing sobbing with joy as Merkut looses her terrible tremolo keening, *Aliannai, aliannai!*, Herron in tears now lurching ahead of her and Kruger, who sees the others' tears before he feels his own salting his inflamed cheeks.

Herron kneels to kiss the salt-and-pepper bridge of the huge muzzle, the little toy ears. The hunters look baffled but seem prepared to see this as some sort of tribute. Jamka crowds into the emaciated flank and sucks at the mouth of the larger wound. A shudder runs through the body lying among its splayed limbs. As Jamka and Herron and the others recoil, the black eyes open and then glass over, a rattle flows from its throat like the ghost of a growl, and its breath-smell—that human hunger smell, precisely the same!—fills the windless air.

For several days they remain on the floe as it erodes. The rain quickens the wasting and soon dissolves the meagre shelters and wind-breaks that Ebierbing and the men scrape together from what little snow remains. They're all soaked to the skin and the rain keeps lashing at them out of the northeast. Now and then, for variety, they have a snow squall—so Tyson quips grimly. Everything is softening to grey, oozing slowly back down into the sea. Only the raw bear-meat, gnawed on constantly, keeps any heat in them.

They launch in the battered boat and try to follow a narrow lead toward shore, but the wind shifts against them and the lead closes. Of *course*, Tyson's tight, oddly satisfied smile seems to say. His face now like a fist shaken at the sky—though not without a certain zest. They haul up on another, smaller floe already on its way to pash. But a steep hummock survives on it, maybe thirty feet tall, a vantage point from which to search for more openings, bears, the land, or steamers.

Kruger is on watch at dawn with Hans's rifle slung across his back. For miles eastward the cloudline and the broken ice are veined and softened by a diffused fuchsia glow. No sound but the steady, sly crackling of tons of melting ice. Below, the others are huddled in the boat like street arabs in a Brooklyn areaway. The desk, offloaded to make room, stands beside the stern as if waiting for somebody to wake and pen a version of these unfinished events.

He hears the raven from a long way off.

Oh good, you've come back to us.

A heavy cold has taken most of his voice. The raven passes close overhead, frankly perusing him and the boatful of dying sleepers. The slow whooshing pulse of its wings. It wheels and flaps off, finally alighting on the pinnacle of a small iceberg about a rifle shot away.

Kruger climbs a few feet down the back of the hummock, out of sight of the boat; Tukulito might wake, or one of the children. It takes some time to get the piss trickling out of him, weak and orange, as if tainted with blood. He turns his head at a crunching sound. Anthing stands above him, skylined on top of the hummock, his curly head haloed with rosy light and his panting breaths.

Ah. Krüger. I assumed you'd deserted your post.

Guten Morgen, Kruger whispers hoarsely.

It has gotten painful, hasn't it?

To talk?

I noticed yesterday that you'd lost your voice, Anthing says. But, no, I meant painful to piss.

Anthing whisks the *ulu* from his outer pocket and descends on Kruger, who is too busy working himself back into his trousers to unsling the rifle. Before he can finish he has to retreat down the steep flank of the hummock, but his feet are swollen numb, he stumbles backward, falls, sledding headfirst on his spine, the rifle trapped under him. The leather strap that Hans's family have been gnawing on for weeks splits and the rifle is gone. Anthing picks his way down, stooping to collect the rifle as he comes. Kruger has rolled onto the flat ice at the bottom, not twenty steps from the floe-edge. Winded, he stands, fumbling with the front of his trousers while Anthing chuckles above him. The hummock like a wall between them and the others in the boat.

How did you get her knife? Kruger rasps. If you've harmed her . . .

Can't hear a word. Why not wait till I get a little closer?

Kruger, backing, repeats himself as best he can.

Ah. Don't worry, not about that. She didn't wake. You've worn her out, I think. She even looks pregnant, with the child inside her coat.

If you mean to skin me, Matthias, I'm afraid you'll find little fat for the lamp.

No sign Anthing has heard him. Almost spry, he trots the last steps down onto the flat ice. In his frost-burned face the eyes look eerily fresh and alert. Kruger has run out of backing room. Anthing weighs the rifle in his bare hand like a harpoon, then arcs it over the floe-edge. The slush-clogged sea ingests it without a sound.

In fact, Anthing says, you must have more fat and meat on you than any of us.

I hope you mean to share me with the others, then.

Anthing's gapped grin stays in place, but his eyelids grow heavier. And give your heart to that nigger squaw? You'll be going into the sea, like an animal. You're not one of us. I believe it was really you, the thief. Not Hans Christian.

What does it matter now, the supplies were . . .

Speak up!

All the supplies were returned!

But why ever should you go unpunished? You are a looter. A traitor.

Lieutenant! Kruger tries calling, but he only gets off a throttled squawk.

You never cared to be one of us, Roland. Like a, like a scholar of some kind. Or a Gypsy. Or a Jew! Why, you even have the colouring of a Jew.

If men like you despise Jews, then I'll be a Jew.

With sudden petulance Anthing tilts an ear toward Kruger. *Was hast du gesagt?*

Think of me as a Jew.

You believe the future is for men like yourself, but it belongs to men like me!

Those are Meyer's words, Matthias, and Meyer is mad.

No! The Graf Meyer is correct!

I never said he wasn't correct.

What? Anthing steps closer, the *ulu* trembling by his blood-matted beard. Kruger's impulse—the only form of retreat left—is to kneel, shrivel down into the ice. But that would look too much like begging. *I was perfectly alone. I'd become meat—nothing more than meat.*

Anthing says, You probably don't even *miss* the Fatherland.

This has nothing to do with Jews! Kruger exclaims in small, rodent tones, or the Fatherland, or with pilfering! You just crouch in ambush behind the principles. You only want power.

Anthing swipes the *ulu* at Kruger's throat, Kruger ducks, and now he is on his knees.

And in my heart I'd remain a German even if men like you destroyed Germany. But my mind is another matter. My mind is a free man.

He has to break off, bottling up a sneeze. The raven with its active instincts appears over the hummock where it hovers attentively, then lands. And Kruger begins to sneeze, severely, helpless to stop. This is Anthing's moment—yet he doesn't act. Kruger peers up at last. Anthing's eyes, empty as bubbles, growing larger, seem liable to pop with enough force to tip Kruger over on their own. His words are slow, subdued, remote. I always had nothing, Roland. . . . Go on, your country is that way . . . nowhere.

It seems he wants to avoid soiling the *ulu*, or getting fresh blood on his boots and parka. Of course, blood would be evidence. They stay in this position for some while—Anthing unable to finish the job, Kruger refusing to jump. Anthing studies his odd weapon, then breathes on his shivering hands. Neither man speaks, as if they're seized with a sudden shyness, or embarrassment. And in this truce of hesitation Tukulito appears. Rounding the hummock she pads toward them with her small rapid steps, feet placed one in front of the other, quiet and deliberate. She holds the cocked revolver straight in front of her like a duellist. Her parka is filthy and blotched. Her eyes are puffy. Her large plate-like face, creased with sleep, is gaunt, pale, hard, implacable. The most beautiful thing Kruger has ever seen.

April 28. 4:30 P.M. A joyful sight—a *steamer* right ahead of our boat and bearing north of us! We hoisted our colors and pulled toward her. She is a sealer, going south-west, and apparently working through the ice. For a few moments what joy thrilled our breasts—the sight of relief so near! But we have lost it! She did not see us, and we could not get to her; evening came down, and she was lost to sight.

We boarded, instead of the hoped-for steamer, a small piece of ice, and once more hauled up our boat and made camp. A new moon, and the stars shining brightly. The sea is quiet, and we can rest peaceful;

for, although one steamer has passed us, we feel that we may soon see another—that help can not be far off. We take all the blubber of yesterday's seal, and build a fire on the floe, so that if a steamer or any vessel approaches in the night, she will see us.

We are divided into two watches, of four hours each, except for Meyer, who is too ill; Jamka, whose feet are too swollen to stand on; and Anthing, who has sustained a head blow, apparently in a fall. We had a good pull this afternoon, and made some westing. The hope of relief keeps us even more wakeful than does the fear of danger. To see the prospect of rescue so near, though it was quickly withdrawn, has set every nerve thrilling with hope.

April 29. Morning fine and calm, the sea quiet. All but the injured men on the lookout for steamers. Sighted one about eight miles off. Called the watch, launched the boat, and made for her. After an hour's pull, gained on her a good deal; but they did not see us. Another hour, and we are beset in the ice, and can get no farther.

Landed on a small floe, and hoisted our Stars and Stripes again; then, getting on the highest part, Joe fired his rifle, and Hans his pistol—which he has received, for hunting, from Hannah, Kruger having somehow contrived to lose Hans's rifle in the sea!—hoping by this means to attract their attention. The combined effort made a considerable report. They fired three volleys, and seemed to hear a response of three shots; at the same time the steamer headed toward us. Now we feel sure that the time of our deliverance has come.

We shouted, involuntarily almost, but they were too far away to hear our voices. Presently the steamer changed her course, and headed south, then north again, then west; we did not know what to make of it. We watched, but she did not get materially nearer. So she kept on all day, as though she were trying to work through the ice, and could not force her way. Strange! I should think any sailing ship, much more a steamer, could get through. She being four or five miles off, we repeated our firing, but she came no nearer. All day we watched, making every effort within our means to attract attention. Whether they saw us or not we do not know, but late in the afternoon she steamed away, going to the south-west; and reluctantly we abandoned the hope which had upheld us through the day.

April 30. At 5 A.M., as I was lying in the boat, my watch having just expired, Herron on the look-out espied a steamer cutting through the fog, and the first I heard was a loud cry, "There's a steamer, lads! Lads, there's a steamer!" On hearing the outcry, I sprang up as if endued with new life, ordered the guns to be fired, and set up a loud, simultaneous shout; also ordered the colors set on the boat's mast, and held them erect, fearing that, like the other ships, she might not see or hear us, though she was much nearer—not more than a quarter of a mile off when we first sighted her.

I also started Hans off in his *kyack,* which he had himself proposed to do, to intercept her, if possible, as it was very foggy and I feared every moment we would lose sight of her; but, to my great joy and relief, the steamer's head was soon turned toward us. But Hans kept on, and paddled up to the vessel, singing out, in his broken English, the unmeaning words, "American steamer!"—meaning to tell them of the loss of the *Polaris,* I suppose; but they did not understand him.

On her approach, as they slowed down, I took off my old Russian cap, which I had worn all winter, and waving it over my head gave them three cheers, in which all the men, except perhaps poor Meyer, heartily joined. It was instantly returned by a hundred men, who covered her top-gallant mast, forecastle, and fore-rigging. We then gave three more, and a "tiger," which was surely appropriate, as she proved to be the sealer *Tigress*—a barkentine of Conception Bay, Newfoundland.

Two or three of their seal-boats were instantly lowered, and the crews got on our bit of ice, shook our hands, and peeped curiously into the dirty tins we had used over the oil-fires. We had been making soup out of the blood and entrails of our last little seal. They soon saw enough to convince them that we were in sore need. They took the women and children in their boats, while we tumbled into our own, bringing Captain Hall's little desk, but leaving behind all else—and our all was simply a few battered smoky tin pans and the *débris* of our last seal! It had already become offal in our eyes.

On climbing on board, I was at once surrounded by sealers filled with curiosity to know our story, and all asking questions of me and the men. I told them who I was, and where we were from. But when they asked me, "How long have you been on the ice?" and I answered, "Since the 15th of last October," they were so astonished that they fairly looked blank with wonder.

One of the *Tigress*'s crew, looking at me with open-eyed surprise, exclaimed,

"And was you on it night and day?"

The peculiar expression and tone, with the absurdity of the question, was too much for my politeness, and in spite of myself I laughed and laughed—painful though that forgotten exercise was—in fact finding it no easy matter to stop.

The captain came along and invited me down into the cabin. There we sat talking of our "Wonderful," or, as he called it, "Miraculous" escape, some half an hour, and I became very hungry, having eaten nothing since the night before. And I wanted a smoke *so* much; but I saw no signs of either food or tobacco. Finally I asked him if he would give me a pipe and some tobacco. He soon procured both from his mate, or "Second Hand," and I had a good long puff—the first I had had since many dreary days in our hut. This "Second Hand" then quietly offered to bring me a "breakfast dram" of spirits, but this I declined. In course of time breakfast came along—codfish, boiled potatoes, hard bread, and coffee. I fell upon this plain food with a keenness which the reader may find it hard to grasp; in truth, no subsequent meal can ever surpass it to my taste, so long habituated to raw meat, with all its uncleanly accessories. No one, unless they have been deprived of civilized food and cooking for as long as I have, can begin to imagine how good a cup of coffee, with bread and *butter,* tastes! Never in my life did I enjoy a meal like that. Plain as it was, I shall never forget that codfish and potatoes.

On board the Tigress, *May 1.* How strange it seems to lie down at night in these clean quarters, and feel that I have no more care, no responsibility! To be *once more clean*—what a comfort! Captain Bartlett has all his boats down this morning, sealing. Numbers of seals are to be seen lying on the ice. Our tireless Joe has joined in with them, and is in all his glory. God bless the good and kind Captain Bartlett! He is very kind indeed; so are all the ship's company. We sail, in a few more days, for St John's.

May 1, Here in v. simple quarters, stench of Seal fat ambiant yet can think of no finer Luxury! No sweeter Joy! And savoured alone, in one's own small v. clean Cabin. All are safe. Ice-Master Woodfine says Jamka's 2 Ft. must be amputated on arrival St J's perhaps up to the Knee or worse. But he & Meyer shd Live! & in 2 nights time under covered Deck theres to be a "Ball" in honor of Rescue. A last Irony for none of us I believe will have strength for a single Reel, or Square!

Tukulito has fixed her hair for the occasion, her braids prettily redone with Punnie's help, looped back behind her ears, a plain woad dress of homespun wool on her, pinned up at the sleeves and the hem—a forgotten ship's dress of Mrs Woodfine, who used to accompany her husband to the sealing grounds every spring, until the children came. Ice Master Woodfine has made a gift of it to Tukulito. Tukulito, working overnight and through the day, has sewn a little dress for Punnie from a tartan wool blanket that Captain Bartlett has given her. A little brown Highlander she looks now, says the captain, who has loaned Tyson his dress uniform, the one he usually saves for the morning of their return to St John's, which will be in less than a week now. Woodfine and Second Hand Squires have lent Meyer and Kruger some plain, decent clothes, but the rest of the crew have only their fur trousers and their washed but tattered sweaters, and whatever spare things the sealers can find for them. Ebierbing and Hans and his family remain in their sullied furs. Says Woodfine, I can't recall no other occasion any lot made our boys look so damn fine.

There's an accordion, a fiddle, spoons, and the younger sealers get straight on the pace, of course, because the ship's hold and forehatch and even this topdeck's edges are baled with good pelts and the voyage ending and the captain turning a blind eye to the circulation of rum, tots of rum fortifying the tea in their tin mugs, and at first the men jig or hornpipe, solo—the clatter of planking flashed over the deck to shield it from hobnailed boots—and a few other men jump in and now the natives are among them, sweeping the floor clear, parents and children square-dancing in the bounding, boisterous style they've adapted from the Arctic whalers, with ease turning these tunes to their purpose, so the sealers must either dance with them or move aside and watch. Some choose one, some the other, but above all they watch Tukulito, dressed as if to teach the dance to the other Esquimaux, but not moving with a teacher's measured, monitoring air, she's flushed like the little ones and equally possessed, abandoned, which strikes the sealers as unexceptional, they've heard of this native exuberance, this love of the dance—and they haven't spent the last two years with her. Her white fellow-survivors are dumbstruck. As she gallops and stamps down the reel-road with her shrieking daughter, to the chugging of the squeezebox and the fiddle's skirling—dumbstruck. Loose planks slapping under the dancers' boots. Seal-oil lanterns swinging on their pegs. And Kruger, lax-jawed, also stares, then feels his face stretching, mirroring her delight and displaying his awe at this latest revelation. Interpreter, mother, mender, marksman, master butcher, burglar, stepmother, diplomat, rescuer, now passionate dancer. Loving her is like loving the population of a small city. You can see the lightness of relief in her, as if she's abruptly exempt from the force of gravity. And Tyson, standing squared beside Captain Bartlett across the deck, the toe of one polished boot tapping—he looks years lighter too.

Herron launches himself on this whirling herd and his cheeks, already starting to plump out again, are the jocund red of Madeira, his full-lunged laughter rising over the sealers' stomping and clapping, their chorus of "Dear Doctor John," your cod-liver oil is so pure and so strong, and now Jackson joins with Herron, a borrowed, too-big felt cap low over his eyes, skull shaved clean, and together they gallop down deck through the yipping gauntlet, I'm afraid for me life I'll go down in the soil, if me wife don't stop drinking that cod-liver oil. Lindermann clumps into the reel, flap-footed, the biggest figure on deck, Madsen and Lundquist the next to yield. Only a few of the watchers are silent. Seated on stools along the gunwale with mugs of spiked tea are Meyer, palely shaved and groomed, his cheek on his hand, elbow on his knee—a pensive general in exile—and Jamka, his doomed feet swathed in bandages. They stare glassily, though less in rueful defeat, it appears, than a kind of burnt-out serenity. They're alive. Only Anthing, slouched against the gunwale smoking, wears a bitter look. Only he seems outside the jamboree. His bandage has been removed, head shorn, and except for the lurid welt at his temple, the dome is white as a toadstool. Kruger wonders if he and Tukulito might have spared the world some small, future misery by finishing him when they had the chance.

But Kruger can no longer resist the rhythm, the release, the riotous delight of the dancers, and he is out among them, biding his moment, then slipping in and pounding down the long reel-road with Tukulito, wanting to move faster and wilder in the elation of the act, yet also slow things down, to make the passage last. It does last long enough that, face to face, and with a row of other faces blurring behind her, she smiles deep into him, a real smile, and it hits him that never before has he fully seen her teeth—stubby, small as a child's, but straight, nearly white—let alone this flash of the glistening red gums.

And there is a moment, some hours later, Kruger pitching, yawing drunk though he has had only four or five tots, when he meets her between decks, by the rope locker, she returning from the head, which he is trying to find, or is it she he is trying to find, and as they come face to face he is brought up straight, as if by a pinch of snuff or a dunking. Dim lanterns sway at either end of the passage. From the deck above, stamping and the clatter of the raw-boards. He reaches for her. She closes her eyes and sags, like somebody walking a plank, into his circling arms. He kisses her forehead, hard, feels the heat of her exertion, tastes sweat, grips the back of her head to turn her face up toward his, expecting resistance, but her lips have already reached his own. A firm, humid, clumsy kiss. She pushes him back and mutters what must be a kind of oath, or profanity, in her language.

But I love you, Tukulito.

You must leave me now, sir.

I don't know what else to do, he says. Forgive me.

Please, sir. An amber tear starts down her cheek. With the clipped nail of her trigger finger she flicks it away. As if expert at the practice. Already her face is being reined back to impassivity. The slate has been swept clear. None of this has happened.

Tukulito, he says, I beg of you. Don't leave. This might be our last moments this way.

I must, sir.

This once, at least, let me hear you say my name!

I shall never forget you either, she says.

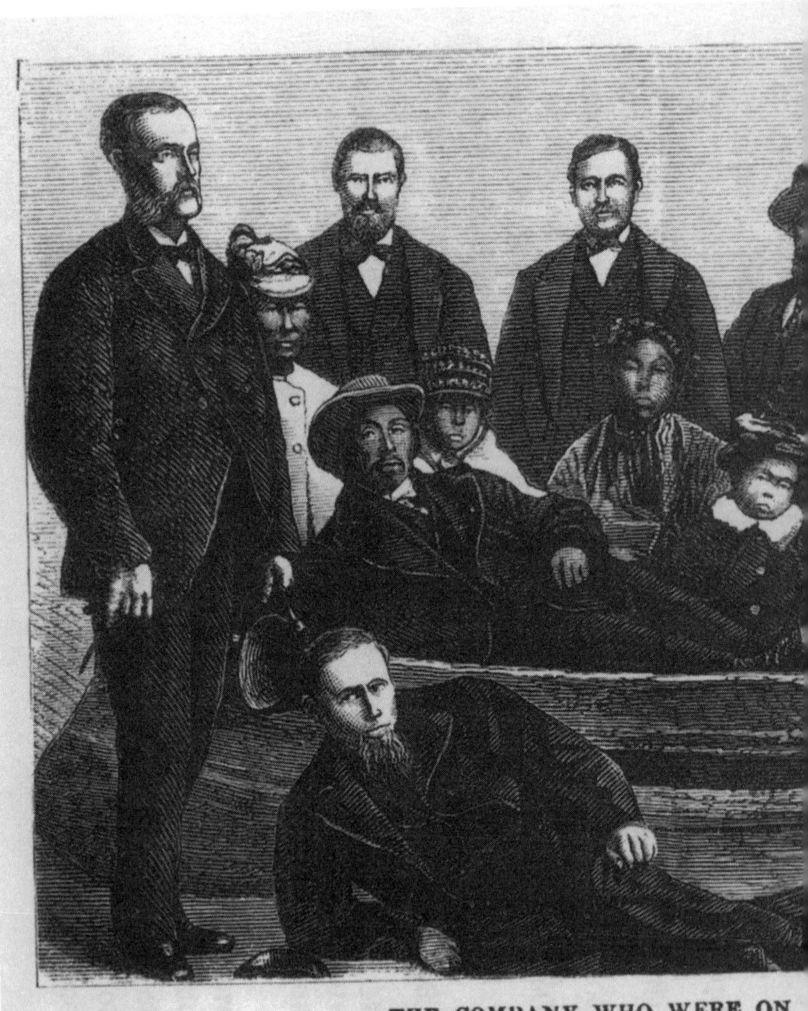

THE COMPANY WHO WERE ON

-DRIFT WITH CAPTAIN TYSON.

THREE

A F T E R

LANDS

It seems to me that the days of the "Innuits" are numbered. There are very few of them now. Fifty years may find them all passed away, without leaving one to tell that such a people ever lived.

—CHARLES FRANCIS HALL, 1864

The noble man will end by having nowhere to live.

—IVAN TURGENEV, 1879

Hoped to shadow the three of you, into the afterlands
of your lives—strange-eyed expatriates (like any survivors)
there for a while in media follow-ups, photo ops, Whatever
Became Of features, but always slipping a little farther
into the public's visual periphery. Tyson finds
a man can't eat homage. Tukulito conjures
with a kind of nostalgia the basalt tors
and ice tongues of Baffin Land, as seen from the floe—
for at least from that point in time her family
was unscattered. And Kruger in Mexico:
how history, the world's memory, seems as difficult
to flee as one's own—as inescapable as the sea,
that eternal kiss-taste of salt.

Hartford, Connecticut, March 1877

INDEED, DESPITE EVERYTHING, I rejoice in this opportunity of returning to those Arctic lands and seas which I have come to know so intimately.

Tyson closes the calfskin folder of lecture notes. Again his hands grip the edges of the rostrum, like a ship's wheel, to keep them steady. Speaking in public has gotten no easier, although he has done plenty of it in the years—almost four now—since his return from the Arctic. Then again, over the last year or so the invitations have been dwindling. This evening the Main Street Memorial Hall is half empty. That means fewer questions from the audience, at least. Tyson follows a script in his lectures, which are carefully revised by the squinting, priggish snuff-addict that Harper & Brothers assigned to help him with *Arctic Experiences* in '73, but answering questions is different. The paying audiences for these fund-raising lectures tend to be educated and upper tier. Forced to improvise, Tyson believes that his humble origins and lack of polish are exposed.

The electric house lights flare on. The moderator, in wing collar and tails, is beside him. A grave, long, sallow face.

Now Captain Tyson, hero of the Arctic, will be pleased to receive your questions.

The familiar tickling heat under his naval collar (he's wearing his dress uniform as captain of the Howgate Expedition, which is to sail for the Arctic in June) blossoms up into his cheeks and forehead and scalp. He rocks slightly from foot to foot, as if itching for crude action: the way he would prefer to deal with certain insolent questions he sometimes receives. It's not just the old problem of the officer who can't adjust to civilians' liberty not to salute and show due respect. It's a matter of caste, too. If the last few years have taught him anything, it's that no success can fully atone for the circumstances of your birth. Make something of yourself and the elite will greet you warmly at the door, even invite you into the parlour for the evening—a social exhibit or adornment, a curio!—but their inner sanctums will remain fastened. That's the world's way, of course, and if it's bad here, it must be that much worse in other countries, but he'd believed that an achievement of sufficient greatness would surely topple all barriers, erase all borders.

And maybe it would have, for another man. Maybe *he* is the problem. He knows that some people have the glad capacity to make others like them, even against their will—the sort of man who could seduce somebody's wife with ease, then charm the cuckold out of a duel or a lawsuit. And how is that done? Tyson wants to be loved as well as respected and feared, but he can't seem to make it happen. He's still trying to win the world over by dint of sheer will. Charm would be a better bet. A sort of anti-charm is what he seems to have. His achievement was to have stood in for this missing aptitude, but it takes him only so far: through the front door and into the parlour of other people's hearts, but not into the inner sanctum.

Yes, please, the moderator intones. The gentleman in the second row?

Captain Tyson, the man says, clearing his throat and rising—a scrawny, elongated man with spectacles and red mutton chops.

What measures do you and Mr Howgate intend to undertake in order to forestall, ah, any unrest among the crew of the *Florence?* Have you signed on any foreigners for this voyage?

Foreigners, Tyson begins, a touch stiffly. I guess you mean immigrants by that. And unrest, on the *Polaris*—why, as you know from my full account—I mean to say, if you've read it, my book—it was only one or two men, mainly. Meyer, Kruger. There's always a troublemaker or two aboard ship and only God Himself could know beforehand who. The unrest, uh, it was dealt with effectively. Unrest is maybe not the word, I think . . . And Tyson blusters on, as if blatantly accused of something.

At the naval inquiry a month after the rescue, he was first made to realize that he could still be demoted to uncertainty, even fear. When the three examiners pressed him, gently and in private, on the matter of his own boozing during the voyage, and whether perhaps the men under his command might reasonably have felt unsure of him, he, George E. Tyson, storied survivor of shipwreck, marooning, exposure, starvation, near-mutiny, assault by enormous carnivores, etc. etc., felt that old unwelcome gut-lurching and chill in the limbs, the quaver of a voice suddenly pitched a few notes too high; the instinctive cringe of a small man, cornered. In this case by powerful authority. On the ice, when threatened, he had been more angry than frightened, but that threat had come in the physical realm, of which he was a citizen in good standing. This was different. This was entrenched society's old threat of disgrace—its most effective resort, against which even a strongman or champion prizefighter is helpless. *We will cast you adrift on your own private floe.*

And God was gone now, too. The final court of appeal.

Gradually sensing what the examiners really wanted—to minimize any stink of failure and scandal—Tyson had rescinded some of his thornier allegations against Budington, the man who had apparently deserted them on the ice. The examiners were then pleased to drop their admittedly minor complaints against Tyson. Delighted, actually. They needed as many heroes, greater and lesser, as possible to float free of the expedition's wreckage. The inquiry ruled that no one had been at fault in the matter of the castaways' stranding; that there had been no mutiny among the crewmen, only some "discord under duress" and a little petty theft; that any drinking among the officers had been minor and had not affected their conduct or command.

The inquiry adjourned without having heard yet from Budington and the thirteen other men on the still-lost *Polaris*. But by the end of the summer they too had been rescued, by a Scottish whaler off the coast of Greenland, where they had been stranded and helped through the winter by the Esquimaux. On their return to America they were brought to Washington. The questioning was brief. The Navy, satisfied with how its preliminary inquiry had concluded, was not inclined to have fresh testimony affect it. The German doctor was briskly exonerated in Commander Hall's death. Captain Budington was quietly reprimanded for his drinking and allowed to go home, having testified that the *Polaris* was separated from the castaways by a storm (as Tyson had stated himself), after which, he said, he had been in no position to rescue anyone, as the ship was damaged and gradually sinking. The thirteen men who had been with him backed up his story. So did the evidence. Had his, or Tyson's, drinking on board led to the problem in the first place? The question was not asked.

What society doesn't whitewash, history whites out, like a polar storm. After his lectures, Tyson is sometimes asked about some of the expedition's minor characters, who are already fading back to oblivion—mainly Meyer, Herron, Kruger,

Budington, Joe and Hannah. He tells what he knows. Frederick Meyer has been interned in an asylum for the insane near Woodstock, in the Catskills. Herron met a young woman in St John's in their two weeks there after the rescue and has returned to Newfoundland to marry her. As for Kruger, he has fled the area, perhaps the country—Tyson can't say where to. Maybe back to Germany, like several of his compatriots, Anthing, Jamka, and some of the other Germans, the ones who wintered over with Budington. Budington himself has retired to Groton, his nautical career ended in the wake of Tyson's book (in which Tyson stood by the allegations that he'd had to retract during the inquiry). As for Hannah and Joe, they also settled in Groton, but in time Joe grew restless and returned north with another expedition. He was absent when the child, Punnie, died of consumption last November. His ship might possibly return late this summer to Groton, where Hannah remains, weaving and also making fur garments for local people gripped by the current interest in all things Esquimaux. The other natives have returned to Greenland. Lundquist has gone west to Wisconsin, Lindermann south to Raleigh, Madsen north to Canada.

Nobody asks about the Negro, William Jackson. Tyson believes he has joined the army and been shipped west to fight Indians.

The moderator says, You, sir. Please rise.

It's a bald, clean-shaven man seated toward the back of the auditorium, though there are hundreds of vacant seats closer up. The man stands but doesn't get much taller than before. He has a baby face, squashed-looking and sour. His voice is boyishly high and yet forceful and crisp, like the voice of a conceited little prodigy.

Captain Tyson. One hears that Hannah—Mrs Ebierbing—is

not only alone but also ill, and in rather straitened circumstances. Do you know this report to be true, and, if so, what can be done about it? One doesn't wish to see a guest of this country, who has so loyally served it, having to—

I haven't neglected Hannah. I'm aware of her condition, sir. In fact I only recently, ah . . .

I say nothing of your having neglected her, Captain! The man sounds a little surprised. I ask only what can be done.

She is, as you say, she's not been well, and she's . . . (He pauses for what seems to him half an eternity) . . . I believe she misses her home. I did call on her, last month. I offered to take her north with me when I sail in June, Cumberland Sound being her home country, and, ah. We may find her husband there. But she said she, she . . . informed me that she wouldn't leave Groton. I believe that she. . . . Tyson doesn't know whether to quote her word for word, his lack of instinctive decorum again vexing him, like an intricate dance he can't master. Most others seem born knowing the steps. He hears her saying, in a mild and tightly managed voice, *I thank you from the heart, sir, for I would gladly see my husband's face and my home country again. But I cannot leave the grave of my little daughter.* On the last words her voice barely sustains. He takes her small, rough hand into his. He swallows to keep his own throat from clotting. In his lumbering way he too had loved the child.

Here now, in public, he wonders if her admission is too sacred to convey.

Well . . . I believe she fears she'll not see him—her husband. If he returns south as she sails northward.

And her circumstances, Captain?

He stiffens, losing what's left of his patience. He's about to reply curtly when he seems to spot Hannah herself, at the very back of the auditorium, a score of rows behind the questioner.

Small, in black weeds and black bonnet, dark of face—easy to miss in the dimness. For a second he wonders if his memory of visiting her could be conjuring spectres. He squints out. There's no doubt.

Captain Tyson? The moderator speaks levelly but with a catch of concern; Tyson has gained a reputation for awkwardness in the question period. Now he answers, I was unaware that she, that her circumstances had become difficult. She said nothing of it, to me. I believed the Navy and the Budingtons were seeing to her needs. But, of course, the *Budingtons* . . . He stops himself in time, remembering that she cares for the Budingtons very much. I'll, I shall certainly try to help her out, at once. (He has a commission and a new uniform and a published book, but very little money.)

The audience is dead silent. Hannah's own silence, stillness, like Banquo at Macbeth's table, seem to accuse him of various things. Tyson too has a single child he is afraid to leave behind. And now a mistress, a beautiful widow named, of all things, Mrs Meyers. She too wears black, in public. He is never seen with her in public and will not be until he returns again from the north. His one or two years up there will surely complete the rift between himself and his wife that the *Polaris* voyage started. When I sail for the north, he has told Mrs Meyers, I will actually be sailing toward you.

And away from little George, forever.

On this voyage he must achieve something bigger. Only that way will his divorce be publicly overlooked, or even forgiven—who knows?—and his prospects not all destroyed. His prospects must not be destroyed. He will have two households to support.

If there aren't further questions now, he says brusquely before the moderator can invite anyone else to rise, I'll thank you for your attendance this evening. Good night.

He remembers to shake the moderator's flaccid hand and tries to excuse himself—he wants to hurry off, find Hannah, maybe she is here to speak to him, surely she didn't come up to Hartford only to hear his lecture, she must mean to ask for his help, she may have decided to come north with his ship after all. He prides himself on being in a position to help. And he owes her and Joe at least this much. The moderator's grip tightens. His other hand on Tyson's gold-braided epaulette: Captain, they would like to meet with you, several of the audience, fellows of the Hartford Geographical Society, to escort you to their club for punch and sandwiches. Tyson nods impatiently. Fine, thanks, but I must speak to Hannah first. Quizzically the man cocks his head. Hannah, says Tyson—Esquimau Joe's wife. She's here. He pulls his hand free and gestures toward the back of the auditorium. People filing slowly up the centre aisle toward the main doors. Tyson can't pick her out.

Are you certain you saw her, Captain?

Another man in wing collar and tails blocks his road. I do hope you'll be able to join us, Captain!

It would be a pleasure, he says tersely—the right words, the wrong tone and delivery, Tyson as always yanked between scorn for these pompous landlings and a yearning to be admired by them, inducted into their inner circle. It stalls him now. The man saying, I enjoyed especially your depictions of the polar night and the aurora borealis, sir, which I daresay must have been rather a difficult phenomenon to (etc. etc.), while Tyson nods and tries to smile, glancing around the building in search of her. She's gone. The seats are empty. The aisles emptying too. Of course—he'd informed the whole Goddamned auditorium that he meant to help her, at once! That drove her away. She is half a New Englander, after all. She'll have slipped out the doors the moment he finished. *Salvaging my pride at the price of hers.*

I did find your book to be the most fascinating and accurate of all such recent volumes, Captain, and there have been a great many indeed, as you will discover at our club, they take up a full wall of our library . . . (etc. etc.).

Helplessly deflected by the praise, Tyson allows himself to be led off.

Groton, Connecticut, March 1877

Last November the child's walnut coffin was lowered into the clay of Starr Hill, like a small lifeboat over the side of a foundering ship. March is the mirror-season of November. Same winds, stripped hardwoods, scuttering sepia leaves, stubble fields; each year the funeral will have two anniversaries. She has not been up to Starr Hill for several days, and this morning she missed the Reverend Cowan's Sunday service. Through her parlour window a baluster of thin, late afternoon sunlight slopes in. The window looks onto Pleasant Valley Road, near the Four Corners, on the town's scattered outskirts. Across the road, beyond a split-rail fence, an acre or so of Mr Copps's farm: a fallow hillside with gravelly snow lingering in the hollows.

She has been too tired to walk up to Starr Hill. Just a mile there and back. The cough is steadily gaining on her, as it did on the child, and the grieving part of Tukulito (and what part of her, really, is not grieving?) almost welcomes this progress. True, there's still the corner of her heart that hopes to see her husband again, yet at the same time she fears his grief, fears to relive through him the first week of her own wild grief, when her heart, it seemed, was being footed out, the way the hunters of Cumberland Sound, having killed a mother caribou, will kill the fawn: running it down, then pressing a boot firmly over the ribcage until the pressure stills the heart.

On Monday afternoon Mrs Budington comes to her with a letter from Mexico; for the last few weeks the woman has been picking up any mail for Tukulito, at Daboll's store. This is a favour Tukulito can accept because she can repay it with immediate hospitality. As they sit in the draughty parlour sipping tea, served with the currant scones Tukulito has baked for the visit, Mrs Budington attempts to interest her in the envelope's odd, furzy yellow paper, and the cochineal postmark, which looks, she says, as though it were made with a child's potato stamp. (Tukulito's throat narrows and throbs.) A former schoolma'am, she's very tall, big-shouldered and -bosomed, with a warm brown tone to her unwrinkled skin. She wears hefty schooner-like hats over chestnut hair streaked with grey, and leans well forward over any table as if impatient to be right upon her companions as she condoles, exhorts, instructs, protests, her gaze fervent and fixed. Forgetting herself she will wrap her large hands around her teacup, as if for warmth, while Tukulito always holds the little handle as she learned to do in England: pinched lightly between thumb and forefinger, the pinkie daintily extended.

Do open the letter, Hannah! the woman finally says, with an almost manic vivacity. Our poor Mr Kruger—driven out of his adopted country by that awful liar! But *we* shan't be driven off, shall we, Hannah?

No, ma'am. Tukulito has learned to say nothing of Mr Tyson, simply allowing Mrs Budington to purge herself of the gathered acid until her natural warmth of character returns.

Well, let us hope he never gets home from his next voyage. He don't deserve to! Maybe this time his crew will do for him properly. If only he'd taken *Micks* last time, instead of Dutchmen!

Do you care for another scone, ma'am?

They're very good. Will you not open the letter, my dear?

Tukulito elects to interpret this pushiness as benevolent, an aspect of Mrs Budington's desire to divert and encourage her, not the nosy fascination of a gossip. Besides, the woman can have no idea of the sentiments Mr Kruger expressed to her on the ice, and aboard the *Tigress;* nor, for that matter, of her own sentiments.

Not that his letter will make any clear reference to such things.

Ma'am, I am most anxious to hear our friend's news, and I shall read his letter to you when next you visit—but for now I should prefer to save the letter, until such time as I have but my own poor company for amusement. Your presence here is too welcome to interrupt.

Mrs Budington's calf-brown eyes brim with affection, but also, it seems, with admiration of Tukulito's diplomatic eloquence. Admiration flecked with the usual surprise. The same look Tukulito used to translate from local faces when Punnie would perform her Mendelssohn.

After Mrs Budington's departure she still does not open the letter. She will save it. She has piecework to finish: a pair of sealskin kamiks for a clam fisherman in New London, for which she has just finished chewing the skins, in the Inuit fashion, to soften them. Now she must cut and sew together the parts on her cherished machine, a Howe & Singer with a webwork cast-iron treadle. This wondrous American invention shares the front parlour, the house's main room, with a table and chairs, the box-like cast-iron stove that she no longer troubles to keep properly fuelled, and Punnie's spinet, a gift of the Budingtons before the *Polaris* voyage, when the Budingtons were still fairly prosperous. She may have to sell it before long. She cannot sell it. Nobody has touched the keyboard since Punnie's death, not even the child's piano teacher Mr Chusley, on his occasional visits, when he sucks on cloves and blushes and fidgets with his saucer and can hardly stammer more than a word.

In the two months after Punnie's death, and especially around Christmas, visitors came often, neighbours like the Budingtons, Mr Copp, the Reverend Cowan, Mr Daboll, Dr Steiger, and Miss Crombie, the schoolma'am. The Walker sisters, Punnie's classmates, would sometimes stop by, bringing their mother's fresh bread-loaves and soda biscuits. But over the brunt of the winter these visits died off. A cruelly cold winter. She feels this seaboard cold in a way that she never felt cold in the north. Or could it be her increasing thinness? And Punnie alone in that snow-clad earth, wrapped in her counterpane but unprotected by her own mother. . . . At some point she began to avoid the front window in the morning and late afternoon when the children would chatter past on their way to and from the Skunk Lane School.

On Tuesday Mrs Budington brings another letter. On foot, she's on her way to visit an ill friend. *Another* ill friend, is how she actually puts it (eyeing Tukulito with conspicuous concern) before catching herself, biting her underlip, her embarrassment obvious in a childlike way that both moves and amuses Tukulito, as it often does. The woman then turns her gaze sharply on the letter, which she holds by its corner like a soiled handkerchief.

If he means to invite you to return north again, do repeat your refusal, Hannah. Enough of us have set a curse on that ship, he'll be lucky to clear Nantucket before he goes down.

I shall stay near you, Pretty Mother. (Her old name for Mrs Budington.) Won't you come in?

But she can't, not today. After a hurried exchange she bustles off, swift despite her size, leaning forward over the road with her skirts hiked as if fording a gutter, showing high black button-hook boots turned out like a soldier's as she walks.

Tukulito assumes this letter from the lieutenant must contain money, the immediate help that he promised at the end of his lecture. She feels she must not accept it. She took the train up to Hartford not to seek his help but to hear him tell their story again, and to hear him mention her Punnie, which he did, twice. And how her heart had flown at each utterance, as if at a sunlit flash of the beloved face. In a much smaller way it pleased her, too, to see the lieutenant's own face again. She bears him no real grudge over anything he wrote in his book. She knows how the madness of winter confinement and hunger can turn any tongue strange and baleful; and in the later, crucial time, he had acted like a man, and led them all well. As for his slander of Mr Kruger, she feels that the lieutenant has hurtfully leapt to conclusions, but she also believes that Mr Kruger has made too much of things. True, he lost face, but that was several years ago: and did he not always suggest that the opinions of society meant nothing to him? In some mental crevice, perhaps, it satisfies her to find that even he cannot bear being set apart from the tribe, in shame. For now more and more she feels there is nothing but the tribe, only blood and kindred, the little nation of one's firmest affections. And foreigners, even such good folk as her neighbours here in Groton, can only help for so long. They don't quite understand, in the end. In illness she is losing the strength to keep her feet planted in two worlds—on two different floes. More and more difficult, to interpret herself to others. Some things she can say only in Inuktitut. Surely this is what a tribe is for.

She is adrift, then, waiting for her husband.

She opens the letter from Mr Kruger, written just after the New Year in a place called Maria Madre.

Dear Madam,

I send my most sincere wishes for your good health, & for the renewal of your happiness. May your Husband soon return from the North to lend you the company for which you must long, in such days as this! As best I can, I share your loss & mourning still.

As for me, I can not say where I am likely to arrive; for now, I am content to be just a traveller. It is odd that having travelled to this place so very different from the North, I am nonetheless strongly reminded of it, & of some of the people I met there, by certain sights and events, from time to time. And so dear Madam, this letter to You, which I do trust will reach Groton, & find you in the very best of Health.

As ever, I remain your most loyal, & obedient,

R. K.

She reads the letter several times, then folds it and places it back in its envelope and neatly sets it down.

After some moments she carefully slits open the lieutenant's letter. It contains a piece of vellum cardstock, tightly folded. When she opens the card, a ten-dollar bill slips out.

Dear Hannah,

I am told you are facing certain dificulties at present. I hope a small gift will be of some help. I shall certainly write at once to the Secretery of the Navy to urge they should see to your needs better! For few have served more loyally than yourself & Joe. Again I offer you a berth on my Florence, we sail out on June the 21. If Joe be sailing south at the same time, the odds that we should miss him are slight, as we shall be on just the same rout & shall certainly hail & speak any other ship we incounter.

I shall await your reply, & whatever it be, please believe Madam, I am all ways your

Most humble & devoted servant

Geo. E. Tyson

But the gift is impossible, a frustration. The sharing, the receiving of fleeting bounty that seems appropriate and utterly unshameful in the North seems unacceptable to her here. Living in the white world—even now—she must live as a white woman, asking and accepting no special favours. She is a sort of emissary, an emblem of her people, who will be judged according to her actions, perhaps even reconsidered. She knows the white world conceives of her people as brave, but also lazy, dirty, greedy, improvident. This ten-dollar bill feels like a further test of her providence and self-reliance.

Also a deep temptation. It has been months since the U.S. Fish Commission, on one of whose boats her husband now serves, has dispatched a letter with some money. The Budingtons seem all but ruined and she would not accept cash from them anyway. Meanwhile a small mortgage remains to pay on the house. Maintaining this modest house—robin's-egg clapboard, with a parlour, a kitchen, a small bedroom and a workroom on the ground floor, a dormered-gable bedroom above—for her husband's sake, for his homecoming, seems one of her few remaining duties. He must not return to a graveplot on Starr Hill, a few feet of earth, and nothing more.

She turns her thoughts back to him whenever the impulse to end her own pain overcomes her. If he should return to nothing but *two* graveplots! Although at times she thinks it would be no more than he deserves. To add her own death to his beloved daughter's. She was raised to see a hunter's chronic absences as a fact of life, but Ebierbing did not need to leave here, he had work enough as a carpenter and a fisherman; no, he wanted to go, he was restless, partly, she knows, for Cumberland Sound and partly, no doubt, for its women. His philandering has always hurt her, and was the thing that first made her determined to try living in the South, where such adventuring would be impossible—so she had confided to Father Hall. But now he is gone again anyway. And the government agency that was to have sent her a monthly portion of his pay is silent. She is afraid of what this could mean. His ship might be missing, feared lost.

She cannot bring herself to write a note of inquiry to Washington, both out of pride in her independence, and for fear they will confirm the worst—and with this recurring fear, her anger resolves back into the love she has borne for him since a girl of twelve, twenty-six years ago. Again she sees that she must not hasten her own death. Not that it would be a sin, in her own people's eyes. In their vision, heaven is not unlike the Christian heaven, a bright and joyous realm high above, a place of eternal song and festivity, while hell, far below, is always gloomy and sunless and bitterly cold. The kind people of Cumberland Bay go to heaven, the unkind to hell. But their Afterlands differ from the white realms in one important way: any Inuk who dies by suicide will certainly go to heaven.

For some minutes she sits staring at the ragged bill, grainy, almost fuzzy with age and handling. Mr Franklin's eyes are worn to a look of ancient blindness, as if by cataracts. At last she picks it up along with the lieutenant's letter and passes through the small kitchen into the downstairs bedroom, where the restored escritoire—Father Hall's writing desk—waits under the window. She can see her breath. She sits on the adjustable stool, takes one of her last envelopes from a sliding over-drawer, slips the bill into the envelope and coughs violently, too suddenly to cover her mouth, so that flecks of bloody sputum strike the front of the envelope like a spattering of red ink. She pulls a handkerchief from her apron-fold and dabs her lips, places the barely stained envelope in the wicker trash basket, and gets out another. From the lap-drawer she takes a notecard, a small bottle of indigo ink and a pen.

Dear Sir,

Grateful as I am for your most generous gift, I must now return it to you. You have been misinformed in this respect Sir, for my circumstances are not such as to require this generosity. Never the less, I am moved. Further I thank you again for your kind offer of passage North, on your FLORENCE; how ever I can not accept this further kindness; I believe I did explain something of my reason for remaining in Groton. I thank you, finally, Sir, for inquiring after my health. I am well enough, and am kept busy here. Should you encounter, on your journey North, the schooner RACHEL, bearing my husband home to Groton, I beg you, Sir, say nothing to him of our little girl! He must learn of it from me. Please say only that his family awaits him with impatience, and expectation.

Sir, I remain, as ever, your most truly loyal and humble Servant,

Hannah

Tukulito blots the note dry and seals the envelope. She returns to the parlour, undrapes the sewing machine and seats herself on the stool. These kamiks can be finished by dusk if she can forgo an afternoon rest. She is behind on her piecework only because she has been needing, badly, to rest every afternoon. But these boots she will complete, and then make a start on the short fur jumper that she has agreed to sew for a Budington cousin: a

Yankee style, but made with caribou furs softened in the native fashion instead of wool. She foots the treadle, legs heavy and stiff, then hears the whir of the flywheel, the jigging hum of the needle, a vital domestic din to contradict the stone-silence of the house. These sounds can soothe her into a trance in which her burden seems to lighten and float somewhat free of her, while she works automatically, but in recent weeks, throes of dredging coughs have put her off the rhythm, shredding the spell, or else the machine's hypnotic droning weighs her head and her eyelids in mere fatigue, only the needle's stab shocking her back to vigilance. . . . Already dreamy, in fever, she is joining the hide sole to the fur upper, fingers framing and guiding the seam under the needle as if stitching a coastline from far above, a raven's view, grey hide for the bouldered shoreline, white fur of an ocean still cowled in ice.

Purificación, Chihuahua State, March 1877

SLEEPING ON WATER AGAIN brings Kruger bad dreams. Or call them something else, the compulsive flashbacks of a survivor. One night, on jolting awake in the houseboat, he describes to Jacinta the one about the bear, the white bear scooping the dome off the crewmen's snowhut and bobbing giant paws down at them. It has returned to him several times since the fiesta in Maria Madre; Jacinta refuses to believe it is anything but a nightmare of the sort any of her three children might have, especially in the sleeps preceding the full moon, which—she points out with a languid gesture, a groggy note of triumph—it now is. He stares up into the roofless rectangle of sky framed by the houseboat's walls. No moon is in evidence. The crowded stars (including, yes, the Great Bear) are beginning to dim. It must be near dawn. So he has slept through the night, finally.

And often the children, they too feel it has really happened—the Padre on his horse has caught up with them. I suppose you will want your comfort now.

She says it with a sort of coy annoyance.

This transaction of savage narrative and wry incredulity is complicated by language, or its shortfall. Kruger, swift to learn, has gained much Spanish in the weeks since leaving Maria Madre and journeying south, but his ability remains modest.

Jacinta herself is at best adequate in the language. Her father, like most of the villagers here, was pure Sina, and as a child she mainly spoke the Sina tongue, certain key elements of which she is trying to entice Kruger into learning. It's probably more for her own amusement, Kruger guesses, than for any ultimate motive. Bodily parts. Bodily functions. Clearly she has no illusions about converting him into a husband so as to pre-empt time and allow her to retire from her profession in dignity, before age forces her out. For one thing, he is an outsider. For another thing, he has no property and little money and no prospects, and he professes little concern with such things. Still, she's very fond of him. She always calls him by his surname, strongly trilling both r's. Krrugarr. Krrugarr, I have never had such a *visitante* as you! Her word for what he is to her. She says that business has dwindled here, become at best sporadic. The village is shrinking. The highway that Lerdo built after the death of the great *indio* Presidente Juarez means that travellers must now pass a half day's ride to the east.

Purificación is a village of cubic, cocoa-coloured adobe huts and a domed church hunkered in the crook of a river looping down through high desert out of the sawback western range of the Sierra Madre. Built upon and out of the same desert earth, the clumped huts from a distance could be seen as an accident of nature, a minor and localized irruption of the land. Perhaps the village would rather not be seen. Kruger knows the feeling.

The houseboat is really just a pine crate open at the top—a bed on floats walled in by iconed planks, with a skylight of stars, and for the August rains a ceiling sheet of oilcloth folded on the tiny deck. A man from Gallego built it as a shop that could be floated downriver from village to village and then shore-hauled back upstream by burro, but soon after opening it he was beaten to death at the cantina. A difference of opinion, involving soldiers.

Jacinta had then claimed the houseboat and for a while she was kept busy enough. But for the past few years the only men who have visited the boat are silver miners coming down from their encampment twelve miles upstream and occasional peddlers and soldiers—the troops of the liberal Lerdo replaced just after the new year by troops of the *caudillo* Diaz, as if in accord with an elemental process, the forcible change of government as natural as the parade of the seasons. Jacinta has told Kruger that he is something of a godsend. Not only is he gentle—except for his starved, incessant biting, which she happens to enjoy—but also it is rare for visitors to remain more than a few days, let alone weeks. There is little here for an outsider besides the high desert's aloof beauty, and the few who come through the region are not here for that.

Kruger loves the desert for its silence and its daytime heat, but this scoured *páramo*, these fading ranges and the air's clarion transparency remind him too much of the arctic wilds where they buried Captain Hall. And the nights are cold. He hopes to reach the Pacific coast by late spring. He doesn't say that he hopes to find in the strong sun and the heat a forgetting of the Arctic with its weather of the grave, and, in the South's fabled levity and disarray, asylum from the world's closing tangle of flags and marching orders. He says he's not looking for gold or silver, or smuggling contraband to Chihuahua City, or seeking the bounties on Lerdo's fugitive partisans—for he himself is a sort of fugitive, a refugee from his own name, his disgrace. And from certain other memories, he adds gruffly. Here he pauses, smiles slightly. Of course, that can be said of any traveller.

Jacinta informs him that he is well liked here, though naturally everyone knows him to be one of Diaz's spies. All the same, she tells him, they are truly fond of you. Now, had you asked them to conceal you when you arrived, they would have taken you for one of Lerdo's men, *un fugitivo*, and driven you away. Given you water and food perhaps and driven you away. But as you insist on sleeping in a blanket by the river and eating minnows and *tuahmec* and smoking *macuche* and drinking *pulque* in the cantina, and making visits to me, they deduce you are a gentleman spy, pretending. And of course they *enjoy* the pretence. . . . She says they love especially how he clowns with the village children, amusing them with his funny Spanish, allowing them to teach him new words, to catch and tackle him en masse. How he is not afraid for his dignity. Their belief that it's all a cunning act does not deter their appreciation. They are flattered to have their own spy. They know besides that there's nothing here for any spy to learn.

Kruger quits gnawing on her plump upper arm, so peppery by the armpit, for long enough to say, One of Señor Diaz's spies is exactly what I would never be. Not his man or anybody else's. I'll never wear another uniform.

If gringo spies wear uniforms when they work, you people are even more foolish than we thought. Still, it's not impossible. None of you knows the first thing about concealing your feelings when you must. As if you don't care enough about them to hide them safely away!

Surely you don't all really think I'm a gentleman?

I suppose I believe you, but there's no convincing the others.

Couldn't I be simply a vagabond? A thief?

Spies are *always* gentlemen. And they know you must have money to be travelling like this—peddling nothing along the way, performing no useful work.

In the darkness her smile glows faintly as if with starlight. That grey front tooth half-capped with silver. A few grey filaments glow amid her bangs and those thick black braids that she unleashes only when aboard the boat. She's just about to do it. She kisses the bridge of his nose.

And so handsome and tall.

I have blue teeth and I am hardly taller than you. And look at my clothing.

But your boots are always polished.

He grins, giving her her due. That's just old discipline.

Military discipline!

But think of my condition when I came here, he protests—on foot! And these hands. You always complain they're too rough. Ah, and my Spanish. How can I possibly be a gentleman?

But that is the genius of your disguise, she concludes—then adds hastily, Or so the others believe.

So she herself is unsure, clearly. Again he brings up the pension he receives from the German government because of his fifteen-year-old wound. (It's a pittance and impossible to collect anywhere outside major cities.) She has seen that scar, even kissed it. Yet she's as dubious about distant naval engagements and his "pension" as she is about his half year adrift on a raft of ice among the white bears and *indios* of the Arctic.

Tyson's account of those events is one of the few things Kruger carries. He could show it to her. She doesn't read, but the book contains—along with several poor images of Tukulito—an engraving of the party made after the rescue, and Kruger is in it, although his face is reduced and unclear enough that she might doubt him still, or doubt him more, believe he's gripped by wishful delusions rather than a traveller's natural temptation to invent or inflate without fear of being challenged. The engraving was made from a photograph for which he'd shaved off his beard, keeping only a neat moustache. He wears a black bow tie and the vested brown serge suit and fobbed watch that the U.S. consulate purchased for him in St John's. The developing process made him look even darker than he was and the engraving compounded the effect. Given the role that Tyson assigned him in the narrative, this seems apt.

She refuses likewise to believe he is thirty-three. You are forty, she says in a tone of nonchalant finality. One always knows by the teeth.

All right then—he chuckles around the glued stem of his pipe—I am forty. Fifty!

Jacinta will not say her own age, although he guesses close to thirty. She is tall for a local, lushly padded, and her shrewd, amusable eyes are so dark that the pupil and iris seem one. In the dimness or when sleeping she reminds him, of course, of Tukulito, but any resemblance is shattered by the slightest movement or speech. Jacinta's proud face is variable where Tukulito's was stoically still; Jacinta is impatient and playful where Tukulito would always seem unruffled, enclosed.

The houseboat is moored dubiously to charred pilings sunk in the river's steep banks. Two flitches of rough-planed cedar bridge the gap between the shore and deck. Between the boat and the adobe house where Jacinta lives with her mother and two daughters and little boy (her husband was borne off some years ago by an army press-gang) stretches a half acre where the children dodge among scraggy fowl, hyena-like mongrels, and a goat that vapidly crops and munches the scourgrass. The mother in her black shawls sits glowering on a ladderback chair in the doorway. Hunched forward with mummy-brown hands spread on her knees, slippers planted firmly in the dirt, she seems forever poised to stand up. She never does. She smokes small Mexican cigars. For Kruger, who tips his dented derby to her, she reserves a glare of medieval enmity and malice.

Jacinta seems to feel that her mother's watchful presence, from sunrise onward, is the reason Kruger seldom stays until morning on the houseboat, as she would prefer. Nobody, she declares, sleeps alone who can avoid it. He agrees, but then reminds her of his half-year struggling to sleep with the floe ice grinding its teeth under him, and the watery upheaval under the ice; and he complains of the chill he feels rising out of the snowfed river in the last hours before dawn. At times it triggers those bad dreams—or call them flashbacks. Wakes him to that cold skylight of stars. She dismisses all his complaints: he is far too easy and amiable, at least during the day, to have endured such an ordeal.

But you, he says, kissing her breasts—he's constantly lapping, teething, rooting at her heavy breasts, the long black nipples, while the beefy Christ on the crucifix nested in her cleavage eyes him forbiddingly—You've had—he stops and pulls back and clears his throat—you've had much worse than what we had.

Losing children is a mother's lot. Husbands grow ill or are buried in the mine or fall into the river drunk or are forced into the army. For Mama it was exactly the same. This is simply one's life.

Again she asks how he can possibly prefer rolling up in a horse blanket in the fly-infested grove up the river. How trying it must be for a gentleman to maintain such a facade!

I have my fire and my pipe, he says dryly. Also, one of the village dogs has appointed herself my guardian.

He prefers a fire and a bitch to a woman.

Come sleep with me there, he insists again, earnest now—*es un buen lugar.* And again he tells her of the softness of the leaf-strewn sand under the rustling poplars. She tilts her head back and lifts fierce eyebrows; no respectable woman with a house and children will lie with a man out of doors.

Days he carries out chores for her and fishes and bathes, briefly, in his grove of cottonwood poplars. On their frail stems the leaves, palpitating with a sound like rain, give evidence of winds so faint he can feel nothing. The dog lies limp on her side in the checkered shade, a fog of flies around her. Rising she leaves her shape in the sand. He has fished since boyhood and though the river hardly foams with life and his rod and tackle are makeshift—a bent brad for a hook, a musket ball for a sinker—he has some success, even trading the odd catfish or *tuahmec* to the cantina for a meal. For the rest, whatever he doesn't fry up with cornmeal and scrounged peppers for himself and the dog he brings to Jacinta in the evening in lieu of payment. Not until he gets to Chihuahua City will he be able to get his next pension cheque and he has only a few pesos besides. Food for the favours of her body. There is a simple rightness to this elemental exchange. And she *enjoys* making love with him, he believes, though how can he be certain of anything about a people who, as she has told him herself, have had to learn to disguise or conceal so much? She says he is her favourite visitor. *Visitante*, he says, yes, that's what every man is, whether he's married to the woman or paying for her love.

I wish you spoke Sina, she says irritably. I never understand your Spanish.

A man is in a woman's body, he says, speaking slower, and for as long as it lasts he knows nothing else, but then he is . . . *¿qué? Como un exilado.* Forced out again—back into the cold. *¡Como odio ese momento!*

So he delays it as long as he can. Several times he has shuddered awake from his dreams to find that they're still nested in their embrace and sweetly socketed. The discovery is a solace, even with the boat drubbing against the pilings, and the gargling rush of the current below like the sounds of the *Polaris*'s bilges in flood. Sometimes, as if sensing he's awake and thinking of sneaking back to his thicket and his dog—although when he wakes like this, departure is far from his thoughts—she too will partially wake and they make love with an astonished rough suddenness, warm odours of bedstraw and smudged piñon and her dense peppery sweat and his own sweat gusting from under the serapes, a sensual fiesta, and he revels in it all, remembering how in the worst of the polar cold you smelled nothing whatsoever, as if your senses were congealed, as if the men sleeping beside you were frozen corpses. Any smell would have been welcome then. He bites and gnaws at her constantly, savouring her flesh, needing to reconfirm through his mouth her wondrous solidity (the ice has turned him into a sort of cannibal after all). At times she does things he never imagined could be done and always she is wholly silent, the habitual home-courtesy of one who used to entertain *visitantes* in the mud-walled house where children, mother, and ancient father (may he rest in God) slept but a few feet away.

During his month in Purificación, soldiers and miners sometimes pass through and Kruger is displaced—exiled, back into the cold—while Jacinta indulges them serially, sometimes several a night, earning, as she puts it, pesos instead of *pescados*. She is philosophical about it. Or maybe resigned would be the word. Kruger pretends to be untroubled, although gradually, as the days and weeks pass, the pretence becomes more of a test. At times when these brief exiles end he's less tender with her. Sometimes even rough. All right, he finally admits to Perra—a slender russet bitch with a pointy muzzle, prick ears and a full brush tail, as if a dog could be part fox—I'm a little in love with her. But she has her life here, and I have my road. Weeping without tears he lies wrapped in his blanket in the grey sand that after dark holds the heat of the day until suddenly it does no longer and from then on it holds the cold of the night, while Perra, muzzle between forepaws, lies between him and the embers, cocking her ears and her hackles at any sound and growling low in her chest, and at times those sounds are the breeze-borne whimpers and puffing and sobbing of the miners on Jacinta's bed. When it's soldiers, the night is quieter. Maybe it's considered ill luck here for a soldier to make a lover's sounds, since they are pretty much the same ones you hear from the wounded and the dying after combat.

The quiet is welcome, although he's always troubled to see soldiers.

On the road south from Maria Madre to here he had an encounter. He was aboard the scabby, moulting grey mule he'd acquired in Pecos, Texas, in trade for his seaman's overcoat. The trader had told him that between luck and the lash the thing might see him as far as the border, but Kruger had treated the mule with Franciscan forbearance and it had regained some strength. Their road emerged from the cool gloom of an arid gully and swerved south. In a collarless workman's shirt with the top button open, sleeves rolled almost to the shoulders, Kruger felt the sun and the warm air on his throat and inner arms as voluptuous, a vagrant's blessing. The beginning of forgetting. We are happy, he informed the mule. The sages are wrong. A man *can* run away from his troubles. The mule's jackrabbit ears, now accustomed to German, waggled affably.

In the open a hot wind was waiting for them and, sweeping north with the wind, as if equally elemental, a troop of Mexican cavalry cantering two abreast, their bannered lance-heads glittering in a tight, bristling shock, dust and convection blurring them. Far behind to the southwest, a broad mesa like the prehistoric grave mound of a chieftain. The troopers by now must have seen him; he could only ride on toward them. He was about to urge the mule rightward off the road to give way, when the animal in its own private discretion veered left at a spry trot, then came to a halt. It stood on slightly lower ground. As the company pounded past with the bass-heavy thudding of hooves and the clinking of spurs and scabbards and carbines and trappings, the giant chargers and the riders in their tall plumed shakos loomed even huger. For a moment it seemed they would continue riding, perhaps in some pursuit, because the leader—dressed like the officer at the bear and bull fiesta but wearing what looked like a cleric's low, wide-brimmed black hat—didn't seem to notice Kruger. An unarmed man on a decrepit mule hardly would warrant notice. The *lanceros* stared straight ahead as they posted by, pair after pair, wooden wind-up soldiers on mechanical stallions. They wore red sashes and tight short jackets of baize green, their white trousers with gold-buttoned seams fell over star-spurred boots. The nostrils of the horses seemed inflamed like large unhealing wounds and their manes and tails streamed back in the wind like bunting. Kruger got the mule walking. He heard the officer crack out a command. Sharply the men reined in their horses and sat them in loose formation. Kruger, bobbing slowly past the rearguard, thoughtfully tipped his hat. He pretended not to hear the rider galloping up behind him.

¡Alto!

The officer in the priest's hat. Kruger managed to rein in the mule, then tried to make it turn to face the man. It would not. It started trotting away, due south.

¡Alto. Alto en seguida!

Kruger twisted round on the saddle, shrugging, gesturing helplessly at the mule's bald, pistoning rump. He yanked again on the reins but was carried on. The officer called another order. There was a pummelling of hooves. The officer and two *lanceros* hurtled past him, their horses' ears laid back and veiny necks stretched into the gallop, then the men reined in hard and wheeled around in the road, blocking the way. The mule came to a stop, its head sullenly down, ears twitching like antennae.

Kruger squinted up at the men. His palate and tongue were sticky, teeth clenched on the stem of his pipe. The *lanceros'* chin-strapped shakos masked their eyes in shadow and black drooping moustaches concealed their mouths. The one on the right gripped a lance with a red guidon under the blade. The one on the left aimed a carbine at Kruger's heart. Between them, on a sorrel mare with a diamond blaze, the small fit officer in his hat and steel-rimmed spectacles seemed a sinister hybrid—the head of a stern scholar or Jesuit grafted onto the body of a soldier. A captain's stripes were on the sleeve of his gold-braided tunic. He was clean-shaven, a great rarity here, and the glare on the little round lenses hid his eyes.

No se mueva, he said, or seemed to say. His lips had barely opened. He seemed a man with little or no outward modulation; his voice, though penetrating, was toneless, and he was as upright and unmoving in his saddle as if held by a photographer's spinal brace.

May I ask, Kruger said in his fast-improving Spanish, but the captain cut him off with a remark too brief and flat to make out. Kruger shrugged nervously. *No entiendo.* The right-hand *lancero*'s bay stamped and nickered, flaring raw nostrils at Kruger. With his kid-gloved hand the captain made a slow clawing gesture across his mouth. Kruger shrugged again, as if still uncomprehending. The *lancero* spurred lightly and approached, lowering his lance, and as Kruger watched, paralyzed, the man thrust the blade at the centre of Kruger's face and at the crucial instant jerked it sideways, smacking the pipe out of his teeth. Under Kruger the mule flinched and shuddered. The *lancero* reined his charger to one side. There was a crunch as one of the forehooves trampled the pipe.

Speaking to a superior with something in your mouth, the *lancero* announced, as if reading a charge at a court martial.

Behind cupped hands Kruger made a quick lingual inventory of his teeth. All there. But I have done nothing, he brought out in a voice audibly shrivelling—and how that shamed him, incensed him. No matter how you exerted your reason the body could still be intimidated by weapons and uniforms and rank—by the colonels of the world, even if they resembled pale clerics. Yes, especially if they'd once broken you. He straightened himself on the mule, pushed his hat back off his brow, trying to appear both uncowed and alertly cooperative.

The captain said, You are American.

I am from Prussia. From Germany, Señor. Do you speak any English?

From Germany! The captain's smile exposed a bank of very long, clean teeth. He lowered his face as if to study his gloved hand resting on the pommel and when he looked up again the smile was gone. Is this true?

I grew up in Danzig, yes. In Prussia.

A very great nation, Germany. A great empire.

Kruger shrugged, his indifference sincere.

Your Bismarck has done wonders to unite it and make it modern. Of course, he had but a single people to work with. Here it is different.

Kruger nodded slightly.

The captain pondered him.

So a citizen of the great German Reich finds himself mounted on an old mule.

The *lanceros* framing the captain chuckled loutishly. The captain's face seemed neither pleased by this, nor irked. That same mineral stolidity. Kruger stared up and said nothing, fear and defiance combining to lock his jaw.

Answer me, the captain said in his stiff, ventriloquist's manner.

I did not hear a question, Señor.

After a few seconds the captain looked down, removed his spectacles and with close attention breathed on either lens. He passed the frosted glasses to the right-hand *lancero* who, planting his lance in the dirt, received them and drew a white silk cloth from a pouch on his bandolier and polished the lenses with a rapid pinpoint motion. The captain's eyes, blue as the base of a flame, studied Kruger from far back in the sockets. The *lancero* finished buffing and returned the spectacles with a smart salute and folded the cloth and tucked it back in the pouch. Without shifting his gaze off Kruger, the captain put on his spectacles, carefully stretching the wire arms behind his small, neat ears.

A German here in the desert, days from anything, riding about on a mule. Why.

Kruger fought to curb his long-aggrieved pride; always this hard striving. And then he heard himself say, In general I prefer mules. From the back of a mule, or walking at its side, one has no temptation to . . . He meant to finish, *block up the roads and molest harmless strangers*, but he lacked the Spanish. It was just as well.

As for the desert, I find it generally peaceful.

The captain's lean jaw seemed to flex. He said, The desert is filled with *primitivos*, some in open defiance of our authority, and with Lerdo's guerrillas and spies.

Kruger swung his eyes across the land. A sun-cracked vista of lunar desolation. Here and there stood clumps of olive-coloured scrub and Spanish bayonet and the weird, beseeching forms of saguaro cactus.

They are cleverly concealed, of course, said the captain, and a corner of his mouth curled slightly upward; an ironist! Or they are killed. Or, perhaps, in disguise. Tell me where you stopped last night.

At the far end of the canyon. You will find my camp about three hours up the road. Or maybe only an hour, on your horses.

Say "Señor" when you address the captain, said the one with the lance.

Señor, said Kruger.

Always.

What is that in your pockets, the captain asked.

From one trouser pocket Kruger dug a handful of unshelled pecans and from the other a roll of stale tortillas wrapped in cornhusks. The *lancero* with his lance-head firked the tortillas and then the pecans off Kruger's upturned hands. The edge of the blade sliced into Kruger's left thumb. The husks flitted away and the tortillas scattered. The pecans in their red shells as they hit the road made a faint hollow clatter and rolled like marbles.

Tell me what you are doing in this country.

Travelling south, Kruger said stiffly. Señor.

For what reason?

Fisting his hand around the bleeding thumb, he winced a bitter smile. Because it is not where I was before.

Now the captain spoke in a much swifter, brusquer voice, presumably to the *lanceros*, although he was still watching Kruger with blank lenses. If he thought Kruger was a spy, and therefore fluent in Spanish, surely he wouldn't do this? Unless it was a trap.

You will show me your documents. And the captain unholstered an immense revolver and held it slackly, like something unclean and disagreeable, pointed at the road by the mule's forehooves. It looked wrong in his fastidious kid glove. The *lancero* with the carbine snugged the stock of it tighter into his armpit as Kruger felt in the saddlebag and brought out a folded sheaf. He leaned forward over the mule's neck and extended his right hand and the captain's mare shied, nickering, showing Kruger her stained human teeth, rolling back eyes out of a painted crucifixion.

Calmly the captain stroked her neck. He didn't bother coming forward. The first *lancero* skewered the sheaf with his lance, just missing Kruger's other thumb, and passed it to the captain.

Through his teeth Kruger said, They are in German and English unfortunately. His thumb throbbed in time with his heart's slamming. The captain's spectacles were halfway down the bridge of his nose and his eyes scanned the documents with minimal movement. *Jawohl*, the captain said at last, in lightly accented German, *Ich weiß*. Kruger's jaw unhinged. The man continued riffling through his Prussian naval pension records, seaman's certificates, U.S. immigration papers, his *Polaris* contract with the U.S. Navy. Finally he murmured something to his men. Digging their rowels in with boyish zeal they shot forward, one to either side of Kruger, and grabbed him by the biceps and swept him out of the saddle, off the back of the mule. Flat-backed he slammed onto the road, his head smacking. Before his eyes a white door with a soldier on either side, the door of the inquiry room in Washington, he about to enter, the door opening and Tukulito and her husband emerging, she wearing a poke-bonnet, head down, so that his final glimpse of her is of her chin and her sealed, impassive mouth. *Good day, Mr Kruger.* With a jolt of pain the medieval skyline of Danzig appears, a cutlass moon setting over the Gothic spires and cupolas seen from a porthole in the sick bay of a ship returning him from the Danish War with his freeing wound. For he knew that as soon as he was discharged he would be leaving his country for the New World, like so many other Germans. . . . Wheezing, he peered around through a spindrift of dust. The second *lancero* had grabbed the mule's reins and was towing it along beside his charger, the mule hobbling quickly with legs rigid, head lowered, ears flat. The captain, still sitting his own horse, was peeling off Kruger's punctured credentials one by one and flinging them toward him, or, more likely, just feeding them to the hot wind, which sailed them dreamily over his face.

Maybe there was no New World.

Failure to answer the questions of an officer in a prompt and clear manner, the remaining *lancero* stated. Failure to address an officer of the Seventh Regiment of the Cavalry of the Republic with due respect. And with a nasal cry, a drumroll of thudding hooves, he too was gone. Kruger tried to sit up, then decided to lie still. His eyes half closed. A centaur shadow glided over him. There was a dense humid whiff of horse-breath like a field of sodden hay. Far above, an eyeless face hovered in its black brim halo, deep sardonic creases bracketing the mouth. Instead of the *coup de grâce* the captain was holstering his revolver and, to Kruger's numb wonder, speaking in virtually unaccented English. You appear to be an intelligent man but your actions are not intelligent. In the future do not be so cursed with courage—like the *primitivos.* This morning you are fortunate. I shall order my men to leave your saddlebag and cantina in the road. They would be unlikely to think of that by themselves. Senseless cruelty does appeal to them—as opposed to necessary measures. And yet, I must have them. Here he frowns, thoughtfully. There is work to be done. I should advise you now to depart this region. *Auf Wiedersehen.*

A nudge of the spurs and the blazed sorrel mare thundered off, horseshoes chipping sparks off the stones of the road. In this way Kruger's mouth and eyes were generously refilled with salt dust. By the time he was able to look again, the captain had caught up with his troop. The men of the Seventh Regiment were receding in the heat, the little grey mule lost among stallions, Kruger's saddlebags jettisoned in their wake. How easy for a life to become mere flotsam. He got up bleeding and reeled about in the road, trying to corral his identity papers and books, his tumbleweed hat, the fragments of his pipe, the latest note he meant to send Tukulito from Chihuahua City. And slowly walked on, ever southward.

In that part of Mexico the women of those times would pin back their hair with fragile white combs made from the sternum and sharpened ribs of jackrabbits, roadrunners, even *tuahmec.* Every night on the houseboat when Jacinta releases her smoky hair she stands a few of them on the candle-ledge of the icon—a gaudy *Pietà* nailed to the wall over the bed. She keeps a good half-dozen combs there. Last night when Kruger slipped out with one of them in his hand, she was on her back snoring gently, the sheet pulled to just below her nipples, crucifix glinting, her mouth ajar as if to drink the fluid moonlight pouring onto the bed. At her feet a passionate aftermath of blankets. Now it's only in hardest sleep, with her face calm and solemn, that she reminds him of Tukulito; otherwise she has become herself to him. Maybe he really can escape his northern past. He bent to ease a serape over her, drawing it to the scooped vale of bone at the base of her throat.

In the comb a few wiry sable hairs were caught, and this morning he wove them among the tines and wrapped the comb in his handkerchief and put it in the breast pocket of his jacket. He has been thirty days, a whole moon, in Purificación. Having spent his last few centavos, he's altogether broke, and Jacinta must start saving for the new poll tax that the Padre will be coming to collect in the autumn. By Padre she means not the village priest but the scholarly officer he met on the road; everyone in the district fears him, this Captain Luz, Maclovio Luz, not only because he seems to be everywhere at once, but also because he speaks a little Sina.

Kruger must go on to Chihuahua City and try to claim his next puny remittance. Then he'll make his way southwest up the traders' trail into the sierra and through the deep copper gorges to the Pacific. I have always wanted to see the Pacific, he has told her, fearing that he might soon tell her more—the rest of his story, what came after the rescue. The temptation is growing. One night he might prowl up from the cantina after a few mescals and tell her the full story and suckle whatever sympathy he can get and be on the way to turning into his father—dyed deep with grievance, poisoned with self-pity. *Think of surviving such a sustained assault by Nature, only to find it brutally renewed by Society!* It would be that easy to import his mess into Purificación.

At sunup he lashes the saddlebags onto a makeshift travois that the vulpine dog draws, her hazel eyes flicking up to his expectantly, her plume of a tail erect and wagging between the traces. She seems to rejoice at being fastened so physically into the journey. Kruger's own heart, being human, can't quite restrict itself to the moment. No *humilliado* ever forgets himself entirely. His bluchers are freshly shined. He wears his frayed brown suit and round collar and black bow tie, his hair reared vertically over his brow as if pomaded with clay.

Down the path to the village among tufts of sage and creosote brush they proceed with their shadows stretched long before them like stick-figure silhouettes on cave walls. Around them Sinas in yellow field pyjamas are turning the earth for the spring planting. The skies have a scoured clarity; to the west the slopes of the cordillera arch up toward their own separate weather of storm clouds. Jacinta is in the yard, bent over a washtub and a pannikin of soap, her skirts hiked up and her sleeves rolled, thick forearms plunged in suds. Her mother is stationed on her chair in the doorway. On a green serape the first daughter kneels with a bone needle and thread, stringing chillies while her sister squats behind her, gravely braiding her hair. The little son, chin high, dispenses handfuls of corn to the chickens with an air of sovereign pomp and largesse.

Jacinta straightens from the tub and dries her hands on her skirts, beaming her wide silver-capped smile. She greets him as always, *¡Qué milagro!*—what a miracle, what a miracle to see you!—a greeting that struck him at first as mere rustic quaintness, another instance of Latin hyperbole and social theatre. He has come to see it as appropriate. He rumples the rumpled hair of the boy, Mateo, who ducks from under his palm and bolts away, red poncho flapping, chasing Perra and the jouncing travois through the yard.

There can be no goodbye embrace here, ashore, in the open. Last night before sleep she held his face close to hers by pressing the middle fingers of either hand into the sunburned hollows under his cheekbones, as if to memorize the form of his bones. Maybe the local women do this for purposes of future identification. Now she cocks her head back and narrows her eyes at him, scolding him drolly, her voice low, for him alone. Why had he not remained the full night with her when it was to be his last night on the boat? *Su última noche.*

I intended to stay. The dreams were especially bad.

Always leaving the bed! It's a miracle to me that you gringos are so many. Of course the people don't want you to leave. There have been no funerals in the month of your staying. Stay! The *barrancas* are full of cavalry and *primitivos.* (Her word for other *indio* tribes, all of whom she hates.)

He says wryly, You will be faithful, I trust, until my return.

If you are returning tonight.

He smiles, with closed lips. Her smile seems more truly amused—a sort of Esquimau acceptance of whatever might befall her. He doubts he ever will return. Perra is approaching with her panting grin and lolloping sirloin tongue, gamely leaning into the work as she drags the travois with Mateo lying in state aback Kruger's saddlebags. Hands on his chest he gazes with glistening black eyes into the blue immensities high up there, his heels sketching twin furrows in the dirt.

The little church bell peals the matin mass, a silvery chain of sound in the sky, as Kruger and the dog make their way out of town, turning southward along the track to the city. Mateo and his grubby chums, lightly armed with sticks, escort them some distance, nattering in Spanish at Kruger and tormenting the dog, though with little commitment, and turning back one by one until only Mateo remains.

You come back to Purificación, Señor Kruger . . . ?

It's not clear if this is a question.

Someday, I hope, says Kruger.

The boy adds earnestly, You must try not to be killed!

Kruger smiles. I've always been a bit of a failure in that line.

¿Mande?

Being killed. You go back to the village now, Mateo. Goodbye, Mateo.

And the boy answers in Sina—farewell, or return soon?—with tears magnifying his eyes.

The peaks of the mountains are still in winter, dark timber in the folds. Keep the sierra always to your right, Jacinta told him, drawing from her apron a roll of corn tortillas wrapped in a clean rag. Turning back to her tub of laundry she'd added, Someday you may be sent up here again, to spy over us. Maybe then you can give back what you have taken.

Groton, Connecticut, June 1877

THE AFTERNOON OF MR CHUSLEY'S VISIT is so windless and still that you can hear, through the open front window, the faint clicking and crunching of the paper wasps chewing at the wood of the porch columns. In this heat she is too weary to go out and shoo them away. Her visitor seems not to notice them. The noise, to her, is increasingly pronounced, aggressive as the buzzing of a horsefly trapped in the long funnel-front of the bonnet she always wears outside at this time of year, to keep her face from darkening in the strong, southern sun of New England. She has not been beyond the front gate for some days. The vegetable patch is suffering. Her pallor is not far off Mr Chusley's; as if this white world is fully inducting her at last, while nature, in the form of the wasps, deer mice, and the scouring effects of another hard winter's passage, takes the house back to nothing, bit by bit.

It is not easy to concentrate on Mr Chusley's words. In part this is an effect of his stutter, but also there is her own grasp of English, which seems curiously reduced. Lately, when she speaks to Mrs Budington or the Reverend Cowan, stray words in Inuktitut will insert themselves in place of the intended English. Her skin may be lightening, but that older world is returning for her. She knows she is dying. She assumes her visitors must see it as well.

Still, she has dressed properly for this visit, in a brown delaine dress with milk lace collar and cuffs, a brimless hat of black straw, cocked with hatpins at a jaunty angle, a sprig of baby's breath on the crown. How she will miss her southern clothing, the variety and complexity of it, the slow, delicious ritual of dressing, even the corsets. . . .

As Mr Chusley chatters nervously, the parlour behind him half-revolves and returns, revolves and returns, as if suspended from the ceiling by a chain. There is the crackle of the paper wasps' chewing. Beyond Copps's knoll, now green in young maize, vast-piled sumptuous summer clouds pillow upward over the Atlantic, invisible a mile to the south. *I hope he will find his own place down there, in the hot countries.* Her visitor is trying to speak, she realizes, about Punnie's playing.

Now now, now I think I know what it was. The pup, piece her hands were playing, on her, her little coverlet. At the end.

Please have more coffee, sir. I do wish these were better.

No—w—wonderful!

They are yesterday's. I had no more powder. I have some of Daboll's soda crackers, if you . . .

His hand lurches out, apparently to grasp and reassure her own, but then it stops, trembling, tentative, as if looking for something, cream or sugar. He begins to move the short, red-bitten fingers slightly, as if at a keyboard—as if he'd meant to do this all along, a demonstration! She watches the hand in remote absorption. His sentences are clipped as he tries to outrun his stutter.

Even then I knew. But dared not believe. I, I . . . I had only *shown* her the music. *Schu*mann! She'd not played it!

Yes, sir.

I'd not taught her, you, you. You understand she'd scarcely seen it! Yet, somehow she . . .

He looks at her urgently, as if for assistance. His soft brown eyes shine uncharacteristically. Wide and red-edged eyes. Moved now, she extends her hand. She touches the doughy, hairless back of his hand. It's as if the touch releases him:

Oh—what we have both lost, Hannah!

She looks down instantly, catching her breath, trying to hold herself in.

Indeed, sir.

After some seconds: Forgive me, Hannah. I had no, no. Had no right.

Not at all, sir. Please, I am quite well.

Only, you see. Only—you see when I'm with you I feel. I *feel.* He pauses, takes a breath, then blurts the rest as if in angry defiance of his impediment:

I *feel* I am in the presence of something *strong* beyond my understanding!

After a pause filled with the weird sizzling din of the wasps, she says, I am really not so strong these days, sir. Then she regrets the words, surprised she has uttered them. Perspiration is dewing on her scalp under the hat. She seems to detect the hard cool edge of the hatpin against her scalp.

I'm in love with you, Hannah.

I should not have said that, sir, she says, referring to her own last statement; then his declaration reaches her, seconds late. Mr Kruger's declaration returns to her, too.

Of course! says Mr Chusley, scarlet to his hairline. Of course I should not have! I am so—I am *sorry*, Hannah.

That is not what I mean, sir.

She ought to have gone with him, perhaps, into the rope locker aboard the *Tigress.* For her husband has abandoned her. Perhaps he has a new family up there.

I am sorry, her guest repeats. Please. He rises from his chair—

a small, soft, clean-shaven man in a rumpled suit and poorly tied cravat—and stumps across the parlour to the spinet.

May I please, please—may I play for you? Schumann's "Träumerei."

Or perhaps he is dead.

Apparently she has answered because her guest is on the bench, hunchbacked over the keyboard, playing with eloquence. Outside a brougham or buggy passes with a clatter of wheels and a beat of hoofs. The tune shifts constantly from major to minor to seventh to suspended chords: not so much like the dreaming of the title as like actual life. This sad bachelor has doted on her for several years—perhaps because she has never shown any impatience when he stutters out his words. Her compassion swells with the tears she constrains as he plays Punnie's final song, though there are notes besides compassion in this heart's chord: a clear note of anger at her husband, another of loneliness, notes of listless apathy, surrender and, strangest of all, a faint high note of desire. As sometimes when she works the treadle, thighs rubbing, and feels the hum of the machine deep in her lap. She is almost delirious, worsening. This must be how it feels to be drunk. Uncaring of all consequences. She can see no reason not to be generous to such a kind, and famished, man. The reasons have all disappeared. She rises, still dizzy but not heavy of limb, in fact she feels almost weightless, lets the rolling chords and melody float her across the parlour to Mr Chusley's side. He looks up, the tune dying under his slowing fingers, as she places her ring hand on his shoulder.

Enough, sir. Do come with me, sir.

Hannah! he says.

His panting breath smells of coffee and cloves.

Some while later she asks if he would see himself out. In an agony of self-consciousness he is fumbling to re-tie his black cravat; whatever she tries to look at becomes the spindle around which everything else whirls and slurs. She feels she can't move from where she lies under the sheets. Move or meet his serious brown eyes, which for their part seem unable to meet her own.

I shall ask her, sir, she says. When I meet her again.

Hannah? He kneels beside her, his pale brow furrowed.

I shall ask her if it was the piece she was playing. When I meet her again, in my people's *quvianaqtuvik*. And she thinks: For I'll not be permitted to enter the white one, not now.

Hannah—I'll call on you, to, to. Tomorrow. If I might.

Tavvaavutit, she tells him, as a goodbye. Though in fact the word is only a general form of salute; in her tongue there is really no word for goodbye.

By the next morning something has changed. Her lungs feel bloated with a damp, cold humour, like thickly settled salt fog. The fever is worse, her sputum streaked with blood. She is aching, too weak to launder the handkerchiefs, as on the ice floe, how difficult it was to keep clean, when she was on her moon, at least before the hunger stopped the bleeding. The shame of it sometimes. As if in punishment, she thinks, this weakness . . . though the fever's drift makes it seem that her strange liaison with Mr Chusley was but a figment. Or is this punishment, again, for stealing on the floe? Her mind struggles to keep occasions and causes separate. Famished on the ice, on the shores of sleep, there was this same oblique, floating, phantasmal quality to her reflections on her theft of the stores. Such reflections were rare, and the awareness of her actions would always come over her like a surprise recollection—a surprise that would seem to *want* to be forgotten, that would insist on its own fragile implausibility. This cannot possibly be you. (But for this child, there is no law I would not violate, no consequence I would not face.)

A rapping comes, the distant front door, a week's journey from the bed, through the bedroom door, along a tedious sequence of cold and richly appointed, palatial rooms, then down a series of corridors, rounded like gloomy iglu tunnels, to the parlour. It will be Pretty Mother Sarah, bringing the mail. Tukulito cannot face her. Again the thought of yesterday comes, and of her present weakness, which feels vaguely shameful . . . everything vague now. Here in the South she has always had to be stronger than any strength, observed as she is by those who expect so little of her colour. She tries to cough but she is too weak, or the thickening fog in her lungs too heavy, a new condition, she can only wheeze. They think of Indian squaws and Esquimau women as weak—weak in virtue. For years she has been interpreting the insinuations and aboard ship overhearing the men. If Mr Chusley should report anything, it will bring further shame on herself, her family, her people. Yet this fear lacks immediacy, seems muffled in sacks of bedstraw. Her thoughts are thinking or dreaming themselves, at two or three removes from her, like some other woman's thoughts infiltrating the cavities of her ears. . . . Yet that woman can only be herself. A woman alone in a way she has never felt before. The Americans will turn from her, surely, and she is lost to her own people; yet this too seems to matter less and less, she is drifting free of all human concerns on the shrunken, private ice floe of the bed, which is yawing, listing on its sea of fever. The bedroom door gapes, Mrs Budington fills the threshold, dark and large, in her hand a yellow envelope. Hannah! Pretty Mother, come in. The woman stoops awkwardly, sits heavily on the side of the bed, sets a cold dry hand on Tukulito's forehead. Lord help us. Hannah? Do you hear me? I shall be back soon, with the doctor. The room is empty. Then, as if only a moment has passed, the room is full, it's not a large room, with Mrs Budington, and the physician, and Mr Chusley, him as well. The physician wears spectacles too little for his stout pink face, he is stripped to shirtsleeves and a shad-bellied waistcoat. How perfectly round and healthy the body packed into his waistcoat! By the door Mr Chusley sits stiffly, a crease between his widened eyes, his derby in his hands, kneading and twisting the curled brim; as though he is attending the bedside of a neighbour's child whom he has run over in his shay. A thoughtful man, always. She sees he will say nothing. Oh, sir, you must feel no guilt in this matter.

I think, think she may be a. Awaking, Dr Schader.

I believe not, sir. This is the worst case I have seen in much time.

Shall I bring more water, Doctor? Pretty Mother's voice, subdued.

Per per, permit me. Please.

If you would, sir. The doctor's accent is heavily German.

Can you hear me, dear? Hannah?

Yes, she whispers. Pretty Mother. Forgive me.

Hannah?

She feels Mrs Budington's face inclined to hers. The surplus heat it contributes is too much, she is burning up so, wanting space, cool space and water.

Please, she tries to say, a further towel.

Is he bringing the water yet, Doctor?

Ja, ja, he is at the pump, I see him.

Forgive me, Mother. The food I stole.

Hush, my dear! You, ever steal a thing? It's only the fever.

Tukulito opens her eyes. Mrs Budington's bitten lips part expectantly.

Not from Mr Daboll, Tukulito tries to say, but only the last word comes clear.

Daboll's shop? Rest, dear, please! You are the most honest creature God ever made!

She may have said Devil, the doctor says in an undertone perfectly clear to Tukulito. They are quite superstitious, these people, one hears. Thank you, Chusley.

You are mistaken, Dr Schader, Mrs Budington says. Hannah is different.

But, she has here in the bed with her this fetish!

It's an Esquimau doll, Doctor.

It was her daw, daw, her *daughter's* doll, Mr Chusley tells the doctor, with force.

Put one other pillow under her back. Like so. And he whispers: If she cannot cough, she will drown from within. Chusley, bring more camphor oil.

It's in the kitchen, by the washbasin, Mrs Budington says.

God help her, the doctor mutters.

Some would call *that* a superstition, Tukulito hears Mr Kruger remark, as plainly as if he were here in the room by her ear.

Could they be, Mother? The ones from the ice. I do hear him. And the lieutenant . . .

Don't you fret about Tyson, Hannah. You must try to cough.

But the cloths, they all be soiled, Mother!

Here I have a clean one, my dear.

Ah, *qujannamiik!*

Her English is regressing now, back through the years of steady, laborious gain, much as Punnie's speech regressed near the end, the child reverting to words and making sounds that she had not formed since she was six, then four, then two—sounds she had entirely forgotten—as she retraced her way backward to her birth time, and the absence before birth, her mother, helpless, watching her recede.

Odd sounds are coming from inside her. When things go

badly wrong, naturally one wonders about broken taboos. Now one would listen to an *angakoq*'s words, as much as this physician's, although the whiter, southerly districts of her being still mistrust those primitive ways. The borders between districts are breaking down, however. All moments, past or near-present, are now present, like the hours of her conversion, which she undertook partly for Father Hall and partly because she loved the Baby Jesus so, in the stories. *Sweet Jesus . . . Lamb*, she whispers experimentally, and Pretty Mother loudly, as if in triumph, relays the words to the others: Sweet Jesus, come, she said!

Some time after the birth of King William, her second baby, she and Father Hall discover a woman entombed in an iglu. Queen Emma, the woman is called. She has given stillbirth to a tiny infant, hard as soapstone, and has tried to conceal the birth, burying this little statue in secret, and so she has been entombed with three ancient women of her tribe who are chanting to her night and day, forcing her to fast, to purge her of her transgression. She is dying. Father Hall tries to intervene, hectoring them about the White God's forgiveness and the cruel error of their superstitions, and Tukulito translates it all to the crones, at first diplomatically, muting the man's bluster, but later, as Queen Emma sinks into delirium and as she, Tukulito, comes to agree with Father Hall and *to deplore these savage rituals*, she translates directly and with passion. To no avail. The woman is dead. Angry and defiant, Tukulito resolves to accept Father Hall's repeated advice and abandon some of the tight constraints on her own diet as a nursing mother, beginning to take cold water and bread and coffee along with the traditional stewed caribou meat. Hall is elated with this victory of civilized good sense over brutish shamanism, though when little King William himself sickens and dies, Tukulito endures agonized second thoughts, allowing the vindicated and spiteful *angakoq* to punish her.

Some time has passed, a new mist of voices in the room. The feeling in her chest is colder and thicker, sluggish, less like fog than like the grey pash of melt-ice. The Reverend Cowan is here. From far away a faint, drilling hum, as of massed paper wasps, then horses and a vehicle, hoofs clapping, the shimmering tinkle of bells, and though she cannot open her eyes, memory furnishes the scene, on disembarking with Mr Bowlby in Hull after crossing the ocean, she fifteen years old, Ebierbing eighteen, and among all the marvels that throng their eyes in the crammed hours that follow, none can rival the spectacle of enormous horses, a twosome drawing the buggy of a merchant, the sun flashing on the bend of their arched necks and gleaming along their glossy sides to curve again on their great, round haunches. The biggest, most *naked* land-creatures they have ever seen: slim legs moving quickly, like trotting caribou, hoofs scratching sparks off the ground which is floored with stones like a tight-cobbled beach. Turf-coloured manes and tails dancing in the wind, their harness trimmed with small brass bells and yellow tassels, while behind them, scarcely less marvellous, a shining machine clatters, a sort of dogsled high up on wheels, like the wheels of the cannon on Mr Bowlby's ship, but larger, blood-red, webbed with bone-like rods like a bloodstained crystal of snow . . . and this wondrous sled has a glistening black roof as well. . . .

Soon after their wedding in Mr Bowlby's vast parlour they are in a room even grander, in London, seated at a gleaming table around which half of the folks they knew in Cumberland Sound could have been gathered, dining with the Queen and her husband, the German Consort, and the two men are silent, Ebierbing because he considers his English too poor, the Consort because it is his nature to say little, or so Tukulito interprets, while the Queen, who is just a little taller than Tukulito and similarly large of head and small of shoulder, asks question after question about herself and her country and her impressions of England, then listens to her brief, careful answers with unblinking interest, her head cocked slightly to one side and her small hands holding her cutlery still, just above her plate, till Tukulito has finished speaking. We wish to know all of our subjects well, she says, and you are the first whom we have met from the northerly parts of our America. Tukulito is fascinated and a little amused by how the Queen seems to speak both for herself and for her silent husband. She likes the Queen and can feel the Queen's liking for her, although the woman has a peculiar way of smiling, somehow keeping her upper teeth covered with the skin above her lip, which barely moves even when she is talking. And were you afraid in Her Majesty's presence? she is asked later by Mr Bowlby and by others. This question she finds puzzling. But the Queen, she be a kind lady, she answers in her still-imperfect English. Her house be a very fine place, sir, I assure you.

Hannah.

Mrs Budington is peering down, her cheeks ruddy and her hair hung around her face in wisps. Lamplight. It seems to be near dawn. Somewhere a ripple of thunder, the burdened clouds clearing their throat.

Mother, Pretty Mother. Care for the house. For Ebierbing.

Oh, Hannah, my dear! Sydney is here now . . . you've been another daughter to us.

Hello, Hannah.

Sir.

Don't try to speak, girl, he says slowly, as if to a foreigner or a child. Cough.

You be all so kind.

She is observing the moment from a high corner of the room where a spider has worked its mansion of a web, and there she is, tiny under the grey coverlet, lungs crackling, Pretty Mother on the bed next to her, sidesaddle, Mr Budington behind his wife, standing, his stovepipe hat gripped behind him and his free hand—red, knob-knuckled, gold-ringed—on her shoulder. A penny-smell of whisky. Everything is so clear. The yellow envelope with the cochineal postmark on Father Hall's escritoire. The doctor bunched over in the chair where Mr Chusley sat before, the tiny spectacles tucked in his waistcoat fob, elbows propped on his knees, steepled fingers rubbing the bridge of his nose between tight-shut eyes. Other voices from the parlour. The thick smell of coffee, like turned brown earth. (It is hot here under the roof, enmeshed in the web.) She wishes she could see who is in the kitchen. He loves fresh coffee, her husband does. Has he returned then? Her blood bounds for the joy of it but then comes the thought that there is some reason she should not rejoice in his return, although the reason evades her. There is too little food in the house; he always returns famished. *Very spare and gaunt the Wolf is.* A peculiar verse on the label of the small, flat tins of lobster meat that she purchases from Daboll's, twelve cents the tin, *To the Full Moon in the Marshlands, through the Warm Night sang the Bullfrog: Very spare and gaunt the Wolf is: LOBSTER is a Fish delicious!* As a child she would sometimes help the women gather mussels from the seabed under the ice. The tides were high in Qaquluit so that at low tide, in certain ledged places along the shore, you could chisel open the ice hole they would use all winter and slip through and crouch along under the ice, then stand fully, the adults holding small qulliqs for light, and attentively you would wander in that gloomy-green underland, searching the fluted, crusting seabed and icy tidepools for mussels and dulse, fronds of bull kelp, gathering them in sealskin bags. Sometimes the adults would pry open a few shells for the children and let them slurp the mussels fresh, salted with brine. The sound of the withdrawn sea like a distant wheezing, repercussing through the caves and chambers formed farther out by the reef and the boulders of the sea floor. An impatient, constant, predatory sound. As the women stoop down and gather, faster now, the smaller children cling near, within the wall-circle of the qulliq's glow. This is their playhouse, large and flat-roofed like the empty warehouse built by the whalers, or they are Nuliajuk's little ones, in a room carved in the foot of an iceberg, in fear awaiting their mother's return, for she is always vexed. The louder growls and whooshing alert you, the tide is stealing back, wave by sly wave, and the roof's creaking like spars or rafters and sometimes, look up now, the lamplight will show a blue seam that darts through the ice like lightning, that miracle her people see but once in a decade. Something, Pretty Mother's hand, is cool on her forehead. *Put me below with my daughter.* That other night's near-bitterness is dissolved, for these people have indeed loved her, after their fashion . . . and did she not just realize her husband was here? She must have heard him, before, so as to realize such a fact. Her being is tiny, is shrinking, a collop of gristle wrapped in layered furs. *Ja*, I am sorry. You must now take your leave of her. The voice could be Mr Kruger's but she seems to remember that he is far away, perhaps aboard the *Tigress*, still whispering certain things to her, before his kiss, *No, please, never say that, Tukulito, I believe you have saved us all* . . . and in the still air his words hover like a fog of cotton but his face despairs and passes and he is not here under the ice with them, rapidly gleaning mussels, although something else, what is it, is deeply amiss, but now Punnie appears out of the dark where she has been lost for many hours, scooting up the mud slope from the lower caves and chambers where the tide is clawing in, her small face solemn with fear, thin-lipped and big-eyed, as her mother kneels in joy on the cooling seabed and opens her trembling arms.

Chihuahua City, Mexico
22 March, 1877

Dear Madam,

I hope this Spring may find you in good health, although I fear it may be Summer before this will reach you! I am making my way towards the Pacific Coast, & am finding the road a congenial home still. To be sure this City has its charms, not excluding the welcome anonymity it offers one such as myself.

But enough. I write again to wish You a return of the contentment you so well deserve, & of course, of your Husband. And, Madam, Tukulito,—if you will pardon this indiscretion, I wish also to tell You that I still think of You often, in spite of the many distractions of travel; indeed, I believe it is not too much to say that I shall think of You often for the rest of my life.

Wishing you the best in this, as in all Seasons,

I remain, as ever, your own

R.K.

In a quiet moment a few hours before the funeral Sarah Budington slits the envelope with a paring knife, and through hazing eyes she reads the letter quickly, several times, before slipping it through the kettle hatch of her stove. Oh, I knew it anyhow, she says under her breath, to nobody.

56°21′ N., 57°44′ W., June 27, 1877

A CHILLY MIDNIGHT, no fog, firm westerlies, the pewter moon a sliver shy of full. Despite the hour, enough of the day's light lingers above the horizon to see even without the moon. The stars are faint. The coast of Labrador a rumour of glacial blue along the horizon some hours to the southwest.

The continuous pre-dawn limbo of these June nights generates in Tyson a mood of expectancy. Something is about to happen. He sleeps little, treads the deck at any hour, even when he is not in charge of the watch. Tonight he is in charge. With his naked eye he detects the schooner—another small berg, he thinks initially—when it's still several miles north and bearing down on them. O'Coin, on watch in the bow, calls it to his notice a few minutes later, as Tyson at the port rail examines it through his spyglass. Her name is difficult to read, but it seems to begin with an R and to be five or six letters long. He goes on pondering the letters. Almost certainly the *Rachel.* Apart from the lantern in her bow, no sign of activity: another ship of sleepers, like his own ship. He's jarred by a vivid glimpse of Joe in the snowhut, face down, snoring in his quiet and regular fashion, more or less unwakeable. Tyson inserts himself into this vision, waking Joe—or, no, having him wakened—to inform him . . . of what, now? Hannah is dead now too. He learned the news a few days before his steamer, the *Florence*, was to depart, and he was far too busy with the usual harried late provisionings, preparations, meetings with the Navy and the Smithsonian and the New York Geographical Society to travel up to Groton for the funeral, as he'd wanted to. Well—his absence must have gratified the Budingtons. And here Tyson's jumpy mind, instead of pursuing the important matter of what he should say to Joe (if indeed he should say anything, having promised Hannah that he would not mention Punnie's death)—here his mind begins sorting through his various spats and grievances with the Budingtons, the disgraced Sydney even now continuing to write letters to the newspapers, no doubt drunkenly, in his vicious campaign to discredit Tyson and reinstate himself. What sweet reprieve, Tyson feels—despite his memories of the floe—to be steaming north again, away from that America of scurrilous editorial pages, thinly attended lectures, dinners with chattery, effeminate patrons, epic fundraising engagements where everybody is drunk (to the point of thinking themselves charming) except the reformed Tyson (who can see they are not).

He's also sailing clear of his now insupportable marriage. No man is a champion to his wife, it's said, yet celebrity always seems to promise a special exemption from the old givens; or, failing that, a chance for another start. And some must be Captain in every room of their lives.

He misses only his son and widowed mistress.

When he was younger, before gaining any niche of command, he used to relish the hushed attention, the fleeting power to be seized and savoured on delivering some item of bad news. For a spell, however short, it would seem to make him the captain of others—even of the ship's captain himself. He was commanding an audience. Now, out here, where he holds authentic rank, he would much rather deliver good news if possible, for on this voyage he would rather be *liked*, at least from a distance. Yet he knows he must tell Joe about his daughter, now that Hannah is gone, too. Wake and inform him of both deaths. In the snowhut, face skewed into the pillow of his bundled fur trousers, Joe would sleep like a child and wake like a child, face blank, vacated—altogether boylike save for that wispy Mongol moustache and the deep vertical creases from the pillow. Now, as the schooner slowly nears and Tyson makes out the rest of the name RACHEL, it strikes him that he can't do it, can't steal from Joe a night's placid sleep, steal from him the last ten days of peace that he will know for a long time. (Is this compassion, or is it cowardice?) Assuming that Joe is aboard the *Rachel*, assuming he's not dead himself, his state of mind will not be just peaceful but also excited, impatient—or as impatient as an Esquimau can be—to see his home and his loved ones. And Tyson knows that state, has known it: returning with your affections refreshed, heart longing again for the common comforts you'd grown almost to despise. Resolved to be a better man. Tyson almost envies Joe, because he, Tyson, now at the start of a journey, is on the starting side of that lengthy arc, and will never be on Joe's side of it again. When Tyson sails home it will be to *divorce* his wife. So, like Joe, he will be returning to a lost family, but in full foreknowledge of the loss.

How can he now inflict this grief on Joe—Joe returned to a state of boyhood by slumber?

Tyson walks aft to the pilot house. His step gains steadiness as he goes. He orders the helmsman to turn to starboard.

Ain't there a schooner out there means to speak us, sir? I heard O'Coin call out. I think I see her now.

I know that vessel, Mr Fluvis, and we shall have to avoid her. Take us two points to starboard. And make steam for ten knots.

Aye, sir, as you ask, sir.

The man's averted face, lamplit, has a furtive, curious look. But he says nothing. A quiet elder who asks few questions. He ratchets the engine telegraph and leans into the wheel. Tyson strides toward the bow of the turning ship. O'Coin, running back from his post, meets him by the berth-deck hatch.

Captain, sir, why are we turning?

Because I ordered the second officer to steer us clear of that schooner. Tyson speaks in a curt but hushed voice, as if scolding somebody in church. Through the deck the *Florence*'s engines throb.

You don't mean to hail and speak her, sir?

Keep your voice down, Mr O'Coin. I suggest you return to the bow and watch for ice.

But Captain—we've letters to send south.

A note of personal distress here; O'Coin is recently married. Well, Tyson has certain letters of his own to send south. All the same he hears himself improvise: I know this schooner's captain well. It's best to avoid him. He sponges food and supplies from every ship he hails. We'll pass other ships, whalers, to take our letters back, probably tomorrow.

O'Coin remains there with his head to one side, frowning down at the hatch. He wears a wool watch-cap and has large triangular sideburns, a large nose of the same shape. In this light his eyes look beady, hard and black, like a wharf rat's.

The bow, Mr O'Coin. You are the middle watch.

Begging your patience, sir, this ain't usually done. Suppose she does really need supplies?

She flies no colours of distress.

O'Coin looks northward over the rail, squinting, as if his captain's word isn't enough to settle the matter. Only Tyson's faint sense of being in the wrong, having just lied, keeps him from chiding the man for this little gesture of insolence. (So Tyson construes it.) The *Rachel* seems to be making to port as if to intercept them, but it won't work, she has only her sails and the *Florence* will soon be clear of her and steaming on to the north-west, against the wind.

This ain't a bit usual, O'Coin mumbles from between his shoulder-blades as he turns back to the prow. The wind carries a bell's frantic, plaintive clanging, the *Rachel* trying to draw their notice.

You've something to say, O'Coin?

Nothing, sir.

Tyson pivots on his heel and makes toward the stern.

Naturally the man will relate this incident below decks the next morning. And, over the next fourteen months of compound failure, it will seem to be the hinge point that the crew keeps returning to, superstitiously, recalling how the very next day the fair weather and mostly ice-clear seas they had enjoyed were replaced by unseasonable gales and heavy ice; how for the very next eight days they met not a single whaler or other ship to take back their letters and news; how from that moment on, they succumbed man by man to a baffling fever, only partially regaining their strength, all except for Tyson, whose choleric energy never lagged; how Cumberland Sound remained glutted with ice until a month later than the average, so the expedition's work was badly delayed; how hundreds of twenty-pound pemmican tins, over half their store, turned out to be ineptly soldered and the meat decayed in the hold; how the contractors had crammed the hold with enough beams and plankage to construct a town half the size of St John's, but neglected to include enough nails to hold together a privy; how, as the carpenter rushed to fashion hundreds of pine pegs to replace the nails, the food began to run short, along with their time, and Tyson, much against his will, realized that he could never insist they overwinter in the little slaphammer slum they had managed to build.

Not that they would have agreed anyway. The crew, demoralized by assorted disasters and having on hand neither the Secretary of the Navy nor the gods of the weather to blame, naturally blamed their captain. Above all, they remembered his strange failure to hail and speak the last ship they had encountered on their way north. Hunger, fever, increasing darkness deepened their superstitions. Some began to see him as a sort of demon. Not fully human. There was something behind his pale, hot eyes that seemed both dead and preternaturally alive; coldly withdrawn yet thrusting to the fore. How did he keep his health when all others were sick? (Sheer will, in fact.) His abruptly sensible decision to flee the thickening ice and return south did appease them for a few days, but then, toward the mouth of Cumberland Sound, in freakishly premature cold, they were jaw-caught in the worst autumn ice that any of them, including Tyson, had ever seen. *Again, my Goddamned luck.*

So there in the open they must overwinter.

Tyson now passes months in a sort of delirium of disbelief; it is all happening again. But this time, despite all that he and the ship's doctor can do, he is losing men, about a man a month. By February he hardly seems to sleep at all, only to doze now and then. His determination to return to Mrs Meyers, and not to grant Budington the satisfaction of his failure and death, keep him going. Perhaps neither love alone nor hate alone would have been enough to see him through, but the two together are potent. Fear and tedium are an equally potent mixture, though. Days and nights, weeks, blend together. Then in the middle of March—the Ides of March!—a moment flares to clarity out of the gloomy, coal-lit blur of those months: a figure pads up behind him in a lightless passageway and shoves him headfirst into a bulkhead. He wrenches round to face his attacker. There's not even enough light to suggest the man's general shape, or to glint off the blade that now nudges coolly into Tyson's abdomen, just under the breastbone. He bellows and flails out. The figure seems to retreat—a slight lessening of the dark's density—then flees with quick spatting footfalls—he's barefoot or in his socks. With an animal sigh Tyson slides down the bulkhead into a seated posture. His life pulsing rapidly in the wound. With each pulse, pain eats into his flesh like acid. A lantern lights the end of the passageway. Dr Bowen in his greasy nightshirt holds it at arm's length, squinting timidly. A few of the men appear too, as if rousted from their bunks, tallowy faces peeping over the doctor's shoulder. One of them is O'Coin. All of them wear boots.

Later, each man will sullenly insist on his innocence, and his ignorance of any plot, so that for the rest of the voyage Tyson—slowly, improbably recovering—will barricade his cabin door and carry his revolver whenever he has to leave the cabin. To him, the crew itself has become that faceless assailant. The *world* itself. Why is it so difficult to be liked?

In mid-June the ice, on its own time, on its own terms, frees the *Florence*, now damaged and leaking. The starved captain and remaining crew, at last unified in intent, work her south at a reckless pace, damn the icebergs, manning the pumps the whole way. For a week they make excellent time, but off the Grand Banks they encounter a spate of tremendous gales that blow them days wide of St John's and almost finish them. The *Florence* that wallows and coughs into the Brooklyn Navy Yard on the evening of the Fourth of July—spars and hull battered, funnel like a crushed top hat, a squad of zombies staring over the rail—seems a sort of anti-mascot for the national holiday, though the stars and stripes she flies is in sterling condition, Tyson having kept one stowed, along with the midnight-blue dress uniform he is wearing, for the triumphal return.

But how did you know to be here? he asks Mrs Meyers. Nobody else is on the wharf, the crew having fled at a feisty hobble, in search of food and booze. Nobody else is on the wharf because nobody knew they were coming. And who would have been here anyhow? America is off celebrating bigger things. And just now, on this rotting side wharf, Tyson sees his future—how in a land where success is a kind of religion, his latest, crowning failure must sign an end to his dream of fame. Still, with his mouth full of fresh-baked and lushly buttered currant-roll, this fate seems secondary. Mrs Meyers has brought the roll. She holds his hands in hers and leans back, as if to bring him into focus and decide if he's an impostor, or else in contempt at his wasted state, although he has scrubbed and shaved and puffed himself up for the arrival, in case anyone should be here. She stares undaunted from out of her clean atmosphere of Saturday baths and well-fed health—her terrestrial assurance that life is more than a starved, helpless drift through freezing seas. But then again . . . surely it *is* more. Her hands are so wonderfully plump, firm-boned, clean and cool. The skin of her cheeks glossed with the evening's heat, hair pinned back off her neck and blushing ears, she'll never look more beautiful than now, seen by a man who for thirteen months has looked only at his own face (a pair of sunken yellow eyes above a greying matted beard) and his ghoulish crew's. Even her nose, upturned, freckled, with large-bored nostrils—the one feature he could never quite love—looks fetchingly made. She's in her widow's weeds and a black velvet pillbox cap. And for this one moment, a first time, simply being alive on the earth is enough for him. As the incontestable fact of his return settles through him, down from his head through his thawing heart and into his feet, nailed at last on fixed land, it strikes him that she needn't always dress for Death. The sooner they marry—provided she still wants him—the sooner they can both rejoin the gaudy, enthralling human parade. I'll not be returning to sea, he mutters. For surely he needn't always dress for Death, either. Surely half a lifetime is long enough.

You are too young for this black, Laura.

He says nothing yet. This public encounter, even in the absence of a public, is deeply reckless on both their parts and marks a fording in their lives.

I've failed, however, he says.

Your presence here is a *complete* success, she says in her wry, incisive voice.

Laura, how did you know to be here?

I didn't, for a fact. There was no word from St John's. But I gambled on the off-chance. I've been here as often as I can, these past weeks.

As often as you can! Tyson repeats the phrase faintly, tears welling, overcoming him. But she seems to hear his broken exclamation as a question. She looks him in the eye and says, with a kind of fond exasperation, Why, yes, George. Every day.

Chihuahua State, May 1889

CLIMB INTO THE MOUNTAINS at any latitude and eventually you reach the Arctic.

Tonight Kruger and the old bitch, Perra, huddle by a meagre, spitting fire of deadfall and fir cones. They have hiked up past a small green lake rimmed with dwarf conifers and draining to the west until they reached the end of a second lake, crowded with rotten floes and pash and narrowing to a stream descending eastward. The stream's meltwater is icy cold, sharp to the taste, though the rush of its cascade makes it oddly mild to his fingers.

Kruger is returning to Purificación. He will stop there for a few days, he thinks, then continue north to the Rio Grande. For six weeks he and Perra have been trekking through the ancient transcontinental scar of the Barranca del Cobre along Indian trails, or the tracks and skeleton trestles of the unfinished Chihuahua Pacific Railroad, leaving behind him the remains of his third life, as a family man, in La Paz. That remote and forgotten little city, in the grip of a century-long siesta, sated with sun, crossed by balmy salt breezes and the music of bells and guitars, its calendar a rosary of fiestas—La Paz has been transformed by the cholera into a site of macabre, medieval scenes. He recalls little of his last days there but even that little is too much. In early March he crossed to the mainland with other orphaned or widowed refugees, then parted ways with the rabble, fleeing up into the *barrancas*. Besides the fox-like dog—now filmy-eyed, grizzled around the muzzle and brows—he had with him a burro, saddlebagged with food and a few domestic souvenirs, although little money, as Kruger had always spent most of what he earned in La Paz as a pearl-lighterman, ferrying divers out to the rich oyster beds, his strength at the oars an advantage in the daily dawn regatta. And how good it was simply to spend the pesos and centavos as they trickled steadily in—to be free of the North with its natural hoarding compulsions, its rationing of time, food, affection, its anxious striving for status and capital. Caches secreted against future lack and loss. (And wars.) The pleasant climate and isolation of La Paz encouraged a sense of sufficiency. There was no winter to hoard for. Oysters, mussels, coconuts were there for the taking. Yet the losses had come anyway.

As darkness settles over the lonely breadth of Mexico, small asters of light begin to quiver far down in the distance, in the U-shaped section of desert framed by the canyon's vast walls. The burro, maimed in a fall, is long since eaten. Perra is increasingly stiff in the hindparts. Kruger remains numb with grief. Yet nothing curtails his appetite. On a propped stick over the fire he's roasting a scrawny hare, trying not to feel or to think; maybe these few bites will help him to stop dreaming of dogmeat. Now Perra tilts her head and pricks her large ears. She rises, growling low in her chest, staring into the night from which footfalls, human and animal, are approaching from the east, then glances anxiously at Kruger as if to say, Do something!

Kruger has no fear left to make him care. A small shambling figure enters the orbit of the firelight, leading a burro. Kruger sighs and removes his disintegrating straw hat.

Buenas tardes! says the figure in a cracked, heavily accented treble.

Good evening, Kruger murmurs, continuing to rotate the hare. You are American, I think?

Yes! Yes, we are!

At this "we" his heart sinks further. There are more of you?

More? The little figure looks hopeful. On the other side of the fire he stands shivering in a dark vested suit and porkpie hat, these items ragworn and far too large. The owlish eyes have a fixed, feverish gleam. Both are pouched and battered. The white hair is cropped unevenly short. And Kruger sees that the figure is a woman, maybe sixty-five, with a small prim mouth, set far down her face, crammed with long yellow teeth.

There's none but I and my husband, she says.

Kruger glances from the woman's face to the lowered snout of the burro, its stoical eyes—the beast now shying back from Perra and the flames—then looks again at the woman's face. Perra growls again but with little conviction. There's a smell of burning meat. Kruger yanks the flaming hare from the fire and waves it between himself and the woman to extinguish it, as if performing some odd, primitive greeting ritual.

Hungrily the woman eyes the doused hare.

Your husband . . . he is then following?

How's that?

Pardon me, he says, I've not spoken English for many a year.

My husband is dead! she snaps. May we sit down?

Kruger eyes her briefly, then extends an open hand toward the ground.

I believed we were being pursued, she says, sitting quickly. But evidently not! They're far too occupied with their *work* down there.

He looks past her and again sees the twinkling lights of the desert villages.

She says, Those are fires. Of course, you might well sympathize, you might well be of their own stripe—another spy!

He smiles unhappily and says nothing.

You look Mexican enough. *Criollo?* You're swarthy, yet your eyes . . .

A dozen years I was in La Paz, he says. I had a home there. A young family. He nods at the ring hand resting on his knee. She considers the silver wedding band, then the rest of him. Out of one side of her pinched mouth she says, It was a spy must have betrayed us. But of course, you ask, what were we *at* down there in the desert in the first place? I told him that, I warned him. Didn't I tell you that? We're missionaries. We came south to bring the Word to the Tarahumara natives, up here in the sierra. The Catholics never have, you see. Nobody has. Yes, and now we know why, don't we!

Kruger sets the smoking hare to cool on the stones by the fire. Perra whimpers and bellies a few inches closer to the meat. The burro remains where it stands.

Because they are impossible to find, that's why! Eighteen months we spent up here and the only ones we ever succeeded in catching and herding into the fold were the poor lepers who reside in the cliffs, way over yonder. Of course, many of *them* haven't even got limbs!

I passed those lepers some days ago, he says.

And did it appear to you as though the conversion had taken? Her expression is crafty and peevish.

I'm afraid I can't judge, he says. They wished to be left alone, that much was clear . . . and now I seem to prefer that also. He's whetting his jackknife on a stone etched with fossils.

And we, through all of this, we imperilling our lives to get to them! As for the healthy ones, we barely caught sight of them, ever. We came to doubt that they really existed. We would come upon Tarahumara hamlets—deserted! Firepits—carefully snuffed, nobody there! A parable of the Lord's dogged pursuit of the wayward soul, you might think, yes—only this pursuit was ever fruitless. We came to doubt our own sanity. We'd brought the Lord's Word up here and were endeavouring to convert a nation of wraiths. Of course we wondered if the Padre might have exterminated them—them as well! Have you spied any Tarahumaras on your travels?

Only at a distance, watching me. And he adds wryly, They are said to be tremendous runners. This Padre you mention . . .

In time of course we conceded the vanity of our mission. I wanted to return to Pennsylvania, my husband insisted we try instead to gain converts away from Rome, down there, in the desert. No good can come of that, I said—but you wouldn't listen!

Perra growls at the empty spot beside the woman, whose credulous gestures seem to be convincing the dog that something is there; or something is amiss.

In the end, as ever, we acted in concert. I believe one of the Padre's spies betrayed us, down there. Or one of the Roman priests. The natives would never have. Please now, please give me a little taste of that coney!

This Padre, he says, holding the knife, not yet reaching for the hare, he's not a real priest?

Almost worse! A captain of the Mexican cavalry. In fact now a colonel. Still they call him *capitán.*

Capitán Luz, says Kruger, straightening.

You know him—Maclovio Luz. His lancers murdered Ezra! She shows her feral eye-teeth. These are his clothes I'm wearing. My own they sullied. So I burned them, when the villages were all afire. I am going to reside with the lepers now, they've need of our ministry now, we shall build them a house of worship and we—

Have you been to Purificación? Has Luz been there?

What?

It's a Sina village. Has he been burning the villages?

We were sowing the Word among the Pehues. The Sinas we were next to visit.

But has Luz been there?

I don't know, I don't know! Has Luz been there? Again she speaks from the side of her mouth, twisting her shrivelled torso to that side, then looks back at Kruger in befuddlement.

Nobody knows if the Padre has been there!

It's where I'm going, tomorrow, he says. Here, take some meat. He hands her his own tin plate and fork and the extra cup. I have no more coffee, he tells her, it's water in the kettle.

The devil, she says—stuffing her mouth, not using the fork, her long fingernails cracked and filthy—he deems the region his private domain. A Herod. The natives who won't flee into the sierra he burns out or slaughters. Mestizos as well. *La Purga*, it's called. The Purging. There was another tax here. Many refused it. For the railway. She closes her eyes as she swallows, then says hoarsely, Ah, God keep you, it's days since I've tasted food! The last was a corn-loaf. There were loaves afloat on a river, I remember, somewhere . . . they were shaped like coffins. Doubtless from funerals.

It's a Sina custom, I think, he says softly, glancing past her at the desert fires.

God forgive me but I took one. We did love them, the natives. Like children. He died for them, my husband. Stood between them and the horsemen with his Bible in hand. So brave you were!

She looks back at Kruger accusingly.

What have you done with your family?

My family?

I always know a lie when I hear it. There, you've been warned.

Kruger looks down, slowly filling his cup from the kettle. She leans toward him over the fire and whispers, *The hoot-owl's calling alerts me that we are being observed from a distance.*

Over the rim of his cup he studies her as he drinks.

He says, It was the cholera.

It's in Californee now, too! she exclaims.

The popping of the campfire and her rapid chewing fill the silence.

I found a place in the sun, he says, off the edge of the world. For nearly a dozen years, nothing happened. Nothing! Every day was really the same. How wonderful that was—to be outside of time that way.

He cuts her more meat and gives Perra another bone.

And to think, when I was eighteen, all I wanted was to be recruited into time, the future. History.

Well, nobody can hide anymore, she says. Not in these modern days. Except perhaps the Tarahumaras—for now. By and by, somebody will catch them up, for all they are good runners. As God caught up with you. At least you yourself were spared. A man can always begin again, unlike a woman. It was a large household?

For a moment he regards her with something close to hatred.

We had a daughter and a little son, seven years and five.

And we too, she says, chewing faster now. We dared hope for children still!

She's clearly far past the age.

He says, As for being spared, I think I've had enough of it. It seems to be my only talent. I was second mate with the *Polaris* expedition, sixteen years ago.

She shows no surprise, no suspicion. Yes, of course—with Captains Hall and Tyson! I never forget a name. Ezra and I attended one of Captain Tyson's lectures, in Altoona.

I saw one in Brooklyn. I thought it wonderfully inventive.

A true hero, she says, like my husband. Like my husband, Faith kept him strong. But then he did something disgraceful. He is dead to God now, dead to the Lord.

He's dead—Tyson? Kruger feels faint, then sick. But I am on my way to—

I don't know! Is the captain dead? We don't know if he's dead!

She flinches back, as if threatened. Kruger has not budged.

How long is it that you've been gone? he asks.

Three years two months and nine days! I'd not heard he was dead! *You* said he was dead! She looks increasingly alarmed. He, he wrote a book concerning the *Polaris.* I suppose you must be a character in the book. Yes—now I know your accent—you must be one of those Germans!

Kruger nods slowly. He says, I have that book still. Did you hear anything of Tukulito?

She stares vacantly, chewing.

Hannah, I mean. And Joe. The Esquimaux who were with us on the ice.

Oh, the poor Christian natives! I'd forgotten their names.

Poor? What do you mean by this?

We did mean to read the book. We bought one at the lecture, but we were too occupied with other things. Then he disgraced himself! What was your name in that book?

I'm Kruger, one of Tyson's villains. But about Hannah . . .

Her eyes ignite as though she's meeting Crazy Horse or Billy the Kid. No one is drawn to a famous outlaw the way a do-gooder is. But then her gaze narrows in a canny way.

Now I remember! The papers all declared you men to be agents of the Kaiser!

Yes, yes, but do you—

He's in Washington now. I remember.

Tyson?

There was a divorce. We thought it disgraceful. There was a scandal. He divorced his wife. We thought it disgraceful the Navy should employ him after such an act! And in *Washington.* Our government is not God's government, Mr Tyson, but in time that day may come. We've heard nothing of those natives, not for some years. Their daughter the Lord took away. A fine little musician, it's said. It's said she would play on the piano nothing but the old-time hymns! That she knew them from the beginning, without the slightest instruction. Her last words were, "Sweet Jesus, come bear your poor creature home." Or were those the words of the mother . . . ?

The words of the mother, Kruger interprets, *at Punnie's deathbed.* He's too relieved by the woman's confused telling to inquire further. Let the good news, no news, stand.

The child's sombre little face appears to him.

I attended her funeral, he says.

We did think of going up.

To the funeral?

To the *Arctic,* where we were needed, by the Esquimaux. Will you travel on with me tomorrow, to the lepers?

He shakes his head. I'll be going the other way at first light. You are welcome to sleep here, by the fire. Please do.

After gnawing at the hare's cooling ribs he stuffs some *macuche* into his pipe bowl—his tobacco is long exhausted—and lights it with the end of a fir twig. Watching the woman lay out her scorched blankets on the other side of the fire, meticulously spreading and squaring and flattening and rearranging them over and over while muttering as if Kruger is not there, he wonders if she poses any danger. Apathetically he decides not.

❧

The woman's hand and Perra's soft growling wake him. As on the sleeping ledge of the crewhut he is vised in, warm bodies on either side: Perra as always on his left flank, the woman on his right. She smells of piñon smoke, mule, and dried menstrual blood, although she looks far too old for that. At any rate, blood. Her hand is under his blanket, crab-walking among the conch-shell buttons over the remains of his husbandly paunch. Perra growls again from one side, the woman hushing her from the other.

Kruger clears his throat and sits up between them. Madam, your hand. Perra . . . *basta!*

It was so cold over there.

She hurries her hand lower, peering up at him in the light of the embers and the half moon and the cold-sharpened stars—an eerie little manikin in her baggy suit, with huge, creaturely eyes. Their bruising is like the makeup on the old whores he would pass years ago outside the disorderly-houses on Bleeker Street. Sometimes, of course, he would enter.

Oh! she says, you're cold as well.

Gently he removes her hand. I am a widower. Please.

We're very like in that—we're even the same age.

He's not surprised to hear that she thinks this. No doubt she's less old than she looks. No doubt he looks as old and empty as he feels.

I can't find my husband anymore. I've tried.

Perhaps in the morning you can find him, he says quietly. Where the lepers are.

Maybe it wasn't *he* I saw murdered! And you—how can I know you're not a spy? The Padre speaks German! The Padre speaks every tongue!

But rest now, please—and he pushes his arm under her head so she can pillow it there. The bristles of her cropped hair prick into his temple. She holds herself stiff. Perra squirms territorially closer. Wedged between a smelly old mongrel and a madwoman in a ruined suit, Kruger hums a Mexican lullaby while shifting his lower body away from the woman, protective of his numb, grieving genitals. Difficult to imagine that part of him ever revived and inclined again. There's nothing sexual or romantic in his desire to see Jacinta, and above all Tukulito, one more time. He now feels as he did on the deck of the *Königsberg*, badly wounded twenty-five years ago: dead, but still able to hear and to see. A ghost intending to haunt the ones he has loved—and, in Tyson's case, hated—one more time before he finds peace.

Love and hate, a survivor's fuel.

He wakes shivering, his right side chilled. Perra, completely moled up under the serape, snores on his left, her acrid breath warm on his throat. A few last stars are fading like the remote, pinprick cries of children in a dream.

The woman and her burro are gone. By the dead fire his saddlebags lie splayed and open. He crawls to them and picks out the boy's homespun stocking that holds his wife's jewellery. The thread that tied it closed has been removed but the pewter-and-pearl ring and earrings are still inside. His wife's wedding Bible, with the naïve image of a blue-robed Madonna sewn onto the calf cover, is still in the bag. The rosewood schooner he carved for his son is still there, and the pearl-lighter he carved for his daughter—but his daughter's corncob doll, dressed for the fifth of May fiesta, is gone, along with the almost empty sack of cornmeal, his papers, and the Tyson book, *Arctic Experiences*.

She stole even the damn book, he mutters, still on all fours, looking coldly at Perra who is pushing her head out from under the serape with an innocent yawn. Useless, flatulent old thing. For a moment it enrages him that an animal as short-lived as a dog should have outlived a whole marriage, a family—a family which, in a way, this dog residually embodies. With smarting eyes Kruger peers to the west, then gets up and walks to a boulder on the shore and clambers up. A membrane of night ice has knitted a few feet out into the lake. Some distance off, a mile-long reach of trail is visible, worked into the side of a cliff now brightening from rusty brown to copper in the gathering dawn, and there's the madwoman in her porkpie hat and masculine rags, astride the burro rather than sidesaddle, plodding west toward the invisible Tarahumaras, seeking souls.

Souls or children.

He shoulders the lightened saddlebags—Perra is now too old for such work—and continues slowly east down the canyon. Ahead, toward Chihuahua City, an inflamed sun is scaling the long rungs of cloud just above the horizon. The far villages now resemble smouldering firepits—charred points scattered across the floor of the desert, smears of greasy smoke on the rise.

For eight years he has been, by marriage, a kind of accidental Mexican, a circumstantial Catholic. Now he's truly and finally homeless, stateless, unaffiliated. In his twenties he grew to believe that only the solitary and the uninvolved, the un-enlisted, could think and act with true moral independence, and be a loyalist only to Truth. But such a solo, arduous path—surely it's better left to the young and the strong. The dogmatic. How is an abruptly old man to inhabit an abstraction?

In late morning he makes out an insect procession thousands of feet below, filing up the switchback trail toward him and the dog. Either soldiers or fleeing Indians. By afternoon, resting in the shade of a ledge, Perra sneezing out the alkaline dust churned from far down the canyon, he can see they are Indians.

At dusk he leads her off the trail and up a steep bouldered draw into a copse of stunted firs, where they camp fireless. The Pehues will be in no mood to encounter a solitary white man, and Kruger's business is not with them anyway.

At dawn he and Perra watch from their blind as half-naked Pehues of all ages, with their starving goats and dogs, though no visible possessions, stagger up the canyon trail in silence. Some are on crutches, with swaddled wounds. Even the animals are silent. When the last stragglers have gone by, Kruger and Perra pick their way down the scree and through the boulders back onto this trail of tears. Perra's nose is animated, her tail flapping. Every so often as they stump along, a black clot of vultures will erupt off the trail in silence and Kruger and the dog will arrive at the corpse of a Pehue man. The vultures have been furthering the work of the bullets. Kruger knows nothing about the Pehues—whether they bury their dead, burn them, or something else—but normally they must do more than simply abandon them where they fall. Perra yaps hoarsely, makes little hobbling dashes at the dispersed but waiting scavengers, then sniffs at the carrion she has claimed. With a cringing smile, her gums bleeding, she looks up hopefully at Kruger, who cuffs her muzzle too hard, as if to scold himself out of his own troubling hunger.

Dusk comes early in the vast shade of the canyon's walls. A large white gull, or swan, or something, appears ahead among a sudden updraft of vultures. They reach the eyeless and naked, gelded body of a man about Kruger's age. The white bird, an albino vulture, slouches in a niche in the canyon wall, like statuary in a satanic chapel. Its bald gory head is half turned away, as if feigning disinvolvement or anonymity.

They emerge out of the canyon the next morning. Along its far wall, several miles south across the *páramo*, tiny figures labour with pick and shovel, laying track, extending the railroad up into the canyon to meet the line coming down from the west. He thinks he can make out soldiers too. There's a dull, remote thump as dynamite explodes somewhere in the cliffs. Kruger and the dog swerve north toward the Sina country, sticking close to the upland flanks and spurs of the Sierra Madre. In an incinerated village at the foot of a broad, loaf-shaped spur, he loots some cornmeal and scorched peppers and cooks a kettle of mush over the fallen, still-glowing main beam of a house.

The Padre's purging looks to be a complete success. The country is mostly desolate. Here and there he does see untouched, presumably more cooperative, villages. Every so often squadrons of *lanceros* pass in the distance, riding north, their wakes of khaki dust rising and leaving a haze in the lower air for hours. . . . From the top of a mesa, behind a blind of chickweed and creosote bush, Kruger and Perra look down on a besieged village on the banks of what must be the lower Purificación. Pehues, again. The Indians have ringed the village with a rough low wall of cottonwood trunks, bales of straw, and adobe. A few dozen half-clad men with bows and arrows and historical firearms man the near part of the wall, exchanging sporadic fire with a handful of *lanceros* who sit their horses out of range among the flattened maize-fields a few hundred yards off. Behind them, on a scrubby knoll, men in the white cotton pyjamas of peons or *campesinos* unhurriedly load a small fieldpiece. A troop of *lanceros* and some infantry appear to be taking a siesta on the far slope of the knoll, out of sight of the village. It's a leisurely siege. Possibly they are waiting for reinforcements, or waiting for the Pehues to pack up and flee into the sierra; the soldiers have made no effort to cut off the village from the rear. Assuming the Padre can still be identified by his broad-brimmed clerical hat, he's nowhere to be seen. Either he has been killed or is leading another attack elsewhere.

With a clipped, barking sound the fieldpiece bucks and flares and the shell, trailing a cloudy comet-tail, arcs over the wall screeching and explodes unimpressively near the back of the village in what looks like a chicken coop. Women and children rush out of the church with buckets of water, others darting through an opening in the wall to fetch more water from the river a few steps away.

A hundred feet down the side of the mesa lies a foot soldier, another pyjama-clad peasant, face down, dead fingers clawing at the slope, apparently shot as he tried to climb it and get away from the fight. A methodical vulture and three crows are crowding into him. The Pehues couldn't have hit him with their muskets at this range; he must have been deserting, and the *lanceros*, or his own messmates, shot him. His rifle is trapped under his body. A simple matter to slip down the face of the mesa, return with the rifle and ammunition, and open fire on the attackers. Kruger, the lone spectator of this casual siege, feels as much disgust at the attack as he is still capable of, yet the thought of sniping at pyjamaed adolescents who will be largely *indios* themselves, likely conscripts, or even killing some of Luz's haughty *lanceros*, sickens him too. The idiot willingness to choose sides is what feeds the abattoir of history. How long has it been since he has needed to form a thought like that? And he forms it, something like it, in German. In La Paz he came to think mostly in Spanish, his melodic language of forgetting—language of a new life. He seems to get a faint whiff of the corpse now. Or maybe just the thought of killing a man has done that. Leave the rifle. Leave the battle, which is not yours.

He has to reach Purificación.

At dusk he leashes Perra to one of the sturdier bushes and warily seat-slides down the mesa, braking with his boot heels and the heels of his hands. At his approach the vulture and the crows flutter and hop back a few paces from the corpse. They stand watching with a patient and formal air, a bald priest and three portly mourners in black tailcoats, their hands behind their backs. He has to roll the body over to get at the haversack and water gourd. The broad dark face with the sharp cheekbones and soft moustache puts him in mind of a very young Ebierbing. The suddenly old flesh is just beginning to smell. Kruger closes the calm, evacuated eyes.

In the stained haversack, tortillas and a bag of cornmeal.

After eating the bloodied tortillas he and the dog plod a few more hours north in darkness before collapsing by a snowmelt creek reduced to a trickle by the season's advance. A pregnant moon floats up out of the *páramo*. In its glacial light another mesa appears, miles to the northeast. He recognizes this one—low and very wide, a mesa visible, he remembers, from Purificación. Tomorrow then, he tells Perra. And in this night's dream he is sternly interrogating Amelia, asking in German why she would choose to leave La Paz and "the very earth itself" with their children. And as she begins weeping, unable to understand him, he hugs her and joins in her tears.

Mesas, the loneliest of landforms.

At first light the Padre is there. Kruger sits up and throws off his serape. This action brings on a sharp collective snapping as the many rifles aimed at him are cocked. He's ringed by mounted *lanceros* in baize-green tunics and peaked pillbox caps. Barefoot soldiers in dirty white pyjamas and sombreros. Colonel Maclovio Luz peers down through his spectacles from under the black brim of his hat. He seems little changed: mounted on the same sorrel mare with the diamond blaze, unnaturally straight in the saddle, fresh-shaven, small and fit, holding the reins with white kid gloves. His skull-cropped hair is a handsome, metallic silver.

Dónde está la perra? Kruger asks.

Without shifting his gaze Luz nods his brim slightly to the side. Squinting, Kruger looks between the figures of two teenaged foot-soldiers, a few paces away, training their shaky barrels on his face. Perra is on the other side of the creek, frantically tearing and gnawing at a heavy slab of some meat. Beyond her, to the east, a large force of men wait in a straggling line, south to north, with pack mules, ox-drawn *carretas*, a few fieldpieces spread among them. Their flags hang limp in the windless dawn.

Mi capitán, this one is not she! shouts the *lancero* on Luz's right.

Claro que no, says Luz and his lips barely move. What is your name?

So Luz doesn't recall him. That's unsurprising. It was a minor incident, long ago, and Kruger has not aged as kindly as Luz. Kruger is not much afraid but would prefer not to jog the man's memory. He says the first name that finds his tongue.

Tyson—my name is George Tyson.

English? American?

American.

Your accent is odd for an American. You sound . . .

I spent some years at sea. With Dutchmen, Germans.

Luz ponders him for a few seconds.

Also, sprechen Sie Deutsch, Herr Tyson?

Ja, mein Herr, he says woodenly, as if it's a struggle. *Deutsch auch*.

Let me see your papers, Luz says in Spanish.

They were stolen, Señor. Up on the pass, in the *barrancas*.

By whom?

He hesitates, weighing another lie—something more plausible than the truth—but decides not to press his luck.

It was a woman, in fact.

The *lancero* on Luz's right looks sharply at Luz.

Describe this woman, Señor Tyson.

She was very small. She was—dressed like a man. He hesitates, wondering if he is betraying her somehow, then he reflects that she's days away and headed in the other direction. She too was an American, he says.

And when did this encounter take place, Mr Tyson? Luz has switched into precise, lightly accented English.

Four nights ago I think, Kruger replies in Spanish. Maybe five.

Impossible. Five nights ago this woman killed and mutilated another of my sentries.

Kruger sees the woman's sun-dried little face, asleep next to his.

It must be four, then, he says.

You are lucky not to be dead. You may speak in English now. I would prefer that you do. These infantry are terrified of the woman—they believe her to be a, what is the word, a witch. She was bearing westward?

Yes, he says.

Luz pivots in his saddle and projects his voice, telling his men in Spanish that this gringo saw the woman riding west in the Barranca de Cobre, and, as the eastern mouth of the *barrancas* is now being cordoned off, it will not be possible for her to return. When the fighting is over, he adds, he will send some of his best *lanceros* in pursuit.

The foot soldiers jabber among themselves, the word *chingada* repeated often.

Luz looks back at Kruger and removes his spectacles, actually a pince-nez, exposing his deeply embedded blue eyes. In English he says, This woman and her husband, whose names we do not know—missionaries of some kind—they were attempting to . . . interfere in our efforts. The local peoples have been in a state of mutiny—in particular the *indios.* We sought to re-establish order in a Pehues village. Her husband, who interfered, was inadvertently killed. The woman escaped that night and was concealed subsequently in other villages. Then evidently she sought a revenge, dressed as her own husband. A religious zealot. No doubt she was mad before they ever arrived here.

Well . . . it was obvious that your men mistreated her in certain ways.

Luz replaces the pince-nez. That is to be regretted, he says. These men are a somewhat resistant material. To shape them into an orderly and disciplined force is no small task. However, in time. How old are you and what are you doing here?

I am forty-six, Kruger says—and then he lies, fearing that if Luz knows he has lived twelve years in Mexico, he will be dragooned into this army. My ship ran aground off La Paz, he says. No other ships were docking or sailing, because of the cholera, so we had to wait there. My shipmates began to fall sick and die. I fled La Paz, and now I hope to walk north to the border, to go home.

You appear older than forty-six, Luz says. Your accent is odd, for an American. What was your rank on this, what . . . whaler?

Coal steamer. The *Sirius.* I was second mate, Señor.

Luz's hatbrim dips slightly. Something of a leader, then—very good. As you are going north in any case, you might as well accompany us partway. You are too old for infantry but you will do, I think, for a sergeant. That woman zealot stabbed to death one of my sergeants. We are on our way north to oppress the Sinas.

Is this a glancing error, or a sly, grim joke? His toneless face and voice give no cue.

I would prefer to continue alone, Señor.

We will furnish you with new clothes and shoes. We are always prepared for new volunteers. Those boots and this suit are obviously finished. Your saddlebags you can place on an oxen cart.

He issues quick orders in Spanish. Within a minute Kruger receives from two panting Indian boys a set of white pyjamas, a red sash and bandana, a sombrero and poncho, leather sandals, a sabre, and a revolver and belt.

But, Señor . . .

Please strip and dress, Sergeant Tyson, we leave immediately.

What about the bitch?

The dog?

She *must* come with me, Kruger says in a rush. She was our ship's mascot, Señor—a reminder of my former comrades. On the ship. Many of them now dead.

Pensively Luz strokes the neck of his mare.

I see no reason why you should not keep the bitch.

A flagstaff propped heavily across his collarbone, he leads his scarecrow platoon of eighteen men, both grizzled and young, mestizo and *indio*, north across the sunburned *páramo* toward Purificación. The dog trots beside him with her tail high and her milky brown eyes flicking up at his, so delighted by all the new company, and her packed belly, that she doesn't sense his darkening mood. *I'll never wear another uniform*, he hears his younger voice telling Jacinta. The wind keeps catching at the banner and jerking the staff, as if he's struggling with a kite. Aside from one dusty Mexican tricolour borne by a *lancero* up at the front, the banners are all the same: on a white ground a stylized lamp with a long sword-like yellow flame, and to its right a black cross which, on closer inspection, is composed of two cross-hatched lines, like railroads intersecting on a map. It seems that this army is not so much a Mexican army as it is Luz's army. Or is it the railroad's? Kruger and his men shuffle along in a ragged procession of maybe three hundred infantry and a hundred *lanceros*.

From behind come the clattering anapests of a horse galloping. He glances back. The men and boys of his platoon stare round-eyed at him—a foreign stranger—for reassurance. Luz, the Padre, the Colonel, *El Capitán*, this leader of many names but one immobile face, reins in beside Kruger, then walks his mare at Kruger's speed. The snorting mare swings her head low and hard to the left, against the reins, as if to spook Perra back, or else dazzle Kruger with the diamond blaze on her face. Luz murmurs something to calm her. Her smell is fresh and pleasant, clean-curried, unlike the smells of the cowering dog, the platoon, and Kruger himself.

Sergeant Tyson, Luz says—and for a moment the name is a shock to Kruger. How are you managing so far? This in English.

Kruger tries to look up at Luz but the sun is over the man's shoulder.

Well enough . . . though I believe these men need more to drink.

No reaction to his failure to say Sir or Colonel, which Kruger can't seem to bring himself to do. Luz says, We will reach the Upper Purificación soon enough. These men are used to such lacks. However, I am pleased to hear of your concern with their welfare.

This is sarcastic, Kruger assumes; but then Luz adds, For a good leader is like a, what is the word, a stepfather to his men. Stern, but solicitous. And every soldier is a kind of orphan.

I thought soldiers were more in the business of creating orphans, he thinks, but setting his teeth he says nothing.

Most of these men I have redeemed from peonage, Luz goes on. A corrupt and antiquated institution which I intend soon to eliminate in this state, along with many other remnants of the past.

But first these peons will have to die? This time Kruger has thought and spoken at once.

Not peons. These are now paid men. And Sergeant, understand that I would never send a new volunteer like you, or your platoon, to fight professional troops. The Indians are ill-armed and ill-organized. Our casualties will be light. It is a pleasure, Sergeant, to have occasion to speak another tongue with someone. And a tongue of the future, I feel. Here one speaks only Spanish and the Indian tongues. You seem a man of some intelligence—something of a linguist.

Kruger is repelled, but he's also intrigued by Luz's cleverness and eloquence. Also puzzled by his indulgence. The Indian tongues must be difficult, he says.

The temporal modes are highly complex.

Some of these men appear to be pure Indian, Kruger says. Are you not uneasy, asking them to attack an Indian village? Maybe it would be better—

Most of our Indian volunteers are Pehues, or Nahuas. Our local tribes mainly despise one another on an ancient footing. In fact, they would have exterminated one another long ago, had they but possessed the proper arms.

The modern world brings them great benefits, then.

Kruger can feel the man's eyes on him.

I should have thought an American would have more understanding of our campaign. Did your Indians not try to prevent your own railroads into the West?

I suppose so. But this is Mexico, and I'm not Mexican.

This campaign, Luz says, entails a principle that sweeps across national borders—indeed, makes national borders all but irrelevant. Everyone's allegiance is to one side or the other. It is a matter, quite simply, of the future being locked in battle with the past.

And if one is for the present?

Kindly explain your meaning, Sergeant. The man sounds not irritated but intrigued.

What if one's allegiance is to the present—the moment as it lives?

The Padre chuckles evenly. A solid rank of white teeth in the shadow of his hatbrim. Very good, Sergeant Tyson. So you're a, what is the English term, a hedonite by nature. And something of a Jesuit in debate. Only be sure to be a sergeant in battle. Lieutenant Ortiz will be instructing you today, and overseeing you and your platoon tomorrow. Afterward, if all is well, I may make you an adjutant in some capacity, if only to have the pleasure of speaking English more often, and with a thoughtful man. Or perhaps German next time, Herr Tyson?

I could try, Señor.

Very good. Luz slips a pocket watch from a fob in his green tunic and glances down. With a slight, concise tug on the reins he veers his mare away from Kruger, then spurs and gallops on along the ranks toward the front.

In early afternoon the army reaches the broad lonely mesa to the south of Purificación. They swing around it to the east, and finding a fringe of shade under the mesa's steep flank they halt and throw themselves down among the pokeberry and sage and creosote brush. Kruger, unused to the pace, his feet in the tiny sandals blistered raw, wants only to close his eyes, but he has to think matters through. Purificación is less than half a day's march from here. He could try to slip away during the siesta, to warn the village—but surely the dirt clouds produced by such a body of men will be visible for miles, and the Sinas will have been expecting Luz anyway. And his *lanceros* would ride Kruger down long before he could reach the village. He ransacks his baked, throbbing brain for an idea, some way to avert war, as he and Tukulito in unconscious alliance helped to do on the ice.

On top of the mesa, etched against a hot zinc sky, the Padre in his hat holds what looks like a pair of opera glasses to his face with a gloved hand.

As Kruger re-scours his plate with a fifth tortilla, Lieutenant Ortiz arrives on foot in a festive jingle of spurs. Stripped to a white blouse, snug lightning-rod pants and high boots, he advances with a rolling, randy strut, bowlegged as if having to provide more room in the crotch of his pants. He's hatless, a polished-bald young dandy, skin bronzed, big sideburns running down from his fringe of hair, eyes black and flashing. His moustache is waxed upward at the tips like a permanent smirk cartooned on his face.

In Spanish: If you wouldn't mind obliging me by just stepping this way, Sargento Tyson?

Si, mi teniente! Kruger's instincts urge instant courtesy. Maybe they're the instincts of a spy after all. Tossing the rest of the tortilla to Perra he leaps up stiffly, saluting, and Ortiz looks pleased, the older *yanqui* according him due respect.

Now, I understand you have a certain young person in your platoon—that one, just over there. Ortiz nods at a boy unconscious on his back, hands folded over the dome of the straw sombrero resting on his chest. His hair is a coarse and rumpled pelt, black with red highlights. His skin *café con leche*. Black down shows above the corners of his lips.

I haven't quite learned all the names yet, *mi teniente*. It's Marco?

Mateo, in true fact. Now I'd ask you to keep a careful vigil on him tonight, and for tomorrow as well—he's a Sina.

A Sina! Kruger's surprise is genuine.

He did execute his orders sufficiently well on Friday, Ortiz says in his dandified Spanish. His blue-shaved chin juts as he inhales through flared nostrils. His lips are disturbingly red. *My* orders, in fact. I was conducting the siege of a Pehues village, near the mouth of the *barrancas.* They were quite numerous, these Pehues, and sufficiently well armed, now that I consider it.

Kruger fakes an attitude of admiring curiosity. And did the village fall, sir?

I took this village by storm, after a thorough siege, and I inflicted severe casualties upon the insurgents before they dispersed!

This is excellent news, sir.

Your accent doesn't sound especially American, Ortiz says with a slight frown, drawing a cigarillo from his shirt pocket and inserting it, just under that smiley moustache.

And your own losses, sir? Kruger is thinking of how he considered adding to them.

Ortiz lights the tip with a lucifer and takes a flamboyant pull. He says, Apart from one deserter, a Pehues youth, I suffered only five killed, and them all infantry, of which three, now I consider the matter, were Sinas. So that only this one here, this Mateo, remains. I ordered the Sinas to proceed first, you understand, because I was aware of the fact that we were destined here next, and I much preferred not to have to rely on them against their own people, if you receive my meaning.

Exhaling smoke through his nostrils he eyes Kruger with the expectancy of a vain man who requires the periodic reinflation of praise—from anyone.

Brilliant idea, sir.

Nonetheless, our casualties tomorrow may be somewhat more substantial. Purificación is a larger town, and well protected on three sides by the river, although fortunately, or so I understand, they're insufficiently supplied with provisions. With a little encouragement they may well disperse, like the Pehues. Nevertheless it's a certainty that we shall have to launch some kind of assault, and naturally your platoon will perform a role. So, do watch Mateo. In all likelihood he will perform his duty, but he *was* recruited from this vicinity—possibly he could try turning coat, it's a risk with all the recruits who weren't peons.

He hauls on his cigarillo, retains the smoke, slowly exhales, theatrically solemn; it is now his duty to have to say something unpleasant, but say it he certainly will, for he, *Teniente* Ortiz, is not the sort of man to shirk a difficult duty.

Be certain that you order this young person to proceed first to the assault. If he disobeys, naturally you'll be required to shoot him, but I very much doubt that he will, he has seen what happens. Order him in, and he'll either block a bullet for us or the Sinas will recognize him and hold their fire, which naturally would assist us even further.

Another splendid idea, sir.

At this latest ovation Ortiz can't restrain a little cherry-lipped smile—a smug mischievous schoolboy smile just under his smirking moustache.

Yes . . . and Sargento, tonight you yourself are to keep vigil on him, if you would. So he doesn't slip away. *Muy bien?*

Claro, mi teniente.

Ortiz offers him a smoke. His fingernails are trimmed and clean. He wears only one ring, a gold wedding band with a small ruby. Kruger snatches the cigarillo as if it's edible. In a changed tone—joking, sociable—Ortiz says, I've heard that men your age don't really require as much sleep anyway!

We have less physical beauty to maintain, sir.

A second's hesitation; then Ortiz helplessly smiles. He says, But now that I consider it, Sargento, you do look a little fatigued. Go now, try to take some rest.

⁂

They camp that night on the banks of the Purificación, about a mile above the town. Kruger remembers this bend in the river, and so, it seems, does Perra, who is sleepless and agitated, turning in tight circles and lying down, getting up, sniffing the air, peering at him expectantly. After the meal, Kruger limps around behind the perimeter of men's backs ringing the fire and sets his hand on Mateo's small shoulder. It's trembling.

May I have a word with you?

The boy looks up anxiously. *Conmigo?*

Por favor.

Si, mi sargento!

He leads the boy into the dark interval between the fire and a neighbouring one—a larger, cheerier fire where there's singing in Spanish, the softly plosive strumming of a guitar. Beneath the sentimental *corrida* runs the bass droning of the river.

You are Sina? Kruger asks.

Si, mi sargento.

Firelight from either side shows the bones of his face in chiaroscuro. Yes, I see it now, Kruger thinks. His mother's bones. And the age is right.

You're from this very town, aren't you?

I was born here, *mi sargento.* How did you know, *mi sargento?*

Are you the son of Ignacio and Jacinta Soquomac?

Mateo's eyes, so dark that the pupil and iris seem one, grow rounder. Who are you?

I met your mother when I was here, twelve years ago. You look like her, I see it now.

I do not, he says in a small, dignified voice. *Mi sargento.*

I stayed here by the river, for a month. Please tell me, is she still alive?

The boy's lips, Jacinta's full lips, compress, almost sneering. So many visited my mother in those days! I didn't understand until I was older. It was shameful! I can't remember all the men . . .

He stiffens to attention, face impassive. Forgive me, *mi sargento.*

At ease, Kruger says after a moment. How long have you been gone? You've heard from her?

Not since I left, *mi sargento.* Two years ago. I left this place with the Padre—the Colonel!

You were . . . were you forced to join?

Mateo averts his eyes a few degrees, glances back, away again, and then blurts out, I *chose* to join the Colonel, *mi sargento!* I was ashamed of her, my mother! My father I never knew.

She was only trying to feed you, Mateo.

The eyes gleam black, like young ice. Surely he reviles all her *visitantes*, as well as herself? *Hijo de puta. Hijo de la chingada.* Now something hits Mateo—his face aged backward to the unguarded softness of a small boy—and he whispers, Your voice . . . you were that German man!

That's a good way of putting it, yes.

The German man with the dog—that old bitch there, is that the one? But your beard, it was so black! You'd tell us about the *indios* of the Arctic, I remember now. For years after, my mother would mention you. The villagers, they all thought you were a . . .

Un espia. The boy stops himself—has frightened himself, it seems.

Mateo, now listen to me. I've been ordered to send you in first tomorrow, when we attack Purificación, assuming it happens and our platoon is used.

Mateo's shoulders start to slump until he catches himself, stiffening.

Si, mi sargento! I shall do as you require!

Yes, but Mateo, this is your own . . . these people are your people! Are you . . .

Colonel Luz is our father! He is the Lamp of our Future! The boy's eyes flit to Kruger's and away so fast that Kruger is unsure of what he has seen. Jacinta always maintained that a Sina would make a perfect spy: so much better than foreigners at dissembling feelings, when necessary. The boy is either loyal and determined, even eager, to help the Padre crush the village—and thus growing suspicious of Kruger now—or else he is willing to desert and waiting for a sign from Kruger. Or does he fear that Kruger may be a spy for Luz, trying to trap him? He may have heard about Luz's lieutenant taking Kruger aside today, while he slept. His face betrays nothing. He must be as unsure of Kruger as Kruger is of him. Nothing more can be said. If Kruger is somehow to help the village, and Jacinta, he can't risk being caught out now.

Helping the boy, this one too, may be impossible.

In a suddenly aged voice he says, Well . . . it may not come to a fight tomorrow. The villagers may slip away tonight. We'll hope so.

Si, mi sargento!

But if we do go in, you're to keep low and stick close to me. This is my order.

Si, mi sargento!

In the small hours of his vigil he dozes for a second or two, then jolts awake, finally sure. The fire is dead. There's no moon, but the wind-polished stars throng the sky. Trying not to wake Perra, he sits up. Perra opens her eyes. Stroking her head he whispers *quédate!*—and she's too old and exhausted to disobey. Mateo is tucked in a ball under his poncho on the other side of the firepit. Sentries, dimly luminous in their white pyjamas, trudge at the camp's fire-lit peripheries. In the centre of the camp, like an angular snowhut, the Padre's large, square tent softly glows.

This is not a Mexican army. This is Luz's army. Cut off the head and the body collapses. He reaches into the firepit and grips a handful of warm charcoal. Under cover of his poncho he smudges it over his pyjamas and his hands and his ankles, his feet and face. He takes up his sabre—leaving it in the black leather scabbard—and rises barefoot and creeps away from the fire. Everywhere his body is stiff and sore and cold and his feet a blistered mess but the strength of decision is in him now, and something else, a memory of stealth on the ice floe, slipping out to the cache. As if he was always preparing for this. His heart is kicking its way up into his mouth; yet the pleasure of stealth returns too. The dark earth between the dim fires of other platoons offers a winding path and he follows it quickly, hunched low. The sentry on his stool at the door of Luz's tent is slumped back against the canvas, his bayoneted rifle across his lap. Kruger approaches slowly, then crouches. The figure remains still. There's a softly buzzing snore. Kruger eases the sabre from the scabbard, lays the scabbard on the ground. Hunched nearly double he lopes forward and tries to duck through the slit of the tent door. The canvas holds, tied from within. His momentum forces the tent's front wall to push in slightly so that the sentry, leaning back against it, sags farther with the motion. His snore catches and stops. The point of his bayonet, inches from Kruger's knee, wobbles. Kruger steps backward and stabs, slashes at the tent door, feels something sever on the inside, ducks through. Blood beating in his chin, he squints and crouches with the sabre raised. Outside, behind him, the sentry resumes snoring. A kerosene lamp burns low on a folding field-table with stools around it. On the table is a map, its corners held down by books, and a bottle of something dark with a few small crystal glasses, neatly ranked. The crystal is the only visible luxury. The feeling is simple, Spartan. Behind the table, a grey nap of canvas hangs from ceiling to floor, running from the tent's north wall almost to the south wall, leaving a kind of doorway into its darker half. He goes to the opening and through it and Luz is right there, in full uniform, faceless, rigid, his sabre at his side—then the mirage resolves. It's a legless mannequin on a stand, blank-featured, dressed in Luz's green tunic and clerical hat.

In the shadows of the corner, a small figure is nestled on a camp cot under a blanket. Kruger steps closer. His eyes readjust to the half light. Luz is asleep in his boots, which protrude from the bottom of the blanket. He's lying on his side furled into himself, childlike. The plain blanket covers much of his face. Only his deep-pitted sockets are in view, so dark that his eyes might be open and Kruger not know. By his head there's a simple end-table where another kerosene lamp sits, this one cold. A carpet woven with the design of his flag covers the bare ground by the cot. A carefully squared stack of books on the carpet. His revolver and pince-nez placed on the stack. Kruger can make out a few spines: MEDITACIONES DE MARCUS AURELIUS. THE PEHUES, SINA, & TARAHUMARA TONGUES. GOBINEAU: ESSAI SUR L'INEGALITE DES RACES HUMAINES.

All this Kruger absorbs in a few seconds, but those few seconds are enough. He hesitates. He has never killed a man. If only Luz would wake up, shout for help, grab at his revolver! In heroic stories, killing is a simple thing. But to decapitate a sleeping man, this man, seems not only cowardly, it means violently taking sides—that idiot temptation he so despises—when the one small wisdom he has gained from his life is that, when flags start to wave, someone must always refuse to join in. To kill Luz will be to murder his own beliefs—a negation of his life. And yet, this thing must be. The sabre whispers in his fist. The sentry's bee-like snoring has stopped. Shoes scrape on the gravel outside. Kruger steps up, arcs back the blade. The sentry yells *Ay—ayúdenme!* and Luz's eyes pop open blindly, he sits up on the cot, the blanket flops off him and he's naked from the waist up, lean-muscled. The two men stare. In this slowed moment, Luz's face regains its calm. The tent shudders as men, still out of view, crowd through the door behind the partition. You, says Luz. Kruger steps to the right of him, slashes the canvas wall, ducks through the long wound, drops the sabre and runs faster than he has run in years, faster than he would have believed he could still run. Shots crackle behind him. Muzzle flares light his path, a zigzag through the dozing cookfires and the stirring troops. Bullets sigh and purr around his ears. He tumbles down the steep riverbank in a heedless panic crashing into the water where the paralyzing current grips and sweeps him away. Downstream a sentry stands on the bank and Kruger dips under and hears the muffled crump of a shot and when he surfaces, gulping air, he's beyond Luz's camp, his paddling hands and feet numb as he drifts rapidly down into a small, familiar grove of cottonwoods. He swims in to shore, crawls up on the sand.

With stiff, truncated steps, he runs toward the village. His old path is shown by the vivid stars and the torches burning along the defensive wall. The Sinas, if they haven't fled, will surely take him for an attacker—the river has washed his pyjamas white again—but he's too frozen to care. From behind the wall a male voice yammers words he doesn't know, Sina, and Kruger raises his hands, still hobbling forward, and a gruffer voice tries Spanish, but before he can call back, the darkness detonates like La Paz on the Fifth of May fiesta as the Sinas open fire. The air zings with the insect whining of musket balls. *No tiren!* he yells, but the Sinas can't hear him, he can hardly hear himself, because now Luz's troops, and presumably Kruger's own men, have opened fire on the village at long range.

A bad night for pacifism. Kruger, hoping to prevent the war, has actually initiated it. He retreats to the river through a gauntlet of fire.

Cottonwoods aren't climbing trees, but he has managed to get halfway up one of the larger ones. He has spent the night trying to hug warmth from the living tree, shivering and dozing a few seconds at a time. To come this far south, he thinks with a kind of dire amusement, only to perish of exposure. . . . But the stars are extinguished now, the sun nearing. From his perch he has a view in all directions through the limp, coarse-toothed leaves. A magpie flaps up out of the willow scrub twenty feet down and lights on a branch above him. It leans over, the keen pellets of its eyes glaring past him, back down into the scrub. It cries a nasal *maa—maa?* as men, soldiers, appear directly below. Seen from this crow's nest they are self-propelled sombreros, hunched and sweat-stained backs, dirty sandal heels, picking their way toward the village in silence, bayoneted rifles pointing the way. A sergeant comes behind with a revolver in his left hand and a sabre in his right.

To the west, in open order across the plain, a phantom-white army advances on the town. Mateo will be among them. They move with furtive, leery steps, as if they think the village, now half a mile off, is still asleep and they might take it by surprise, though the village is clearly alert and waiting. It looks much as Kruger remembers it: a tight clump of cocoa-coloured adobe huts and a domed church, hunkered in the crook of a river looping down out of the foothills and snowy ranges of the Sierra Madre. But now braids of purple smoke rise from the houses hit last night in the shelling, and a rough, damaged wall of mud shuts the village off inside its bow of the river. And this is a problem. Once the attack begins, there will be no way for the villagers to flee. The low wall is lined with waiting faces—Sinas with yellow head-bands and bare chests, some mestizos in sombreros—and it bristles with firearms as well as bows, machetes, and, God help them, pitchforks and mattocks.

A corner of Jacinta's house can be seen, and beyond it the roofless top of the houseboat, but there's no sign of life in the yard by the river where Kruger once amused Mateo and his pals, and through which he would slink in the moonlight, away from her houseboat, back to this grove. Now behind him the sun blisters up out of the *páramo* and its first, tentative heat is glorious; yet it doesn't embolden him. Another spasm of shivering hits him. His stomach is chewing and tearing at itself. The growing urge to slink off is more than a temptation, it's the compulsion of a man conditioned in the marrow to shun hunger—hunger and cold. From up here he can see Purificación to be another floe: floe-sized, almost circular, icy water running around much of it, and crowded with trapped and hungry people. He can see no way to help them now—to help Jacinta or Mateo—or even to approach the village without being shot. He was a fool to think he could alter this puny, provincial chapter of history. Maybe the best anyone can do is to do no harm.

Well back of the peons, on the edge of Luz's camp, the *lanceros* sit their horses in two tight squadrons, lances hackling, waiting for the peons to soak up the Sina ammunition. Between the mounted groups, three fieldpieces sit ready. Luz, on his mare behind the artillery, holds the opera glasses to his eyes. The camp behind him is empty. A man practised in stealth could easily climb down this tree, slip back upriver into the camp, fill his saddlebags with food, food and blankets, and leave.

The light brimming westward reddens the flattened maize fields and the army tiptoeing across them, nearing the village. The Padre casts a glance at the sun, consults his fob-watch, then draws and hefts his sabre. He swings it down and the fieldpieces fire, spewing flame, bucking backward. Somewhere a drummer and bugler start in. A shell explodes on the earth ahead of the advancing men. A second shell bursts just inside the Sina enclosure and a third whistles clear over the village, into the river near the houseboat, exploding in a geyser of spray. Kruger's tree shudders in its roots, the leaves quivering. The magpie shrieks and takes wing, bolting eastward. Below and in the fields the men break into a charge, yipping like coyotes, the villagers at the wall waiting, holding their fire with surprising discipline, until, at point-blank, they loose a ragged volley. Soldiers tumble. The fieldpieces fire again and a shell smashes into a house behind the wall and another strikes the wall directly, dead centre, swatting flat the defenders, the attackers as well. From across the fields come screams, shreds of dense oily smoke floating, the panicked clanging of the church bell.

The worst fighting is at the smoking gap in the wall, flashes of bayonets and whetted farm tools, the hoarse roaring of combatants. The battle may soon end—the battle outside him. If he means to rob a distracted Luz, now would be the time. He stays where he is. He tries to make out certain faces, figures. Here and there soldiers are trying to clamber over the wall but they are thrown back, clubbed with shovels, shot by defenders kneeling on the flat roofs of houses. Most of the attackers, herded on by their sergeants, funnel in toward the gap. More shells whine in and pummel down behind the Sina wall, then another hits close behind the gap and for a moment smoke curtains everything. It clears on a scene: some attackers milling forward, others trying to recoil, like a civilian mob being fired on in a riot. A sergeant aims his pistol into a slew of fleeing men but they run him down, infected with panic and the spirit of retreat. Within a minute the whole army is in flight. Luz watches from the saddle, his body inarticulately still, though with his gloved hand he is soothing the neck of the mare.

The line of flight is straight back across the plain, the cottonwood grove remains empty. But Kruger stays in his perch. The sun's accruing warmth is reaching him there and the soldiers at any time might sweep back down through the grove. Through the day's rising mercury the shelling continues, while the villagers, men and women, labour to douse the fires and rebuild the wall. He strains for a glimpse of Jacinta and recognizes her repeatedly, through that semaphoric totality of posture and gesture that distinguishes someone at a distance, even years later. Then, repeatedly, he doubts it's her. Another shell makes a direct hit on the wall and opens a new breach. Bodies, a few still moving and making pitiable sounds, clutter the ground in front of the wall. The slain in their deep, eerie siesta.

There's curious activity on the banks upriver, around the spot where he leapt in last night. *Teniente* Ortiz is in charge of five men, who are struggling to the bottom of the bank, awkwardly rolling down a large keg. They lift and prop it on a rock and tilt it over the water. A trickle of clear fluid gleams. They seem to be taking their time, pouring very slowly; or maybe the bung is tiny. Above them on the bank stands Ortiz, smoking a cigarillo, hand on his hip, effeminate in his machismo.

Kruger lets himself down the tree, not nearly fast enough, hot now, dizzy, slipping the last few rungs and tumbling in the sand. He limps to the river and strips off his uniform, as he must, to have a hope. He stoops and drinks quickly, stopping long before he has had enough, then wades out through the shallows—the icy cold now briefly welcome. The current hooks and pulls him in and he swims hard, ahead of whatever is coming down behind him, swimming out of the grove and around the long treeless bend to where the village wall begins, a Sina with a musket standing atop the wall profiled against the sky. Jacinta's houseboat appears ahead. It comes up fast. He grapples onto the stern deck, under the taffrail, tries to heave himself up, but he is too weak and numb. A slab-like pair of hands, red and freckled, clutch his wrists and lug him aboard. He stands on the deck naked and tottering. They look him over, a fat, bearded white man in a slouch hat and an old Sina with a whiskery undershot jaw, like some ancient river fish. The Sina aims a rusty derringer at his chest, the white man picks up a rifle. By their feet are a dozen wooden buckets—still empty.

Busco a Jacinta, he says through clattering teeth. *I am looking for Jacinta.*

The two guards exchange a glance. The old Sina bursts out laughing.

¡Ah . . . un visitante informal!

The white man grins in his orange beard but doesn't lower the rifle. In Spanish with a thick American twang he says, Suppose you tell us who you are.

A spy, says Kruger, with information. I am one of you.

The old Sina lends Kruger his poncho for modesty and walks him across the yard past Jacinta's empty house, into the besieged village. Small women in bright headscarves trot past them toward the river with buckets. While keeping his pistol pressed into the small of Kruger's back, the old man shouts affably into his ear.

Ah, the German, yes! I remember you now! There were no funerals in the month of your staying!

They pass a house crushed and gutted by a shell. Two hunched women in black weeds are splashing bucketfuls of water on the ruins, as if there were something left to salvage. Nothing remains standing but the wooden door frame.

I fear the same won't be true this time, however, the old man says.

Jacinta's son is with Luz's troops, Kruger says.

Yes, this is known. He was in their front ranks today.

Was he hurt?

This way, *por favor!* the old man hollers above the nearing clang of the church bell, the whistle of another shell passing over. You are well remembered in this village. Though naturally you were known to be a spy of Presidente Diaz. We kept expecting you to return to us. I find you are much changed.

You have to believe me about the water.

We will see. Not to drink in such heat would be as bad as poison.

Then save what water you have—let the houses burn!

But, they are not your houses, Señor. What is there to fight for if all the village should burn?

They round the shaded corner of a house into the sun-dazzled plaza in front of the church. Four men bolt across their path, in the direction of the wall. Three are Sinas with long sticks, the tips scorched and sharpened, the fourth another white man, with a new-looking rifle. The men glance at Kruger, then at his Sina captor, but go on running. Kruger asks about the white men; again the old man politely yells, This way, *por favor!*

A boy with a flintlock pistol swings open one of the church's heavy doors and they pass into the cool and lamplit gloom. The sounds of the bell and the artillery are muted. Out of the dimness come voices moaning, sobbing, as if gripped by some violent religious rapture. Kruger's eyes adjust. The windowless inner walls are of stone. Lamps, lampions, ranks of votive candles tremble in the corners and in niches. The altar and sanctuary are dark. Wooden benches have been pushed and stacked against the south wall to clear the floor of the nave where the wounded and dead are stretched under the low, unembellished dome. Among the bodies, small kneeling forms in black pray softly, in unison, and among them other women tread with candles, blankets, buckets. There's a raw and complicated smell. Huddled at the front of the nave by the altar rail, a mob of whispering children.

Jacinta! the old man shouts hoarsely, and her name reverberates through the church. One of the nurses sets down her bucket and candle and pads over. Her bare feet are silent on the clay floor. She has greying braids and wears a spattered apron over a loose dress of some dull, coarse fabric. Kruger knows her now, although she is thinner and seems smaller, with scooped shadows under her cheekbones and eyes. The same faint down above her lip, the same endearingly small feet, although they're untended, the nails curled, the skin like sunbaked adobe.

Qué milagro, he says quietly, shivering.

She looks him over, frowning: a naked skeleton in a poncho. But something in her nimble, liquid eyes is not quite certain he is unfamiliar.

Is this man wounded? One of the Padre's men?

No, Señora! Our spy has returned to us. The German . . .

As she stares at his face, Kruger nods once.

¡Por Dios! she cries, *¡Kruger. Qué milagro!*

He steps forward, extending both arms. She recoils lightly, takes his right hand in hers. Her hand is hot.

Have you come with the Padre's men? she asks sternly.

I'm afraid I did—I was volunteered. Is your son . . . ?

You saw him? You spoke with Mateo?

He was in my platoon, they made me a leader. What happened today?

But—in your platoon? Then why is he not here with you? Why did you not bring him!

It was impossible, Jacinta. It's difficult to explain . . .

She lets go his hand. You mean because he *wants* to be with the Padre.

I couldn't be sure.

For a moment her eyes redden and well; then they dry, as if she has somehow retracted the emotion. Maybe she has learned to. Behind her somebody grunts and calls out in Sina, the sounds echoing liturgically in the dome. The whispering children fall silent.

They tell me, she says, that he was in the front ranks, but then retreated.

We must hope so! bellows the old man.

He was well when I saw him, Jacinta.

She says, You look as if you need to lie down.

She leads him to a blank spot on the floor among the wounded and lays out a serape. He can do nothing except sag to the ground. He curls shivering in his damp poncho while she and the old man confer ardently in Sina, their voices already starting to drift away from him. He catches Mateo's name, the name Luz, his own name, then the name of the *caudillo*, Porfirio Diaz. Jacinta too may still believe that Kruger serves Diaz . . . Luz . . . Ortiz. . . . How a fever reduces all names and words to phonetic gibberish. In the end, if this is it, they signify no more than the unstable names and boundaries of nations. With a hollow booming the church shudders like a sepulchre in a quake, flakes of mortar tumbling slowly out of the dome as if to lid his eyes. *Don't forget about the river,* a voice is murmuring somewhere. His own voice. *You have to believe me.* He floats up into the dome's immense hemisphere as if into a cloud of clay, his eyes shut, feeling somebody is there. The bells and the shelling have ceased. Out of an ancient book beside the sleeping Padre's cot, Marcus Aurelius is whispering, All life is a warfare and a journey in a strange land.

¡Amelia, mi amor . . . Mis niños . . . !

Are you awake, Kruger? *Krrugarr,* she says. He lifts himself onto his elbows. Jacinta is kneeling in her bloody apron, holding a candle to his face. As she leans over, the brawny Christ on her silver crucifix slips out the front of her dress and hangs.

You were asleep all day, she says.

She puts a small piece of something between his cracked lips: corn tortilla.

This is all we can spare.

I came to offer help, he whispers, and I seem to have turned you into my nurse.

This is often the way with men, I find—and she smiles a little, showing that grey front tooth half-capped with silver. But in fact, you have helped us.

You've not been drinking the water?

No—I told them to believe you. Then Sam on the houseboat began to pull dead *tuahmec* out of the river. But we're out of water now, by tomorrow we'll be desperate. Some believe we should start to use the water again now, but there's no telling when they'll poison it again.

Yes. Or if it stays awhile, this poison, on the bottom and the banks.

You can put these on. She hands him the neatly folded field pyjamas of a Sina man, loose trousers and a yellow tunic with an emerald sash. There's a small hole ringed with blood on the right side just under the collar.

We think the Padre will attack the wall tonight, and we're short of defenders. She sweeps her open hand around her, as if suddenly impatient with the dying and the dead. Can you stand? Can you aim a rifle?

He blinks slowly, nods.

One of the miners was badly hurt this morning. Better his weapon go to somebody who can use it.

She's hollow-eyed, her breath stinks of hunger, but when he urges her to rest for a while she frowns at him, clucking her tongue. *Venga . . . apúrese.*

They emerge into the dusty heat of twilight. The western sky is coral over the snow peaks of the sierra, fires are burning low in the many ruins. He carries the Springfield rifle of a dying silver miner—one of several who rafted downriver last week, she says, to help the village, including the big American that he met on the houseboat. The others are Mexican. The priest, too, he stood at the wall with them, she says, when Kruger asks where he is, assuming, since the priest is invisible, that he has fled. Cut down this morning by one of the first shells, his cross brandished high.

I'd always thought of priests as siding with the authorities, Kruger says, chastened.

A faintly fetid sweetness wafts in off the plain. They join the threadbare rank of defenders at the wall. Next to them are the old man with the catfish jaw, then the American miner, a Mexican miner in a battered Stetson, and villagers variously armed or half-armed, women now as well as men. A Sina whose foot has been amputated and the stump roughly dressed leans against the wall, his face pale and tight, clutching a musket held together with rawhide thongs. Everywhere wounded men are propped up, one asleep with his bandaged head on his forearm on the wall.

Kruger says, Who's caring for the wounded in the church, with these women all here?

The wounded are all here too. We left only the dead and the ones who will soon die. Young girls are with those ones and with the children. My daughter is there, for one.

In front of the Padre's camp across the littered fields a long row of soldiers is forming under the flags. Above the line of the men's sombreros, the heads of horses and the green coats and lances and guidons of the cavalry. And in the heart of that bristling mass, which pulsates dimly as the last of the day's heat lifts out of the earth, Colonel Maclovio Luz can be distinguished by his hat.

On the wall she sets her long-dead father's flintlock pistol and stares gape-eyed into the distance. The old man offers Kruger his pipe and though it contains only *macuche* he sucks on it greedily, far longer than he should, scorching his dry throat with the taste of burning cornfields.

The old man says loudly, You marched with the Padre, then, you camped with him?

Briefly, yes.

He is nothing like us! If you see him in a mirror, or his shadow on a tent wall, there are horns! And he coughs up hairballs! This I know to be so. Many have seen this.

One round'll put a stop to him, the American mutters in English, and Kruger levers the trapdoor breech of his own weapon and checks it again. Again he sees himself waking Luz; the man's moment of helplessness; his own humane, fatal hesitation.

Night like a dark fog salted with stars rises out of the eastern *páramo* as Jacinta relates her last dozen years to him in whispers. Her mother has been dead for six. The younger daughter departed just a year ago to work in Chihuahua City, in one of the new cotton mills, and the older daughter, thank God, is still here, married for three years, with a baby son. She and her family live with Jacinta in the same house by the river. The girl's husband is the village brickmaker, a good man, though very thin, and his marriage to Maria has permitted Jacinta to retire from a calling that she is much too old for. (To Kruger she doesn't look old.) She says only a few words of Mateo. How the boy grew restless, bitter, contrary, he had wanted to be a priest but then he hoped to go to the city, perhaps join the hated cavalry, or even to work on the railroad for which they were so taxed! Anything to leave Purificación. More and more he seemed to despise his own people's ways, and above all his mother's ways, her manner of life, when, to a Sina mind, there was nothing especially shameful in her profession. The flesh was simply the flesh. All this naturally was a heartbreak.

Torches are being lit and propped at intervals along the wall. Kruger says only a few things, all he cares to say, or can, about his vanished world in La Paz. His own lost children. He's grateful when the bell's tolling cuts him short. They're moving on us, the American says. At first it's not apparent—there's no sound, no outward motion—but in the dark, that solid white line of men, like a wall of surf breaking on a far reef, is thickening. It's not long before small distinct forms can be made out, seeming to tread the night air. Somewhere a bugle sounds. The forms begin to move faster, up and down, jogging toward the wall, the massed slap of sandals getting louder. Then a high-pitched savage yipping. Somebody calls out in Sina and Jacinta frowns and grabs her crude pistol and, imitating the old man next to her, thumbs back the hammer. Kruger guesses she has never used the thing. He cocks his rifle. The fieldpieces open fire, the shells screech in at the village and one lands in the hulk of a flattened house nearby and Kruger feels his stomach has been butted, his ears boxed. The flash of the explosion shows white figures closing in. He squints out at them, trying to see. A voice screams another Sina command and the defenders open fire—an unimpressive, disordered volley, the old man's derringer misfiring, Kruger and Jacinta not firing at all.

Fire! she tells him, why are you not firing?

For the same reason you aren't. I need to see the faces first.

Fire now! she orders, and turns away scowling and thrusts the flintlock straight out with both hands tight on the handle but still she doesn't fire. The white forms with their long, levelled bayonets are nearly on them. Another round of shells flashes in. The Mexican and the American miner with their toy-sized Winchesters are shooting down soldier after soldier while the Sina defenders fumble to reload their muskets, the old man tinkering with his flashpan, trying the pistol again and then hurling it down at his feet and turning to Kruger and screaming at him in Sina. And Kruger does fire now, though the soldiers' sombrero-brims keep the torchlight off their faces as they bunch themselves low and small, anonymous. Jacinta is still paralyzed beside him. The peon-soldiers are too close to miss. Kruger levers the breech and reloads and again he doesn't miss. He seems to be praying. He aims at their legs—the spindly legs of men or boys crowded on from behind. The fire of the Winchesters and the Springfield is too much for them at this part of the wall and the charge falters a few paces short, wavers, then melts back, while the sergeants holler and shoot their pistols into the air, trying to drive the men on.

From down the wall, where a shell has punctured another breach, comes the bestial uproar of hand-to-hand fighting. They start toward it but then a Sina woman with a field hoe points and cries out. An obscure, heavy mass is pounding, surging out of the darkness: the *lanceros* at full gallop, their lances cocked down and streamers fluttering from the blades. The quaking of hooves comes through the shuddering ground. The Padre leads, standing the stirrups and crouched over the neck of his grinning mare, his right arm thrust out, sabre pointed. Somehow he glides through the mass of his fleeing soldiers without running them down, or scolding or exhorting, yet some of them now stop and turn as if under a spell and follow him back toward the wall, while the *lanceros* trailing Luz make no effort to avoid the clots of retreating or turning men. They simply ride over them. The miners are wrestling their own guns, trying to force in fresh rounds. Kruger gets off a shot and Jacinta finally fires her pistol, but the Padre is on top of them. They tuck down against the wall as the bellies of the leaping horses, sorrel, black, white, dappled, flash overhead. That suddenly the Padre is inside the village. The Sinas and the miners, Jacinta and Kruger abandon the wall and run for the church.

Purity is the mother of evil, the Sinas would say during their mid-spring fiesta, the Fiesta de Caos, and tomorrow would be the day, Jacinta whispers. She feels sorry for the children, she says. It is their favourite fiesta, their favourite day of the year.

Bodies cover the floor of the dimly lit church, the dead and the wounded and the living, all promiscuously strewn. Now and then a child will squeal or one of the wounded will cry out and these sounds along with the drone of snoring transform themselves high in the dome, where they circulate and return, fused to a ghostly communion of sound. The thick-necked American miner snores loudest. No sounds reach them from the outside; the heavy doors are piled and barricaded with benches and charred beams from the outer ruins. Jacinta sleeps under the north wall by her daughter, Quamhac Maria, and her grandson. Her son-in-law is posted at the church's only other opening, a small door for the priest, off the vestry.

Kruger lies on Jacinta's other side, though with space between them. A wounded man in the middle of the nave is prone, licking at the cool clay of the floor. It looks worth a try.

Kruger's thoughts keep returning to that vestry door.

Are you awake, Kruger?

Too much so.

I see him too, she whispers, presumably meaning the man licking the floor. The babies will die first of us, she says. My daughter has no more milk.

We may have to give ourselves up tomorrow, he says.

No! We heard he slaughtered a Pehues village like that.

I think he cares too much for order and rules to let his men kill prisoners.

You don't understand, most of us are *indios.* There are different rules for us.

He says nothing. She may be right. In the silence their conversation is prolonged by whispering echoes in the dome.

I had a chance to kill him, Jacinta—in the camp. I'm sorry.

Many have tried, she says mildly, as if resigned to the impossibility. She adds, When Mateo is older he will not only miss having a home, he will miss having a *people.*

Don't say that yet.

To whom will he speak his mother's tongue? Not that he cares to speak it anyway! His Sina is so poor! She laughs softly, almost fondly, as if at a child's harmless foibles. I didn't see him there tonight, I looked . . . I think they must have kept him back, as a guard.

This is the fourth or fifth time she has voiced this opinion. Her swollen eyes show all the symptoms of crying, but seem too dry to make actual tears. If they did, he would drink them.

She says, The Padre, he's much too smart to make a Sina attack his own village, no? For how could a Sina be trusted?

Jacinta—

In the first attack, it's true, they used him, but he was one of those who retreated—he may even have led their retreat! So, in a way, he might have *saved* the village. They won't want to use him again.

Returning her glazed stare, he nods firmly. Time to be a willing collaborator. Reflecting on how he hates the way men like Luz twist the confusions of youth to their advantage, he says, I joined up at your son's age, too.

And you were wounded! she says.

I'm still here. The boy's zeal will pass, I'm certain of it. He rests a hand on her shoulder, willing its weight to steady her trembling. His hand, unfortunately, is also trembling. He knows that the boy's new loyalty may not pass at all.

Lie close to me, she says. Here.

After some time, during which they may have dozed together, she turns her flank to him and says in a cracked whisper, Go ahead, Kruger. You must need a woman now.

Her generosity at such a moment is touching—also shocking. Though maybe she is also seeking to comfort herself, return herself to a time long before these troubles. Or is this merely some kind of reflex? But her invitation is beside the point. She must be too dry, and that part of his life is now dead. Even her armpits' ripe, spicy smell—the same, the same—does nothing for him. He can picture her sprawled back on the bed in the houseboat, gazing up at him, her fancy white petticoats hiked high and spread around her smooth, open legs. Her brown, almost hairless body. The way she always called him by his last name.

I don't even wake that way in the night anymore, he says.

Then what did you return for, Kruger?

I had something to return to you. No. That's not it. It's as if—as if I wanted to haunt you. If I could have just looked in on you and seen that you were all right, then gone on my way, I would have. I don't seem to want to be involved with people much now.

Sehamic! a man cries, then switching to Spanish, *¡Agua!*

Men only ever returned for the fucking, she says, turning back to face him, seemingly touched. I never forgot you.

Nor I you. There were times . . . times when my wife would say things that reminded me of you. As you reminded me of the Esquimau woman.

For a moment she is still, then her eyes shoot darts of fire and she hisses, Naturally, yes, because we're all dark! All brown women! All just the same!

No, forgive me, it's not—

We don't even *like* the other *indios.* We hate them! How can you—

Amelia was mestizo, not *indio*—you don't understand. I had to leave that northern world. That morgue. The worry and the shame, the wars and the money. They pretend to be rational and civilized, when all that drives them is hatred, and fear. I came south . . .

His voice is drying up.

Here too there's war and hatred, she says.

Claro.

Still, maybe you should have stayed and become a Sina.

I didn't think you wanted that. I didn't think I did.

Mateo was so fond of you!

Yes, he says. And he thinks: It would be very like my life, to finally join a people on the verge of extinction.

He waits until her breathing thickens and then he gets up and, stepping over bodies, not always sure if they're dead or alive, he picks his way toward the vestry, searching. A Sina man groans, rasping words as Kruger steps across him: *Sehamic, timaquis! ¡Agua, por favor!* A little folding knife is tucked in his sash. Kruger stoops and slips it out, opens it to feel the short claw-shaped blade, folds it up again and tucks it into his beard, under the chin.

In the lamplit corridor leading to the priest's entry, more armed sleepers. In front of the heavy-looking door, built long ago for defence, two young Sinas sit on footstools facing each other. They're slumped forward resting their heads on each other's shoulders, blocking the door with their bodies so that any movement will wake them. Their muskets rest against the wall behind them.

Kruger taps the bony shoulder of one of these two, Jacinta's son-in-law. Calmly he peers up at Kruger with the lugubrious long face of a Christ in a Mexican icon. He keeps one hand on his fellow sentry's shoulder and the other hand under his forehead, so the man's position is unchanged, his sleep unbroken.

Please let me through this door, Kruger says.

The soldiers are out there, Señor, the young man says quietly, his manner shy and respectful: Indian to much older white. You can see them through the squint.

Kruger lifts the hinged slat and peers through a judas in the door. It looks straight up an alley which opens onto the torch-lit plaza. Two sentries in white pyjamas guard the end of the alley. Beyond them in the plaza, more figures are moving.

All the same, I have to go out there. I know a way to help us.

I was told to let nobody through, Señor.

You were told to let nobody in. I'm going out.

Are you running away, Señor?

Please don't ask if I'm a spy.

You are running away, the young man says mournfully. Well, you are not a Sina, I can't keep you here if you want to leave. Will the miners leave as well, with their good rifles?

No, they're brave men. Can you see anything in my beard?

After a moment the young man says gravely, No, Señor. Your beard is quite clean, Señor.

Gracias.

De nada, Señor.

Wake your friend, you'll need to close and bolt the door quickly after me.

He is fatalistic—too tired for fear—as Luz's sentries grope him for weapons, then rush him across the plaza lit up with torches and a bonfire, as if for the Festival of Chaos. His beard feels heavy, tugging at his chin. A little mob of peons is shoving and hauling one of the fieldpieces into position in front of the church's front doors. Others are sprawled asleep along the edges of the plaza. A *lancero* rides by, exaggerating his torso, glancing down with haughty half-curiosity.

Lieutenant Ortiz intercepts them, on foot. His moustache tips are waxed upward and his pate looks as if it's been smartly buffed, but he seems preoccupied, his eyes small and mean with fatigue.

Sargento Tyson! You're hoping to switch sides yet again? Your last choice seems to have been a poor one! And your men, they missed you greatly—many of them fell tonight, along the south part of the wall.

Most of them were ridden down, by you.

Cowards, one and all, Ortiz says irritably.

What about Mateo? Is he—

He played no part in the victory. This afternoon he drank from the river, against orders. Old habits, I suppose. He may live.

Kruger absorbs this, then says—can't stop himself from saying—Do you have any water?

So, this is about water! Yes, I'm afraid the local water is not fit for a dog. And it was a hot day, no? The Sinas fought quite well, considering. But it must be rather . . . awkward now in the church, I suppose?

I need to speak with Colonel Luz.

Like the cholera, I should think, Ortiz says with his double smile. And you can speak with me.

I've been instructed to speak with the colonel. It's about a surrender.

You allow yourself to be "instructed" by *indios*! He snickers, and the sentries dutifully join in. This inflates him further. Why, you even dress like them now!

The Sinas are prepared to surrender.

Kruger watches the man in the firelight which, as always, illuminates features and feelings that could be missed in daylight, with its less subtle angles and tones. Clearly Ortiz would like to negotiate this surrender himself, now; he suspects he might get away with it but is worried that his superior will be angry; he is deciding that he had better consult *El Capitán* after all.

Thrusting his jaw he says, Very well, come this way.

I need water. Kruger's voice is faint. Ortiz ignores him. Spurs jingling he roosters off, at a pace he must know will be difficult for Kruger. But it isn't far. Luz's command post is in one of the few undamaged houses in the village—the usual flat-roofed, one-storey adobe hut with a front awning of wood and straw, and for windows a vertical slit to either side of the door. Ortiz raps sharply, cocks his ear, then lets himself in while the sentries stand back from Kruger, aiming their bayonets at his ribs, timidly dodging his eyes. They look about twelve years old.

¿Tienen agua? Kruger asks them. *¡Por favor!*

The boys exchange rattled glances. Ortiz bursts importantly through the door and with a leer of ridicule he looks Kruger up and down, then nods toward the opening. He draws his long-barrelled revolver and steps aside, keeping the gun trained on Kruger as Kruger enters. Then he follows him in. The one-room house has been made to look exactly like Luz's command tent: stools set neatly around the folding table, the lamplit map squared on the table and held open by books, a bottle with a clean rank of glasses, and, draped from the ceiling toward the back of the room, two sheets of canvas curtaining off the bedquarters. Back there a second lamp is glowing, a familiar figure looming in silhouette. No horns.

A sabre pokes through the gap between the canvas drapes and sweeps to the right, parting them wide. Luz, looking fresh and alert, glides through. From the waist up he is naked except for white suspenders, white kid gloves. His hard torso is oiled with sweat. His broad, scholarly forehead shines too, flushed against the steel-grey helmet of hair, his wire-rimmed pince-nez. At his solar plexus is a diamond-shaped scar, as from a spear. He wears his revolver. He has been exercising, clearly, but is not out of breath.

Mr George Tyson, welcome, he says in English. The lieutenant advises me that you have come to arrange a capitulation. *¡Teniente Ortiz—espera afuera!*

Ortiz stiffens. *¡Si, mi coronel!* He backs out the doorway but remains there at attention, looking in.

I must have some water, Kruger says.

Do you care for a glass of port? Luz sheathes the sabre. I keep a bottle here for my officers. I myself do not drink, or eat meat.

Just water. Please.

He feels the weight of the little knife as he speaks.

Yes, says Luz, you must need some by now. All of you. He shakes his head, frowning slightly. My lieutenant took matters into his own hands today. Normally this tactic would be a last resort, so as to end a long siege and avert further loss of life. He is a very poor lieutenant. *¡Teniente—trae agua buena!*

Ortiz blinks, then pivots on his rowelled heel and strides into the dark. A few seconds later, long seconds, one of the child sentries shuffles in quickly with a sloshing bucket in one hand, a tin cup in the other. Luz nods. The boy sets the wooden bucket in front of Kruger's toes and then, trembling, saluting Luz with averted eyes, he backs away fast, out the door. Kruger crumples to his knees; he scoops up water and thrusts it to his open lips, slurping with violence, spilling half the cupful, and for this long moment he cares about nothing, nobody else, all he's aware of is the rapture of that precious, tepid fluid flooding down the *arroyo* of his seared throat, trickling down through his beard. He glances up at Luz, who is closing the door in Ortiz's staring face. *Don't take it away*, he thinks, *please!* He scoops again, again soaking his beard, but this time he drinks more carefully, getting more down. He drinks a third and a fourth and a fifth cup.

Don't drink any more, Luz commands softly. Not yet. You would be ill, and we have some matters to discuss. You say those in the church are willing to emerge without further resistance?

Yes, Señor.

He must get closer to Luz. He wipes his mouth and nose and stands up—then sneezes. The little knife tumbles out of his wet beard and plunks into the bucket.

Luz's lean jaw seems to flex. His eyes peer with deep irony from behind the pince-nez.

Well, apparently you did not come here merely to negotiate a surrender.

Somewhere a rooster crows prematurely and goes on doing it. Luz studies him.

In fact, however—and contrary to what you may believe—you

did not come here to kill me, either. In fact, you have come here simply to save your own life.

This is unnecessary, Kruger says.

Probably you are not even aware of it yourself. And this has fascinated me—how men, even intelligent men, can persuade themselves that they are acting with principle in mind, when in fact they are merely indulging their animal natures. I took notice that you drank this water with exceptional, what is the word, relish. This water and the survival it entails, this in fact is what you came for. Lieutenant Ortiz furnishes a clearer example. He declares to me, and doubtless to himself, that he serves with me in order to clear this region of its primitive insurgents, and allow our nation to have its future among other modern nations. He declares that he serves the valid causes of progress and prosperity. In fact, he is merely a vain dandy, a, what is the English word, a cock, coax . . .

Coxcomb.

A coxcomb—thank you—hankering after a brilliant uniform, a commission, some decorations. A touch of glory, as aphrodisiac. Poorly armed adversaries and facile conquests. Tonight was a shock to him. We encountered real resistance. In the plaza his mount was shot out from under him, whereupon a Sina housewife very nearly impaled him with a hayfork while he lay helpless. She herself was shot only at the last moment.

With his gloved hand Luz unholsters his revolver. His eyes swing down to it for a moment, the rest of him unmoving. Then his eyes light again on Kruger's face.

I know that you are a man of some thought, Mr Tyson. A part of you must have known that you could hardly kill me with this little knife. Last night you could not even achieve it with a sword.

Kruger says, If thoughtful men fool themselves, how can you be sure you aren't just like Ortiz?

Luz's chin lifts very slightly.

And why should I think, Kruger says, that you believe any of those things either? Progress, prosperity, wealth. I've read the Presidente's broadsides too—nailed to the door of every cantina in La Paz. You know as well as I do, Diaz cares only for his power. And whether you know it or not, you, like him, are working for the railroad firm.

No.

How flattering to be seen as the Lamp of the Future—a father to those boys!

Luz's eyes gleam. He bares that array of tended teeth. You think that they want anything else?

Given a chance to live till adulthood, who knows.

People do not grow up, Luz says firmly. There are no adults. Very few adults.

What about you?

The only adults are those who can turn to advantage the natural childishness of the mob. They thus become the parent of the mob. A parent who provides, who protects, who *improves*, who thus in turn begins the long work of elevating it to adulthood. I do in fact believe in these things we speak of, Mr Tyson. Like you, I am by nature an idealist—though by necessity a soldier. I care little for wealth or railroad money. I am not even much of a patriot. Fundamentally I despise the disorder I perceive here, the ignorance and barbarous suffering that ensue from it.

The Sinas are hardly barbarians. You must know that.

Luz regards him with that fixed smile.

I find I rather enjoy this, Mr Tyson. Here I have nobody to speak to. To speak to in this way, I mean.

Kruger says nothing.

In fact, you are correct. I have some respect for the Indians, and the Sina most peculiarly. Their language I respect. They are not without culture. Their time here, however, is finished. Civilization will not realize its entire moral and intellectual possibilities until it has purged itself of all these, how shall I phrase it, these *infantile* elements which constantly revert it into the past. Dirt and superstition and primitive ritual. *Nostalgie de la boue.* Imagine, Mr Tyson, an ordered and rational civilization all of adults! A society where, for example, all men can read and write. Where people like your shipmates will not die of the cholera, because of the wretched condition of our towns. It may be possible, in a future we strive towards. For now, alas, we must pragmatically *exploit* the primitive, as with my own illiterate troops, so as to advance the futurist cause.

Luz holds up the revolver and extrudes the cylinder, examining and spinning and clicking it back into place. The muscles of his arm bulge and knot: a perfectly tooled physique.

Now, in choosing to side with the Indians, you exhibit a curious sentimentality and nostalgia. I find it difficult to understand such self-indulgings in a man who appears otherwise intelligent. Men like you, Mr Tyson—men like you have no notion of the suffering your liberal decencies inflict over time!

Numbly Kruger sees the knife in the bottom of the bucket, the water magnifying it into a more plausible weapon. Through his pince-nez Luz transfixes him with eyes as blue as Kruger's own. The whites are very white. He has grown almost animated.

In fact there are men of thought, and there are men of initiative—of activity. Rarely, one finds men who combine these two properties—men who, upon reaching a hard conclusion by irresistible logic, will then set it into practice, dispassionately, impersonally, like the great Stoic emperor Aurelius, having to deal with the Christians. These are the Adults.

Men like you.

You, however, are a man of thought exclusively. That is why you were unable to use the sword last night. Similarly, you consider the merits of the Sina—I don't deny that they have them—and refuse to face the cruel necessities of progress. In essence the Indians are children, subsisting in the ancient districts of imagination, not fact, not history, and they must be forced to grow up, or forcibly removed. Still, they cannot help being what they are, and in this they exhibit a certain rude integrity. You, however, have made a free choice, a foolish one. Though not necessarily fatal.

Luz cocks the revolver. Kruger remains calm, empty. He has often wondered what has caused more death and pain through history: the brutish lack of any ideas, or the ideas themselves. Luz might find this paradox intriguing, but Kruger can't bring himself to speak, to participate.

You remain unconvinced, says Luz, pleased. He takes three steps toward Kruger, his left hand reaching to grip the barrel of the cocked revolver he holds in his right. With his left he turns the gun around and passes it, steel handle first, to Kruger. Kruger receives it and stares dumbstruck at the weapon in his hand, then at Luz, whose face at close range, shaved perfectly blue, is all irony, deep sardonic creases around the mouth.

Luz bows slightly and with arch formality takes two steps back, leaving a smell of lye and clean sweat in the air.

You came here to save yourself, Mr Tyson, and I shall permit this. I shall permit you, in fact, simply to walk away. However, you told yourself that you came here to assassinate me. And this also I permit. However, you cannot do it. Men are consistent—a matter of science. I stopped you with my will last night and as I look into your face at this time, I perceive it again—you see in me your leader. I have earned you, Mr Tyson. And this, in fact, is what men want, always. I sense that you have been deeply, how shall I phrase this now, deeply *lonely*, no doubt for a long time.

How terribly men need something to adhere to, Mr Tyson! A church, a people, a land, a flag—a leader. A leader above all. As for the leader himself, if he is a true one, a true Adult, he needs only an idea to which to adhere. I think that you understand this, for you yourself, I think, are something of a leader, if undeveloped as yet. So I offer you a third and final choice: a commission in my army. A chance to become more than merely a man of thoughts. Frankly, Mr Tyson, you would be a great relief to me, Ortiz is such a . . . Luz grins dryly as he locates the word: a *coxcomb.* Like a young Santa Anna. To Ortiz and his ilk, conquest is merely a form of . . . of sadistic theatre. To me, it is moral science.

If I join you now—Kruger senses, even smells, the luscious water at his feet; maybe Luz was not totally wrong in his accusation?—would you leave the village in peace? What's left of it?

But that would be to leave a vital work unaccomplished, Mr Tyson! However, I would certainly spare and protect any of those villagers who choose to surrender.

Kruger knows they won't surrender. Those mastering, hypnotic eyes continue to hold his, and as the gun gets heavier in his slackening hand, he feels an odd visceral softening, a sort of voluptuous temptation to yield to his conqueror—this scholar of human weakness, a man bold and assured enough to give over his own weapon. The most primitive seduction. A bead of sweat stings down into Kruger's eye. He tightens his grip on the pistol.

In fact, Mr Tyson, whatever should happen, I shall try to ensure that something does survive of the Sina people. I perceive that this matters to you a good deal. Victors do write the histories, and this confronts them with the obligation to record and preserve as much as possible.

Something distracts Luz. His mesmerist eyes release Kruger's. His brow and lips pucker in thought, just slightly, though on his impassive face the effect is dramatic. With the bemused look of someone ambushed by a fascinating paradox, he says, the Sina tongue, for example—it cannot and will not be extinguished immediately. I myself have learned much of it, you see. In fact, should events transpire as they may have to—these Sina being so cursed with courage—then I myself might be the final living speaker of the Sina tongue!

Kruger's finger jerks, the hammer snaps. Nothing happens. Luz blinks—a microscopic show of surprise, or something—but he doesn't move. A slow smile dawns across his face. He has hedged his bets, the scholar not quite so sure of his experiment as he claimed. This surprises Kruger; as his own action has. Casually Luz reaches and grips the barrel of the gun. He's still smiling, the smile of a man tickled by the spirited anger of some harmless inferior. A woman, a small child. Kruger lets go of the gun and bends and swipes up the bucket by its hinged handle and swings it up and over his shoulder and down. Centrifugal pressure retains most of the water, the weight. The bucket smashes onto Luz's head, cracks apart, water sloshing, slats and the tin cup and little knife and now the revolver clattering to the floor. In the manner of a folding chair Luz collapses neatly. On the floor he sits drenched, his scabbard splayed, blood pooling in the hideous dent in his hair. His glasses have popped off, his pensive blue eyes exposed. He holds up a hand, the index finger raised. Brow knitted, lips parted, he seems to have one further point to make, but can't formulate the words. There's something he means to object to, or rebut. His torso topples straight back and his head hits the floor with a decisive clunk.

Glancing at the door Kruger kneels, grabs the revolver, pops out the cylinder, leans toward Luz's body hoping to find bullets. Then he sees: the cylinder is not quite empty. There's a single bullet. The Padre, it seems, had a vice after all. The door swings inward. It's Ortiz, his mouth forming a little O of shock under the moustache. As the man gropes at his holster Kruger snaps the cylinder closed and cocks the pistol, aims, squeezes. Another click. Ortiz fumbling to cock his own weapon. The two men fumbling a few feet apart. Kruger fans the hammer, the gun fires and Ortiz pitches backward into the doorframe, the astonished look dying on his face. Something on the back of his uniform or belt must be snagged on a hinge-head; he's still on his feet, his torso and head slumping forward and hanging, a demobilized marionette. Kruger ducks through the canvas partition into Luz's bedquarters, where the mannequin sporting Luz's tunic and hat, pathetic now, confronts him. He grabs the hat and returns through the partition and crosses the pooling floor of the house. With a flat, vacant feeling, he steps around Ortiz's limp torso and polished head, outside. The sentries gawp at him, hands slack on their rifles. Others are approaching. Kruger holds up Luz's hat like a scalp.

¡Señor! says one of the child sentries, *¿Es usted el capitán nuevo?*

Listen to me. The *lanceros* are all asleep. Now is the time for you to arrest and disarm them.

The sentry looks shocked and delighted. The Padre is dead?

Yes.

Then you are our *capitán!*

No.

¡El yanqui es el capitán nuevo! another soldier whispers. A crowd is quickly gathering, chattering as word moves among them. Someone says, We must arrest the *lanceros* or else kill them! So orders our *capitán!*

I am not your *capitán.* Go now, disarm them. Your war with the Sinas is over. I'll join you after I take some water to the church—you there, help me. Go, before some of them wake!

¡Viva el capitán nuevo! chants a soldier, turning and holding his rifle high.

❧

On the edge of Luz's ruined and smouldering camp in early dawn he works beside the American miner, helping the Sinas and the peon soldiers to dig a mass grave. The Sinas and the peons—Mateo not among them—work in separate groups, communicating little. At least forty of the *lanceros* were murdered last night on their cots, or as they emerged from their billets, before the rest of them managed to form up and ride out through the broken wall and away to the south. The peons had fired after them into the dark until the last sounds of the galloping had died out.

The chilly air is pervaded with drifting odours of cordite, woodsmoke, the kiln smells of scorched adobe, the stink of shit and incipient decay. The gravediggers' hurry is not out of fear of detection, but fear of the flesh-eating sun, soon to commence its daily onslaught. Toward a widening wound in the desert the peons drag the limp, gashed bodies of the *lanceros* by the toes and tinkling spurs of their boots, while village women, keening and shrieking, dart in to kick at the dead, lash at them with cottonwood switches, even stab and hack with knives and captured sabres. No blood flows from these cuts. How pale and null the dead faces, young now in repose, disarmed and dismounted, appear in the soft gloom.

Luz's face is not among them. In the middle of the plain between the camp and the village a large pyre still smokes, fumes rising plumb into a sky spiralling with soundless vultures, buzzards, and crows. In part because of his mastery of their difficult tongue, the Sinas have long considered Luz a sort of devil whom the weight of a grave mound would never be sufficient to confine, even with stones heaped on top, as is customary with enemies. So they've burnt him. Beyond the pyre, by the wreckage of the village wall, torches flit slowly like bog candles as huddled clumps of women shuffle over the battlefield, searching; Jacinta and Quamhac Maria will be among them, though Kruger has explained to them that Mateo was too ill to have been in the battle. In the dark, after the Sinas had spilled out of the church and while the damaged bell was pealing the strange victory, Kruger had accompanied them on a search among the dead of the village and of Luz's camp—where Kruger found his saddlebags, but nothing else—Jacinta herself kicking and slashing at the dead bodies once she was certain of who they were not.

Seems pretty odd, don't it, the miner says in a subdued voice as he kneels by the water bucket that he and Kruger have almost emptied. Helping all these dark folks, I mean, bury all these white ones. His little pink eyes seem troubled and evasive, as if he fears that Kruger may intend to report him to somebody. He slurps from a dented tin cup, belches. He's bald with a peeling scalp. His red beard hides a mouth that's usually so silent and unmoving, you could wonder if he even has one.

Ain't that I shovelled dirt over no lack of white faces in my life. Whiter than these ones, mostly. I was with Iron Ben McCulloch in the Texas Infantry, '63 to the end. Course by then we'd no darkies with us, lending a hand.

He frowns and starts digging again. Dirt is seamed into the wrinkles of his fat, sunburnt neck.

Why did you come down to help? Kruger asks.

Seemed right to do. I like these Indians all right. Been dealing with them going on eight years. Trading, visiting Jacinta back when. We all love Jacinta. Mostly though I hate that tax—the tax them Mexers were trying to take out of us. I come down here to get away from governments. (He says it like "gumm'nts.") Why did you come to fight?

I didn't, Kruger says honestly.

A blood-orange sun soars up out of the *páramo*, the grave is fed and tons of rock piled preventively on top, and Kruger wanders off, in a trance of exhaustion, to find Jacinta. On the edge of the camp he sees a familiar auburn shape: Perra, half-hidden behind the solid wheel of a *carreta*, tubing her body like a stinging wasp and trembling as she tries to move her old bowels. Kruger approaches. She gazes toward him with moping, martyred eyes, not seeming to know him at all. As she finally finishes, recognition flattens her ears and lifts up her tail, she gives two perfunctory digs at the earth with her hind paws and waddles swiftly toward him, whimpering.

Near another trench being filled with peons, he and the dog find Jacinta, her daughter and son-in-law and other villagers bunched around a foreshortened, purple-faced man who wears nothing but Sina field pyjamas cut off at the knee. He has the medieval bowl of hair that older Sina men favour and his enormous oar-blade feet are chalky with dust, channelled with sweat. As the old man with the useless derringer questions him, he nods and tries to respond, winded, while the others in low tones gravely coax him. Jacinta catches sight of Kruger and pushes toward him through the crowd, her eyes reaching. As she gets free, she seems set to embrace him, but stops short, peering skyward and crossing herself. Formally and softly she says, Mateo must be alive, and again she crosses herself, and Kruger understands—she has to mute her joy for fear of heaven's overhearing (heaven too has its spies), and for fear of provoking the envy of those whose sons are unquestionably dead.

This man has seen Mateo, then?

We think so, yes! He ran to us, this man, from the hamlet far downriver. Among the *lanceros* who fled past in the night were some sergeants, and some peons too, in white, riding two to a horse. He thinks five or six such pairs. One of these men was being held on by his fellow, as if he were ill, though not too ill—still awake. And Mateo is not here. Nowhere.

It must be him, Kruger says hopefully.

The *lanceros* must have captured them, and forced him to go along!

Si, claro.

And the others here, they believe the same.

¡Si, si!

But clearly she herself does not really believe. Not that he left against his will. A crisis of faith made visible: a gradual dimming, a subsiding of features momentarily tautened by hope. She won't look away from Kruger—though normally Sinas, even Jacinta, don't stare for long—because Kruger can still abet her in upholding this wishful fiction. There's no reason that *lanceros* fleeing for their lives would corral a few sergeants and peons and force them to join them—and especially an *indio* who was too ill to ride properly. The boy must have gone willingly. He's a zealot, a convert, as Jacinta herself knows, to Luz's kind of progress.

All the same, he's alive.

Behind them a commotion as the dwarfish messenger collapses among the villagers, who press around him cooing, the women fanning him with their scarves, the old man offering water from his gourd, a puff from his calumet. The old man points at the shade under a stretch of undamaged wall and the Sinas lift and hurry the runner there, at least twenty of them pitching in with near-comic, crowding awkwardness. The old man fits the stem of his calumet between the runner's lips and implores him to puff. The man moans and grimaces with all this help.

❧

Kruger and Perra have been sleeping in the cottonwood grove for several weeks, Kruger sleeping longer and harder than he has in months. He walks down to the grove with Perra each evening after spending long, mostly silent days apprenticed to Jacinta's son-in-law, helping him to make adobe bricks—dirt, water, and straw given form in pinewood moulds and sun-dried among the ruins or along the edges of the plaza. Purificación is being rebuilt. After much public debate the Sinas have decided to rebuild the village here, on its ancient site, with an eight-foot-high defensive wall on its open side, rather than moving it far up into the cold sierra. Kruger thinks this is probably a mistake; Luz may be dead and his power broken, but the railroad and the *caudillo* Diaz remain, and when word of an *indio* victory gets out, they will surely respond. But the villagers know this perfectly well, and the decision is not Kruger's to influence. An honorary citizen is still an outsider. He can only work to fashion stronger bricks for the wall. And though briefly tempted to remain, as Jacinta has urged him, he knows he will be continuing northward once the work is done.

Still, he's enjoying his apprenticeship. Like Goethe's Faust pitching in with those northern villagers to reclaim lowlands besieged by the sea, he's forgetting his sorrows in a large collective venture and hard, simple work. Having little more self and no more family to serve, this, he supposes, is how to live what remains of his time—in service to something else, beyond him and his own blood. This unremarkable conclusion has the power to make his throat throb, his eyes burn and stream. Such tears used to embarrass the Prussian in him. . . . Maybe up in Groton, Tukulito and her family will need him in some way. Maybe they have other children now, adoptive or their own—why not?—and will want to build them a larger house.

Jacinta has been sleeping in the intact houseboat along with her daughter and grandson while her obliterated home is being rebuilt. Her son-in-law sleeps among his tools and bricks in a sapling lean-to on the edge of the plaza. During the day she helps other women and children prepare the trampled fields for the summer planting. The old man, with no apparent tone of grievance or of brutal triumph either, remarks that they are apt to be especially fertile this year.

One evening, with the work of reconstruction nearing an end, Jacinta joins Kruger in the grove and sits beside him while he applies himself to a modest *tuahmec* and a single corn tortilla smudged with *halcumah*, a red-pepper paste. She says she has eaten already. He makes her take a little anyway; the captured oxen and corn and beans are being rationed, and the local food remains scarce. Perra's ribs jut through her balding hide and she cuddles against her master in the night. Jacinta's face more than ever shows its bones, yet she seems not unhappy, knowing Mateo to be alive somewhere, and finding herself, like Kruger, caught up in the age-old satisfactions of a robust communal undertaking.

She sits cross-legged in the sand a foot away from him, watching the river and swatting vaguely at the gnats, a red-and-green striped poncho around her shoulders like a shawl. Her unbraided hair is drawn back tightly and secured with a rabbit-rib comb. This evening, for the first time since his return, she wears her pewter and silver bracelets.

It's at its highest this week, she says as the milky waters drone past. From this week on, it will get lower, and the *tuahmec* will go. You didn't see that last time.

I think I left around this time, he says.

Autumn is the best time here. Food is plentiful, and the sandflies are gone.

He thinks that sounds quite wonderful.

Here's your comb, he tells her.

She stares at it, feels for the comb already in her hair, regards him inquiringly. There's always something potentially ferocious about her black eyes.

I took it from you when I left. Twelve years ago.

Ah!

You never noticed it gone?

I must have noticed, certainly. But a number of the *visitantes* would steal things like that.

She smiles at him, the mocking silver of her capped tooth.

Men want to think their acts are unique, she says. What women do, they know has been done before by their sisters and mothers and grandmothers.

With the shade of a grin, he looks at her aslant. You may be right.

Of course I am.

I took it as a memento, he says, and since I had nothing of my own to leave you, I hoped the . . . sentimental absence of the comb might be a sort of keepsake.

Ah, gifts of absence! The one thing any man can be counted on to give.

And some women, too.

I still wish you spoke Sina, she says, scowling. Stay here and learn Sina! You know how welcome you would be here.

He smiles with some pain, his lips still cracked.

You're a hero to the village.

I told you, he says, I pulled the trigger because his words startled me so much. I flinched and it happened. Till then, I seemed held there. Maybe his words freed me.

She looks impatient.

It was as if I caught a flash, like a glimpse in a bad dream, of some future. Of men who want to become the curator of what they destroy. They're so starved on logic that they need to cannibalize others, whole peoples . . .

What matters is you shot him.

The bucket, he says gruffly, I used the bucket.

No reply. He can't get anyone to believe him. In the village now it is public knowledge that *Capitán* Kruger used Luz's pistol to kill him—for what else could suffice to kill a devil but the devil's own weapon? Not a wooden bucket. In fact, the Sinas are inclined to view Kruger's preposterous story as a kind of boast—excusable, perhaps, in a hero—like claiming to have killed a monster with one's bare hands.

You admit you shot the other?

That was easy, too easy. Like brushing a fly from a wound.

Of course it was.

As if the first killing hardened me, in just seconds.

No, she says sternly. It's because you're a good man, and they were bad.

I might have been better if I'd been a bit worse.

Again she looks baffled. He doesn't say what haunts him—that if he had killed Luz on his first opportunity, the night attack on the village might never have occurred, and many dead might have lived.

She shifts her haunches closer in the sand. He can smell her hair, her peppery sweat.

It might be better for the town, he says, if I'm not here when they come looking for Luz's killer.

We would never betray you or give you up!

If they come, promise me you'll flee into the sierra. Don't try to fight them.

On behalf of the village I can promise nothing. Stay, learn our tongue, and maybe you can convince them yourself.

She leans into his side, her breast to his ribcage, then kisses his cheek. He turns his mouth to her upturned mouth. His hurt lips sting. Her own—dried blood salting the cracks—must hurt as well. There's a stirring in his lap, like a small animal crawling over him. Her fingers dig into the stands of thick hair above his temples, seeming to palpate the bones underneath, as she did on his departure twelve years ago. As if having made a positive identification, she kisses harder. He grips her breast under the poncho and groans to feel it and then he feels its difference from Amelia's—not so much a matter of size or even form but of something more unknowable; lost now.

He retracts his face, draws her hands from his head, gently kisses the palms. They smell of capsicum and his own hair.

It's too soon, he says. I feel almost as if she were here. I mean the river itself. Not *in* the river—as if she *is* the river. I know this is absurd.

Jacinta waits.

Forgive me, he says.

You won't stay, then. She looks surprised, a woman who has learned confidence in her charms, and who doesn't ordinarily invite men, even heroes, to stay around.

There are two people I have to see in the north.

Women.

One of them, yes.

There are others who wish to marry me here. The Texan, for one.

The woman I mean to see is married herself, and a loyal wife.

Ah, the *indio* who was with you on the ice, the Esquimau!

I want to see them again, that's all. I'm not looking for a wife up there.

Even if her husband is gone? Husbands go. They die, they vanish.

It's too soon, he says. *And it's too late.* Yet he keeps thinking of how that dead part of him has been stirred again here in the grove, with her, momentarily. How in the last weeks here he has started to regain a sense of solidity, almost belonging. How the food here is plentiful in the fall.

I'll try to return, he says. I promise you.

She juts her chin, clearly unconcerned that he could be led astray by a mere *indio.* For Sinas consider themselves not so much as *indios,* but—like the Esquimaux themselves—as the People.

Still dressed as a Sina, he departs two days later. Perra he leaves with Jacinta, as a guardian and pet for her grandson, he says. The dog always was one for children, he says. He knows Perra has used up her last round on the heavy trek over the *barrancas.* So let her finish where she started.

On a *lancero* horse, a calm, solid chestnut gelding with a blond mane, a good horse for an unpractised rider, he travels north-eastward, in his saddlebags a little food and his share of the pesos found in Luz's quarters (very few) and among the *lanceros'* things (somewhat more). He carries Ortiz's revolver. Luz's personal weapons he urged others to claim as trophies, but the Sinas preferred to break and bury them with the man's ashes. In Maria Madre, a mestizo town apparently untouched by Luz's purging, he spends an uneasy night. The townspeople are suspicious of him, a foreigner in Sina field pyjamas carrying a *lancero* revolver. There are no *lanceros* or soldiers in the town. When he asks in the cantina about the annual bear-and-bull fight, people seem even more wary. The ritual was banned some years ago, the barkeep tightly explains, by the Padre himself. The Padre considered it barbaric. (Yes, says Kruger.) Of course, now that the Padre has unfortunately been killed, some will want to see the ritual revived. . . . The barkeep carefully leaves it unclear whether he himself would want to see it revived. He adds, The grizzly bear is mostly vanished from these parts, however. As Kruger glances at the other faces, they look away fast, abruptly captivated by their companions' moustaches or the way their own hands rest, with studied slackness, on the tables. Probably they regard him as a spy for Luz, or rather Luz's successor, whoever that might be. That night in his lodging he barricades the door with the deal wardrobe and chair and keeps the revolver to hand. At dawn, going downstairs and finding the horse untouched, he rides briskly out of town.

Before the mule ferry at Ojinaga, he slips off the road, canters west up the Rio Grande until he finds a wider but shallower reach that the horse can ford and swim. Then he rides northeastward cross-country in a sort of absent trance furthered by the unvarying landscape: scrub hills, mesas, terra-cotta plains now and then punctuated by hilltop haciendas and missions like baroque cathedrals built of mud. Sometimes over the horizon huge pillars of dust stand or travel slowly, as if from an army on the move. Cattle. He begins to see work parties in the distance, mauling posts into the ground and unrolling wire from huge black spools, fencing off the open range. Eventually he has to return to the main road. He sleeps in gullies under brush willows and cottonwoods, for him their rustling now the leitmotif of slumber.

San Antonio is full of Germans. Along a street with a German name he rides past German confectioneries and bakeries and dry goods stores, two Lutheran churches, a lushly watered beer garden. In the garden he sits with a brass tankard of lager and a plate of *wurst* on sauerkraut and mashed potatoes, among merry, successful-looking immigrants who chatter in various kinds of German. They glance his way now and then, cautiously. In the barber shop of Winfried Hussel, Kruger's face shrouded under hot towels, these sounds of his first familial tongue have a keen impact. Before his eyes, all is dim and warm as a womb, so the effects of the German, as well as the aftertastes of *wurst* and *kraut*, are undiffused by the input of other senses. Memories mob into his heart and seem to stretch it painfully. From La Paz years ago he tried writing to his mother, his brother and sister, again, and again he heard nothing back. He assumes his mother must be dead. She would be seventy-five now. If she could see Kruger now, she would think her own child a foreigner and a stranger.

Have I made these towels too hot for you, good sir? asks Mr Hussel in English, apparently unaware of his silent customer's origins. Mr Hussel, having pinched up a corner of the towel muffling Kruger's brow, is leaning down, peeking in at him with a large yellow eye, the stropped razor held up beside his hairy ear. No, sir, you must not be too polite to complain if they should scald you! This is not our Texas way!

Kruger sells the good horse in the market plaza and buys a derby, Jaeger woollens, two linen shirts, a brown worsted suit, a pair of bluchers, and a cardboard valise. And a ticket for a train to the North, which he boards that same night.

A "prushun," he learns, is new American slang for a kind of young hobo.

Washington, D.C., July 7, 1889

HIS FIRST STOP, en route to Groton. The missionary woman's remark about the fallen hero enjoying a government position seemed lucid enough, among all her figments. He asks where he can find the Navy Department and he walks there, reconfirming directions along the way. His revolver is in his cardboard valise. He shortcuts through a hovel-town where half-naked Negro children pause their games of tipcat and tag to stare at this neatly dressed and shaved old white man—they must think he is old—passing through their neighbourhood on foot. Over the subsiding tar-stained roofs of the shanties, the high dome of the Capitol, not far off, glows in the noon sun: fresh white of an intensity that will always set Kruger in mind of snow and ice.

The Navy Department is housed in a surprisingly modest four-storey red-brick building on Seventeenth Street. The rotund doorman dozes on a stool inside the front door, which is propped open as if to catch any breeze on this humid, breezeless day. He looks as if he hasn't been disturbed since the last time the country was at war. Years now. He's hatless and his livery is faded and unpressed. Kruger crosses the threshold and softly puts down his valise, not wanting to alarm the man—who needs a shave, too, Kruger sees when his eyes adjust to the lobby's dimness.

The doorman's red eyes pop open and he starts to sit up, but then, taking Kruger in, he relaxes. The folds of black-bristled flesh under his chin flop back over the stiff collar. He looks like a baby with jaundice and a heavy beard.

Have an appointment?

I'm looking for Lieutenant George Tyson.

I always call him Captain, the doorman says in a tired, casual voice. Why do you call him Lieutenant?

He was a lieutenant when I sailed with him, years ago.

Sure, and he's one again now. Lieutenant of the Watch.

The man yawns in his fat.

Then why do you call him Captain? Kruger asks.

Because he ain't really a lieutenant. Lieutenant of the Watch is just a phrase. He was *definitely* a captain, though.

Where may I find him?

You were on the Howgate Expedition with him? The doorman's eyes spark up, though he remains slumped.

No, Kruger says, another one.

The other one? A German, are you? The doorman sits up. One of them Germans?

I'm Mexican, actually.

Sure, of course—your accent.

Kruger's accent is still conspicuously German. The doorman seems in earnest, though.

Who'd have guessed there were Mexicans on that voyage! How many?

Only myself, Kruger says with a kind of subdued Latin dignity.

Must have found it damn cold.

Kruger smiles, picks up his valise. May I see the captain now?

His office is . . . The doorman yawns again, eyes closed, not bothering to cover his wide mouth, though he lifts his hand to signal that he won't be long. . . . It's in the basement, next the boiler room. Number B-8. Says it's the right one for him, always so warm. Stairway's at the end.

The corridors of the Navy Department are still and deserted. Presumably some of the functionaries are lunching elsewhere, yet the quietude seems to go deeper, as if the white plaster walls and ceilings and the faded blue runners of the hallways have absorbed boredom and inertia for so many years, they exhale it like a vapour. In this dead stillness, the rows of heavy doors with brass nameplates seem less like throughways into hives of important busyness than like ranks of headstones. Passing a door that's ajar Kruger sees a beige-haired man in shirtsleeves, behind a massive rosewood desk, peering down through a magnifying glass at a miniature schooner made of toothpicks. His lips are pushed out in concentration as he tries to insert a tiny mast.

The doors of the half-dozen basement offices are more closely ranked, and of pine instead of oak. It may be warm down here in the winter, but now, with the boiler off, it's clammy, mildewed, deeply silent. So this is where the world has buried the lieutenant. Kruger would have expected to feel more satisfaction at the thought of his nemesis reduced from famous hero to factotum—adrift in the postscript of bitter obscurity endured, Kruger guesses, by the formerly renowned.

LIEUTENANT OF THE WATCH G. E. TYSON. The door is ajar. He knocks. He prods the door further and looks in, half expecting to see Tyson asleep, head down on the desk. The office is empty. It's windowless, of course, illuminated by a gaslight on the wall over the small desk. There's a ladderback chair behind the desk and another in the corner of the room beside the door. On the wall where Kruger would have expected to see framed lithographs of heroic scenes from the *Polaris* expedition are two large photographs, one of a petite woman in summer finery, another of a family. He approaches the family. It's a much older-looking Tyson and that woman, now grown buxom and nicely plump, along with baby daughters—twins—and a boy, perhaps three. On the desk, an ash-dish, ink and quills, a half ream of paper, a few letters slit open. A pocket book called *Angling for the Hobbyist.* Kruger settles himself on the chair by the door. He puts the valise between his feet, perches the hat on top and looks up at the woman in the frame. She's confidently addressing her whole person to the lens. Her skin has a summer glow and her wide-set eyes are very pale and fixed. She's attractive in spite of her nose, which is broad and blunt, almost snouty.

Kruger smokes half a bowl of tobacco and then walks off in search of a privy. He starts for the back of the building, some door to the outside, then realizes that such a place must have plumbing, a thing he has encountered only a few times in his life. After a search that takes him into a broom closet and a janitor's cubicle, he finds another likely door, unmarked, and tries the latch. It's locked. After a few seconds there's a muffled sound of tumbling water. The door opens and a man emerges in a billow of smoke, a pipe chomped in his beard, newspaper folded under his arm. He's wrinkled, almost bald, the top of his skull fuzzy. Wire-rimmed spectacles rest at the base of his nose. Over the top of the spectacles he gives Kruger a neutral, shaggy-browed glance, then turns and saunters up the hall. A stout man in a rumpled night-blue uniform, like the old parade kit of a second officer. A moment after he has passed, Kruger knows him. His walk is similar, if far less hurried and emphatic. After ten paces or so the man comes to a thoughtful stop, then slowly begins to turn his shoulders and head, to look back. Kruger enters the water closet and pulls the door closed. The body, as always, has the timing of a joke-teller; he really has to piss before he can confront Tyson. Or whatever it is he came here to do.

Above all, he's afraid to ask about Tukulito.

He stands there for a minute or several, emptying, taking things in: the square wooden seat with the round hole, the wood-handled pull chain that dangles, still moving, from the reservoir. A porcelain sink the size of a water gourd. There's a latrine smell but mostly the warm pleasant sweetness of pipe smoke.

He walks slowly up the hall toward Tyson's office. The door is wide open. From behind his desk Tyson peers up over his spectacles. The face is expressionless. Kruger's valise is splayed open on the desk, his derby upturned beside it. Tyson sits back and pushes the valise forward as if to display the long revolver nestled there among Kruger's things.

It's you, isn't it. Roland Kruger?

That isn't loaded, Kruger says.

Yes, I've just seen. But what am I to make of this?

The voice is unchanged in pitch but there's less of it. He seems out of breath—maybe frightened? He seems to have become a fellow of comforts, there's a sort of blurred softness to his eyes and body, he looks as though he should be wearing slippers. He doesn't hold himself squared, even now, suspicious. His manner could signify either flippant confidence or exhausted apathy.

Don't worry, Lieutenant, I've been involved in something of a war, in Mexico, and I mean to return there. I may need the pistol again then.

But why did you come *here*, Mr Kruger? How did you know where to find me?

I got news of your fortunes, even there.

Fortunes. Mocking, it must sound. Which was not his intention, he feels.

Sit down again if you like, Mr Kruger.

Thank you, Lieutenant.

Tobacco?

I have some of my own, thank you.

A war in Mexico, Tyson says, relighting his pipe. I thought you were a, what was it, a pacifist objector . . . ?

I found I objected even more to certain other things.

Germany isn't involved down there?

I have no idea.

The, ah, German Empire is one nation we watch carefully, here at the department. They're becoming a great power, Germany, involved everywhere.

This little speech sounds perfunctory. The official position of a department trying to justify its peacetime existence in the face of apathy and budget restraints. Tyson looks vaguely sheepish.

As I suppose you must know, he adds.

I'm relieved they've no Indians to exterminate, at least, Kruger says.

You never were an agent for them, were you?

No.

But a thief?

I was something of a thief, I guess. Though not in the way you believed.

But . . . you've come back here to offer me a duel?

Kruger searches his face. The remark sounds like Tyson's all right, but the avuncular beard, skunked with grey, has a faintly smiling look.

I'm not sure why I had to come here, Kruger says.

I drew my conclusions under great duress, Mr Kruger, and I wrote that book in a great hurry. I may have been slightly intemperate. Unjust to you in certain ways. . . . Tyson is talking downward into the open valise, holding his pipe.

He closes the valise.

After a silence Kruger says, It no longer matters, Lieutenant, but I am grateful for your words. And now if you'll accept mine: on our worst night out there, you were a true hero.

Tyson looks up with rheumy eyes, seeming to will himself to believe.

You seem quite peaceful now, Lieutenant.

I think so, yes—I've made my peace with the world. Tyson sits forward over the closed valise; he is almost animated. I did it by *surrender*, you know. Unconditional surrender. Surrender can be a wonderful thing, after all. Too few seem to know that. Of course it's not something to say out loud in the Navy Department—surrender is frowned on here! He grins, really grins. I'm sorry to hear that you're still having to fight, down there. You look as though you'd been through some tough scrapes.

My one knack seems to be surviving disasters.

I'm glad your luck is holding.

Frankly it's a bit of a curse. Kruger takes his pipe from his jacket pocket, reconsiders, then drops it back in.

Lieutenant, I must ask about Tukulito. Hannah. About her and her husband.

Tyson's stare is locked and unblinking, his lips bitten in his beard.

Ah, says Kruger, his heart plummeting.

I don't suppose there's any way you could have known.

Ach, Gott!

I'm sorry to give the news.

After some moments Kruger says, in a flat voice, Maybe I did know, somehow. For years, down in La Paz, I didn't write to her, because I had a place there, a family, but also because of my fear for her. If you write from a place like that, you can't be certain the letter will ever reach its home, can you, so then you may get no reply. Which then will make you wonder if the person you fear for may be dead.

These few words may be the most he has said at one time since leaving Purificación. He looks up. Tyson's attentive eyes are spliced to his.

By not writing to her after a certain point, I was helping to keep her alive. By not pursuing my questions when I met an old woman down there who knew of her, I helped to keep her alive. By coming north to visit once more, I helped to keep her alive—how could anyone be so thoughtless as not to be there to greet a visitor who has come two thousand miles? And by saying nothing to you until just now—by taking your silence about her as hopeful—I hoped to keep her alive.

I wish your superstition had worked.

When did it happen?

Not long after Punnie's death.

I feared it, at the time, Kruger says.

It was early June. Twelve years ago.

And Ebierbing?

Tyson frowns, and for a moment Kruger is sure that he too must be dead.

I can't say. He came back south just as I was sailing north in '77, for the last time. He stayed in the house in Groton and did odd jobs around town, and often he tended the graves, I hear. Next spring he signed over the house to the Budingtons and went north with another expedition. I must have passed him again at sea, or nearly. It was an expedition to turn up relics of Franklin, which they managed to do, even after so long. A grand success. (Tyson doesn't pronounce the words bitterly—though not without irony, either.) Joe served them well, I guess, but I didn't pay much attention to news of it. I'd lost interest in the sea and the Arctic by then . . . like you, I suppose?

Yes, mostly.

He remarried up there—in fact, within a year. They say he gave his new wife the name Hannah.

To have remarried so fast! Kruger says thoughtfully.

One could do worse, Tyson says with a pinch of his old touchiness. Kruger is about to assure him that the remark is not personally aimed when Tyson adds, more softly, If you heard about me, down in Mexico, you likely know about the divorce.

Kruger nods, then looks at the photograph beside Tyson's desk. Your new family?

That portrait is eight years old. Ned is almost eleven now. The twins are nine, Flora and Hannah. Yes, Hannah.

Studying the photograph Kruger says, And all's well with your old family, I hope?

They're well enough. George Junior is a man now—almost nineteen.

Tyson is short of breath again.

And will he go to sea?

No. He's gone west, out to Idaho. Haven't spoken to him in some years. He means to do the very opposite of everything I've done, that's plain as sunrise.

But he's nineteen, Kruger says—not a man yet, really. Around his age I enlisted in the Prussian navy, partly to spite my own father. He may return to you, I think.

You've a family of your own, you said, down in Mexico?

Kruger tells him a little about La Paz—the first real details he has been willing to revive since fleeing in March. How his daughter Aurelia used to sit in his lap in the cool of evening while Kruger would braid her fragrant, fawn-coloured hair, the tint an exotic surprise in La Paz, the legacy of her Prussian grandfather, dead now for years, who had been fair in his youth. Always after the braiding Kruger would express playful disappointment in the outcome, then unravel it and start over repeatedly, fastening the eventual masterpiece with a jade-green ribbon. The girl, carding wool, would sing to him while he braided, then tease him when he tried to join in, because, she said, he was a terrible singer. *Un pésimo cantante.* His wife and son would confirm this. The son, Felix, dwarfed by his sombrero, would often accompany him in the pearl-lighter in the early morning, sitting in the stern facing his father at the oars, the boy dropping pearl oysters in sisal bags when the divers surfaced, panting, Kruger feathering the oars to keep the boat steady.

The marriage was no grand passion (Kruger doesn't say this part), not after the first weeks, but there was always an abundance of fondness, care, and high humour. And Kruger had wanted to make a home. In his life there had been no joy quite akin to being part of a young, flourishing family—one's own small tribe, in fact, with its own language and rituals, customs and difficulties. All subject to extinction, however. Tyson must know this now too—the delight, and also the losing—although he has been lucky enough to start over. This should feel more unfair to Kruger than it does. Something seems to have burnt out in him. Maybe the capacity to envy and resent. He knows only that Tyson, too, has lost a child. In the pit of his belly something is in process, a lush expansion, something like the first leavening effects of mescal. What feels like the start of a love is actually the end of a hatred.

Another silence and he says, I mean to go up to the burying ground, in Groton. I think I'll set out now, back to the station. Thank you for this, Lieutenant.

But, Kruger, you'd not arrive till after dark. Wait a moment.

It doesn't matter.

Tyson stands up. Let me go with you, Kruger—early tomorrow morning we could go. I haven't been up there in years. Not since '78. I went up with my wife—Laura, I mean—but only the one time. I never wanted to see Budington, you see. But he's dead now, the poor souse, died last year. He's buried a few plots over, I gather. We . . . I'd offer you a bed for the night with us, but we haven't one. Haven't the space, I mean. This isn't much of a position, as you see.

Kruger waves off the regrets, which come not as an expression of shame but a statement of fact. Neither he nor Tyson would feel comfortable with his sleeping there anyway.

Tomorrow is Saturday, Kruger says, won't you be here?

It's a half-day, I can be absent. I'm not needed here urgently, as you can see—nothing here is urgent. Few lieutenants, I'd guess, have ever had fewer subordinates than this. He shakes his head, grins, setting down his cold pipe. Two doormen, two janitors, two tea ladies, and the night watchman. There's my full command. And they hop to my every command, Kruger, because they know all about my old reputation. Johnny, up at the door, he's even read my book—which by the way has now pretty much vanished. They must think my . . . laxness is the manner of somebody who knows he'll be obeyed without question. I wouldn't know, I've never asked. The truth is, Kruger, I don't care anymore—not for any of this. I gain a living here, that's all. What matters now is my wife and my family, our evenings and Sundays, our meals together—wonderful meals! There lies all my devotion. I walked away from myself, Kruger. The malady burnt out in me. Or it was frozen out. Or maybe it was just fatigue. Fatigue can be a good thing, too. All I want now is for the world to leave me alone.

Life in La Paz was that way, I think.

Emmaline's misfortune was to have met me when she did, Tyson adds. Before I changed. And people—here he speaks with some firmness, as if anticipating an argument—people do change. Why, you yourself seem different, Kruger—and not just an older, fainter version of what you were.

I'm willing to belong to things now. A few things.

If only one could go back and undo the hurt one did before!

Tyson eyes him feelingly. Kruger slowly nods.

For a while, Kruger says, I wondered if the best one could do was to do no harm. I decided not. I think that to go through life means at times to harm. That must be why good men—from under his brows he gives Tyson a sustained look—always seem the most troubled.

On the four-hour journey to Newark, the transfer, then the second leg to Groton, they talk only a little. Forgiveness is one thing, friendship another. Tyson speaks more comfortably with the others who sit with them in the facing seats, getting aboard, getting off. With a big sullen man who keeps his top hat on, the brim low on his brow, they discuss last year's election, how the Democrat Cleveland lost to the Republican Harrison despite getting more of the popular vote. There's a fine brand of democracy for you, the man says, angling for an argument. It's no use. Tyson finds grounds for accord, even when the man shifts his tack, and even though (as Tyson has mentioned to Kruger) it was President Hayes, a Republican, who secured a position for him during the divorce proceedings in '78, when no one else would touch him. So Tyson feels a great loyalty to the party. Learning of Tyson's position at the Navy Department, the man bewails the fact that in times of peace there is nowhere for a fellow of vital constitution to find honourable outlet. Even the Indian Wars are all but concluded, the man rumbles. Here Tyson remarks helpfully, absently, that there may be trouble brewing with the Sioux again out in the Dakotas—they seem unwilling to keep to their reserved lands.

A phrenologist with a faint Irish accent recognizes Tyson and asks if he isn't going up to New York City to give a lecture, as he is himself. Drowsily Tyson admits that he hasn't done a lecture for years. He adds, Do give us a sample of your own talk, though, sir. And for forty miles the man does.

After sharing with Kruger the dozen good sandwiches that Laura packed for him—smoked oyster with mayonnaise, lobster paste, salt-ham, cheddar and cress—Tyson droops on the bench for the last hour of the trip, salivating a little into his beard, spectacles dangling mid-air by the fine wires that curl behind his ears. Eventually he slumps full into Kruger, who smokes his pipe and stares out the window. Beyond towns and pastures, chrome flashes of the Atlantic, every glimpse a heartbreak.

They step down at Groton at one in the afternoon. A single carbon arc light glows at the end of the platform, perhaps on account of the thin fog drifting in. In the direction of the harbour they walk along a dirt road between square clapboard houses, then turn onto Pleasant Valley Road, where they walked together years ago, after Punnie's funeral. Tyson is out of breath again. Through the fog the sun is dulled, like a daytime moon. Tukulito's house appears: green clapboards blistered, windows boarded, the house and the listing fence and the basswood tree all casting vague, borderless shadows. The men stop at the fence, look in at the framed wilderness of the yard. Where her garden was, along the front porch, phlox and poppies and lavender still throng.

They go on past a small white Presbyterian church—hers, Tyson says, and a minute later into the silence: That was another stone off my heart, losing faith. God was never anything to me but a General.

The Starr Hill Burying Ground rises to their left through the brightening fog. The cast iron gate, with the five-pointed star wrought into it, hangs open. They start up the path. A few crows bickering in the cedars behind them. The graves, Tyson says faintly, will be off to the left. Over near that tree. And he stops in his tracks. His left hand gropes out toward a headstone beside the path, although it's well out of reach. His right hand grabs at the waistcoat over his solar plexus, tugging at it.

Lieutenant?

Tyson's mouth gapes in his beard but he can't seem to speak. Kruger takes hold of him.

Sir?

It's all right.

Is it your heart?

Wincing, Tyson shakes his head. No.

Come to the bench.

It'll pass. I was hurt, on the second expedition. Now and then it comes back, the pain.

Kruger guides him toward the bench.

Exertion does it. Very early mornings.

A girl is skipping along Pleasant Valley Road, whistling without tune, deep inside her moment. If she glanced to her left up the path climbing into the cemetery, she would see two old men frozen there, as if daunted, unwilling to continue into the midst of all those stones. One of them is hunched as if with extreme age, the other appearing not so old and yet old enough—though strong, holding the old man up, his left arm around the other's back, bracing his shoulder, his near hand clasping the other's arm, and his brown, fretworn face close to the old man's ear, saying, May I do anything else to help you, Lieutenant?

Thank you, Kruger, the old man whispers. You have. I'm much obliged.

From the hillside as the fog opens, the two men can be seen departing, walking slowly now for Tyson's sake. There's a handsome tombstone up here—still now, years later—green granite spotted with lichen, on its crown the block letters J & H, like lovers' initials carved in an oak, within a circle under five ivy leaves. Below is the misspelled name JOSEPH EBERBING, and, under an expanse of blank rock, never filled in because Ebierbing disappeared into the North, the words: HANNAH, HIS WIFE, and the date of her death, AGED 38 YEARS.

Punnie's headstone stands eight feet in front of theirs, a small tablet of whitened marble, much of the inscription today illegible.

From this hillside, this remove in time, the two survivors vanish behind a stand of tall, cypress-like pines, retracing their road to the station and back down the seaboard to Newark, then on to Washington, where they will say a brief and reserved farewell. The next morning, trying to get a train south, Kruger will duck and elbow his way through a small Orangemen's parade, but get caught up in it, swept along by men in orange sashes and derbies who, seeing his own hat, take him for one of their clan. Some of the Orangemen carry revolvers. The hatreds of cavefolk but with improving weapons, again. He takes the night train south, steerage, and after a fourth consecutive night reaches San Antonio, where his money—Luz's money—is all but exhausted. After a last visit to Winfried Hussel, barber, he continues southwest on foot, a spy and a thief once more, feeding himself off the stingy land and the odd windowsill. He wades and swims the Rio Grande at the fording place near Ojinaga, still without papers, no legal identity, a border ghost, and he hikes westward, avoiding Maria Madre and the other towns, into the Sierra de la Tasajera and across to the far side.

A *lancero* on horseback finds him on his knees by the Laguna de Encinillas, drinking and filling his canteen. The *lancero* wants to arrest him—he's paperless and uncooperative—and take him back to Gallego. Kruger refuses. The *lancero* draws his revolver and aims it down at Kruger's face. Come now or I'll shoot you.

With no special haste, in a kind of trance, Kruger pulls Ortiz's revolver from inside his coat and cocks it and, while the *lancero* glares in disbelief, shoots the man in the chest.

With a numb, gutted feeling he continues west on the surly stallion until, within a day's ride of Purificación, the horse stops dead, curvets and throws him and then gallops southward, as if for help. Kruger walks on, the wide mesa nearing. Around the village the cornfields have been burned and flattened. With pent breath he plods through the charred stubble. Yet over the village are no circling birds; behind the undamaged wall the houses are deserted. A museum village. The army that arrived must have been too large for the Sinas to think of fighting. He sleeps in the grove under the cottonwoods where the sandflies, as promised, are nearly gone with the approach of autumn, and at dawn he forages a few scraps from the village and walks up into the foothills of the Sierra Madre.

On the first day he happens on a few signs of flight—a half-covered firepit, fishbones, goat dung, a few spent cartridges, some footprints in the scree. He climbs a long rocky draw and by dusk enters dappled stands of larch and Douglas fir, and then, an hour upslope, a rill trickling down to meet him and vanishing into the rocks. He sleeps there. The night air is chill, the tips of the firs piercing at the stars. On the second day as he works higher, the forests thin out, the conifers begin to dwarf and on the pebble banks of the stream the next morning there is frost. On this third day he finds only one covered firepit, then climbs on through an alpine meadow awash in gentian and saxifrage and fringed with child-sized pines and cedars, deep into the sierra now, patches of snow lingering in the shadows, and in one patch a half-melted footprint. Only that. The Sinas are trying to conceal their route and are becoming impossible to track, elusive as the Tarahumaras, leaving no tokens, not even ashes, excrement, or the bones of whatever livestock they have not yet killed. He assumes they would cleave to the stream. He is dizzy with hunger and the sparseness of the shrill air and he wears his blanket around his shoulders while he climbs. On the fourth day, many thousands of feet above the *páramo*, which is lost to view now, a figment, he comes to the headwaters, a sapphire tarn deep in a cirque of bare rock slopes and talus. Small floes and platelets drift in the tarn and by the next dawn a silver rind has appeared along the shore, edging outward. On the fifth day he crosses a pass between two icy peaks and wanders west over a moon-like plateau of rock and frozen tarns and monumental boulders sparged with lichen, and the wind is bitterly dry and cold and carries no smell of anything alive, only snow and stone, and he has lost the trail, can find no further marks. He's starving again. He falls and lies still and then rises and drifts on. . . . On the night of the sixth day, on the further rim of the plateau, swathed in his blanket on a high spur, he wakes to smells, obscure and distant, though with his senses so honed by hunger he can make them out. Woodsmoke, chillis, roasting meat. On the seventh day at nightfall he stumbles down a dead watercourse among scrub firs and crabbed bristlecone pines, a thousand years old or more, and when he crawls up on a boulder to look westward he sees, a few hours off and down, like stars reflected in a still ocean, their fires.

LAST VERSIONS

IN OCTOBER 1906, after a summer of ill-health, George E. Tyson died in his home on H Street in Washington. For some time he had suffered from heart problems. Obituaries, such as the large, respectful one that appeared the next day in the *Washington Post*, attributed his problems to the wound he had received aboard the *Florence* twenty-eight years before. He was survived by his wife Laura and their three grown children, as well as by his first wife Emmaline and their son, George E. Tyson Jr., then thirty-five years old and living in Porthill, Idaho, a small town on the British Columbia border. Soon after the funeral, George Jr. wrote to his mother in Brooklyn. By then he had been estranged from his father for almost twenty-five years.

> *Dear Mother:*
> *The article that you sent giving the account of father's death I did not open until I reached home. In the solitude of my cabin, I read the news of father's death. And when I saw his picture, I noted his face wrinkled with age through the lapse of all these weary years. Then I thought of all the suffering he must have endured during the long Arctic night, starving and freezing. He caused us many a pang, Mother, he caused us many a pang, but he was my father,*

and the news of his death saddened my heart. I often think that the awful hardships he endured affected his mind and caused his heart to wither. The love I bore him when a baby boy, awoke again to life. And I wonder if he ever thought of his boy through the last 20 *years or did he go down to his grave and never a word of me? Poor father, for you I shed tears both of pity and of love. Seek his grave, Mother dear, and place some flowers there for me. And let your loving radiance glow around the place. It was noble of you to forgive him. You are a good mother and I love you, and am proud of you. He is gone now, gone forever. He is forgiven. Let us remember him as he was when his smile was long and his voice was soft and tender. Let us ever cherish in our hearts his loving memory. Peace to his ashes. He bore an honoured name. May it never perish.*

Your loving son, George

Tyson was buried in the Glenwood Cemetery in Washington, D.C. But this was not the end of his reputation. As late as 1976—although no later—his name and a biographical synopsis appeared in the massive *Webster's Biographical Dictionary*:

Tyson, George Emory, 1829–1906. Am. arc. Whaler, b. Red Bank, N.J.; member of Polaris arctic ex. under C.F. Hall; assumed command of a group, 19 in all, accidentally left adrift on an ice floe (Oct. 15, 1872–Apr. 30, 1873) and by resourcefulness and seamanship kept up morale of members of the party until they were rescued, after drifting about 1800 miles, by a sealer off Labrador.

Some years after Punnie's and Tukulito's deaths, a Groton woman named Mary Walker Raymond, one of Punnie's former classmates, wrote briefly of her friend in an unpublished memoir: *She was a good little playmate, and with her broad, brown face, black, shining eyes, and very straight, black hair, with her little fur suit and cap with hanging tails, she makes a pleasant picture in my chamber of memories. Julia, my sister, and I, New Englanders for many generations, taught to conceal our feelings, could never quite understand the long, clinging kiss with which Hannah let her go from the gate in the morning, or the rapturous way in which she was caught up in her mother's arms again at night, to receive many more kisses. . . .*

On Punnie's small headstone, under the particulars of her name (which was in fact Silvia Grinnell Ebierbing, although the name was used only at school and on legal documents) and her place and time of birth and death, there is a partially legible inscription. In March of 2002, I knelt in front of the stone, and with a charcoal stick and a sheet of paper torn from a notebook I did some very amateur rubbings. A number of the words eluded me. The American writer Sheila Nickerson, who must have been there only a year or two before I was, researching a non-fiction book about Tukulito, did better with her own rubbings and has made an effort to recreate the full inscription, including the badly faded last line—a process not unlike translating almost inaudible words from an old recording, in a difficult tongue.

> *She was a survivor of the Polaris Expedition under Commander Charles Francis Hall, and was picked up with 19 others* [sic] *from an ice floe April 30, 1873, after a drift on the ice for a period of one hundred and ninety days and a distance of over twelve hundred miles. Of such is the kingdom of*

The last word remains unclear. I think this is right; I think I prefer it blank, uninterpreted, the beloved child and her mother still alive in the silences. Nickerson remarks that she wanted the word to be love, thought it might be, but couldn't be certain. Heaven, she thought, was another possibility. But she wanted it to be love.

Of Roland Kruger and the Sina people, nothing more is known.

196 DAYS ON AN ICE FLOE.

CAPT. TYSON,

Of Arctic Fame, and late Commander of the

HOWGATE EXPEDITION,

WILL LECTURE AT

CURTIS SCHOOL BUILDING,

Georgetown, D. C.,

Wednesday, May 18th, 1881,

On his unequaled experiences while cast away amid Snow and Ice with eighteen men women and children in charge.

Six months on a Flat of Ice in cold and darkness! Wonderful Stratagems for preserving life!! Final Rescue!!!

told with the graphic power of actual experience.

ADMISSION, - 25 CENTS.

AUTHOR'S NOTE

Concerning the passages from Tyson's *Arctic Experiences* (Harper & Brothers, 1874; republished in 2002 by Cooper Square Press, with a new introduction by Edward E. Leslie)—while I often quote Tyson's published words verbatim, I have also excised, rearranged, conflated, compressed, and occasionally invented, always following the demands of my story as it grew and pursued its own inherent drift. Likewise, the italicized journal entries, or "field-notes," are inspired by what survives of Tyson's field-notes, although here too—here especially—I have improvised according to my needs, while at the same time maintaining the consistent differences, in both tone and content, between Tyson's actual notes and the corresponding passages in *Arctic Experiences.*

Of the real Kruger, little is known. In *Arctic Experiences* Tyson portrays him as a prime troublemaker and mutineer, but elsewhere cites him as one of the few men volunteering to help at moments of extreme danger. From this intriguing contradiction his character emerged—independent, defiant, courageous. His and Tukulito's stories on the ice are largely improvised in the rifts and openings in Tyson's own, sometimes unreliable, account, while Kruger's afterstory—unlike Tyson's and Tukulito's—springs purely from my own imaginary pursuit.

In the concluding "Last Versions," all material is quoted verbatim.

A note about some of the names. A modern, more accurate spelling of Tukulito's name would be Taqulittuq, or else Tuqulirtuq, while Ebierbing is now usually spelled Ipirvik. For the purposes of this book I've retained the nineteenth-century spellings—spellings that Tukulito herself used when writing the names. As for Punnie, the name is a corruption of *panik*, the Inuktitut word for "daughter." English speakers, hearing Tukulito and Ebierbing address their daughter in conventional Inuit fashion as *panik*, assumed at first that it was a name, and spelled it "Punnie." For convenience, the child's parents came to use the word as though it was a name when referring to her in the presence of whites.

The German name Kruger would normally take an umlaut over the "u," but Roland Kruger, like other immigrants to the New World, jettisoned that stigma upon arrival.

Of the many to whom I owe thanks, I want to single out those who read all or parts of this book in draft form—Kendall Anderson, Tim Conley, Heather Frise, John Heighton, Stephen Henighan, Michael Holmes, John Metcalf, Anne McDermid, Michael Redhill, Ingrid Ruthig, Alexander Scala, and Rhoda Ungalaq and John Maurice—as well as those who generously gave advice or information on various matters: Erica Avery, Judith Cowan, Marty Crapper, Jennifer Duncan, Rupert Hanson, Deirdre Molina, Adrienne Phillips, Scott Richardson, Leah Springate, John Sweet, Bill Staples, Roland and Bettina Speicher, Anje and Nico Troje, and Michael Winter. I was also lucky to have Doris Cowan as copy-editor again.

I must thank my terrific editors—Michael Schellenberg and

Louise Dennys at Knopf Canada and Anton Mueller at Houghton Mifflin—for their various astute interventions. I'm also grateful to Simon Prosser at Hamish Hamilton. Likewise my agent, Anne McDermid, as well as her associates, Jane Warren and Rebecca Weinfeld—thank you so much for your help.

I'm grateful to Douglas Glover for choosing an excerpt from this book (pages 31–38) for *Best Canadian Stories 2004*. Also to Sheila Nickerson, whose carefully researched and moving biography *Midnight to the North* will interest any readers who wish to know more about Tukulito/Hannah. Bruce Henderson's *Fatal North* was also helpful, in part by directing me to material contained among the Captain George E. Tyson Papers, at the National Archives in College Park, Maryland.

I'd also like to acknowledge the support of the Canada Council for the Arts; the Ontario Arts Council; the Concordia University English department, which gave me a writer-in-residence position during the 2002–03 school year; Master John Fraser and Massey College, for doing the same for me in the winter of 2004; the Hawthornden Foundation, for a three-week stay at Hawthornden in 2003; and the Pierre Berton House Foundation, whom I thank for a brief but inspiring residency in Dawson City in 2001.

And of course, my first reader, Mary Huggard.

This book is for the Scalas.